DANCING
WITH
TROUBLE

DANCING WITH TROUBLE

A Novel on African Leadership

Omotunde E. G. Johnson

Langdon Street Press
212 3ʳᵈ Avenue North, Suite 290
Minneapolis, MN 55401
612.455.2293
www.langdonstreetpress.com

ISBN-13: 978-1-935204-76-3
LCCN: 2013930645

Distributed by Itasca Books

Cover Design by Alan Pranke
Typeset by James Arneson

Printed in the United States of America

Chapter 1

Donald Bijunga is twelve years old. He loves the piano. His dad, John Bijunga, who greatly enjoys Western classical music and plays the piano himself with some dexterity, is sitting in a nearby drawing room, listening to his son. Donald is working on the three-part invention of Johann Sebastian Bach in G minor. Then the phone rings. John hesitates. He does not want to answer and get caught in one of those lengthy conversations with friends. Not at this moment. It might be someone trying to sell him something, some organization asking for charity, or some politician soliciting campaign funds. Unfortunately, he does not have caller ID. He plans to get one soon.

Something inside tells him the call may be important. Reluctantly, John picks up the phone. It is an international call from his father, Samuel Bijunga, from Nigasilia, a country in the continent of Africa about the size of the state of Virginia, where John lives. Samuel Bijunga also happens to be the president of Nigasilia.

John is anxious when he hears the voice on the other side say hello. His instincts were right.

"Hello, Dad, you are the last person I expected to call on a Monday. What's up?"

"My son, the news is not good. It's about your mother."

"Yes?"

"She suffered a massive heart attack this morning and did not survive it."

"Dad . . ."

"And she did not complain of chest pain at all. I wonder if her diabetes was acting up. She was complaining of her sugar level a day or two ago and I just thought it was her usual worries."

John is barely holding back the tears, his voice cracking. His mother was only sixty-four.

"So what are the plans, Dad?"

"Well, she died only this morning and the plans are not yet set. But we shall most likely bury her Friday, the twenty-third. I will contact your sister and brother. I would like you all to be here."

"Yes, of course, Dad."

"It will be a state affair, so be ready for solemn pageantry. But you, my child, will help me make certain that things are done in ways consistent with our family traditions and your mother's wishes."

"I shall call you the moment I arrange my flights. Donald and William are well and they are both here. They would like to say hello to you."

"Yes, thanks, let me get a word with my grandsons. How are they both doing? I am sure Donald will be ready to show off and to give me a concert when he comes next time. I keep my piano tuned just for him."

John and the boys visited Nigasilia together last summer. Although John visits every summer, the boys do not always accompany him.

John beckons to Donald, who is still sitting at the piano in the living room, hands over the phone, and goes down to the basement to call ten-year-old William. After the two boys are through talking to their grandfather, they pass the phone to John, who says good-bye to his father and turns to the boys.

"Did Grandpa tell you about Grandma?"

"No," they reply in unison.

"When I asked him how Grandma was, he said he just talked to you about Grandma and that you will tell us," Donald says.

John is not surprised. To him, his dad would consider it rather hard-hearted to deliver such a message to his grandsons over the phone. His father would want to have the message delivered in person.

"Grandma passed away today from a heart attack. I must go to attend the funeral. I will leave you boys with Uncle David and Aunt Frances."

Donald grows quiet and then bursts out, "You mean my grandma is dead? Did you know she was ill? Did Grandpa tell you she was ill?"

The two boys embrace each other as Donald begins to cry. John joins in the embrace.

"No," he says, "I didn't know."

John walks up to the bay window in the drawing room and stares into the sky. "If that country had better medical facilities, my mother would be alive today," he mutters. Of course, he does not yet know the details of how she died. But the lack of decent medical facilities has always been the most damaging aspect of life in Nigasilia.

Still, the country is blessed by nature. Nigasilia sits right on the Atlantic coast, with luscious tropical vegetation in the south that slowly dissipates into savanna grasslands in the north. The Atlantic is on the west, where the Caribbean-like vegetation is interspersed with tropical forests that soon take over as one moves into the hinterland, southwards.

Approaching the country from the ocean, the visitor is captivated by the imposing hills of the capital city, Lamongwe, which dominate the landscape. The beaches on the Atlantic coast run along most of the west of the country, and contribute to Nigasilia's enormous potential as a tourist attraction. To attain this potential, the country first needs better infrastructure and the right kind of trained labor.

The British succeeded in colonizing Nigasilia in the nineteenth century. It did so in two stages. Western Nigasilia, comprising mainly Lamongwe, was colonized in the early nineteenth century. Almost ninety years later, after the famous Berlin Conference of 1884-5, when the major European powers divided Africa among themselves, the British colonized the major part of what is now Nigasilia.

John, forty years old and born in Nigasilia, is a naturalized American. He holds a PhD in economics from UCLA and teaches at George Washington University in Washington, DC. While at UCLA, he met and married a fair-skinned Californian, Cecilia, who was an African American of mixed race. Cecilia died two years ago, at the age of thirty-five. She had gone to visit her mother in San Francisco when a truck hit her car.

John wakes from his gloom and approaches the telephone. He needs to talk to his deceased wife's brother. But he pauses, drops the phone, and decides first to go see how the boys are doing.

When John enters Donald's room, the boys are both there, quiet, with their heads down and hands covering their faces. John does not want them to start crying again. He quietly sits on a chair next to Donald's desk.

"Do you guys want me to say anything special to your uncle? I am going to call him now to tell him about my plans."

The two boys hug their father and Donald says, whispering, "No, just say hello for us."

David Simpson, six feet and two inches tall, with a big frame and bulging eyes, is the thirty-nine-year-old brother of the late Cecilia. He and John are very close. David, a journalist, is interested in covering Africa and the Asia-Pacific region. David visited Nigasilia three years ago. His New York newspaper was doing a series on the work of non-governmental organizations in sub-Saharan Africa. The study covered ten countries including Nigasilia, which was one of the three countries assigned to David. He was able to visit Lamongwe, although he went to a number of smaller towns and villages to see firsthand the beneficiaries of NGO work.

In a telephone conversation before he went to Nigasilia, David asked John, "So what do you think was the British colonial legacy?"

"At the end of their century-and-a-half reign, all the colonial masters really left of value were the English language and a fairly decent civil service."

"What do you think they could have done better?"

"Clearly, education and infrastructure. The country is rich in minerals and in cultivable agricultural land excellent for tree crops like cocoa, coffee, and palm trees for palm oil. The colonialists built only the minimal infrastructure necessary to facilitate feasting on all the known natural resources. They educated only enough Nigasilians to help them administer the territory and prevent the natives from disturbing the peace while ensuring the smooth exploitation of the country's resources."

For two weeks, David, on his visit to Nigasilia, talked to the NGOs, government officials, and a selected group of local civil society organizations, politicians, and business representatives. He loved the beaches and hills of Lamongwe. But he could not get over the stark contrast between Lamongwe's poverty and filth and the isolated luxurious sections inhabited by a small minority of professionals; nor could he understand the politicians who did not seem to care about the plight of the masses. Disparity was nothing new to David but it all seemed magnified in Lamongwe. Moreover, even the so-called luxurious sections were little better than the poor neighborhoods in the downtown areas of most US cities. He asked John on his return to New York, "Where is the pride of the people of Nigasilia? Can't they even keep their capital city clean and orderly?" John's reply was brief. "No," he said, "those who have been running the country have no pride and low standards."

Then, David asked John, "So, do you think the colonial legacy on education and infrastructure is still hurting the country?"

"You know, David, I don't encourage Nigasilians to blame the British for their current misery," John said. "The citizens of Nigasilia have had several decades to do what the British failed to do, which is to modernize and develop their country. But the Nigasilians have themselves failed so far. The country is still only a primary producer, surviving almost exclusively on the income from the gifts of nature. There is hardly any industry to talk about and the methods of production in general are rudimentary, except for some segments of the mineral sector dominated by foreign firms. The infrastructure is better than what the colonial masters left, but it is still very basic. Illiteracy is rampant, with over two-thirds of the adult population unable to read and write. Worse still, the Nigasilian political leaders, with their corruption and ineptitude, have succeeded in drastically reducing the efficiency of the civil service and have made it a sham compared to what the British left behind."

That was before John's father became president in 1997. But John keeps telling David that nothing much has changed since. John, in fact, gets cynical. He says the leaders are unable to govern well; they do not have the institutions and the organizational structures to do so, and no one has found a way to put the right system in place, not even his own father. For John, the cause is a systemic disease that needs cleansing.

John goes to the kitchen, gulps down a small glass of water as he collects himself, and dials the phone.

David answers.

"Hi, David, John here."

"Yes, I know. How are things?"

"Oh, so-so. I got some bad news from home. My mother died this early evening, their time, from a heart attack."

"Wow, how sad. Accept my sympathy, John. So, I guess you have to go for the funeral. You know you can leave the boys with us. How are they taking the news?"

"Thanks, I would not think of leaving them with anyone else. They are saddened by the news, especially Donald. I guess that's natural, since he has had the greater time with his grandma. I plan on leaving for Nigasilia this Wednesday, the fourteenth. The funeral is most likely next Friday. I shall then spend a few days with Dad and return towards the end of the month. I hope that's all right. I will fly with the kids to New York this Wednesday and fly from there to London to join my flight to Lamongwe midday on Thursday. I shall ask my brother and sister to be on the same flight so we can arrive together."

"I will try and meet you all at the airport. I hope you will come early enough so that we can spend a little time together before your flight. Frances and I are both on vacation, spending time with the kids before they go to soccer camp."

"You are generous as usual. I shall call you once I complete my bookings."

When John hangs up the phone, he goes quickly to his desktop computer in the basement to book his passage. He keeps a small office down there, with lots of books, though he hoards many more in his university office.

John hurriedly books his British Airways flight from London to Lamongwe. He then compares the costs of the flights from New York to London. He decides on a United Airlines flight. He picks up the phone at his desk and dials his sister.

"John, I called you earlier but got no answer. Dad has called you, right?"

"Yes, he has. Sorry, I was talking to David."

"How are the boys taking it?"

"Reasonably well, but they have been crying, especially Donald."

"Yes, I can understand that. Okay, I shall immediately book the London flight. Are you going to call Peter?"

"Yes. Are you coming alone? I guess you must have been as shocked as I was when the news came. I just could not believe that such a thing would happen to Mom so soon. It still seems like only a bad dream. How are the others taking the news?"

"You know, the moment I stopped talking to Dad, I started to cry, but then I calmed down before I told Mundu."

The thirty-five-year-old Elizabeth has a nine-year-old girl and a seven-year-old boy. She is married to a Nigasilian doctor, Mundu Sasay, who practices in London. Elizabeth herself is an architect.

"Mundu asked me if I wanted him to come and I told him no. It's all too complicated and Mamma would not have considered it a wise move. We would have had to leave the children behind, anyway. Mundu was shocked by the news, really surprised. He wondered if the state of medical services might have had something to do with it."

"Yes, I certainly think the state of medical services could be to blame for Mamma's untimely death. A real problem is the inability to have quality regular checkups. Aside from her medical visits abroad, Mamma could not really do much out there. Anyway, let me call Peter. I'll send you my itinerary."

"Okay, bye for now."

John dials Peter, who picks up the phone almost instantly.

"Hi," Peter answers.

"Were you on the phone?"

"Yes, I was trying to call Elizabeth to ask her if she had spoken with you. I have been trying to call you for some time now. I have been so devastated by the news and anxious to talk to you and Lizzie."

"Oh, sorry, I have been on the phone. Anyway, I wanted to let you know my plans for going to Lamongwe and to suggest that we all meet in London."

Peter is married to a Nigasilian and they live in Toronto. Peter is thirty-four and has been married for only two years. His wife is twenty-nine. They plan to start raising children soon.

John briefs Peter and learns that Peter is going alone. They say good-bye and John dials his dad to let him know the plans.

Samuel always carries his cell phone around. Less than 1 percent of Nigasilians have landlines, which are now mainly confined to offices. In fact, the majority of small businesses use only cell phones. The cell phone industry is quite good and the competition is very lively.

Each business is part of a major international cell phone company. In contrast, the landline company is state-owned and not very dependable or efficient.

"John?"

"Yes, Dad, I am just calling to give you the details on our arrival plans." John goes on to give the president the information.

"Okay, the protocol people will be there to meet you."

"Thanks, Dad. We will all be coming with chocolates, of course, and whatever else we can think of. If you think of anything special you want us to bring, just send us e-mails."

"Okay. I'll be praying safe trips for you all."

John hangs up and calls out to his two boys.

"Do you guys want to get Chinese tonight?"

"Which one?" William asks.

"K Street."

"Good," William says, and Donald concurs. The Szechuan Chinese restaurant on K Street in Northwest DC is only eight miles from their home in North Arlington. It is their favorite Chinese place.

All three jump into John's Volvo and head for DC. Less than a minute into the trip John breaks the silence. "So, I have telephoned everyone today: Grandpa, Aunt Elizabeth, and Uncles David and Peter. Everyone asked about you both."

William looks at his dad. "But we spoke to Grandpa earlier; he knows we are fine."

John does not want to bring up Grandma again, so he does not tell them that Grandpa was interested in how they were taking the news.

"Well, you know Grandpa. He always wants to know how you are doing."

John informs them that he will be traveling from London to Lamongwe with his siblings. "But I will go up to New York with you guys and spend the day with Uncle David and Aunt Frances before I leave to board my flight."

"We can travel by ourselves, if it is easier on you, Dad," Donald interjects.

"Of course you can. I am just taking the opportunity to visit since I have not seen them for many months now."

"Sure," Donald replies in his confident tone, shaking his head in approval. "We are very happy to be visiting them, although we are sad that it is because you are going off to Grandma's funeral."

The traffic on Route 66 is light. They use the Roosevelt Bridge and go past the back of the International Monetary Fund building on Twentieth Street, very close to the White House. In less than twenty minutes they arrive at the restaurant. They already know the menu. William votes for pork, marinated with soy sauce, and Donald for shrimp, stir-fried. John is indecisive. He does not feel particularly hungry.

"I think I will just order white rice for myself and share with you two. If we need some more food, I shall order another dish later."

"Okay, Dad," William replies. After a few minutes, he asks, "Where will Grandma be buried?"

"You mean which cemetery?"

"Yes."

"The one at Bassa Road, remember that cemetery?"

"Yes, I do, but why that one?"

"Because Grandma's family has a big cemetery plot there and she told us that that's where she wanted to be buried."

"Will Grandpa be buried there as well?"

"Probably not, since he is not from Lamongwe. His family may ask us to take him to his native village. If they do, we shall honor that request. Now that he has become president, the village will make a monument for him, and his burial place will become a tourist attraction. If Grandpa turns out to be a great leader, that will also make both the village and the cemetery famous. Your grandma's family is well known, so she will not lose prestige being buried in her family plot."

As they head back home, John says to the boys, "I'm very proud of you two. Well, you know, I am always proud of you. But given what you must be going through inside, I am especially proud that you are handling yourselves so well."

Not so long ago, the boys went through the pain of losing their mother. John suspects this death will evoke that memory and reassures the boys that he feels their pain.

The boys say nothing in response.

Packing for the trip to Nigasilia is easy for John. It is June and so he does not have to worry about two sets of clothing; it is as hot on the East Coast of the United States as it is in Nigasilia. A black suit is the only mandatory attire, but he cannot afford to forget toiletries, since razors, toothbrushes, toothpaste, cologne, and deodorant are very expensive in Nigasilia. He also needs to take lots of cash. Credit cards are not widely used in Nigasilia, and he does not trust the enterprises that do accept cards. He had a bad experience with one of them forging his signature. He also does not need to take any presents. When he gets over there he will change his dollars into the local currency, the *kala*. The locals prefer cash.

He must remember to walk around with small denominations of the kala, since the destitute people who know him will demand money even though they realize he has come for a funeral. John does not really mind. He is one of the few. He rationalizes that the average Nigasilian lives a tough life. Still, he does not like that they beg persons from abroad, and yet show no appreciation when they receive something. "God has blessed you," the natives say, as if the money fell in your lap.

To make matters worse, the locals ridicule their countrymen from abroad, the so-called diasporans. They say too many of the diasporans only drive taxis or have to work two or three jobs to eke out a living.

And yet when these same diasporans go home to Nigasilia on vacation, the despicable locals will line up, conjuring all sorts of tricks to extract money from them.

John's boys are capable and disciplined. Once they return home from the restaurant, they go straight up to their rooms and arrange their clothing for the trip. Their father walks into their rooms some forty-five minutes later, looks at their stuff laid out on their beds, and nods in approval. "Great, you fellows are all done," he says.

The following day John makes the necessary phone calls to his department colleagues at George Washington and to a few close friends who have not yet heard the news. He is not teaching this summer, so he does not have to make any arrangements for students. Most of his Nigasilian friends in the US, of course, have heard the news; his phone rings all day.

On Wednesday morning, John and his two sons board a plane at Reagan National Airport bound for Kennedy International Airport. They leave early, even though the onward flight for John will be at 6:45 p.m. The pre-arranged plan is for John to spend time with David and Frances at their residence in Queens, and then David will take John to the airport. John checks his luggage all the way to Lamongwe; that is one headache solved.

And so it transpires. John, Donald, and William spend a beautiful New York day with David and Frances and their eleven-year-old daughter and nine-year-old son. They have a nice lunch, Frances says, "so John can sleep during the flight and not have to suffer through that airline dinner." Soon it is time to head for the airport. John says goodbye to the others and leaves with David.

As they get in the car to leave for the airport, David hands two books to John.

"John, these are the books I mentioned in my e-mail yesterday. I hope they are not too much of a burden for you to carry. I can always send them by express mail."

"No, they look all right. I do not have much hand luggage anyway."

"I also have a letter for the guy, Ben Kline. You know, he's still there running this NGO called Right to Play, although I gather he is going to be transferred to another African country soon. The books are about games children can play. These books just came out so I'm gambling that he does not have them already. I tell you, before my visit to Nigasilia, I had never heard of this organization. They use sports and play programs to encourage the development of children in the most disadvantaged places of this world. I would have thought there was no need for such a program, but this organization operates in some twenty-five countries. This guy convinced me that these programs really do strengthen communities."

"Yes," John replies in a slightly cynical tone, "I am sure that most communities in Nigasilia need strengthening. I have always been amazed at the sort of NGOs that we have in Nigasilia . . . or should I say the ones we don't have. For example, we have NGOs like Saving Needy Children, Help a Needy Child International, War Child, and the Youth Welfare and Development Organization. Somehow, we don't have NGOs that care about the environment, global warming, and those hefty globalization issues. Even for issues like AIDS, corruption, or democracy, the international community prefers to work with the government, not independently or with the local civil society NGOs. What always tickles me is the fact that the international NGOs have become major employers. I don't think the government even bothers to ask or investigate whether these organizations are effective. The economy certainly benefits from having them there. Those who have money to build nice modern houses are especially grateful for the powerful attraction of our misery. They can rent their houses at high prices and in US dollars!"

As the plane takes off, John opens the copy of the *New York Times* he received from an attendant and pores through it. His mind wanders.

Isn't it amazing, he thinks to himself, *that both my mother and Cecilia are now dead?*

He recalls the last time his mother was in Arlington. It was the summer of 1996; she stayed for six weeks. She and Cecilia got along extremely well that summer, as they had when Mrs. Bijunga had visited them before. Though the two women were almost the same height, the slim Californian was small relative to the light-brown Nigasilian lady, who showed signs of middle-age spread. She constantly complained that the weight must be attributable to her diabetes, because as a girl, her mother worried she was too thin.

Washington was not strange to Mrs. Matinbi Bijunga. She first came there in her youth to spend some time with a Nigasilian friend studying in the United States, while she was a student in the United Kingdom. But during that long summer visit with Cecilia and John, she wanted to absorb the cultural and historical offerings of Washington, including those she had explored before. Many times she would go around by herself, using the underground metro; there was a station only a short distance from their house. John or Cecilia would drop her off and pick her up at the station. She was resolute in her adventure, exploring Arlington Cemetery, the National Gallery of Art, the Hirshhorn Museum, the White House, Congress, Old Town Alexandria, Mt. Vernon, and on and on. She even took Donald and William to the National Air and Space Museum, an experience they fondly recall all the time.

Mrs. Bijunga actually took notes and wrote a long article in one of the local newspapers on her return to Lamongwe about the potential for museums and heritage sites in Nigasilia. She immediately began devoting time to the National Museum in Lamongwe, which was suffering from years of neglect, not fit for visitors with a serious cultural appetite and good taste. John wonders what will happen to it now. *My people, with no imagination or steadfastness, they will let all her efforts go in vain, waiting for some Westerner to come hold their hands. "We have no money," is always their refrain. Fools! Even if they had the money they would still do a shoddy job. On top of that, the donors will have to monitor them so they do not steal the money or waste it.*

Soon, John is asleep. His thoughts of Cecilia and his mother fade away into his dreams. He wakes up for breakfast not long before the flight arrives, some six and a half hours later. Luckily, he is to board the flight for Nigasilia at the same terminal at Heathrow where he arrives. He just needs to go to the transfer desk and confirm his seat. He will then look around for his brother, who should have just arrived from Canada. Their sister will come a little later, since she lives in London.

By the time John gets to the waiting area, it is 8:00 a.m., local time. The flight to Nigasilia is at 12:15 p.m., so he has quite a wait. Soon, he spots his brother, who is walking away from him.

"Peter!"

"Hey, John."

They embrace and find a reasonably quiet location with some privacy where they can sit and chat. It is some distance from where their boarding gate will be, but they have no need to worry about that now.

John and Peter had talked about their mom before they each left for the trip. They do not feel like talking about her now.

Peter asks, "John, did Dad tell you they have set up some kind of Anti-Corruption Commission?"

"Yes, and they are getting some aid money for it, too," John replies.

"So, what do you think?"

"I'm cynical about their plans. I have not seen such organizations work well in any country in Africa. Yes, we could have watchdogs of corruption in government. But then we must be clear on our definition of corruption, we must pass the laws, and we must enforce them. My view is that we should focus on the big fishes."

Peter interrupts. "Isn't that obvious?"

"Yes, but that's why these efforts fail. If a high proportion of your police, your judges, your big politicians, and your senior civil servants are corrupt, then who will catch and punish the big fishes? It's all a waste of money. If international organizations and industrial countries want to give aid, let them focus on infrastructure, education, and skills development."

Peter is not satisfied. "You mean we should not attack corruption head-on? There is nothing we can do?"

"Yes, we can do something. But we must focus on prevention—rules, regulations, procedures, transparency. In other words, we should emphasize institutional and organizational arrangements that make it difficult for public officials to be corrupt. We should not play the game of traffic police, because we are not able to do it fairly and efficiently. We should make it difficult for people to break the law. Having said that, we do need to clean up the police and the legal system as a whole. For that, both prevention and punishment approaches will be necessary. But for the government, I would focus on prevention. That does not mean I would do nothing about punishment. It's all about relative emphasis. Anyway, I think the aid people overpay the head of the Anti-Corruption Commission. His pay is obscene for that country."

"Well, I did read somewhere that many people see the issues the same way as you do and so the aid organizations like Transparency International are putting greater emphasis on prevention. Some well-respected observers and aid agencies believe countries in Africa are making serious progress in controlling corruption."

"Yes, you are right, more emphasis is being placed on prevention, and many African countries are making progress. But not only is it true that many African countries are not making any progress at all, I doubt that any country, apart from the two or three without serious problems to begin with, are making what you call serious progress. Nigasilia is not making serious progress."

"Well, we should ask ordinary Nigasilians about their perspective on this issue."

"I have, and have found the overwhelming number of persons agree with my pessimistic view."

"Yes, I know, you've done research on corruption in Nigasilia."

"Yes, and every summer I go to Nigasilia, corruption is prominent in the discussions I have with people. The same thing is true when we Nigasilians meet in Washington for various events. You know that; I tell you this all the time."

Peter is ready to stop the argument, so they go find something light to eat.

Soon it is 10:30 a.m. Boarding commences in a half hour and the brothers are anxious to see their sister. So John and Peter head for the boarding gate. When they get there, their sister is already looking relaxed and sitting in the boarding area. She sees them coming and waves. They all have broad smiles on their faces. Then, as if feeling guilty, the smiles disappear. John looks at both of them and says, "Well, we have to do our best to hold up." Elizabeth and Peter agree in unison.

The three siblings resemble their mother far more than their father, except they have their dad's smallish oval face. But their light-brown complexion is clearly from their mother.

Peter asks, "How is the rest of the family?"

"Oh, they are well, praise God," Elizabeth replies. "Mundu sends his best wishes. He told me he has spoken to you both." She looks sharply around as if to see whether anyone is paying attention.

"What?" Peter asks.

She leans over and says, "A girlfriend of mine from school days in Lamongwe told me this morning that people are already whispering that Daddy might now start openly dating Rabena. We all have been aware that Dad and his confidential secretary are close. Mom did not mind, but this girl says the whole world seems to think something has been going on. Even the woman's husband was so jealous that the marriage broke down and they divorced last month. But I gather the marriage was on the rocks anyway. The guy was an alcoholic."

"Lizzie, do you believe the story about Dad and Rabena?" John asks.

"Well, with you Nigasilian men, anything is possible. But if this story is true, I would be surprised. Dad is so serious about work, and Mom was a wise and strong woman. If something was going on, she would have sensed it."

"Well, I'll ask Dad," John insisted, "but right now I don't believe the story. What about you, Peter? Do you believe it?"

"No, that's not my dad. He's too cautious and sensible," Peter says firmly.

It is time to board. John has a window seat, as does Elizabeth. Peter prefers the aisle. As John takes his seat he greets the Chinese gentleman next to him. After making himself comfortable, he turns to the man. "Are you going all the way to Lamongwe?"

"Yes," the man replies.

"Will this be for a short visit?"

"No, I work there now."

The plane takes off only fifteen minutes late. They can make it up unless the weather turns out worse than anticipated.

"So what do you do in Nigasilia?" John asks.

"I am one of the deputy managers in a hotel that the Nigasilian government has given us to run."

"You mean like a management contract?"

"Yes."

John knows the hotel he is talking about. He has visited and dined at that hotel since the Chinese started managing it.

"You must have a lot of experience in hotel management, though you look so young."

"I don't have a lot of practical experience in business, but I studied in the US and have an MBA, so this is practical management training for me. I have been in Nigasilia for one year. After another year, I might get transferred to another country."

"You probably want to go to Asia or Europe, right?"

"Perhaps, but actually I don't mind Africa. My problem is I don't want to stay in the hotel management business; I think I prefer to be in industry. But my mind is not made up yet. Maybe I need to go to school again. I want to do more finance—real finance, not accounting. I enjoy finance, but I need more training in that area to feel qualified."

"You know what has become a big topic these days—the Chinese in Africa. Many people, both in the West and in Africa, think that the Chinese only want Africa's natural resources. But I get the feeling the Chinese also want to develop a total business relationship. In Nigasilia, for example, apart from the beach hotel that you people manage, you are in construction, restaurants, and trading of Chinese-made goods, especially furniture and manufactures. Of course, you are in mining and timber also. This is truly a Chinese invasion!"

"Is that bad?" the Chinese man asks.

"Well, it's business. It's not good or bad."

"Yes, I understand," the Chinese man responds, nodding his head.

Then John adds, "You even have a Chinese Chamber of Commerce in Nigasilia. That is remarkable!"

The Chinese man looks at John and smiles. "Are you just going home on vacation?" he asks.

Without specifying who his father is, John replies, "No, I lost my mother, and I am going home for the funeral."

"Accept my sympathy."

"Thanks. Oh, my name is John. What's yours?"

"Yingyi. I hope that's not hard for you."

"Not at all, I know that name." John can't help himself and continues to talk. "There are two other things that people say about the Chinese in Africa. First, there are those who say the Chinese do not care about corruption, restraints on democracy, and human rights abuses in African countries—that they are solely interested in their business relationships. Second, some people say that the Chinese are pushing deals, especially in the minerals area, that are economically unfair to the Africans. What do you think?"

"John, I really know nothing about such discussions. We Chinese respect the rights of countries to control their internal affairs, even though China is part of the international community. China understands it must support certain human rights. Also, Chinese companies negotiate with countries and do not impose any deals."

"Yes, that is what I hear from your people all the time. What I tell my African people each time I get involved in such a discussion is that Africans must learn to bargain well. African countries have nationals, both internally and abroad, who can help them do that. Let them use their best people."

The plane is going through some turbulence, the seat-belt signs have been switched on, and the crew is making the usual announcements. John and Yingyi concentrate on finishing their drinks as the attendants hasten to clear the tables.

Chapter 2

The Lamongwe International Airport terminal is clean but simple. It is never really busy, as not many flights come in on a daily basis. In general, there are no more than ten international flights a day. The airport service personnel can be annoying and not terribly efficient to someone accustomed to Western standards. Only VIPs get competent service. They receive all kinds of courtesies from the airport staff, they do not have to face customs and immigration personnel with their constant attempts to elicit bribes, and on top of that, as a VIP, one gets escorted to the VIP lounge to relax until it is time to board a flight or wait for one's luggage to be retrieved on arrival.

The normal traveler has to face all kinds of nuisance. A passenger will be carrying two pieces of luggage and three or four porters will battle over the suitcases. Then the immigration and customs officials will openly ask for money for doing their jobs. The stories are always the same: "Times are hard." "I have been working long hours without any food." "I have a sick relative." "I'm struggling to pay school fees for my children."

John and his siblings are lucky. They are children of the president. Hence, they are VIPs. They are met by protocol officers from the president's office and whisked off to the presidential lounge where their luggage tags are taken from them. Their bags are soon brought out, and they set off in style for the president's lodge.

The roads in Lamongwe are narrow, one lane in each direction. In Nigasilia, driving is on the right, just like in the US. It is nighttime anyway, and they can hardly see what is going on. To make matters worse, the route is dark. The authorities have not been able to supply electricity on a reliable basis for years. Only a privileged few receive electricity even two nights a week on average. There are generators blasting everywhere. Even the president's official residence uses a generator for electricity supply more often than not. The poor who cannot afford to have generators have to use any kind of lighting they can afford. Kerosene lamps are especially popular.

The trio arrive at the Presidential Hut (as Nigasilians call it) at about 11:30 p.m. The president is still up. He would not go to sleep without seeing his children. As they enter the front door he embraces them, first Elizabeth, then Peter, and finally John.

"Welcome, welcome, I hope you all had pleasant trips." Samuel gives them the well-known look that says "Let's pray" and they make a small circle holding hands. He offers a prayer, thanking God for having brought his children safely to Lamongwe and asking for God to give them all courage to face what lies ahead. He requests that God enables everything to go smoothly in just the way that God knows Mrs. Bijunga would want.

After praying, with a broad smile of joy on his face, the president asks, "So, what can I offer you? Sit down, sit down." He calls one of the servants.

So far only the president has spoken. Now Elizabeth looks at everyone and says, "I think we can all say that the trips were fine. Daddy, you look well." The other two concur, with restrained but clear smiles across their faces.

A servant walks in and everyone orders something to drink. The three siblings order Nigasilian beer; the president only wants mineral water.

"Thank you. Yes, your mother's death has come as a real shock. She had so much planned, not only to help me but also to pursue many projects dear to her heart, especially in education and the arts.

The people loved her, probably more than they like me. She will be a real loss to the country and, to me, irreplaceable. I keep on asking, 'Why her? Why now?' Okay, she had not been in good health for months. Her diabetes and high-blood pressure were acting up, even with medication. But she had survived such an experience before. I tell you, the last thing we thought about was a heart attack. She had planned a trip to London in July to see her physicians. The state of health services in Nigasilia is not great, even though we are improving every year. This is one area that really bothered your mother. She was particularly disturbed by this inequality between the well-to-do and the overwhelming majority of our people."

"Yes, Dad, we know," John interrupts. "In my very last conversation with her, the subject came up and she reminded me that the expected life span in the country is a mere forty-five years, and the infant mortality rate is among the worst in the world."

Peter then asks, "So, Dad, what happened on the day she died?"

Strangely enough, the details of their mother's death had only been given to Elizabeth. She is the only one to have asked their dad and she just assumed the other two already knew the details.

"Oh, she died peacefully. As I was saying, she was not feeling well. So I encouraged her to take it easy and simply rest. If she did not improve, my plan was to convince her to go immediately to her doctor in London. On the day she died, she rose up late, almost midday, and then slowly got herself ready. She had a fair-sized brunch at about 1:00 p.m., the maid said. Then she complained of being tired and feeling weak. The maid noticed that she was quite warm. But the maid said that your mother told her not to call me because she had had such an experience before. That was your mother. Unless it was really serious she did not want me disturbed at the office. So, the maid helped her to bed and left her, checking her every few minutes or so. At about 5:45, the maid checked her and she seemed calmly asleep. But when the maid returned at about 6:05, she noticed that your mother did not seem to be breathing and checked to make sure. It was a quiet passing away."

The president's house is large, even though there are only two levels. Single-family Nigasilian houses do not typically have basements, for geological reasons—there is too much underground water and rocks to deal with. Only major office buildings bother with underground constructions. Even though this is an official residence for the president, they have not bothered with a basement. Some single-family houses will have three stories because they are built on slopes, which allow them to conveniently construct three stories without having to go underground. The first level can then be used for adding a garage to the main building as well as a recreational basement. These three-story homes are very big houses owned by a few people with money.

The Hut has five bedrooms upstairs and a relaxation room for family and close friends, as well as a sizable office. Downstairs is a big reception and family room in addition to the living room, drawing room, kitchen, dining room, laundry room, pantry, and storage room. There is also a large two-level library built as an extension to the main house. Moreover, there is a barbecue house connected to the main house by a covered walkway from the kitchen. The garden has a sizable gazebo and a marvelous combination of flowers, including roses and herbs.

By 8:00 the next morning, everyone is sitting at the table for breakfast. President Bijunga is anxious to go over a few things with his children. "You know, with a state funeral, we are constrained to observe all kinds of protocols. Still, I would like you, my children, to monitor everything very carefully. Your mother's wishes and our own family traditions have to be respected. Don't let any details pass you by. If anyone tells you, 'Oh, this is the way we do it here,' just tell them as politely as you can that your mother had ideas about how things should be done, and that your father insists you follow her wishes. So, I will leave the rest to you. I'm sure John will discuss his tribute with you, Elizabeth and Peter. But John, don't forget to talk to others as well. There are so many people who would like to say something about your mom. But we simply do not have the time to let them all speak. You will have the challenging task of summarizing their tributes. Your professorship will come in handy."

Mrs. Bijunga had been a devout Catholic and wanted a Mass that was very solemn. She had supported certain groups ardently and requested their active participation in the ceremony. The blind school she patronized has an excellent choir and should sing something during the service. The Roman Catholic girls' secondary school she attended has a brilliant band. They must lead the procession as it enters the cemetery. She did not want the military band to dominate the affair. She insisted that the female organizations in which she was a member be allowed certain places among the seats reserved for dignitaries. She did not want the female members of her family and the women's organizations to wear black. She preferred white. She wanted the Gospel reading to be John 5:19-25. And at the graveside, the hymn "Abide with Me" had to be sung. The anthem of the choir during the service had to be something from Handel's *Messiah*. She wanted only one tribute, to be given by her oldest child, John.

The children adored their mother. She had a master's degree in history from Durham University in England, and for many years taught African and British history at an undergraduate college in Nigasilia. In fact, she only stopped lecturing when her husband became president. She was particularly fond of recounting the long march to independence of African countries. Several times, she would sit all three children down and discuss the Pan-African movement. John used to recite, like a parrot, dates that his mother had drummed into his head:

1900: First Pan-African Congress held in London under the leadership of the Trinidadian Henry Sylvester Williams

1919: Second Pan-African Congress, Paris

1921: Third Pan-African Congress held in London and Brussels

1923: Fourth Pan-African Congress held in London and Lisbon

1927: Fifth Pan-African Congress in New York

1945: Sixth Pan-African Congress in Manchester, England—organized by many individuals, including Kwame Nkrumah

1958: All African Peoples' Congress in Accra, Ghana, organized by Kwame Nkrumah and George Padmore. This, she used to say, was the foundation of the Organization of African Unity.

Mrs. Bijunga revered Kwame Nkrumah. She used to say to her children and her students, "If we Africans had listened to Kwame Nkrumah, we would not be like Lazarus today waiting to eat the crumbs that fall from the white man's table, having our peoples barely surviving from day to day, when we are camped on top of so many natural resources and God has given us so much strength." She had no patience for Africans who, after many years of independence, would continue to blame the Europeans for their misery. She would say, "Africans act stupidly and deserve their lot." She was far more revolutionary in her thinking than her husband. But she hated communism and thought that it was a useless and harmful ideology. "Africans are not communists by tradition," she would say, "despite our social systems, which include sharing with and supporting the unfortunate. Africans believe that individuals should work for what they consume and are entitled to only what they earn through their labor. That," she would say, "is the true African tradition."

It will be John's burden to summarize Mrs. Bijunga's thoughts in his tribute. It is a burden he shoulders with pride. He has been re-hearsing it his entire adult life in talking about his mother to all who would listen. During his trip to Lamongwe, as he reflected on how to summarize his mother's attitude toward Nkrumah, he chuckled. *Yes, I once got her to admit that her stance on Nkrumah was based mainly on his tenacity over the issues of African independence and unity, and that Nkrumah erred in his industrialization policies and his dictatorial arrogance towards his detractors. Of course, Mom had the last say—but look at what he did for education and infrastructure in his country!*

John knows that his siblings want him to say something about how they felt about their mother. So as they finish their breakfast with their father, he outlines his tribute to them. They both like what he plans to say.

"Of course, I shall discuss further with both of you as I spell out the tribute in more detail. But is there something you can think of now that you would like me to add?"

"Yes. In my case," Elizabeth says, "I would suggest that you add that Mother was a great confidante to me and was quite frank and open in helping me educate myself as a girl and later as a woman. Mom's emotional support was beyond measure. She strengthened my resolve to be as good as anyone else, particularly in school, and to be self-confident and self-reliant."

"As for me," Peter adds, "you can note that although Mom would call me her baby, she used to say to me, 'Peter, don't let your older brother and sister bully you, now. Tell them you are no baby.' You know, I can recall when I was afraid of mathematics, in the early years, which I am sure you two remember also. Well, here was Mom, who was not great in math herself, but she would sit down with me after school and we would work through exercises together. Mom was extremely patient with me. In fact, whereas sometimes she should have scolded me, she would call me and whisper in my ears, 'Peter, don't make me be ashamed of you, now. What you just did was bad.' Then she would explain to me why such behavior was wrong and even selfish or stupid. Of course, she would sometimes scold me, but not in front of my friends because she knew that I was easily embarrassed."

John then looks at his dad. "So, Dad, is there something special you want me to say about Mom on your behalf?"

John's father bowed his head and closed his eyes as if to pray. Then he rubbed his eyes gently with two fingers, gave a deep sigh, and looked at John with a faint smile.

"She was a rock on which I could count to be there when I needed support and peace of mind. In fact, most of the time, she was very proactive in her support. She would know when I was down or when I could benefit from her good counsel. But what I admired most about her was her terrific understanding of people, her ability to make people feel at ease, and her enormous generosity."

Later that same day, John begins his research. He calls on a number of his mother's friends and leaders of her favorite organizations. They have much praise for her concern, generosity, and energy. The constant theme that flows from all these people is that if Mrs. Bijunga saw someone who would benefit from a helping hand, she would volunteer or inspire others to do so. The one thing Mrs. Bijunga did not tolerate was a culture of dependence. She felt that when someone was being helped, that person should be making efforts to become self-sufficient.

That afternoon, John decides to surprise his father and calls on him at the office. The president, who is sixty-nine, is a lawyer by training, and did his undergraduate work in economics. He has not been in politics too long, and does not have a political heritage in his family. His father was a civil servant and his mother a nurse. But his work as a lawyer made him keenly interested in political activity. After he joined the Nigasilian Progressive Party, he endeared himself quickly to the kingmakers of the party for his national standing as a lawyer who was honest in dealing with his clients and who was willing to fight for what he thought was right. Indeed, as a lawyer, Mr. Bijunga gained national reputation for being willing to put fairness and justice before money. The party needed someone like that. Being in the opposition at the time, the Progressive Party had to give the population enough reasons to kick out the party in power, the United Party. So when Bijunga was selected in the party's convention over far more seasoned politicians, he turned to his good friend and professional colleague, Kamake Tigie, who also had presidential ambitions and was far more seasoned as a politician, to be his vice-presidential candidate.

Since independence, the Progressive Party and the United Party have been the two main political parties of Nigasilia. Other parties tend to show up, stay small, and disappear. There is little ideological difference between the two parties. But their support reflects the tribal and regional divide of the country, even though both parties have supporters from each of Nigasilia's twenty-one ethnic groups. The Progressive Party has its greatest support in the north and the west, while the United Party has its support mainly in the south. The east is more contested, although the United Party has won it more times than the Progressive Party. The two parties accuse each other of corruption and tribalism. But John, based on all the information he has been able to obtain on the activities of the two parties, strongly believes the Progressive Party is far more corrupt than the United Party, while the United Party is the more tribalistic of the two. Hence, apart from ineptitude, which is a general leadership problem of Nigasilia, John conceives of his father's greatest struggle within his own party as the fight against corruption, especially corruption at the highest political levels. The president is a workaholic and remains highly respected and fairly popular. Six feet tall, somewhat dark in complexion, he is healthy and strong. He got gray in his forties, but has dyed his hair since. With hardly any wrinkles in his face, he is looking quite young for his age.

John arrives, unannounced, during the president's cabinet meeting. His father's fifty-year-old confidential secretary, Rabena Karam, knows

John very well. He decides to go see her rather than wait in the general waiting room.

"John, it's great to see you," Rabena says as she embraces him. "Please accept my sympathy. I have been praying for your family that God will give you strength to face this tragedy. I really admired your mother."

"Thank you, Rabena. It's great to see you, too."

John sits down and after a brief moment Rabena asks, "John, can I get you something?"

"Sure, a cup of tea would do, please."

"Chocolate, too? We have some Belgian chocolates."

"All right, thank you."

"So how are the boys?" Rabena asks, after handing John his tea. "Is Donald still working on his piano? And William, have you been able to get him to practice?"

"Oh, yes, Donald is still very serious about his piano, but William is not keen. He prefers to play soccer . . . you know, football. I think that every child should study a musical instrument, but I have no intention of forcing William. He does very well in school, as does his brother. They are both very good in mathematics, which is important to me. So, it's fine."

From the moment John entered the State House, he was struck by how worn and dirty the carpets are. It's as if the traffic is so heavy it is impossible to keep the carpets clean. He has always been amazed at how many ordinary people go in and out of the State House. To John, there is just an unpleasant informality about the whole place. Relatives, friends, and others can just pop in and out without much ado. Yes, they have to go through a guarded gate, but all a worker inside has to do is call the gate and tell the guards that someone is coming and give the name of the person. The person could be a child from school, a cousin who wants to engage in idle chat, or someone who just wants to take a look at the State House from the inside. Even so, John is surprised that the carpet in Rabena's office right next to the president's office is barely neater than the carpets in the corridors.

"Tell me, Rabena, who is responsible for the upkeep of the interior of this building?"

"What do you mean?"

"Just look at the carpets. They look a hundred years old and as if no one has bothered to clean them all those years. Is this where you bring visitors?"

Rabena is a bit surprised at John's remarks because he has been to the office before and never commented on the carpets. She thinks he is just depressed.

"You should tell your dad. He'll listen to you. No one else seems to care."

"I think you people have too much traffic in this place, with all these hangers-on. Why do they encourage people who have no business here to roam all over the place?"

"Which people do you mean—constituents, relatives, friends?"

"All of them!"

"Well, it's not easy to keep the people away. This is Africa, not America."

After shuffling some papers, Rabena asks, "So, when are you coming home to help?"

"What can I do here? I can't even influence my dad. If my mother had been president, I would have been anxious to come home—to help, as you say. But these fellows who run the show here, I will only quarrel with them, including my dad."

"So that's a challenge you should accept. Don't underestimate your dad, though. He is a very kind man and is willing to listen to you young intellectuals. He is very popular."

"Yes, so I hear."

The cabinet meeting ends and the ministers stroll out. They all greet John and extend their condolences. Three of them pull John aside while the others leave—the ministers of Tourism and Cultural Affairs, Agriculture, and Trade and Industry. They want to arrange a meeting with John before he returns to the US, but after the funeral. So John reaches for a piece of paper and makes an appointment with the three. They leave and John steps into his dad's office.

"Hi, Dad."

"John."

"I see you still have your twenty-five or so ministers."

"John, I am not a dictator. The number of ministerial positions is a consensus decision. Sure, I could influence things, but then what will I tell all those ministers who suddenly have no portfolios?"

"Tell them to go find work. They can be farmers, schoolteachers, entrepreneurs, just name it. There is plenty to do in this country. How were they surviving before they became ministers?"

"Too many of them were not doing well, John."

John walks around, surveying the books on the bookshelves in his dad's office. "So now they are making up for lost time and cleaning up the state coffers?"

"Who, John?"

"Your ministers, Dad. Who else would I be talking about?"

"John, do you want something to drink?"

"No, thank you. Rabena gave me a cup of tea." John pauses. "You know, Rabena is very pleasant and beautiful."

"Yes," his dad concurs, "and she is hardworking, efficient, and trustworthy. I am lucky to have found her."

John hesitates but cannot resist spilling out what he really wants to say. "Someone told Lizzie that people won't be surprised if you married her now that your wife is gone. I gather her ex-husband accused you of messing around with his wife. What's all that about?"

"John, people can talk a lot of trash; you know that. Yes, Rabena and I are close. She is my secretary. As soon as a boss is close to his secretary, people bring out their radar looking for some kind of sexual relationship. The husband was simply a jealous fool. What does he gain from divorcing her? He was no use to her anyway. The man deteriorated, simply because his legal practice was not doing too well. He barely escaped being debarred a few years ago. He drinks too much for his own good. He needed Rabena to help him return to his senses. Nothing has been going on between us. Anyway, this is the worst time for you and me to be having such a conversation."

"Sorry, Dad, I agree."

President Bijunga arranges some papers, orders his desk, and then looks up at John.

"Tonight, we shall have the vice president, Kamake Tigie, and his wife, Sama, join us for dinner. I hope that is all right with you. I have already sent word to Lizzie and Peter."

The president stops for a moment, looks up at the ceiling, and then goes on. "Both your mother and Tigie convinced me to bring more young men into the cabinet. But I find them worse than those over fifty, irrespective of their education."

"Daddy, these young men are all broke and most of them are in a great rush to get rich quick. So what do you expect?"

"Then who should I turn to, John?"

"Well, Dad, here is my opinion, for what it's worth. You should look for seasoned persons, with experience both at home and abroad, who are well educated with few financial responsibilities such as having college fees to pay for their kids. My own personal preference is for people with a solid education and experience in the various sciences, engineering, economics, and business. Stay away from people with long administrative backgrounds—you know, the civil service types."

"Despite all your lectures, when I ask if you would like to come home and help, you seem reluctant. America has really got to you. Anyway, we shall talk about this again before you leave. Maybe I shall finally find the right words to convince you to push the engine with us."

Soon after John got his doctorate degree in economics, the University of Nigasilia offered him a lectureship. His parents were excited at the prospect of John coming home to help in the economic development of the country. At first, John was leaning towards coming home. But as he investigated the university, and after a two-week visit, he came to the conclusion that his research would suffer. The library facilities were particularly poor. The economics department staff was thin, which meant that his teaching load would be heavy. He decided he would spend some time at a US university to get some research projects under his belt. Afterwards, he would come home to help. But for John, the economic and political environment in the country deteriorated and he lost interest in coming home. He is still unconvinced that he will be able to make a difference, even with his dad as president. To leave his job in the US and come home would be a worthless sacrifice.

"So what were you discussing in the cabinet meeting? When the ministers walked out they all looked rather morose."

"I'm not surprised. We had four contentious issues on the agenda. First, some measures we are considering to address youth unemployment, which is a very serious problem right now; second, plans for increasing electricity capacity in Lamongwe over the next three years or so; third, progress in completing some major road projects, which are being undertaken but for many reasons are way behind schedule; and, last, the allocation of funds from the budget to the districts to finance approved projects proposed by those districts. As you know, decentralization is an important governance initiative of this government but the local governments have only limited capacity to raise funds. There is a struggle even within the cabinet over the allocation of funds from the central budget to the districts. You see, my son, these are the issues you should be interested in, not the size of my cabinet or idle talk about Rabena."

Just before 7:00 that evening, the president, John, Elizabeth, and Peter greet the vice president and his wife. After the usual salutations, the president's waiters serve drinks. The president's three children have never met the VP's wife before and are delighted to meet her.

Then the VP's wife looks at all three young Bijungas and says, "I am sorry you have had to leave your families behind in such a rush for this sad event. I hope they are all well. Your mother was such a leader and an inspiration to all. We will miss her especially for her work with mass education and the cultivation of the arts and the heritage of Nigasilia."

"Thank you, Mrs. Tigie," Elizabeth responds.

"I hope you young ones will now find a way to stay even closer to your father because, I tell you, your mother was always there for your father. We don't want him to slip now without his strong right-hand person."

"No, Mrs. Tigie, we won't allow that to happen," Elizabeth assures her.

"We have a lot of interesting things going on in this country to which we want young and brilliant minds like yours to contribute. But I know it is hard, once you get used to life in Europe or America, to come home. We used to be lucky; things were not so bad after the British left because there were so many opportunities for the few well-educated Africans like us. We were assured of good jobs and good benefits—housing, cars, bank loans. Now things are not so easy. The demands on government and the few decent employers are enormous. Unfortunately, the development of the country has not kept pace with the rising expectations."

"Mrs. Tigie, you are right," Elizabeth says. "That is the reality. But the world out there, especially in the West, has all these wonderful opportunities for us to feel fulfilled. We don't have that same nationalistic fervor now to counter all that materialistic attraction. You people who were there at independence time are of a different genus altogether."

Sama Tigie then asks, "Talking about housing and all that, Elizabeth, you are the architect; what do you think about the new buildings going up around the city? You know, of course, many of them are being built by people like you from the diaspora."

"Actually, Mrs. Tigie, I like very few of the houses. There simply is too little imagination or artistic air for my taste. My guess is that functionality is stressed while artistic attributes are almost totally ignored. I think that only office buildings should be so bland. More generally, we really should get serious about urban planning in this country. For example, we have modern houses situated right next to tin shacks with no running water or inside toilets. We also need better public health in this country. John and I have concluded that all these do-gooders from Europe and America who talk about bed nets and prophylactic drugs to handle mosquitoes should come here and push for better sanitation."

"Yes, you are right," President Bijunga says. "The truth is we don't know how to control the situation without expelling the masses from the city. But we fear that any such attempt will merely provoke mass protests and riots. We will have to run a police state to keep them away."

The party settles down to a simple three-course dinner of shrimp-and-avocado salad, chicken tomato stew and rice, and ice cream and fruits, with beer and wine as desired. Afterwards, cognac will be served when they return to the living room.

The VP says, as everyone settles down at the dinner table, "No doubt, people love the city life, in spite of the unemployment and the squalor. They enjoy the freedom, they meet interesting people, rub shoulders with foreigners, and they escape the local customary restrictions in the countryside. We need to accelerate urbanization in other parts of this country, so that Lamongwe does not remain this big attraction to the youth. It is the youth, you know, who are most anxious to escape the countryside. A major problem is that we do not have enough jobs for them here in the city."

John adds, "Maybe if development is promoted in a more resolute manner in other parts of the country, the youth could have something that attracts them to those areas. Right now all they have are factors driving them from the countryside and from other small towns, and nothing—nothing at all—that encourages them to stay. It's really dreary outside of Lamongwe. Only the very traditional people are keen to remain in the countryside."

"It is not all that bad out there," the president interrupts. "There are at least four towns slowly emerging into major urban environments. But I agree that we still need to do far more to address the unemployment situation in Lamongwe, in conjunction with promoting the development of agriculture, tourism, and small-scale modern industries in our heartland."

"For that, you need better skills training programs, higher literacy rates, and better infrastructure," John interjects.

"Yes, John, you are right," the president says in an unmistakably agitated tone. "We are currently trying to develop a coherent program for the youth that would include especially literacy as well as technical and vocational education and training. Unfortunately, a major challenge will continue to be the jobs. Where will the jobs be? And will the available jobs be where the youth want to go?"

The VP, as if to clear the air, turns to Peter. "Peter, you are the civil engineer. I hope you will be able to travel around a little after your mother's funeral so that you can see the progress we have made in our road development program. I remember that before you decided to stay in Canada, your dad told me that you had planned to come here and, among other things, run a consultancy firm with your engineering friends."

Peter replies in a soft, quiet tone, and speaks slowly as if weighing his words carefully. "Yeah, I should really travel around. I have not gone to the interior since I first left for Canada in 1984. That was sixteen years ago."

The VP, who like the president is a member of the Lamongwe Golf Club, then asks, "Lizzie, Peter, and John, can I invite you three to come to the golf club next Saturday? I am sure your dad's driver can bring you. As you know, we have golf, tennis, and squash at the club, and our beautiful course is eighteen holes. I am not great myself, but I enjoy the game. We don't discuss any business at the club. After playing, we sit around—outside when the weather allows—drink more than we should, and argue about world affairs and sports."

All three young Bijungas have been to the golf club before. The president winks, encouraging them to accept the invitation.

"Thank you, VP," Elizabeth says, smiling. "I am the only golfer among the three but we will all be there."

Mrs. Bijunga would have been elated by the show. Her body is beautifully laid out at the Catholic cathedral in Lamongwe, and the service begins promptly at 1:00 p.m. Two church choirs participate but the anthem is sung by the cathedral choir. There are ten priests, and the Roman Catholic archbishop of Nigasilia, who governs the two dioceses of Nigasilia, presides. The army band is there as well. The president is a Freemason, so there are representatives from five lodges. Several female organizations participate, as do beneficiary institutions of Mrs. Bijunga's charity work. John's tribute brings tears, smiles, and laughter and the archbishop's homily is kept brief, stressing Mrs. Bijunga's preoccupation with lifting the dignity of the average person and giving the opportunity to all to reach their full potential in life. The service lasts for two and a half hours, and then it's all over, in grand style. The cemetery is not too far away but it takes an hour to get there with the full motorcade.

by the usual repast. Quite a number of John's
ry school friends who attended the church
quet. The same is true for Elizabeth and Peter.
te friends is Nathan Bang. A medical doctor,
and returned only a couple of years ago to be
r and to see if he could give something back to
. Nathan's wife, Gertrude, is with him. She is
German, teaches mathematics, and is one of those idealists who would
like to help Africans develop their countries. Nathan is fed up with
the state of things in Nigasilia. His mother died a few months ago
and now he wants to return to Germany, where he has naturalized
citizenship. But his wife wants him to stay a little longer.

"You are joking," John says when Nathan mentions leaving. "Why?
They have so few doctors here. You don't feel guilty?"

Nathan is shocked that John would say such a thing when he is
abroad in the US himself.

"Well, they have so few economists here, your dad is the president,
and you are still in the US. Don't you feel guilty?"

"Actually, no," John replies. "These people have no interest in
economic development. They are mainly interested in enriching themselves. The only thing I am willing to give my dad is that he is not
corrupt. But most of those around him are corrupt. The problem I see
with my dad is that he does not have the nerve to take the tough decisions on governance that would turn things around in this country.
He says the people will not support him if he becomes too tough."

"Well, have you told him that as a leader he can motivate the people
to do better?" Nathan asks.

"Every month I mention Lee Kuan Yew of Singapore. His reply is
always the same: 'Give me the people of Singapore and I will govern
like Lee Kuan Yew.'"

"Interesting," replies Nathan, as his wife gives him a wry smile. "So
we Nigasilians are just hopeless, eh? That's what I've been telling my
dear wife. But she thinks I'm too harsh."

John presses his question. "So, why do you want to go back to Germany now? Is it because your mission here is accomplished?"

Gertrude interjects. "Yes, John, ask him. I really think he should stay a little longer. Our son and daughter are doing all right in boarding schools and can visit us here during the summer months in Germany, and even for Christmas. We still have our apartment in Germany and can visit as we want. I enjoy teaching the students here. Two to three more years won't hurt. There is a serious shortage of mathematics teachers in this country."

"The real problem," Nathan says, "is that the whole system in this country is designed to annoy you, unless you are masochistic or ultra-idealistic like my wife. Of course, I am leaving out the corrupt and powerful manipulators of the system who are precisely the ones pulling the strings that rub the rest of us the wrong way. If I want, I know I can join these powerful and corrupt manipulators. But I cannot do that and help the common man. Why should I be a doctor only to the small class of people who are well-to-do? In that case, I might as well return to Germany and ask them to come see me there, which they can afford to do. As you well know, I have not even touched on the day-to-day frustrations of ordinary living. Things have seriously deteriorated in this country from the days when we were growing up. Anyway, I am sure you know what I'm talking about, so I am not going to say any more."

"I'm afraid I agree with you completely. So, when do you plan to go back?"

"That's what I am still negotiating with my wife. Let me have your e-mail address and I will send you the answer."

John turns to Gertrude and asks, "What school do you teach at, again?"

"Nigasilia Grammar School."

"I should have guessed," John says as he looks at Nathan, and both burst out laughing. That is the all-boys secondary school they both attended; there had always been a significant percentage of female teachers there.

Nathan asks, "When was the last time you visited the school?"

"Actually, two years ago, soon after our university year in the States ended, because I wanted to talk to some of the students before they closed school here for the long break. Apart from that, I wanted to see their lab and library facilities. The old boys in the US send funds to help with lab facilities and books for the library. I wanted to see for myself what was happening here. The books were there but the lab facilities were disappointing. Maybe we should send them the lab equipment and supplies rather than the money."

"That may not be a bad idea," Gertrude interjects.

"I think so, too, but my other alumni friends think it's too much of a bother. So we send them the books, since it is easier for us to buy the books there than for them to do so here. Anyway, I would like to visit you two in Germany and, of course, your whole family is most welcome to visit me in the States. Incidentally, I have two boys, twelve and ten. My wife, unfortunately, died two years ago in a road accident."

"Oh, sorry," Gertrude says sympathetically. "Was she Nigasilian?"

"No, she was from the States."

Peter beckons to John from a distance. He would like them to go home now. Nathan and John exchange e-mail addresses, and John says good-bye.

On Saturday, John, Elizabeth, and Peter go to the golf club with Vice President Tigie and his wife. A large number of members have their club membership dues paid for them by the companies for which they work. Then, of course, there are the men who work for successful small- and medium-sized businesses, who are also members of the Chamber of Commerce and Industry. Besides those groups, the club members tend to be those Nigasilians who are retired from many years of working abroad, all of them well-educated professionals. It is an elite group. There are also many members who hail from foreign countries, both within and outside Africa.

Every person John talks to has the same two questions: "How do you find Lamongwe?" and "When are you coming back to help us in Nigasilia?" But the big topic at the club on this day is Tiger Woods' impressive win at the US Open at Pebble Beach. They all watched it on TV and were in awe. Many of them, though, are still grieving over his failure to win the Masters earlier in the year. They have no doubt that he will win the British Open at St. Andrews. "No other golf course in Britain is more suited to his game than St. Andrews," says one of the leading golfers in the club. Everyone agrees and drinks a toast to that. Then the waiters come by to take the orders for lunch. No one is playing golf until 2:00 p.m., when they begin to pair off for their nine holes.

Elizabeth and Peter decide to roam the course and socialize with different players. John decides to walk with Stephen Mongo and his wife, Betty, who will be playing together. The wife is a better golfer and she is far more serious at it than her husband. John and Stephen were in class together in secondary school. Stephen is now a senior executive at the second-largest commercial bank in the country and Betty is a chartered accountant.

Stephen pulls out a driver and hits his ball into some light rough. "John, are you still mourning or have you met another girl?"

"No, I have not met another girl." John turns and looks at Stephen, smiling. "Why?"

"Oh, no reason," Stephen says. He walks to his ball and whacks it with an 8-iron into a bunker near the green. Then, as he watches his wife hit her ball onto the green some fifteen feet from the hole, he says to John, "Well, there are some beautiful and well-educated Nigasilian women who would be very delighted to meet you. I can introduce you if you want. I'm sure you will find one of them highly suitable to be your partner in marriage."

"I'm sure," John replies. He really does not want to continue with the subject and Stephen can see that.

Stephen loses the hole, and all the other eight holes. As they head for the clubhouse, John asks, "Stephen, does Betty always beat you like this?"

Stephen replies, rather nonchalantly, "No, she usually wins but never so decisively. She sure wanted to impress you!"

To that Betty responded calmly, "Actually, John, he does not practice enough, and often comes here just to sit and drink while I go play with other people."

John smiles. "How is work, Betty?"

"Oh, hanging in there." Betty works for the local branch of one of the big five international accounting firms. "It is a lot of fun and very challenging, but the workload is heavy. We audit most of the state enterprises and that is demanding work."

John continues, "I hope at a minimum they keep their accounts up-to-date."

"Why do you ask, John?"

"Well, all the audited accounts of the government and the state enterprises that I see published are three to four years behind. It seems there is no pressure to maintain up-to-date accounts."

The state enterprises and the government have to publish their audited accounts in the *Nigasilian Government Gazette*, which is an official publication.

"Well, the pressure is building, and they all hope to improve on that performance."

"It's good to hear that. Anyway, what really is disturbing to me about the state enterprises is that they don't seem to be self-sustaining. I really do not understand why the electricity and water company and the state telephone company, for example, require subsidies on an ongoing basis. So, of course, they do not typically have enough funds to make capital investments or even to replace machinery. For those, they need government money. When I ask the question to some people who are in a position to know, they tell me that the explanation is a combination of corruption and poor management. What do you think?"

Betty, with raised eyebrows, turns to John and looks at him straight in the eyes. "I don't think poor management is a big factor, unless you define management in a very broad sense. Fundamentally, the political environment these enterprises face, including interference in their decision making and the arrears of the central government, is the real source of the problems. So, yes, there are management problems, because the managers are not given enough autonomy to manage. But the managers cannot be blamed for that."

"You have a point, Betty. But even when the managers are left alone, they still do not succeed. That's what other well-informed people tell me. My view, then, is that the managers of these enterprises have been spoilt by a succession of governments that have not fired the heads for incompetence and inefficiency. These enterprises should be completely privatized or handed over to private entities under management contracts."

"Well, your dad is president. Why don't you discuss it with him?" Betty suggests. "He'll probably tell you that you sound like the World Bank and the International Monetary Fund."

"Yes, he and I have been through that already. I will continue to tell him, anyway, that some degree of privatization will help make these enterprises successful."

They soon reach the clubhouse and say good-bye, promising to continue the conversation some other time.

Sunday rolls around. John is Anglican like his dad, but the family attends the Catholic church where the solemn Mass was held for Mrs.

Bijunga. A number of relatives and other sympathizers join them at the 9:00 a.m. worship. All the female mourners are still in white. After church, President Bijunga invites those in the mourning party to light refreshments in his garden. Many accept the invitation. Rabena came to the service and decides to go to the reception as well.

Having left promptly after the service, the hosts are home to welcome their guests. Some of the people sit inside, some relax on the veranda, while others roam the beautiful large patio next to the garden of flowers. Rabena, after greeting the hosts, walks down the stairs to the patio. Elizabeth notices and hurries to grab hold of her before someone else does.

"Hello, Mrs. Karam." Elizabeth salutes as she approaches Rabena.

"Oh, Lizzie, Rabena is quite all right," Rabena responds. "How are you? Your mother was such a vivacious and gracious person. She was so motherly in her instincts. We will all miss her."

"Thank you, Rabena. My mother admired you, too. I remember when she mentioned your divorce in a telephone conversation; she was really torn up about it."

"Oh, the marriage was not working anyway. It was better for both of us to stop pretending."

"How's your daughter taking it?"

"Rosie is eighteen. She saw what was going on and knew the end result would be separation. So she is handling it very well."

"Well, I am pleased to hear that she has such a mature attitude to the whole thing. In the meanwhile, you yourself are looking so good. I can see that my father is not exhausting you. I hope you are enjoying your work with him. Everyone comments that you two get along very well and that he adores you."

Rabena smiles softly. "Thank you, Lizzie, you look great, too. For me, I follow the doctor's orders. I watch my diet, I exercise, and I try to have enough sleep. When I have to work late, I just give up on other social activities—even church group meetings. I also don't have too many domestic responsibilities now. My daughter is very helpful and she is serious with her schoolwork. You know, she has even won a scholarship to study in the US at Cornell University. She starts this coming September. Anyway, about my work, 'enjoying' is an under-statement. You know, when I first applied for that job—and your dad was the first president to have it advertised—many people, including my husband, asked me, 'Why do you want to leave teaching and go be a secretary, with your honors degree in English?' I told them I was not going to be a typist. A confidential secretary is different. In fact, Lizzie, I have two regular secretaries that do most of the typing and the filing in the office. I type mainly highly confidential material. I even draft memos for the president, arrange his meetings when several senior people are involved, and I attend most regular cabinet meetings. And to crown it all, Lizzie, your dad is a super boss."

"Yes, so I hear," Elizabeth says. After a moment of hesitation, she adds, "Everyone tells me you two are very close."

"Yes, it seems as if only your mother was not suspicious of the closeness between your daddy and me. That's because your mother knew your dad well and trusted him. Those two really belonged with each other. I wish I had a man like your daddy."

Elizabeth turns towards the house and says, "I think I must go and circulate a bit. Rabena, it's been great talking to you. I'm not sure I'll be able to talk to you again before I leave for London, but I'll send you an e-mail. Take care of my dad now."

"Sure, Lizzie. Thanks."

As Elizabeth steps onto the entrance, Peter and John are standing by. She pulls them to the side and says in a low voice, "Nothing has been going on between Dad and Rabena, but she is in love with him."

"How do you know?" Peter asks.

"Woman's intuition."

John arranged his meeting with the three cabinet ministers for midday on Monday. They meet in a private dining room at Bokubo Hotel, one of the hotels on the oceanfront. Sanjo Manray is the minister of tourism and cultural affairs. Mahdu Kontana is the minister of trade and industry. Dumomo Frah is the minister of agriculture. Of the three, John has met both Kontana and Frah before, during his summer visits to Nigasilia, usually at the houses of mutual friends.

Everyone arrives in their chauffeur-driven SUVs, and Sanjo, whose secretary had made the booking, leads the way into the hotel. The waiter arrives promptly, gives them their pre-arranged menu, and asks them if they want drinks to start. They all order beer, look over the menu as if to remind themselves, and begin their conversation. Sanjo has the honor.

"John, we know how much your dad loves and respects you. We also know your views from talking to some of your friends and those who know your academic work. Kontana and Frah, of course, you have met before and they admire you. We must warn you, though, that we are the frustrated minority in the cabinet. But we do not want to give up the battle and certainly not the war."

The three ministers are among those determined to do something about corruption and mismanagement. They are particularly suspicious of a group of ministers close to the vice president whom they see as particularly corrupt. They are worried the president is not aware of what is going on. After a bite, Sanjo continues.

"Our party won a hard-fought election and your daddy still remains popular, very popular. But our popularity, as a party, is seriously declining. You dad is a brilliant man, has lots of good ideas, and wants to better the lot of the average person in this country. But when it comes to implementation, he is weak. He does not have a system to hold accountable his ministers, top civil servants, and senior managers and administrators of state enterprises and statutory bodies. It is not totally his fault; he inherited a bad system. But he has done nothing to change things. Our Parliament cannot be an efficient watchdog, because it is weak and full of people expecting favors from the government. So, it is up to us in the executive branch to do a good job if the governance of this country is to improve significantly."

In Nigasilia, the Parliament tends to be weak relative to the executive, partly because much of the revenue for government expenditure comes from minerals, import duties, and foreign aid, over which parliamentary control and approval have been perfunctory, almost by tradition. Even more important, most of the parliamentarians look for favors from the government, in the form of aid to their districts, employment for their friends and relatives, and even contracts for businesses in which the parliamentarians or their friends have interests.

John has a wry smile as Sanjo speaks, because for him the whole institutional environment in which these people operate is just a virulent and stinking patrimonial web. Anyway, he says nothing, just giving the impression he is enjoying his meal and keen to hear Sanjo, who with a surprisingly calm look on his face, continues after stopping to take a bite.

"At the ministerial and deputy ministerial levels, we have some of the most incompetent and corrupt individuals that this country has ever seen. What really gets me and my colleagues here is the way some branches of the government are able to negate or neutralize the good work that other branches want to pursue. We have a big problem; we must reform the whole system if any part of it is to work well. Your dad is reluctant to implement anything without consensus in the cabinet or support from powerful people in the country, including the chiefs. That's fine. But then he does not engage these people in a debate so that those of us who are in favor of some policy will have the opportunity to convince the opponents. We discuss these issues a lot, especially when we have our usual bull sessions at parties or in restaurants to discuss Nigasilian problems. We three here have now come to understand that it is a matter of finding a way to compensate those who think they will lose something from a policy change. In that case, we should discuss how we can buy those people out. But no, your dad takes the soft approach and simply says, 'Well, so-and-so group will not like it.' That's not the kind of leadership we need in this country."

The hotel is situated on the estuary of the largest river of Nigasilia, just where it opens into the Atlantic Ocean. So the hotel is not only on the western side of the city but it is situated close to a beautiful beach as well. The water is calm at this time and there are several small boats with passengers enjoying the view. Two of the boats are racing and quite a few of the hotel restaurant's clients are fascinated by that. A couple of people are skiing, each being pulled by a different boat.

Mahdu Kontana decides to enter the serious conversation.

"You know, John, things that go on around here are really disturbing. For instance, the deputy minister of finance in charge of expenditure refuses to sign vouchers unless the recipients bribe him. These are people who have performed services for the government and they need to be paid. In fact, if he does not like somebody for whatever reason, that deputy minister can delay signing for six months or more. Then you have the minster of lands and country planning. He insists on reviewing all survey plans in Lamongwe before they are signed— this is the minister, not some third secretary! You know how tense the land situation has become in Lamongwe, since this is where anyone with money wants land. So the minister's approval is now for sale and costs real money. In fact, in some cases, if the land is big enough, he will not sign unless the owner gives him some of the land for free! I can go on and on. The wonder is that all these things are open secrets. But no one is going to write about them in the newspapers. Residents— Nigasilians and non-Nigasilians alike—are afraid of retribution if they speak out in public. The president has heard these rumors and we have made suggestions about ways he could investigate. Why is he reluctant to launch investigations? We don't know."

John only sighs while the other two shake their heads in disgust. But Kontana is not finished.

"Not to waste more time, John, but there is another big issue that is important for agriculture, industry, and tourism in this country that we want you to help pressure your dad to resolve. It is the reform of our customary land tenure system. I know that you are also passionately interested in this subject."

When the British instituted the second phase of their colonization, they decided to make a major change in the land tenure system of that part of the country; that is, the non-Western part of Nigasilia. The land was owned by extended families and sale of land was not allowed; but the system was going through an evolution towards individual ownership similar to what occurred in other areas of the world. John is convinced that such an evolution toward private individual ownership of land would have continued if the British had not interfered with the system. The British decided to place guardianship of all the land under the traditional rulers, mainly the chiefs. This move gave the chiefs power over land, which they did not have in the traditional societies. Now the chiefs don't want to give up that power. John thinks the chiefs are using that power to concentrate use of land in the hands of a few powerful people and to lease land to foreigners with much of the income going to the chiefs themselves. John, for one, wants to abolish this system, returning full control of the land to the extended families. He also wants the families, with some government oversight, to be free to decide how they want the ownership structures of their land to evolve. John thinks it will evolve towards private individual ownership.

"John, you have a keen interest in reforming our customary land tenure system," says Minister Frah. "I have come to appreciate your views on the matter. Our colonial masters thought they were protecting alienation of the land from the local people by preventing sales of land to outsiders. That all sounds rosy. But the colonial masters made one crucial mistake: they gave guardianship of the land to the chiefs and elites of these communities. Now, we are talking about 80 percent of our land in this country. When foreigners are asked to assess the system, all they seem to see is that people from those traditional societies have inalienable rights to land. They notice that the small man has access to land. What they don't see, and this has been one of the points in your writings, is how restricted that access is in practice for the ordinary person in traditional society. The big people have a disproportionate share. You are right, John, when you argue that what we are observing, in fact, is a disorderly form of privatization. Now, all three of us ministers here are among those big men who gain from the current system, but we have come to see your point."

Several years earlier, John wrote an article in one of the daily papers, the *Daily Times*, arguing that it was possible to develop a strategy that allows evolution towards private property rights while protecting the true extended family owners from exploitation.

"John, we want to push for a discussion on reforming the current system. Too many of the chiefs and the other big men are opposed. They see only losses for themselves. We have to think of a way to convince your father that we need a national debate on this issue."

"Yes, Minister, I agree with you that we should find a way to openly debate these issues at the highest levels," John responds. "I will have to discuss this, and the general leadership problem that Minister Manray raised, with my dad. I have myself raised similar concerns with him, since the problems have been clear to even the casual observer. My dad thinks that many of the suggestions will not receive adequate support to be smoothly implemented. I must confess that each time I discuss governance problems with him I come out with the impression that a dictatorship, with the right kind of leader, may not be bad for this country. The problem is that, in Nigasilia, the dictator must have qualities beyond the single-mindedness, tenacity, and sound policy intentions of a Lee Kuan Yew of Singapore or a Park

Chung Hee of Korea. Maybe some additional degree of ruthlessness is needed as well. Why? Because in Nigasilia, the forces opposing change are more powerful, greedier, and far less enlightened than the opposing forces those leaders had to face. I have almost given up on our country. Anyway, you do inspire someone like me."

"Well," Sanjo responds, "no one wants a dictatorship now, in Nigasilia, but we want strong leadership."

"John, before we end this meal," Kontana says with a smile, "you should find yourself a Nigasilian girl. I know you are a good Anglican, but Cecilia has been dead for three years now. You must start looking for a girl again. I have a young cousin who is very fussy about the man she wants. She is thirty-three, beautiful, and a graduate in biology. I can introduce you to her. Poor girl, she says that most of these Nigasilian men are not very serious. They just want sex and then move on to the next girl."

"Well," John replies, smiling, "I'm taking my time. But thanks. Your offer might come in handy when I am ready."

"All right," Kontana replies as they all get up to leave, "but don't wait too long now."

Chapter 3

John, Elizabeth, and Peter have a couple of days to roam around, sightsee, and socialize with friends and relatives before they head back home. They cherish the opportunity to be together and explore a bit. The only problem is that since they will not have the time to do much visiting, they have to decide who to visit and what excuse they will give the others. Today, Tuesday, not long after breakfast, they take their father's private SUV and drive around to see how the city is looking these days; they will make up their minds on the run regarding who they want to call on. They decline a chauffeur so they can talk freely with each other. Peter volunteers to do the driving. All three enjoy driving in the countryside, but only Peter doesn't mind driving within Lamongwe.

In the central area of the city, traffic is very slow; it is stop-and-go, between ten and twenty miles an hour on average, because of the volume of traffic. In addition, the pedestrians are partly on the sidewalk and partly on the road itself, since the sidewalks are woefully inadequate. Street vendors have their wares on the sidewalk, from ready-to-eat fruits to solid foods cooked at home and sold right on the street in bowls and basins. For the most part, the vendors on the sidewalks deal in light consumer goods, especially used clothing, shoes, radios, notebooks, various pots and pans, pens and pencils, and music CDs and videos. Those selling the CDs will usually be blasting their music, which can be heard in neighboring offices and houses. The people in those places have stopped being disconcerted by all that noise. There are laws controlling noise in Lamongwe. No one is able to enforce them.

Hawkers walk the streets with their wares. They could be selling water or soft drinks, or light consumer goods like cell phones, cell phone chargers to be used in a vehicle, radio batteries, pens, pencils, or notebooks. Right in the middle of the city, the Bijungas soon get stuck in traffic. As they come to a stop, one of the peddlers walks up to their vehicle on the driver's side. He lifts up his wares and looks straight at Peter. Peter rolls down his window, looks at the wares, and notices fifteen to twenty cell phone chargers. So he says to the young man, "How many of these do you have to sell to make a living?"

"Oh, don't worry. Me, I will make enough money to buy a vehicle that is better than yours." The boy spits on the street in disgust and walks off.

An old man then walks up to the Bijungas' vehicle, his hands held by a small boy. The boy halts the old man near the rear of the car where Elizabeth is sitting. The man is supposedly blind and says, "Ah, for God's sake and blessing to you, please let me have something so I can eat. I am hungry and this child is hungry, too."

Elizabeth rolls down her window and says to the boy, who seems to be around ten years old, "Are you not supposed to be in school today? What are you doing here? Do you want to be a beggar when you grow up?"

"No, ma'am, but we need some money to buy food. I also need to pay my school fees before they will admit me into class this term."

"Where is your mother?" Elizabeth asks.

"She went to sell in the market."

"Is this man your father?"

"No, ma'am, he is my uncle. He is my mother's big brother."

"Where is your father?"

"My father is up-country."

"Does he not send money for you and your mother?"

"No, ma'am, he has a wife and two other children with him. He does not send any money for my mamma."

"I see." Elizabeth takes out some kala and hands it to the boy, who puts it in a pouch that he is carrying. The traffic starts moving.

Elizabeth turns to John. "John, just as I expected, all your friends here want to find you a girl. Aren't you lucky to have such caring friends?"

"Yes, indeed." All three burst out laughing. "Maybe I should organize a competition."

Peter asks, "Who will be the competitors, the women or the male matchmakers?"

"Well, the women, of course. What do the men have that I want to see?"

"You make it sound like a dog show," Elizabeth butts in.

"Oh," Peter retorts, "haven't you heard of those African chiefs who line up the women and select the ones they want as wives?"

"Who has been spreading that rumor, Peter?"

"Elizabeth, where have you been?"

Elizabeth ignores Peter and turns to John. "So, have you talked to the boys these last couple of days?"

"Actually, I called them yesterday. They are fine. Their aunt and uncle took them to a movie and they were just getting back when I called."

"You know, I have not spoken to David or Frances for a couple of months now," Peter says. "I have been running around so much. This big road contract that my company has with a couple of our provinces is keeping us all very busy. Kiraney tells me I talk a lot in my sleep these days and it usually is about some road project. You know, she is anxious to be pregnant and thinks I may be too stressed out to impregnate her. She even suggested I go for some test. I told her I may be working hard but not that hard."

Elizabeth asks, "Do you want me to talk to her?"

"No, not yet. If it comes to that I shall let you know. She respects you and, of course, your husband being a doctor, she may want you to ask him a few questions. Her mother is not helping. She is a great mother-in-law but she keeps asking her daughter what she is waiting for. Anyway, I am not too worried. Kiraney will get pregnant soon and the worries of the old lady will come to an end."

"That's the right attitude," John says. "Anyway, you guys, can we drop by to see Stephen? His bank is just down the road here. Or do you want to eat something first?"

"Actually, I'm not hungry," Elizabeth says.

"Nor am I," Peter concurs.

They ring Stephen Mongo to tell him they are dropping by and he is delighted. He is happy to show them around, and offers some coffee, tea, and biscuits. As they take their seats in Stephen's office, Peter asks Stephen how easy it is to get loans to start a business. For example, if he wants to come and set up an engineering consultancy firm, how easy would it be to secure a loan?

"Actually," Stephen explains, "it's not easy. To tell you the truth, we make good money investing in government securities, because the interest rates are 15 to 20 percent. Apart from that, we support mainly import and export businesses. These are very liquid and safe loans."

Elizabeth asks, "So how do the banks help in the development of the country?"

"Well," Stephen responds, "the plain truth is that the banks are not helping as they could, mainly because we are rather conservative. In my view we have little alternative, because of the risks involved. Most of our local businesses in Nigasilia do not keep proper accounts, they do not have good collateral, and they do not have much credit history, if any at all. So banks won't touch most of them and it becomes a vicious circle. For someone like you, you would have to show a healthy balance sheet to start, which means a lot of seed money from you. The government and the central bank are working on a financial sector development program to increase the ability of the banking system to contribute to development. Look, the banking system is all we have for a financial system."

"Anyway, Stephen," John says, "what I wanted to ask you is what you hear from all these business people about the leadership of our father."

"You know this is a difficult question. Overwhelmingly, they like your father. They think he has the interest of this country at heart, that he is not corrupt, and that he has a clear vision of what needs to be done. But they think he does not have enough good and strong people around him to do a good job running this country. That is, as far as economic development is concerned. They are also not sure that he is strong and able enough to clean up the government and to motivate the people in civil society and business to work together to bring about the changes that are needed. The only thing saving your father is that they cannot think of anyone in a position to take over who would better lead the country."

"So, what do these critics want to see?"

"They would like to see major organizational and personnel changes in the public sector, and action by the president to bring in civil society and the business sector to develop ideas and implement them."

"So how would you suggest my father start the process?" Peter asks.

"By talking to civil society and the business people and asking their views, both in open forums and in closed, even confidential, discussions."

"But," Elizabeth interjects, "that won't help him with the action part."

"No," Stephen agrees. "For that he will need real courage and disciplinary fervor."

"Stephen, thank you," John says. "We have taken enough of your time today. Hope to see you again soon."

The Bijungas decide to stop by to see an aunt, Marie, who is a cousin of their late mother. As they drive to her house, Elizabeth asks, "So, John, are you thinking seriously of coming to help Dad?"

"Why do you ask?"

"Well, Dad has been talking to you about coming home, and I hear you asking around about his leadership."

"Actually, I would like to come and help, but I am not convinced I would make a difference unless Dad is a stronger leader than I think he is. But I am trying to be fair. I have never had much opportunity to observe him firsthand or interact with his team. With civil society and the business community, I don't see him doing much—that is, really lead. That's why I consult people whom I know will be honest with me. I want to know if I am being unfair to our dad when I say that he does not impress me as a strong leader."

"John, here's something else you are forgetting. Dad wants you to come and help because he thinks you can help him be a better leader. A general needs good captains and lieutenants. Dad is unsure whether he can trust many of the people around him. He wants to build up the quality of the economics team, which is why he wants you to come. In my view, in spite of all the downsides, I hope you do help him. You can take leave from your university post and send the boys to boarding school if you do not want them to change educational systems."

Peter glances at John and smiles. John raises his eyebrows, but says nothing. Elizabeth thinks she has been convincing. She knows her brother very well. He will come if his dad makes a good offer.

Auntie Marie is a first cousin of the late Mrs. Bijunga. She lives in a one-story house in the south side of the city. She is a widow and her daughter, who never married and is a cashier at one of the local supermarkets, stays with her. The daughter has a son who also stays in the same house. The small house, fully owned by the aunt, is about seventy years old. Three bedrooms, a living room, a dining room, and a pantry form the main body of the house. Adjacent to the house is the only toilet, a separate bathroom for showering, and the kitchen. There is a covered pathway along which one walks to go from the main body of the house to the adjacent facilities. Barbecue and cooking facilities are outside in the back yard.

The Bijungas park on the street just outside the house. The house is fenced but someone can see who is at the gate from a small porch at the entrance to the house. One needs to climb a flight of stairs of five steps to enter the house via the porch. When the Bijungas knock on the gate, Auntie Marie's daughter, Safie, who happens to be at home, lets them in. Her brother, Santigie, a self-employed painter, is also at the house today, just visiting. He lives about two miles away with his family. They had already seen the Bijungas at the funeral, but they did not have any time for conversation beyond the usual condolences. Auntie Marie could not attend the funeral because she was not feeling well.

"Elizabeth, Peter, John, you are welcome," Safie says as she embraces each one. "I'm so glad you have come. Mamma has been longing to see you all. Come in. Santigie is also here. Mamma is lying down, but she can get up to talk to you."

The Bijungas tag along behind Safie as she leads them into the house. As they enter, Elizabeth says, "Oh, Safie, don't wake Auntie if she is asleep."

"No, no, no, she is not asleep. She is only resting. She must see you. She wants to. Yes, yes, yes."

Safie brings Auntie Marie out from her room and then goes to the backyard to fetch Santigie, who is chatting with some friends from the neighborhood. In the meanwhile, Auntie Marie embraces the three visitors.

"Oh, it's so good to see you all. Your father told you to come and see me, eh? You young people, you always just go about your business."

"No, Auntie, we wanted to see you," Elizabeth replies. "Safie told us you were not well when she came to the funeral. We are just here for a short time and so we wanted to see you."

"Well, I am happy you came. You may not see me again, you know. I don't know how much longer I will be alive. All of my body aches. I have arthritis all over. But now the doctor says I have an enlarged heart and I am anemic. What kind of trouble is this? I cannot even afford to see my own doctor for a regular checkup or to buy the medicines he is prescribing."

Santigie has since walked in and greets the visitors.

"Auntie Marie," Peter says with a restrained smile, hoping to cheer up the old lady, "you will be all right; don't worry."

"Peter, look at you. You are a big man now. I have not seen you for a long time. I see John more than you and Elizabeth. Why don't you two come visit Nigasilia more often? Peter, you have children now?"

"Auntie, no, I do not have children yet, but I will soon. Anyway, Elizabeth and I will come home more often now, and each time we will visit you."

"Why, you think I have many years more? John, you are so quiet."

"Auntie, I am very happy to see you. You will be around for a long time. You are not going anywhere. You have been handling the arthritis very well. The other things you can deal with also. You just need to follow the doctor's advice."

Santigie interjects, in a rather embarrassed and soft tone of voice, "The medicines and the doctor's fees, they are hard for us."

"Don't worry; I will help. Who is your doctor?" Elizabeth asks.

"We do not have a doctor right now. We used to go to General. Now we just go to a pharmacist and he advises us on what medicine to buy for her."

Nigasilia General Hospital is the largest public hospital in the country. In principle, no fees should be charged for the doctors' services in the public hospitals. But you have to go buy the medicines privately. People with means do not like going to the public hospitals because the service is slow. It can take hours of waiting before one sees a doctor. Hence, for serious ailments, many of the doctors will advise patients to see them "privately" if they want adequate services. This could mean going to the private clinics of the doctors or seeing them in the public hospitals as "private" patients. As a private patient, the person must then pay the doctor a service fee, which is not publicly controlled or even reported to the hospital administration.

"Okay, I shall call Dr. Mondeh. He is a good friend of mine and Mundu's. And with the heart problem he can always talk to Mundu."

Elizabeth calls the doctor and arranges for her aunt to see him for treatment. The doctor will send the bills to Elizabeth via the Internet. She will wire the payments to his bank account in Lamongwe. If her aunt needs particular specialists, the doctor will arrange the visits and Elizabeth will pay all expenses. Such bills are usually only a fraction of what would be charged in the US or UK. Elizabeth writes down all the relevant information and hands the paper to Safie.

"Auntie, please continue your rest," Elizabeth says. "We will keep in touch, I promise. We are very happy to see you. You will be all right."

They stop next to see Borbor, a first cousin on their father's side. He also lives on the south side of the city only about a mile from Auntie Marie. He and his wife and two children live on the second story of a two-story house; they are renting. It is a complete flat, modest but self-contained. It was built some twenty years ago by a well-to-do businessman. The dining room, full bathroom, and kitchen are all contained in the body of the flat. In similar situations, many Nigasilian landlords have to share kitchens and toilets with the tenants on another floor. This is mainly because the houses were originally built as single-family homes. As the population increased, particularly in Lamongwe, many homeowners found it profitable to turn such houses into multi-family units.

Borbor is a carpenter and has been doing miscellaneous jobs for the past two years. Before then, he was working with his older brother who is a building contractor.

"Peter, Lizzie, John, it is good to see you all. We were at the funeral, but we could not make it to the cemetery or the repast. I don't have transport."

"Borbor, it's good to see you," John says. "When we were driving here I wondered if you would be around, because people always tell us that you and your brother go all over the country doing construction work. How are you two doing now, and how is the family?"

"Things are not going well. But please, come in, sit down."

"Borbor, you have a nice place here," Elizabeth adds.

"Yes, but things are rough now. I am even struggling to pay school fees for my children. Sorry, Tinkoko is at work. She would have loved to see you."

"That's okay. We should have warned you, but really we didn't know what time we would have," John says.

"Yes, I understand."

John is surprised that Borbor is struggling to make ends meet; Tinkoko has told him nothing about it. "So what has been going on? Why did you not contact Dad to see if there was some way he could help you? Dad has always been kind to you and your brother."

"Yes, John, I know. Uncle has been very kind to us. But the situation is not easy and I don't know how to approach Uncle. I am too ashamed. John, my brother has run away. He has a British passport and some friends in the UK, so he fled. He won a government contract to build the main building of a new elementary school in Moyembe.

"John, he did a bad job on that contract, buying cheap materials and hiring inexperienced people to do the work, because he did not want to pay for experienced people. He failed to take my advice. He told me that some people had not paid him for work done and so he was in debt. He saw that as an opportunity to make some extra money. Unfortunately, soon after he finished the building, there was a thunderstorm in the area and the building collapsed. Upon inspection, his crime was uncovered. Of course, there were some jealous people who helped the inspectors see the bad job my brother had done."

Peter jumps in. "So what happened to the company?"

"Well, the government closed it and says that Alfred must show up and give a full account. Alfred has since got a visa for the US but I doubt he will settle there. Look, what is really a problem now for me is that, in the bidding process for the contract, Alfred received the help of Maigo Bang, the minister of works, housing, and infrastructure. So I have been ashamed to go talk to Uncle. Otherwise, knowing your father, he would have been willing to help me with school fees for our children."

Borbor has a son and a daughter, both in secondary schools.

"So, how are the two of them doing?" John asks.

"Very well. They both want to do medicine."

"Excellent."

John continues his intervention. "Look, Borbor, we will help you with school fees. But you have to find a way to go talk to Daddy and apologize. Let me give you my e-mail and telephone number in America. You can just flash me and I will call you back." This would prevent Borbor from having to pay for the expensive call.

"Also," John continues, "I'll leave some money with Daddy's confidential secretary to give you for next year's school fee. I will give you her telephone number also. Pay the whole year at once, for both of them. Your kids must have only a couple of years left, right?"

"Yes, two years and three years."

"Borbor, you are a carpenter. You can set up a good business of your own."

"That is what I am trying to do now, John."

"Okay, keep trying. Maybe we can help you with some start-up money. But no monkey business, now."

"Ay, John, you know me, I am hard-working and serious. I'm not going to deceive you when I know you are only trying to help me. You have to work hard for what you have."

∞

As the Bijungas relax at home for dinner that evening, Elizabeth asks, "How was your day, Dad?"

"There were all the usual matters, most having to do with economic issues. But I had two very relaxed sessions, with the ambassadors from France and the US. The French envoy is new, just arrived about a week ago. Particularly important today, though, was a visit I made, on the advice of the minister of health, to General Hospital to see the progress being made in renovation, as well as some new equipment. I also talked to the doctors about their problems. Of course, as you can imagine, the discussion ended up being all about medicines, pay, inadequate facilities, and long hours. The message was that we need to act and do something before we drive all our good doctors from public service."

The old man pauses, looks at each of the young ones, and asks, "So how was your day? I hope you people had a good tour."

"Yes," Elizabeth responds. "We basically just drove around the city. We came down only to visit Stephen Mongo, Cousin Borbor, and Auntie Marie."

"Did Borbor tell you about his brother?" their father asks.

"Yes, and we were disgusted."

"Well, you should be. We'll get hold of him sooner or later and I will not protect him. How is Auntie Marie? They told me some time ago she was ill. But then, I did not see her or even hear from her until I talked to Safie at your mother's funeral. I then found out that she was quite unwell. I asked Safie to come around, even at the office, to tell me how she was doing and to see if there was any way I could help. But I never heard from Safie again, so I assumed that she was all right. You know that your aunt does not like to impose on anyone."

Elizabeth explains what they had found and what they had done. By now they are already well into their dinner. Even though she has so far dominated the conversation, Elizabeth decides to pop the question, mainly to see how her father will react.

"John," she says, "all my friends are asking me why you do not come home and help your dad."

"You know, engineers and architects have a lot to contribute to the development process, too," John retorts. "I hope your friends are asking you and Peter the same question."

"Well, of course, they are," says Elizabeth. "But they understand my constraints—my husband is in England. It is you they are most keen to see around. They say that without good economic policy making, a lot of other things cannot be made to fall in place."

"Sure," John says. "Well, I don't rule out the possibility that I could return some years from now. Maybe things could change enough for me to find this place attractive for retirement. Right now, I don't see how I can fit in, as far as work is concerned, especially work involving economic policy making. These politicians are not interested in development, but only in their own power and wealth."

"Well," Peter says, "you are an economist; you should not mind self-interest."

"Of course I don't," replies John. "But I do mind it when there is nothing protecting the public interest from the theft and inefficiency of those in public service. In more fortunate environments, institutional arrangements and mechanisms perform such a function, constraining certain types of behavior and providing the appropriate incentives for more socially productive behavior."

"Well, there you go, John," his dad interjects. "You just drew up your own terms of reference."

"Oh, I don't really want to be a minister around here. Not yet, anyway."

"You want to be an adviser?" President Bijunga asks. "That's easy to do."

John had known this subject would come up and had rehearsed his strategy. Yes, both Elizabeth and his dad think it is a great idea for him to come and help in economic policy making. But John thinks his dad will not want to take his advice to rule with a strong hand—not dictatorially, but by putting the burning issues squarely on the table, and forcing national debates that John believes can result in good economic policy making. John also thinks his dad is weak in pushing the corrupt politicians and senior state employees out of office. Moreover, John wants his father to reform the appointment procedures for leadership positions in government and in state enterprises so that highly competent people will be appointed to those posts. John has told his father all this before. He wants to insist he would consider coming to help the president only if his father could promise him all of the above. But it would be disrespectful to demand that his father promise these things up front. After all, he can always take leave of absence, and then if things don't work out he can return before his leave ends. After serious thought, John thinks he has found a compromise. He will come if he is given a position that allows him enough access and authority from which he can build adequate evidence and support to force his dad to act in ways that will improve governance in Nigasilia. John knows he has bargaining power, because his dad really wants him to come. Elizabeth has assured him of his bargaining power.

So without any hesitation John says, "Here's my offer, Dad. I shall seriously consider coming home, at least for a couple of years, if you give me a position like chief economist to the government, which would have the rank of a cabinet minister. As chief economist, I should have the authority to review the economic policies of all the ministries and government departments to ensure coherence and rationality. I should participate in all international economic policy decision making—including aid, trade, and investment negotiations—as well as in relations with the multilateral financial institutions. I should be involved in reform programs designed to clean up the government and make it more efficient in its supply of public services."

"Et cetera, et cetera," the president jumps in, chuckling. "Sure, you want to be the economic policy-making czar of Nigasilia. I get the point. I'll discuss your offer with the vice president. He'll have to be the referee in the contests between you and the ministers, especially the minister of finance and development and the minister of trade and industry. I am too tied up to give enough energy to that kind of task. But of course I will support you enough for you to do your job as chief economist and be my right-hand man in economic policy making. We just have to find a way to deal with all those I do not fully trust, but who at the same time are very important in keeping me and my party in power. That is where I will need the VP's help."

Peter looks at both his dad and John. They seem relaxed. He wants to be sure they are really on the same page, so he asks, "Dad, did John or Lizzie tell you that we have invited the Gelegumpo dancers and singers to perform in the backyard tomorrow? Apparently the group has been eager to do something for us before we leave. The members want to show their appreciation for all that our mother did, sponsoring them and raising their profile in this country so they can eventually be launched onto the international stage. Mom had it all figured out. You should discuss sponsorship with your minister of tourism and cultural affairs. John thinks that Sanjo Manray is one of your more enlightened ministers."

"Yes, yes," Samuel replies. "Manray will try. But you know it's not easy to get our cultural groups to prepare themselves for the big stage. Achieving sponsorship abroad is also a hurdle; not impossible, but not easy. Yes, enjoy them tomorrow. I won't be here, because duty calls. But I get to see them more regularly than you, anyway. Last year, your mother invited them over twice. I plan to continue the tradition."

Wednesday afternoon, the Gelegumpo dancers and singers have arrived and are all set for their performance. The Bijunga siblings have invited about fifteen of their friends to join them, former schoolmates who are still around in Lamongwe as well as friends from their church where they still make contributions. They plan to entertain their guests with some light refreshments after the performance. For now, the attention is on the Gelegumpo performers, a fair-sized group of some thirty acrobats, dancers, singers, and instrumentalists playing drums, cymbals, xylophones, sansas, native horns, flutes, fiddles, lyres, and koras. The total membership of the group is more than twice as large, but they do not always perform together.

The guests are all thrilled. It is amazing to John and Elizabeth how many of these locally educated residents never bother to attend live performances. They conclude that part of the reason is that the groups do not normally perform at locations pleasant enough to attract the elites. The financial contributions at such performances are strictly voluntary, with no gate or entrance fees. Not much revenue flows from such an approach. John wonders why there is not a greater attempt to gain commercially from all that art.

After the show, he turns to Elizabeth, who takes a keen interest in the arts. "Lizzie, why don't our performers of high native art exploit their artistic and cultural talents?"

"Well," Lizzie replies, "the performers see these dances and songs as elements of larger ceremonies, festivals, or rites that have deep cultural meaning. Our people are not aware of the commercial potential. It is this aspect that the Ministry of Tourism and Cultural Affairs should help them with. Still, I am quite surprised that as a people we have failed to recognize the value of our native art for pure relaxation and for building national pride. We would rather go to Covent Garden and watch Billy Budd or to some symphony or ballet performance in Washington or London. We have not considered cultivating our own serious performing arts, or building theaters sophisticated enough to attract the best in our societies. Thank goodness a few African countries are beginning to see the light. Nigasilia, unfortunately, is still in the dark."

At dinnertime, all three young Bijungas have nothing but praise for the majestic and beautiful performance. They urge their father to take seriously the promotion of the performing and visual arts of Nigasilia.

While his children were enjoying the performing arts event, the president had a conversation with the vice president that morning, on the topic of John coming on board as chief economist.

"Kamake, as you know, I have been trying to get John to come on board. I have finally convinced him to come. He is willing to take leave from his university, you know, since he is not sure how it will all work out. I think we should give the ministerial ranking so that he could broadly cover all economic policy making and have the ability to speak with the ministers on equal terms."

"Samuel, I support you wholeheartedly, but we have a potential management dilemma. The role of the chief economist could become so broad that John could control the whole of economic policy making. So far, the Ministry of Finance and Development has felt that it had the overall economic policy-making role. So we would have to be clear on the role of the chief economist versus the role of finance and development."

"Kamake, you are right. But what I see is that the chief economist would not get into monitoring implementation of policies. That would be the role of finance and development. It is when it comes to development of strategies and approaches to policy making and the design of economic policies that the chief economist office would take the leadership role, working with the various ministries concerned."

"The chief economist office and finance and development will need to work closely."

"Yes. There is another matter. You know my son is analytical. He is not a politician. So you might have to help me resolve conflicts that are bound to come up between his office and the various ministries. In addition, they would need to give him information when he needs it and be willing to discuss this information with him when he requests it. I would like you to talk to our ministers, and I will do the same, of course, emphasizing that such cooperation is essential to improving policy making and implementation in the country. I don't want John to have to spend a lot of time lecturing these ministers on the value of such cooperation. You know John; he will do so as politely as possible, but also as resolutely as necessary. I don't want the pride of the ministers to be hurt."

"No problem, Mr. President, I am happy to play the middleman's role here. I like John and have a lot of respect for him."

Recalling this conversation, the president now informs John that the vice president is thrilled at the prospect of his playing the part of czar of economic policy making. He asks John how soon he can come. John replies that he could try to make it by the end of January, which is almost exactly seven months away.

"John, congratulations," Peter says.

"Yes, John," Elizabeth adds, "I am very pleased it has all worked out."

"Dad," John asks, "did the VP think it was wise to give me ministerial ranking?"

"Oh, yes, he was quite comfortable with that. Otherwise he would have told me so. I have encouraged him to speak frankly with me. I chose him to be my vice-presidential candidate and we were good friends even before then. Look, John, given the task and the level at which you would be operating in Nigasilia, you cannot come in at a lower rank."

Elizabeth glances at John and her father and concludes that the discussion is now exhausted. So she turns to one of her favorite topics in African politics; namely, the role of civil societies and what African countries can do to strengthen them.

"You know, Dad, one African president, I gather, is officially promoting civil society activities by giving the societies logistical assistance and offering to help them attend select conferences abroad. But in Nigasilia, like in the vast majority of the African countries, civil society is a joke."

John snickers. Everyone turns and looks at him, surprised, since they did not find anything funny in Elizabeth's statement.

"In all honesty," their father says, "I don't think that African governments should be in the business of financially and logistically helping civil society organizations. Governments should simply not obstruct them as long as they act within the law. I also think that a government should encourage serious civil society activists and organizations to express their views on government policy and even be proactive in making suggestions to the government on any policy on which they feel they have expertise. We of the Progressive Party do nothing to impede civil society activity."

The main dish has been braised lobster in cream sauce on white rice. Just before the waiter interrupts for dessert, which is a choice of vanilla ice cream, pound cake, or fruit salad, Peter says, "Dad, this lobster was especially delicious tonight."

"Well, it's only a small variation from what you had the other night. Anyway, my cook is simply very good, and as you can see, he does several international dishes. The bookcase in the kitchen is full of cookbooks."

After the dessert orders have been placed, Samuel continues. "The truth is that our civil society organizations are a farce. Part of the time, they organize hoping to get money from sympathetic organizations in the rich countries. This happens all over our continent, if I may say so. In Africa, the so-called civil societies that claim to be working for good governance or democracy are often themselves very corrupt. Governments are able to buy their leaders anytime they choose, because the leaders are usually financially strapped and power-hungry. We have seen them in Nigasilia. Right now, in fact, we try to keep track of their activities, not so that we can suppress them but so we can expose them when necessary and to warn gullible foreign organizations that want to throw money at them. So, we ask them to register properly, keep regular accounts, report their fund-raising activities to the Internal Revenue Authority, and make public their officers and organization addresses. Other than that, we welcome them here. But I have not seen a solid one yet in Nigasilia—one that is not riddled with tribalism and corruption. In fact, their personnel are often very poorly educated. So, if you are interested in strengthening them you will be doing a great favor to the country. But you will perform a greater public service if you ignore the imbeciles we have right now and start afresh, from scratch—that is, if you are that interested."

"Oh, Dad, you've said it all. Civil societies in Nigasilia lack funds, are bedeviled by tribalism, and sometimes face government restrictions and sabotage—all factors hampering their growth."

Peter cannot help but ask, "So, John, do you think that someone in Nigasilia should try to assess what we lose by not having a truly vibrant civil society?"

"Actually, Peter, that's not a bad idea at all, because civil society activity fosters cooperation and the building of trust, which are good for economic development."

Elizabeth shows her frustration with a heavy sigh. "Yes, Dad, unfortunately, everything you say is most likely correct. I would like to see us succeed in making civil society organizations flourish here because they are very important in all democratic societies. Also, as John and others have been arguing, we need civil societies to pressure governments in Africa to come up with, and implement, sound economic policies."

"Well, you know what to do, then," her dad responds. "Those of you who strongly believe in the value of civil society should organize and act. If someone like you, Lizzie, does not act, who should? Look at me; I am president and all my three children are diasporans. How can I preach to other young people abroad that they should come and help in the development of their country?"

The three young Bijungas look at each other and raise their eyebrows, signaling they had better not say anything. Their father has told them repeatedly that all three could succeed if they came home. There is no reason to stay in the US, UK, and Canada, as far as their father is concerned. Unfortunately, he understands also that Nigasilia is a very difficult place to live and that many of these excellent professionals of

Nigasilian origin think they will be unable to get adequate professional satisfaction—it isn't simply a matter of money. Elizabeth makes that point all the time. But her father argues that if a sufficient number of diasporans return home, they can help improve the standards in their professions and somehow garner more facilities to make things more palatable and professionally appealing for all.

Peter looks at his brother. "John, you are collecting the boys in New York? Are you going to spend any time with David and Frances again?"

"Actually, I booked in such a way that I will not be flying out of Kennedy but rather out of LaGuardia. David and Frances say they will come to Kennedy with the boys and we will all drive to LaGuardia from there. We will have enough time to talk, unless my flight into New York is very late."

"Do the Simpsons have a piano for Donald?" Samuel asks.

"Yes, and both of them play a little," John replies.

"Greet them for me. You know, I never saw the articles David wrote on the NGOs. I guess I could have downloaded them online. To tell you the truth, I completely forgot about it all, though I really enjoyed talking to him. I remember he looks so much like Cecilia."

"Yes, he does. I will get copies of the articles for you. In fact, I will get soft copies and e-mail them to you."

"Okay, thanks." Samuel looks at his children. "Don't you guys need to pack?"

Peter laughs quietly. "I don't know about the other two, but I am just going to throw everything in my suitcase."

"I guess that's the advantage when you are going home. I have the same approach," John admits.

As expected, the parting on Thursday afternoon is somber. But as the siblings sit down for lunch, Rabena walks in.

"Hi, Rabena," each one says as they embrace her. They invite her to join in the lunch.

Rabena asks, "So when do I see you people again? Soon, I hope."

Peter responds first. "Well, maybe Kiraney and I will join the diasporans' homecoming this year."

Nigasilian diasporans in the West typically go in great numbers to Nigasilia during Christmastime. The bulk of them usually go between December 15 and January 15. In fact, a couple of the European airlines schedule additional flights into Nigasilia during that period.

"That would be great," Rabena says. "I have not had the opportunity to meet your wife, you know. If you do come, please don't forget to let me meet her."

"Certainly, we will make sure, Rabena. She wants to meet you, too."

"Lizzie, greet Mundu for me. He used to come every year, he told me, but he seems to have stopped doing so. Am I right?"

"Actually, he has not come for the last two years. This is the longest he has been away. He feels guilty, because he has not seen his parents during that time. His work is keeping him busy. He'll try, perhaps in the next year, to come. To tell you the truth, he hates coming during the holiday period. Lamongwe is just too busy and noisy for him."

"So, what about my man, John? When will you grace these shores again?"

"Just for you, Rabena, I'll come soon."

"I'll be waiting ."

As they finish their meals, the president turns to them and says, "I know you still have some time before you will be getting yourselves together. Maybe we should say prayers for traveling mercies before Rabena leaves us."

All four of the Bijungas have tear-filled eyes as they make their little circle and their father begins the prayers. He chokes up a little, swallows, and then gets to it.

"Almighty and merciful God, we thank you for the strength that you have given us during this difficult period. We pray now that you continue to guide and protect us as we move forward without our greatest source of strength and inspiration, Matinbi. Now her three children are to travel back to their families. We pray that your angels guide and protect them and deliver them safely to their destinations. We ask this, oh God, in the name of your Son, Jesus Christ. Amen."

John's agenda is clear. He must negotiate his leave with the university, and tell his boys about his plans to go to Nigasilia. Then he must find appropriate boarding schools for them. He will talk to schools in New Hampshire, Massachusetts, and Connecticut. He has friends in the United States Agency for International Development, who leave their children in boarding schools while they spend time abroad, and David and Frances live close by in case of emergencies.

John's flight arrives on time at JFK. The Simpsons pick him up and after the warm embraces all around, they drive to LaGuardia. William asks, "Daddy was Grandpa sad when you were leaving?"

"Yes, very sad. But he knows I will be in touch regularly."

"I'm sure Uncle Peter and Auntie Lizzie will also be talking to him. You think they will go to him at Christmas?"

"They might, but they have not decided yet."

"And you? When will you go visit Grandpa again?"

"Oh, I don't know. Grandpa will tell me when he wants me to go."

John thinks it would be rather unkind to just drop the news of his big move in such a casual manner, especially after having been away from the boys. But he is struggling for the exact words to use now.

"You can go when you want to, can't you?"

Donald looks at his brother with a frown, and his brother thinks Donald wants him to stop talking. So he does.

No one says anything until they reach LaGuardia. Once they arrive at the appropriate terminal, John tells the boys he wants to talk briefly with their aunt and uncle. So the three grown-ups find a space with some privacy, not too far from where the boys are standing.

"I finally agreed to go home and help my dad," John says to David and Frances. "I will only take leave for two or three years, because I am not sure how things will work out."

"This has been weighing heavily on your mind for a long time. What made you finally agree?" David asks.

"Three things, I would say. First is my guilt. I have been raving about the bad governance in Nigasilia. Now here is my father, elected as the president, and he invites me to come and help. I no longer have the heart to say no. I am convinced that he wants to improve things. I think I owe it to him to give it a shot. Second, my sister urged me to go. She says my father told her that he does not know who to trust when it comes to those giving him advice in the interest of the country. Moreover, my father wants to improve his economics team. Third, my father agreed to give me the post of chief economist with the status of a minister."

"But you are still hedging."

"My worry, to be honest, is about myself. I am too impatient and I am afraid that the pace of change will never be satisfactory to me. I am worried that I may not be happy. But I am determined to give it my best shot."

"Well," says Frances, "I can see your point. I can see why you feel you should go and help but still be cautious."

"Yes, but you know my dilemma."

"Yes," they both answer in unison, "the boys."

"We will help you in any way we can," says Frances.

"Thank you, Frances, I don't doubt that. I shall broach the subject with the boys in a day or two. I prefer boarding school for them, right here in America. I don't trust the facilities in Nigasilia, especially the science programs."

"On that I agree with you, John," David assures him. "I also support your helping your father. It's a privilege for you. Here you are, a Nigasilian economist, having his dad as president and the opportunity to go be chief economist. I would jump at the opportunity if I were in your shoes."

John and his boys arrive home safely and find everything in order. John visits the chairman of his department, Charles Wilkinson, the next day and discusses extended leave.

"John," the chairman says with an excitement in his voice, after John tells him of his father's offer, "look, this is a great experiment for us. I don't think we know of another case in Africa where the president has a son who is a highly reputable economist. Even the State Department would be excited at this opportunity to observe what happens. We don't want to lose you, of course, and hope that you will come back to us. But whenever academics have the chance to bring research knowledge to policy making, they should always jump at the opportunity. How long will you be away?"

"I think up to three years. My dad's first term ends in a couple of years. If he is reelected, I will at least stay a year or so and see what happens."

"Well, John, as you know, we do not give leave of absence longer than three years. Once that limit is reached, we usually ask people to resign and renegotiate to come back if they so wish later."

"Yes, I am aware of the policy. I will not ask for a special favor. You are already being kind. But I do have one more request. I am overdue for sabbatical and wondered whether I could have the first of my three years away considered a sabbatical year."

"Yes, John, I think that is possible. I shall verify with the dean and get back to you. I will support you if we are within the rules."

"Thank you, Charles."

"I assume your teaching for this semester is not affected by all this?"

This semester, John is scheduled to teach an undergraduate course in microeconomics and a graduate course in African economic development. "That is correct."

"I just have one question for you, a difficult one, perhaps," Charles says, as he looks at John straight in the eyes. "You have always argued that most African countries, Nigasilia included, are on a slow evolutionary path, because their fundamental political and economic institutions are not likely to change easily. Do you think you will make a difference in this regard?"

"To tell you the truth, I am not optimistic. But I find it difficult to say no to my father. He keeps telling me and my siblings that we should not merely talk about what needs to be done, but act. Now he is ready to challenge me by giving me the opportunity. It is an offer I cannot morally refuse. So, I shall try. If I find myself failing, I shall withdraw from the battle."

"Well, I certainly hope you succeed."

At breakfast the following day, John makes the kids some easy-over fried eggs and sausages. The boys get the feeling from looking at their father that he does not want to talk about the funeral. As they sit quietly, John decides to break the silence.

"So, fellows, how would you like it if I go and help the people of Nigasilia?"

"Really, Dad?" Donald asks.

"Your grandpa says I should take leave from my teaching and go help the country of my birth."

"But you said you don't think the people of Nigasilia are serious," Donald retorts.

"Yes, but your grandfather says I am wrong. He says the people want someone like me to go over and help. He says that, as president, if the people want his son to go over and help, he has to listen to his people."

The boys are of two minds. They love their grandpa and believe that what Grandpa says must be correct. But what about them? What happens to them now? Their mother passed away just a few years ago. And now their dad wants to desert them for Nigasilia? Or does he want to take them with him? If he does, do they really want to go? They do not mind Nigasilia, in general, but what does it mean for their schooling? They look at each other, baffled. They love and respect their father and do not want to upset him. They have never been faced with this challenge before. Donald especially feels the pressure to say something.

"Dad, can't you just advise them from here?"

"Of course I can. But I need to help them act on what I advise them to do."

Donald persists. "You mean they will not do what you advise them to do if you are not watching them?"

"Yes, Donald, I'm afraid so."

"Why?"

"What do you mean, why?"

"Why can't they simply read what you want them to do and act? If they do not understand, they can talk to you on the telephone."

"Donald, in politics some people may not like you or what you want done. If you are there every day from morning until night to make sure your supporters carry out your program, your opponents will have less chance of seizing the upper hand."

"You mean they will not try to sabotage your program when you are there?"

"They will, Donald, but I shall be around to stop them."

"They might still win, Dad."

"Yes, they might. But if I am around they might not. If I am not around, they will win."

Donald glances at his brother. "Sure, Dad," Donald says.

"William, what about you? What do you think?"

"Okay, Daddy, if Grandpa needs you, then go. Do you want us to go with you?"

"I am thinking of placing you both in boarding school here in America. But if you prefer to come with me, I can take you to Nigasilia. They have good schools there, too. Do you want some time to think about it?"

The boys look at each other. William shrugs his shoulders. So Donald says, "Boarding school is not bad. Michael Stewart will be going to boarding school next year because his parents are going to work in China."

"Can the two of us attend the same school?" William asks.

"Well, of course," John replies, with a big smile across his face. "It is better for me, too, that you both attend the same school. We will have to go for interviews and visit the facilities. You will start in September."

"Sure, Dad," says William, glancing at his brother.

July turns out to be a very busy month for John and the boys. But things work out well. Both boarding schools to which John applies are willing to admit the boys. The boys are coming from a first-class private school in Washington, DC, have good results and excellent recommendations from the school, and John is not asking for any financial aid; the schools are very glad to have them. Both schools explained their academic curricula, stressing mathematics, science, and foreign languages. They also underscored their library and science and computer laboratory facilities. Then they showed off their extracurricular activities: choir, music, diverse sports, and field trips. Finally, they took the Bijungas through the boarding facilities. The boys were amazed when, at the first school, they observed untidy rooms. They have grown up being told to keep their rooms neat and tidy.

As they drove home after the visit to the second school, John asked the boys, "So which one do you prefer?"

The boys had already discussed it while their dad was having discussions with the admissions staff. They like both schools, as each has the curriculum they want, but the second school in New Hampshire boasts a better soccer program. As it turns out, that same school also has a more pleasant-seeming piano teacher. So there it was.

John and the boys spend the rest of the summer together, realizing that in a few months they will be separated with John going off to Nigasilia. Both boys attend a one-week soccer camp in Washington, DC, and Donald participates in an all-day Mozart Festival, in northern Virginia, where he plays the first movement of Mozart's Piano Sonata No. 3 in C Major. They also go twice to see the Baltimore Orioles play, and visit the National Gallery of Art and the Natural History and Air and Space museums. They cap the summer with a trip to Thomas Jefferson's 5000-acre plantation at Monticello. John has a friend from college days who is a professor at the University of Virginia and they stay at his house for one night.

Soon it is the end of summer and the separation time has come. The night before they are to leave for the long drive to New Hampshire, John says, "Well, I hope you guys have enjoyed this summer as I have. I am glad I was able to take you to a couple of baseball games. It's been a long time."

"Yes," Donald replies. "With soccer and piano and museums, we have not had time for baseball or basketball."

"Yes," William says, "I wanted to play baseball, but nobody was taking me."

John looks at his son. "William, that is not true. I enrolled you with a team soon after your mom died."

"But you didn't come. You let Jacob's father take us."

Jacob is one of their neighbors; his father, Michael, was the coach of the team.

"Sometimes I did go watch you."

"Then after one year you did not encourage me to go anymore."

John realizes he underestimated how much baseball meant to his son.

"But William, you were not enjoying yourself. In fact, when I did not encourage you to go, you kept quiet. I have been taking you to soccer and I see the difference. I think you enjoy soccer far more than baseball. Also, those silly teammates of yours picked on you if you dropped a catch or struck out, and you did not like that. I thought you were happy that I saved you from them."

Donald looks at William and says, "I think you prefer soccer anyway, William, no?"

"I do, but I wanted to show those boys that I can be good at baseball, too."

"Okay," John says, in a consoling tone, "don't worry about it. Your new school has baseball. Just tell them you would like to play to improve your game. After all, you should play for fun. You don't want to play baseball to impress anyone."

Donald, to support his brother, adds, "I will come and watch you practice."

William is pleased. "Thanks, Donald."

"That's very nice, Donald, thank you," John adds.

The following day, John drives the boys up to New Hampshire. It is an uneventful trip and he spends the weekend in a nearby hotel, making sure the boys settle in before driving back down to Arlington.

On his return, he attends to some important details. He needs to rent out his house. He solicits the help of a realtor to manage the property while he is gone. He will contract to rent on an annual basis. The house is big and fashionable enough to attract senior executives in business or embassies. He prefers those. They usually are willing to pay more than the average tenant and will take better care of the house.

John requires a good storage company, and that's no problem. He knows a number of people who have firsthand experience with such companies, and the realtor will have suggestions as well. He telephones three storage companies for estimates. He tells them he could be away for up to three years and requests a yearly storage rate. He is not sure what to do about his car. He will lose money to sell it but he does not want to pay to have it stored for so long. If he were going for one year he wouldn't mind. After some thought he decides that because the car is six years old, he might as well just sell it.

John needs to arrange shipment of some personal effects to Nigasilia. He has no intention of buying much over there in the form of clothing and will ship enough to last him for up to three years if need be. He will also take some cooking and dining hardware; things that are rather expensive or unavailable in Nigasilia. Then, of course, he will need to take a good laptop. He uses the storage company to do his shipping. Part of the shipping will be by ordinary freight and part by air. Among the perquisites of his new position, he will be given a three-bedroom house built solidly of stone and cement, for official use. The house is equipped with modern facilities, including air conditioning. He will be given an official vehicle, and a chauffeur, all paid for by the government. Still, he decides to buy and ship a Nissan SUV over to Nigasilia. In such a situation, with him going to assume a senior official post, government policy allows him to import one vehicle duty-free. John wants to avoid the risk of being excoriated by the media and the opposing party for exploiting his position for private gain, and thus of corruption, which he would certainly be guilty of if he were to use his official vehicle for private trips.

John is amazed how quickly the first semester has gone. He enjoys his teaching on the whole, though he is tired of the challenge of getting the students to study. Then there are those who, no matter at what level, want to take only objective tests. John hates objective tests. He does not like grading on a curve, either. He has great freedom to indulge his approach only when he teaches the graduate courses. So whether it is microeconomics or African economic development, he prefers the graduate-level courses. But, he also believes it is good for his constant improvement as a professor to be involved in undergraduate microeconomics as well. He certainly does not want to teach African economic development to undergraduates. His technique is to make sure the students know they have to study, so they do not think of the African course as an easy elective. That way he gets only those students who want to study and work hard. John once told the chairman of his department, "If all the students want is a course at the level of the *New York Times*, I don't want them in my class."

Soon it is Christmastime and the boys come home from school. John is all organized and ready to leave after the holidays to go to Nigasilia. So he has time to relax and enjoy Christmas and New Year's Day with the boys. They plan to do what they always do: shop, go to Christmas Eve Mass, watch the ball come down in Times Square, and spend time near the fireplace watching ball games on TV.

On Christmas Day, just the three of them plan to be together. Year after year, John wakes up late, so the kids can never open their presents early. This year John's father is missing his wife terribly. Samuel wakes up early and cannot go back to sleep. He has an irresistible urge to call John, and so at about 8:30 a.m. in Washington, he telephones his son to wish him a Merry Christmas.

When the phone rings, John jumps out of his bed. "Hello?"

"Merry Christmas, John," says the voice on the other side.

"Dad, Merry Christmas. . . . Is everything okay?"

"Yes, son, I was just thinking about you and the boys and I am sitting here alone. I went to church last night and I woke up early this morning just thinking of your mother."

"Oh, Dad, I'm sorry. But are you all right?"

"Yes, I am. Where are the boys? Can I talk to them?"

"Let me see if they are awake," John replies. He opens his door and the boys are right there in the corridor, still in their pajamas, quietly looking down the stairs at the Christmas tree. John cannot help but smile.

"Boys, your grandpa wants to talk to you."

"Grandpa!" William exclaims with great excitement. He grabs the cordless telephone from his father. The boys both wish their grandpa a Merry Christmas and, after his turn, Donald hands over the phone to his dad.

"Your sons are excited about opening their presents," Samuel says.

"Yes, Dad, they are. I will surprise them this year and we shall open up the presents soon after breakfast."

"Well, we are all here waiting for our New Year's present."

"What present is that?"

"You, John. We are looking forward to your arrival in the New Year."

"Daddy, I am, too. I am also praying that it all works out."

"So are we."

On New Year's Eve, John and the boys spend the time quietly together, enjoying the warmth of the fireplace, the crackling of the wood, and the usual entertainment on television. John orders some Nigasilian dishes from a small Nigasilian diner in Washington, DC. After the delicious dinner, the boys decide to roast marshmallows in the fireplace.

After a couple of marshmallows, Donald looks at his father. "Dad, are you not going to try some? One, maybe?"

"No, Donald, I have never liked marshmallows."

Donald looks over at his brother. "Well, do you people want to play Scrabble?"

"Donald, it is 11:00 now," William protests. "We won't be able to finish before midnight."

"Well, if you two keep to the time we will."

"No, I'm too tired," William objects. "I just want to watch the people having fun on TV."

Just before midnight, John quickly stokes the fire as they watch the ball drop in Times Square. All three stand close together, as if ordered to do so, staring excitedly at the TV as the ball begins to drop. When it reaches the bottom, they embrace, and say "Happy New Year" to each other.

Chapter 4

On February 1, John arrives in Lamongwe. Once in Nigasilia, John has the arduous task of setting up a new department, that of the chief economist, and developing a working relationship with the rest of the government via the cabinet ministers. John is quite relaxed now. He will try to make the experience successful. If it fails, he is determined to have the satisfaction of having honestly done his best to make it all work.

The plan he hopes to sell to the president is to make the core activity of the office essentially that of an economic policy think tank and economic policy formulation unit rolled into one. John's idea is that the chief economist's office will work closely with government departments, statutory bodies, and the central bank. John has thought hard about his plans and how he will proceed. Even though he arrives rather late in the night, John is ready to begin serious discussions the next day.

As John enters his father's office to attend his first meeting with the president, vice president, and minister of finance, Rabena hugs him.

"John, my man, I'm so happy you decided to come. You are welcome and I will be praying that it all works out for you and for us as well. The three of them are already in there, but I have to tell you something." In a whisper, Rabena says, "The VP and Tubo Bangar are not good friends. I don't know if anyone told you."

"No, no one told me."

"Well, Tubo is admired for his brilliance and is very popular among the educated youth of the country. He is seen by some in the party as a possible successor to your father. Because of that, the VP, who you might imagine wants to be the successor, does everything he can to put down Tubo. So watch out."

John is totally unaware of all this intrigue and looks at the door cautiously.

"Go, so you don't keep them waiting."

As John enters, he greets the VP warmly and then turns to the minister of finance and development.

"Bangar, you and I have not talked enough, I know. Anyway, I am here now and we have lots to talk about."

An economist by training, Tubo Bangar taught for a little while at the university of Nigasilia. But he was too keen on becoming a politician. Not too big in stature, with a rather big head and short neck, Tubo is still a handsome and imposing figure.

"Anyway, Mr. VP and Mr. Minister, thanks for coming. I asked for this meeting because I wanted to explain my plans to you, as I would like your views. The way I see it, the chief economist office should operate as a think tank in addition to being an economic policy-making unit. In the latter role, the chief economist's office will work in close collaboration with all the departments, and especially with the Ministry of Finance and Development, the Ministry of Trade and Industry, the Ministry of Agriculture, and the central bank.

"I know that, right now, you work in the context of five-year development plans. Correct me if I am wrong, Tubo, but the economic analyses that go into those plans are not very thorough. Hence, the economic management and governance arrangements to implement those plans are not well thought out. One consequence is that the development plans look almost like wish lists and sales plans to raise foreign aid."

Tubo interjects. "John, you have a point, but you most likely are underestimating the quality of the economic analyses that go into the five-year plans, especially how they fit into the annual programs and budgets. Anyway, you and I can talk about that later. For the time being, you were going to tell us how you wish to organize your office and how much staff you are going to need."

"Ideally to start," John explains, "I need two to three senior economists, three economists, two economic statisticians, and two to three research assistants. Then, of course, I would need an administrative assistant, two to three secretaries, a receptionist, and a couple of dedicated drivers for the office, which will all be in line with normal government rules and regulations. We also need to start developing a small library. So we will need library space and librarians. The library would be available not only to my department but to all economic departments, such as Trade and Industry, and Finance and Development."

Tubo looks at John and says, somewhat bewildered, "Is that all?"

"The senior economists should all be PhDs in economics with proven research and publication experience."

"And where are you going to find these senior economists?" Tubo asks.

"Most likely, abroad."

"And where will you get the money to pay them to work in this hardship post?"

"Well, Tubo, you are the expert, you should tell me about the money part. I can find the people from universities, research institutes, and central banks in the US, UK, Canada, and continental Europe." After pausing, John adds, "Incidentally, it may not be a bad idea to get one PhD political scientist and one PhD sociologist to join my team. Again, they must have research credentials."

John presses on. "Apart from the fact that all these people need equipment, namely computers and econometric programs, I need to pay these economists far more than the miserly sums you pay around here. We do not have the money, I know, so I recommend that the minister of finance make a plea to the aid donors. I can come up with the budget to be financed on an annual basis. I shall also be happy to survey our foreign aid intake and associated expenditure, and to make recommendations of funds that could be better used in my shop. If Tubo disagrees, he and I can discuss at a technical level and try to reach an agreement."

Tubo looks somewhat uneasy but controls himself. "John, I understand your problem, but let us stick to ways to get more aid for your department. No other department has surplus funds. I am happy to consider your proposals and to work out with you a strategy to solicit more aid dedicated for your department. Otherwise, you may need to cut back."

So far neither the president nor the vice president has spoken. John glances at both of them. "So Mr. President and Mr. VP, what do you think?"

The president responds first. "Well, how do you, John, respond to Tubo? We need to find money for your office. We do not have much of it and need foreign aid. So, yes, draw up your request in a coherent way: the objectives of the office, how they fit into our economic policy making, how they are going to work, and why you need all that staff and equipment. Then, between you and Tubo, you will lobby with the aid donors."

"Yes, John," the VP adds, "this is the reality of our situation in this country."

John is not surprised at the reactions. "I'll send my written proposals to all three of you in a couple of days. I am quite willing to do the legwork with the donors, starting with their representatives here in Nigasilia. I also can write universities in the US and the UK directly to ask them to help. Some of them will be willing to come here on sabbatical; some will take leave and come if we are able to find the money to remunerate them. The aid agencies will then be lobbied to pitch in. I shall tell them they would be promoting economic growth and good governance in Nigasilia. At least two or three of them will jump at the opportunity, I'm sure."

"John," the president says after a big sigh, "I hope you will find foreign economists who are truly interested in policy formulation work. We've had some bad experiences in this country with many of these academically oriented economists from Europe and North America. Too many of them are interested mainly in getting access to data and to the authorities to enable them, I mean the researchers, to have enough information to write papers for publication in academic journals or books. They are interested in our countries the same way biologists are interested in rats."

"I know exactly what you mean, Dad. I also will watch out for those types. I will make sure they do not come anywhere near my office. There are many first-class economists who are genuinely interested in helping with economic policy making in our countries. Those are usually keen to assist the authorities of countries like Nigasilia in developing their capacity for policy making, and to have a direct input into policy-making debates in these countries. If they end up being able to write research papers as a result of their access and experience, then that would be a bonus rather than the primary motivation of their interest."

"Okay, John, go ahead and finish your proposal, and the VP and I will review it. I believe we can wrap up for the time being."

John and the central bank governor, Victor Kunongo, have known each other for some time. Since he became governor almost three years ago, Victor would bump into John each time John came to Lamongwe for summer vacation. The governor is on the tall side, and well-built, but he has been working on his weight. He is quite dark with big, bulging eyes and a round face. He has shaved off all his hair.

As John steps into the governor's office, they greet each other warmly.

"So, John, what did you do with your two boys? I gather you left them in the States. You did not want them to come and suffer here? It would have made them tough, you know."

"Well, it was not that easy. I didn't want them to have to adjust to a new education system."

"I assure you there is not much difference these days. Anyway, that's not why you are here."

"I wanted to touch base and say I look forward to our working together. The central bank is important and I hope to initiate discussions with you on issues of access to finance, especially for small and medium enterprises. We need to do something to boost the private sector in this country and the small and medium enterprises are struggling. Of course, they have other problems, too, but those are outside your area."

"John, you are right. I have a few initiatives I am discussing with the banks and I will invite you to the next meeting on this subject. I am trying to see what we can do to help the banks, whether such help is in the form of analysis, data collection, a database to help with risk analysis, or special central bank lending facilities; in other words, anything except controls on the banks."

"Good, I'll be very happy to be involved in the discussions. But in general, how are things going?"

"Well, as you know, we are struggling to keep the exchange rate of the kala relatively stable, our foreign exchange reserves are not as high as we would like in relation to imports, and the pressure to lend to government is still strong. But I must confess that your dad's government is staying within the law. Our ambition, though, is to have the government move away, even if slowly, from any direct borrowing from the central bank. If your dad lasts for two terms I'm sure we will make progress in that direction."

"Good, I'm happy to hear that. How is the family?"

"Well, my wife is still with me and running her own clothing store. As you know she took early retirement from teaching. She says the students are getting more and more unruly by the day and the quality of the new teachers coming in keeps going down. If your father doesn't know this, please let him know. At least he is aware of the school certificate results. They have been going down steadily over the last ten years."

The school certificate is awarded for all high school academic subjects of study. Students must attain a minimum grade level in international exams set by a number of African countries that cooperate in the process. Hence, the certificate has good international recognition. For each subject passed, the certificate specifies the grade level attained. Students who attain a certain grade in a minimum number of subjects, usually six or seven, are eligible for entry into colleges and universities. Students are sometimes allowed by their schools to repeat the exams when they have not met the grade—for instance, if they do not have enough subjects or simply want to raise their grades. More often than not, the schools will not admit them again into regular classes and the student will have to arrange for private lessons and take the exams as "private" students at locations specified by the government.

"Yes, he knows everything. It is high on his agenda but I don't know when he is going to see the results of any efforts he puts in. To make it worse, I am not so sure how much reform he will be able to achieve. The problems are huge, from what I have been told. My father, as you know, has established this commission, which is looking into the problem so they can present us with suggestions for national debate and, hopefully, government action."

"Yes, that's right. What about you, John, with this chief economist assignment, are you optimistic?"

"No, but I'm hopeful. I will also do my best to make it work, because I don't want to look back and say I did not try hard enough."

"I understand. So how long do you give us before you decide if you are succeeding?"

"Three years."

"Good, that's fair. I wish you luck. You will have your father on your side."

John has an early dinner at a restaurant in the central area of Lamongwe with the heads of two state enterprises—Energy and Water Resources, and Telecommunications. But, on his way from the bank to his office, he decides to drop by Mahdu Kontana's office just to say hello. They have spoken on the phone but have not seen each other since John arrived.

As they embrace, John notices a young lady sitting rather relaxed in Kontana's office. One look at her and there is a twinkle in John's eyes that Kontana doesn't miss.

"John, I would like you to meet my favorite cousin, Jamina Tamba. Jamina, meet our chief economist, John Bijunga, coming all the way from the US to help us."

"Jamina, very pleased to meet you."

"So, you are the famous Dr. Bijunga. My cousin has been talking about you and how pleased he is that you decided to join the forces of good governance."

"Oh, well, that's your cousin for you. I am very grateful that he is here to help me through the rough waters. I have never actually worked within our country's administration. Even my father is sometimes difficult for me to understand."

"You know, John, Jamina's father is a chief, so you better be careful what you say around her."

"Don't mind him, John. I also criticize the chieftaincy institution."

"Anyway, she is also a schoolteacher, and teaches biology," Kontana adds.

"Well, I always enjoy meeting female science teachers."

"Do you know many?" Jamina asks.

"Unfortunately, no. But the few I know are not only committed to their subjects but also do their best to encourage girls to go into science."

"Yes," Jamina says with excitement, "because most of the time, whether we are talking about parents or school administrators, girls do not usually get the same push as the boys. It usually starts with not encouraging them to practice their mathematics the same way the boys are pushed. Then when girls are timid or squeamish about dissecting animals, these science teachers don't try to find a way for them to overcome that obstacle."

"I'm afraid you must be right, because I have heard the same stories from women in the US."

Jamina gets up suddenly and says, "Oh, Mahdu, I must go. I have to stop by Vivienne's before I go home and I have homework to grade."

"Okay, dear, we'll talk."

After she steps out, Kontana turns to John. "How lucky! She wanted to leave a few minutes before you came, but I could not stop talking. Pretty and smart, eh? What a combination. John, she's made just for you. She also has a wonderful personality. What a coincidence that you bump into her right here in my office. She is the one I mentioned when you came for your mother's funeral. I'm at your service, John. I can arrange a lunch for the three of us, so you can meet her properly and make up your mind whether I am right that you will love her."

"Kontana, you win. Yes, I do want to meet her 'properly,' as you say."

"Good, I'll arrange it. Now how are things going so far?"

"So far, so-so . . . Maybe a little better than so-so," John says, narrating his meeting with the president, the vice president, and the minister of finance.

Once he is finished, Kontana says, "That was not a bad meeting. I'm sure you did not expect the government to provide you with the staff and the facilities you justly require. We are an aid-dependent country. That is the reality. We cannot afford books, computers, and highly qualified technical people."

"Yes, Kontana, at a minimum I am that realistic."

"So now you are going to send the draft plan. I would recommend you send it to all three and get your father to call a meeting if any has a problem. Give them a deadline by which you expect a response—make it at most three working days. If they need more time, they will ask."

"Thanks, Kontana. Now you must let me go. I have a date with a couple of director generals."

"Yes, talk to those guys; we need shake-ups. I'll arrange our lunch with Jamina soon. I feel very excited already."

John rushes to meet the two gentlemen of the public enterprises at one of the most popular restaurants in the middle of town. Sanfani Abuye is head of Energy and Water Resources, while Kimah Sandeh is head of Telecommunications. They are both engineers, and Sanfani Abuye also earned an MBA in the US. They are both on time, as is John.

"Gentlemen, thanks for coming," John begins. "As I indicated to you over the phone, I am interested to hear your thoughts on two subjects. First, I'm interested in your relations with the government and what you would like to see changed or improved. Second, I would like to know your views on the privatization of state enterprises. But please, go ahead and order. The waiter is looking at us."

The two guests order from memory. Only John glances at the menu and orders a main dish and a soft drink. When the others recognize a couple a few tables away, the two gentlemen get up to go greet them, leaving John all by himself. That is Nigasilian society for you—jovial and informal. When the two gentlemen return to their seats, Kimah asks, "John, are you comfortable here? We can move to another table you know. The upstairs is very nice."

"No, it is okay; I don't think they will hear us. They are talking so loud anyway."

Kimah Sandeh continues, responding to John's questions. "You know, we don't have a problem at Telecoms. We are monopolizing only the landline. We are also in the cell phone business and are an Internet service provider as well. But the market for both is open. If the government wants to bring the private sector into the landline business, it's okay with us. We could use the investment funds as well as the technical and managerial expertise. A public-private partnership arrangement would be perfect. I'm not so sure the private sector will want to go it alone, because the landline market is not that big. The majority of our people have no landlines, as you know."

"Yes, I know," John responds. "Incidentally, the food is here. That was fast."

"Well," Kimah says, "as you know, these people already have the food cooked; it's just a matter of serving."

John clarifies. "Yes, of course, I know that. But in some of the other restaurants, the service is still so slow."

"Yes, I know what you mean," Kimah says. "Anyway, to continue with your questions, in the case of the first issue, the biggest problem is government and public sector arrears. You know, the government departments and the public enterprises are the biggest users of landlines and they are always late in paying. Sometimes they owe quite a lot, especially for international calls. In addition, when it comes to making investments in new equipment or in staff training, we depend on government financing; there again, there are constant delays."

"So, you think a public-private partnership arrangement will help."

"Yes, but only if the public sector pays its bills on time."

John looks at Sanfani. "What about you?"

"Look, John, I think our problems are worse than those of Telecoms. We not only have problems with arrears and getting funds for investments, but a big problem has to do with rates. Government should give us greater freedom in setting rates. Government could, as a validation procedure, have experts analyze any suggestion for rate changes on our part before giving its approval to the changes."

Sanfani suddenly stops talking. There is a heated argument taking place at a nearby table between two people who support two different teams in the local soccer association. The teams are about to play a friendly match this coming Saturday and the two men are arguing over which team will win. They soon realize that everyone is gazing at them and quiet down. When they do, Sanfani continues.

"John, I am dead set against major privatization. I don't mind looking for some public-private partnership arrangement. We can, maybe, allow about 20 percent of private investment in the enterprise and, of course, use the private sector more in maintenance activities. But turning over the management of the enterprise to the private sector I would oppose."

"Why is that?" John asks.

"Because the private sector will want to earn a high rate of return on their investments and they can get away with it because energy and water will stay a monopoly. The poor people will suffer."

John looks at Sanfani and smiles. He then says as forcefully as he can, "But Sanfani, right now the poor people are suffering. There is a serious water shortage and the electricity supply is woefully inadequate. There is a constant blackout in most areas of the city. Only in a few reasonably well-to-do areas do you have a decent supply of electricity."

"But John, that is because we lack capacity. Government investment can take care of that."

"Sanfani, everyone in Nigasilia knows that you are also not doing well on maintenance and you are not collecting rates that are due from a lot of the population, especially the powerful people. I bet you at least one of today's papers mentions that."

Sanfani is a bit irritated. "Yes, John, I was coming to that. The reason is because we are handicapped by government obstruction, such as when we want to cut off the powerful people. Government can simply give us more freedom to do our work, including the collection of rates. And there is more. When it comes to water, we are struggling with the cost of fuels and chemicals, workers' inefficiency, and illegally connected pipes. In all these areas, government is a problem. We need adequate autonomy in our management."

"So, you do not think that if we privatize, the problems will disappear?"

"It might, but private capitalists then bring other problems that will increase social tension. We have no use for that now."

John sees no resolution. "Well, let's leave it at that for the time being. I think I am going to explore some serious privatization of your public enterprise."

Sanfani smiles. "You won't win, John. All the powerful people in this country will oppose you and all the poor people will oppose you. You will be left with no one to support you. Not even your father will support you, because his party will lose if they argue for privatization of energy and water."

"We'll see," John says, as he beckons to the waiter for his bill. He is unhappy, because he is fully aware that Sanfani is right, and it is a battle not worth fighting.

On the following Monday, February 5, at the end of a special cabinet meeting, Kontana pulls John aside. "John, I called your office earlier today but there was no answer. You should give me your cell phone number. I assume you have one already."

"Yes," says John, "but I don't even remember the number. Let me ring you right now, and you can record it. Was it anything important?" John pulls out his phone as Kontana continues the conversation.

"I have arranged our lunch date with Jamina. I took a chance that you would be free on Saturday. Can you make it? We will go to Bokubo except this time we shall sit outside."

The outside restaurant, with covered roof and a surrounding low wall, is the largest dining area at Bokubo Hotel and is officially named Rambana Place.

"I can make it. Thank you, I'm grateful."

It is one of those dry, sunny, hot mid-February days in Lamongwe. As Jamina steps out of her vehicle, which she has driven herself, Minister Kontana beckons to her. John stares at this slender, glamorous lady, attired in a simple, elegant, yellow cotton dress, with ruched sleeves and a conservative V-neck. *She is so perfectly proportional*, John thinks. That had not struck him when he first met her. At that time, he had noticed her beautiful face, somewhere between round and oval, with prominent cheekbones and a complexion that matched his. Her lips are thin, and when she smiles, she shows off vividly white teeth. She has a lot of hair, which John will one day find out she inherited from her mother.

With a broad smile, John approaches Jamina. "Jamina, it's good to see you again."

"Hi, John, it's nice to meet you again, too."

Jamina says hello to Mahdu Kontana, who embraces her and leads the way. As they climb the steps to a large platform area with tables and a view of the water, a waiter approaches and leads them to the table reserved in a choice spot. This is Minister Kontana's favorite restaurant for his important guests.

The waiter hands them the menu and they order drinks. The two men order Nigasilian beer, while Jamina asks for mineral water. It takes them only a few minutes to choose their lunches. They all prefer seafood—lobster, fish, and shrimp for Jamina, John, and Kontana respectively. The restaurant has a blend of Nigasilian, French, and Indian styles in its cooking. They all request steamed rice and vegetables; today's vegetable selection includes green peas and carrots, which all three especially like.

"How is my uncle, Jamina?" Mahdu asks.

"He's well, I assume. I have not heard from him for a week now. And I have not been good enough to call him, either."

"John, I did not tell you that Jamina's dad is a chief, did I?"

"Yes, you did. I have to talk to your father someday, Jamina, especially about the government's decentralization program."

Transferring powers to the districts and chiefdoms should, in principle, increase the government's accountability and so should help democratic development. But many Nigasilians are skeptical, arguing that the big men of the local government will capture the power and the money for their own use. Hence, instead of spurring democracy and accountability, decentralization beyond a bare minimum may only worsen corruption.

Jamina obliges. "When you are ready to talk to him, let me know. I'll arrange it."

Jamina smiles gently as she looks at John. She already thinks of John as an engaging person and one she could encourage a close relationship with. But she is rather cautious in her dealings with men until she gets a feel for their intentions. She is old-fashioned in that way.

John returns the smile and says, genuinely grateful, "Good, I will. Thank you for the offer."

Kontana turns to John. "You know, John, Jamina is one of the most vocal critics of what is going on in the secondary schools today. No secondary school has a decent science lab of any kind or a good library by any respectable standard. The average class has over fifty students to the teacher. As for mathematics, every year it is going down; even the mathematics teachers are leaving in droves. When it comes to hygiene, the rubbish is amazing—not enough toilets and those they have are not kept clean. The kids, Jamina says, are being reduced to pigs. Tough language, perhaps, but it reflects her frustration."

John, smiling, asks Kontana, "So what are you people in government doing about all this?"

The response does not surprise John. "There is not much we can do. We cannot raise fees, because the parents cannot afford to pay more. We don't have the government revenue to increase subsidies. Teachers' salaries are low and we cannot afford to increase them. To make matters worse, we cannot afford more teachers or facilities. It is a sad situation."

John responds in a serious but quiet tone. "Maybe as part of my job I shall find a way to let those responsible know that government can raise more revenue by widening the tax base and improving tax administration. We can also be more efficient in the allocation of government funds—much more efficient. But no, we Nigasilians just want to go around the world with our begging bowls. Well, many in the donor community are getting tired of us. In my teaching and research I interact with those people on a regular basis and read many of the things they write. Moreover, everyone knows that the citizens of the donor countries are weary of paying taxes beyond a certain low threshold."

Jamina wants to change the subject. "My cousin was telling me that you have two sons but that you lost your wife. I'm sorry to hear that. If only our schools were better here, this would have been a great time for the boys to come and understand their father's country. Being a man, is it better that you do not have a daughter to deal with?"

"I never thought about that, really," John replies, with a slight grin. "I always wanted a girl. It just seems natural that if you have two kids, one should be a boy and the other a girl. Of course, at the end of the day, you take whatever you get and love them just the same."

"Yes, of course."

"The boys know most of their close relatives here already, especially the relatives of similar ages. They also have a number of good friends from past visits. So, they are quite comfortable in Nigasilia. To tell you the truth, they are usually far more relaxed here than I. In fact, they sometimes have to resist my attempts to protect them."

"Protect them from what?" Jamina asks.

"From the poverty and filth. I cannot protect them from it all, of course. The plain truth is that I am afraid it will affect their self-esteem. They might begin to wonder why there is so much dirt and poverty in the only black man's country that they know. I also think they are not as streetwise as they think they are and will not know how to deal with boys who want to pick a fight."

"In that case, just make sure they go around with their relatives and their friends. Do they come often?"

"Yes, they have been coming regularly, for about a month every summer holiday for the last three years. Before that they came once every other year."

"Good, that's really good."

The three gaze at those having their boat rides on an estuary that opens onto the Atlantic Ocean. Bokubo Hotel sits just at the end of this estuary of the largest river in Lamongwe, which flows all the way from the northeast of the country some three hundred miles away. The hotel is one of three sitting at the water's edge. On the immediate west of the hotel, its wall gets washed by the water. On the south there is a three-mile-long beautiful beach, Lumpimo Beach, which begins about fifty yards from the hotel's compound. On the north about the same distance is part of the estuary as it gets to its widest point, merging with the ocean. On the east is Lamongwe, with its beautiful hills.

As the three of them watch and eat, two guests stop by to greet Mahdu Kontana as they head to their table. Kontana introduces Jamina and John. But the guests do not stop for a lengthy chat and simply continue on to their table.

Mahdu, who has been quietly enjoying the conversation so far, asks as they finish their main dish, "How was the food?"

"I like the way they did the lobster," Jamina responds. "This is the first time I have tried it with garlic and vegetable oil. The lemony butter sauce is just great. I think they added some cumin or turmeric, and a couple of curry leaves."

John says, "Yes, my fish was good also. It was barracuda cooked in our favorite sauce. It is difficult to go wrong with that."

John means that it was cooked in the style of a traditional Nigasilian stew, with onions, chili pepper, tomatoes, tomato paste, and thyme, in any light oil; the pan-fried fish is cut in steak-like slices and immersed in the sauce towards its simmering end.

"Yes," Kontana agrees, "my shrimp was the same, except mine was slightly curried."

The waiter clears the table and brings them each a fruit cocktail. The two gentlemen order coffee and Jamina wants tea.

"So, John, how is your work here going so far?" Jamina asks.

"Well, not any faster than I expected. Building up the office will take some time. I really will have to work very hard to get the qualified staff I need. I shall try to stay optimistic. Still, I cannot leave matters in the hands of my honorable colleagues in the cabinet. I will have to take charge sooner or later. Since the government has no money, I will have to eat up my words, pack my begging bowl, and go chase some aid money—all so I can build up a staff that will then explain to this government how to grow, save, and finance our development without begging. When you beg you are at the mercy of the donors. They can cut off your aid and bring you to your knees anytime they choose. Look at the treatment of African countries in the global community—our countries are treated like dirt. A major reason for that is our aid dependence."

Jamina smiles approvingly. "You know, I agree with you. I don't know why we aren't better at managing our affairs, with all these natural resources at our disposal. Instead, I hear these Western economists, almost in unison, talking about our 'natural resource curse.' What do they mean? How come natural resources are a curse for us but a blessing for them?"

John does not really want to get into that subject. It could end up becoming a long lecture because it is a topic that excites him. "I hope I shall have the pleasure of revealing that secret to you one day. You will see that, if there is a curse, it has nothing to do with the natural resources but with the Africans and their weak institutions. In the meantime, I would like to know what interests you apart from teaching biology."

"Apart from reading—mainly science books, the old literary classics, history—I am a member of the Conservation Society of Nigasilia. And, I play squash."

"So that's how you keep so trim. Where do you play squash?"

"At the golf club. I'm not a member but I get invited to play every Saturday and Sunday and I go most of the time."

"Very interesting. Tell me about the Conservation Society. What do you do there?"

"Right now, we basically do three things. We point out in great detail all the destruction taking place in our environment from soil erosion to deforestation to problems left by mining companies, and show stark pictures in the newspapers and over the Internet. Second, we explore several aspects of our natural sites—forests and the vegetation and wildlife, lakes, mountains, hills, and islands. Third, we work with the government and international groups, guiding the construction of wildlife sanctuaries and reserves. Many of these sites are just breathtaking. You know, even our beautiful beaches need attention from the conservation authorities, if they are to retain their pristine qualities."

"In that case," John is quick to suggest, "I can't wait to have the privilege of your being my guide."

"Oh," replies Jamina with her charming smile, "My colleagues at the Society are better experts than I am, but I will be pleased to take you on a tour of the sites. It would be best to arrange something during school holidays."

Minister Kontana, who is delighted at the animated conversation between John and Jamina, decides to join in.

"John, what do you like to do apart from reading economics?"

"I like to read history, philosophy, political science, and sociology texts. I enjoy watching golf on television. In the US, I even go to professional golf tournaments. Apart from that, I am a classical music buff. I play the piano and I go to the opera and the symphony. I enjoy the theater. I go to movies now and then but I really prefer theaters with live actors. You can see how I am going to suffer in Nigasilia— hardly any theaters, no symphony or opera, and no decent bookshop or library. We should be banned from the community of civilized nations!"

Kontana chuckles and says rather cynically, "No, John, you are here now. You will show us how to do such civilized things."

"I am sure all you old hands are familiar with such problems and have initiatives in place to improve things." John winks at the minister and turns to Jamina. "Jamina, do you mind if I call you next week and ask you for a date?"

Jamina turns to her cousin, who nods gently in approval. "Sure, John, I'll give you my phone number. We can arrange something. As you know, we teachers are very busy during the week and I have other commitments as well. But you are a pleasant person to be with, or so it seems."

John takes out a small diary from his pocket and hands it to Jamina with a pen, watching her as she writes down her number.

Soon after, they finish their lunch. John and Minister Kontana add a generous tip, but not before going through the pain of counting bills. As Kontana counts, John jokes, "You know, this is one thing I still have not adjusted to. We have no denomination larger than the equivalent of five US dollars and, to make matters worse, the majority of the bills are dirty. Sometimes I wonder if I count two to three hundred of these and put my fingers in my mouth, will I fall dead?"

Jamina bursts out laughing. "There are many things that will kill you more easily than our money. No, John, it's not that bad. But I agree, you should tell the central bank governor that we need larger denominations."

"I have, every time I see him. He probably does not hear me anymore. Anyway, Jamina, thanks a lot. I'll give you a call. You have made my day."

The Chamber of Commerce and Industry people have been keen to talk to John. They see him as the new governor on the block, and one who could make a difference in the business climate of Nigasilia. Today, Monday, February 12, five of them have come to treat John to lunch—the chairman, the secretary, and three other executives. The event will take place at one of the private dining rooms of the Tamra Conference Building, up on one of the lower hills of Lamongwe, with a beautiful view of the west side of the city, which borders the ocean.

John already knows the chairman, Baba Tey, and the secretary, Paul Sutu. He is introduced to the other three, Malika Kaykai, Tarik Day, and Raboya Bami. The menu for the luncheon is already arranged, but they order cocktails before the meal. When the drinks arrive, they raise their glasses. The chairman begins to talk, in a deliberate and serious tone, as if delivering a lecture.

"John, you economists talk all the time about the cost of doing business in Nigasilia. Well, we talk about the frustrations of doing business here. What we see is that the whole system in this country is geared toward discouraging regular business enterprise—businesses that will promote rapid development in this country, help with technical and vocational education and training, create good jobs, and allow the government to collect real tax revenues instead of the meager sums they come up with now."

The food arrives and the chairman takes a bite. No one says anything, waiting for him, as it were, to finish his speech.

"Just look at the nature of the businesses we have in this country. We have lots of importers. Nothing gets made here for export. We have our minerals and agricultural commodities, plus aid, to provide the foreign exchange for the imports, in addition to remittances from our diasporans. The things we make here are strictly for local demand. These, generally, are things requiring little skill. For the most part, any machinery used is simple or requires little maintenance. When complicated machinery breaks down, we call someone from abroad to come fix it; enterprises don't use complex machines that require constant vigilance and maintenance. But still, the things made here will not survive without protection. Even with protection, we still cannot attract serious industry. If you cannot make a profit, what is the use of protection? That is the problem. So, we go round and round and end up with certain kinds of services—retail, restaurants, hotels, transport, foreign exchange bureaus, housing construction. Even with construction, how many modern houses are we really building every year? Not that many, really, when you think about it."

The chairman looks up at the others as if to say he is finished. John glances around and puts in a word. "So is this all about infrastructure and education and the skills of the labor force?"

"It's about those, yes," replies Tarik Day. "But it is much more than that. It's really about everything. It is about customs, the ports, the legal system, the attitude of the workers, and the apathy that the government departments and state enterprises show with respect to their incompetence and corruption."

"Yes," John says, "I understand, it's a miserable picture."

Malika Kaykai then adds, "I think we should stop pretending we are interested in attracting foreign investment or even in having our diasporans abroad come home and invest. What serious multinational firm will want to invest in this waste yard with all the alternatives around the world at its disposal?"

There is a deliberate pause, as if to ease the tension. John puts on a faint smile and grits his teeth. He knows the others want him to say something. He believes they are trying to send a message to his father through him. So what message are they trying to send? It cannot simply be that they are unhappy. No, that's too simple. It cannot be that they want his father to know the problems. No, that's nothing new. They must tell him what actions they want his father to take.

"What can the president do now to change the situation that you so effectively and vividly portray?"

Raboya Bami volunteers a response. "You know, the president, your father, did not create this. He inherited it."

"Yes," the others concur in unison.

Bami continues. "My personal view is that he has not shown any indication that he is aware of the gravity of the situation and the importance of acting with vigor. And yet he is aware. That's our problem."

"So, where do we go from here?" John asks.

Raboya explains further. "Well, look at all the areas we have just highlighted. In each one, he can map out a strategy and a set of actions to alleviate the problem. He could review progress regularly to ensure things are moving forward. He should be willing to hold people accountable. But I don't mean he should sign management contracts with his ministers. That's all hogwash. Those contracts never get implemented and the ministers don't get fired. The contract approach also downplays the interdependencies within the system. Look, John, many of these ideas have been discussed widely in this country. These are not my ideas only."

"I agree with you, Raboya," John says. "The government departments should find a way to work as a team, while leaving certain details and the day-to-day implementation to the individual ministries. That way, they can cooperate better and keep an eye on each other's efforts. You do not have to be a genius to realize that conscious and planned coordination is extremely important to achieve any objective in these ministries."

Chairman Tey jumps in. "So, John, we all know your father respects your views, and your reputation precedes you as a sound economist and one who is impatient with the rut in this place. We are at your disposal, but we are also interested in buttering our bread."

"Is that it? The government is bumbling and you want me to tell my father, the president, that he is not getting his ministers to do what they are supposed to do to prevent this country from remaining backward?"

"Yes," Baba Tey responds, shaking his head and faintly smiling, "to confess, that's it, no more and no less."

"Then you do not need to send me. You can meet directly with my dad and tell him yourself. I can arrange a meeting for you."

"John, we have been through that. We requested a meeting with him a few months ago. He asked us what we wanted to discuss and we sent him a note outlining the issues. He sent the VP to represent him. The VP invited us to the State House and we stated our concerns. He then said the government was doing everything it could to improve the situation. Then he gave us a long lecture about how we were simply interested in our short-run profits and that we were making things difficult for the government by not responding earnestly to government initiatives. He went on and on about how we do not manifest any initiative or innovation in our business ventures and how we are afraid of taking risks. He said that when we talk of corruption we should look in the mirror if we want to see major contributors."

"So how did your team respond?"

"We suggested an open forum on these issues, organized by the Chamber and the government, because neither party is perfect. We suggested inviting a few knowledgeable people, including aid donors, to participate in the forum."

"And what did the VP say?"

"He nodded several times and said something like, 'Okay, that is a good idea, a really good idea. I shall let the president know about this suggestion and get back to you.' That was some three months ago and we have heard nothing since. Nothing at all."

"Do you want me to follow up on that? The VP knows about this meeting, you know."

"In that case," Baba Tey says, looking rather obdurate, "you will, because the VP will ask you how it went."

"But I meant more than that. Do you want me to see if we can organize the sort of forum that you asked for? I can include it on my initiative."

"No, John," says the chairman. "We want the VP or the president to take leadership in organizing this forum. If not, we will organize it ourselves and not invite the government. And we will invite people and organizations we know will be very critical of the government. Moreover, we will make sure the newspapers are there to cover the forum."

John thinks it's all a bluff. He is certain the vast majority of business people in the Chamber do not want to confront or annoy the president, because they depend on government patronage. "Okay, Chairman, I will not do anything on that front. I will, of course, continue to interact with you, since it is certainly important to get the Chamber's views on policy initiatives under discussion. I would also like to encourage you to send me directly any suggestions you have on economic policies or call me for discussions. I am at your service."

On Wednesday, the vice president calls a meeting with John; he does not waste time in presenting his concerns.

"John, have you noticed that when we discuss in cabinet the issues you raise, only Kontana, Frah, and Manray will comment? The others stay quiet or simply ask you questions."

"I assume it is because the others either do not like what I have to say or they do not understand."

"Well, partly, yes. John, many members of the cabinet are worried about your attitude. They think you are too radical for this place. In fact, a few of them think you are arrogant, that you believe you have all the answers. Some believe you think they are nothing but corrupt and inept. This idea of the cabinet being too large just drives them mad. They say if you compare Nigasilia with other African countries, we actually have a small cabinet. Most of these ministers say they will not even read your suggestions. They will simply give your scripts to their staff and let their staff decide. They have no interest in discussing anything with you directly. Of course, they will not say so in front of your father, but they are frank with me. So, I want to put you on guard while I convince them that their attitude is not appropriate."

"Mr. Vice President, I hear you. But remember that I just came. I have been here for only—what?—five or so cabinet meetings. To tell you the truth, I am not so sure I care right now what those complaining ministers think. And I know exactly who they are, all six or seven of them. Not one of them is fit to be a minister. They *are* inept and I suspect they are corrupt as well. I will soon find out. Mr. VP, I have a lot of respect for you but this is the way I feel. I am not going to compromise with people I don't respect."

"Well, John, they can fight back, too. And they will not hold back. Be careful how you take sides and how you deal with malicious gossip. People can be very nasty here."

"I keep forgetting I am in the jungle now," John says, clearly annoyed.

The VP gives a deep sigh, and decides to ignore the comment.

"There is one more thing. You told me you were going to have lunch with the Chamber of Commerce people."

"Yes, I did. And actually it went well, very well." John gives an honest account of the discussion, without identifying who said what.

The VP appears quite agitated. "Look, we have very good relations with the Chamber, and most of them use their connections with ministers and senior civil servants for their own benefit. So they can say anything when they meet people like you. What bothers me is when people accuse the president of being weak. What they see as weakness, I see as wisdom. The president has to balance many opposing forces in his policy making. The man is doing at least as well as anyone can. Yes, he could insist that things be done a certain way. But in this country he won't get anything done without support. If the people are unhappy with what he is trying to do, they simply will find a way to spoil it.

Sometimes the president has to give people something in return for their support. Your father's wisdom lies in recognizing this. So don't listen to these people who say your father is a weak leader, and don't take seriously these businessmen who come crying to you that they have all the answers. They have no interest in the country."

"Mr. Vice President, I understand. But the Chamber of Commerce has legitimate concerns. My father has to demonstrate by his actions that he understands those concerns and is capable of doing something about them. Yes, business people are mainly concerned about their profits and, yes, they also participate in corruption. But my father can address the corruption along with their legitimate concerns. The Chamber of Commerce has asked for some kind of forum and you promised you would help organize one. My humble advice to you would be to keep your promise. Doing so would build your prestige not only among the Chamber but in the country at large."

John was deliberate in saying this. He thinks the VP is at least somewhat disingenuous. He also remembers from Rabena's tip that the VP wants to succeed his father. That's not a crime as far as John is concerned. Politicians should be ambitious.

The VP, six feet tall with a big frame, dark complexion, bushy eyebrows, and a handsome smile, has been steeped in politics for some time. His father was in the delegation that went to London to negotiate the independence deal, and was the minister of foreign affairs in the first government after independence. The VP, a renowned lawyer, studied political science before law school in England. He initially refused all cabinet positions. But when his party lost an election, he felt he had an obligation to lead the party back into power. Unfortunately, in the competition, he lost out to his good friend Samuel Bijunga.

"John, I did not give those fellows any timetable for a response. Your dad and I have been very busy and we have had no time to discuss the possibility of such a forum."

"Mr. VP, may I suggest that you delegate some of the tasks involved, given that you are so busy?"

"What do you mean, John?"

"You have ministers who can handle that issue. They can agree on the agenda and date of such a forum. If you or the president cannot attend, the honorable ministers can report back to you."

"Yes, John, you have a point. I will take that into consideration when I discuss the matter with the president. But I first have to let him decide how to proceed."

"I'm willing to help, if you want me to."

"Thank you, John. Please, my office is always open. I care about you, for your father's sake if nothing else. I admire him. But I also respect your brilliant mind."

Chapter 5

John would like to do something special for his first date with Jamina. So he comes up with the idea of taking a trip with her to the countryside. In particular, he thinks it would be a great idea to go to one part of the country not far from Lamongwe where he used to visit regularly when he was growing up but has not visited for many years now. He particularly wants to see how the ordinary people in that area live and cope with the current economic problems of the country. When he comes to Nigasilia he stays mainly in Lamongwe and visits a few of the larger towns in the east, north, and south of the country. He has avoided the smaller towns and villages for a long time. When John telephoned to ask if she was willing, Jamina said, "Yes, I think it's great. I know that area very well. It will be my pleasure."

On the Wednesday before the drive, John asks his chauffeur, Samura Sonenge, "Samura, when I want to go out on my own and I am using my own car, are you able to drive me sometimes?"

"Sir, I'll be happy to do it."

"How much will you charge me?"

"Sir, I won't charge you. You just give me anything you like. And anytime you want me, just let me know. That kind of work, we poor people like. You see how things are expensive here. People like me are just managing to survive. So anything you want to give me, thank you."

John expected that answer; it is the traditional response. The chauffeur knows that if he is good, he will get rewarded at a far higher rate than he could normally charge for such a service, and certainly better than the rate of his official pay.

"Okay. So is this Saturday all right, the whole day?"

"Yes, sir. Just tell me when I should come."

Samura is prompt on Saturday and John arrives early to pick up Jamina at her beautiful house on the west end of the city. When she opens the door, he embraces her warmly and kisses her on the cheeks. She smiles in return.

"Are you ready for the adventure?" she asks. "Things have not changed since your boyhood days, I assure you."

Before they leave, Jamina takes him around her home. It is a beautiful house. It has four bedrooms, each with modern bathroom facilities, a veranda upstairs, a family room, and a living room. The kitchen and the dining room are both quite spacious. There is an adjoining small house with a barbecue space and a laundry room. The connecting corridor to the main house is covered. Jamina explains to John that she had bought some of her furniture from a neighboring African country, some from the US on a visit there, and some from local Lebanese furniture stores. She informs him that the land on which she has built was given to her by her deceased maternal grandfather who was a businessman. He ran a retail store and was also a wholesale importer and distributor. Jamina's mother, Fatima, was his only child. The grandfather left Jamina money—lots of it—some of which she invested into this house.

After the short but efficient tour of the house, they step out. Jamina tells the driver where they are going; Sonenge knows the area well.

"For much of the journey the road is excellent," Jamina assures John.

They are going to the Benefugo area. They will get to some important junction. At that point, they will veer off the main road, which continues up-country, eastwards.

"Oh, I'm not too worried about the road. Bad roads don't bother me, as long as they are motorable. You know, it's been a long time since I went to Benefugo. My mother had relatives there and we all used to go there and pick fruits off trees. I used to climb trees—mango, avocados, and cashew trees, especially. There were also papaya, guava, orange, tangerine, pineapple, banana, and plantain trees. Then there were various types of plums. As children, we would collect various fruits, depending on the season, and bring them home. We ate everything. I wonder if all those fruit trees are still there. I remember also that people used to do swamp rice farming in that area and some fishing, too."

The area is not far from the Atlantic and there are some beautiful beaches not too far away.

"So you were quite a normal Nigasilian boy, John," Jamina said, smiling at him.

"But, you know, I have actually forgotten the names of the very small villages. I left this country for university studies when I was almost twenty years old and since then I have not visited the area. That was more than twenty years ago."

"Yes, Mahdu mentioned that to me—that you left for the US some twenty years ago."

"I have been visiting the main towns over the past few years. To tell you the truth, I have been impressed. We have made good progress on our main road arteries. Those colonialists left us hardly any decent roads."

They drive some fifty miles or so on good tarmac roads and then veer off the main highway onto some rugged patch to get to the main cluster of villages in Benefugo.

The first village they stop to visit, famous for its fishing, is located right on the west coast; in fact, it is but some thirty miles south of the edge of the estuary of the large river that opens into the ocean. They stop to observe the fishermen. As the boats dock, young men jump into the water to help bring the catch to women who are waiting to bid for portions. The fish is loaded onto big basins, which are then carried on the head and dumped on the ground to be sorted out by the fishermen and the buyers. Some fish are set aside for the porters as a group; each will have to fight for his share.

As John watches the scene, he slowly begins to recall similar scenes from his boyhood days. He is amazed that nothing seems to have changed after all these years. The porters still have to fight for their share of the pay.

Pointing to the boat and the heaps of fish on the ground, John says, "At least they have a jolly good catch." After a moment he elaborates. "Those fishermen who labor nearer to Lamongwe seem to be running out of fish. They blame Europeans and even Asians who come into our waters with their trawlers. When I asked my dad about it, he said an underlying problem is that we do not have the resources to police our waters. And, of course, we want foreign aid to acquire those resources!"

Jamina laughs. "You know what the fishermen say? They say that if the government uses foreign aid to patrol the waters, our enforcers will simply negotiate a payoff each time they catch a pirate trawler, and the trawlers will still go away with the illegal catch."

"Yes," John says, "that's for sure." Then, he adds, in a cynical tone, "I guess the only good will be that our enforcers will become richer and spend the money here building houses and supporting their families. The poor fishermen, their livelihood will still not change one iota."

A young man walks up to John and Jamina. "Mister, Madam, you want some fish, I will give you a good price."

Jamina looks at him and gives a broad smile. "Sorry, we really do not want to buy anything."

"Madam, help me, I have snapper, I have barracuda. Any one you want, I shall give you a good price. If you go to the market, you will see, you will not get my price."

"I am sure you are right, but we have no place to put the fish." Jamina whispers to John, "do you have a cooler? If so, I can buy a couple for the driver."

"I don't. Don't worry about the driver. He won't feel bad."

Jamina turns to the boy. "Sorry, we can't help you. But I'm sure you will sell everything soon. Look at those market women buying over there. Why don't you go to them? You can sell your whole pan soon."

"Okay, ma'am, thank you."

After some minutes of watching the process unfold, John and Jamina leave. They continue in their SUV towards the next village, away from the coast. Jamina has met the headman of that village before and they decide to stop by and talk to him. He seems to be in his early fifties and has been headman for some ten years now.

"So, what does a headman do these days?" John asks.

"You know, sir," the man replies, "a headman is supposed to settle disputes and to keep order in the village without involving the regular courts. The headman also organizes the villagers in community efforts to clean the village, the village cemetery, and the village streams that supply our water. When people want to buy and sell land, they can have the headman sign the documents. Using the regular government offices and facilities takes time and costs too much money. The headman's fees are much lower."

"So, nothing has changed, then, over the past twenty years. Can I see the stream that supplies your water? I'm sure nothing has changed there, either."

"Sure," the headman says. He takes the seat next to the driver and shows the driver the way. After less than two hundred yards he tells the driver to stop. They walk a couple hundred yards down to the stream. The water seeps out of the ground like a spring. The villagers have separated the section for drinking from the section for washing clothes and taking baths. The headman explains that certain young men take turns monitoring the water hole to make sure that everyone follows the agreed-upon procedures. The villagers make voluntary contributions to a pool of funds from which the watchmen are paid.

John scratches his head and blows air forcefully, as if trying to blow a trumpet. "Nothing has changed after all these years of independence. People still collect the water using small bowls, pour the water into their buckets, and head home with the buckets on their heads. There is no purification of any kind. Time has stood still for generations upon generations. The colonialists built no water treatment infrastructure and we just let things continue exactly as they left them."

"I'm afraid you are right, John," Jamina replies.

John asks, "Do these people just drink the water like that?"

John remembers that when he used to come to these villages they would come with their own water in bottles and flasks.

"Yes," the headman replies.

"Is the water that pure?"

"Well, it is spring water of a kind and it works for them," Jamina replies. "I would not recommend that you drink any of it with your dinner tonight, though. No one has done a scientific study of the potability of this particular water."

The headman informs John and Jamina that the village has two such water holes. He explains that their village is in fact the luckiest around, in two respects. First, they can see the clean water bursting out of the ground and can shield the immediate area around the springs for drinking. In some villages around, the people are less fortunate and have to drink water flowing from some upstream area with human traffic. Second, the headman explains, many villagers have to dig wells to get water. "You don't need to go too far down," he says, "to get to the water table. But the well water I see is not very clean. The people of those villages insist their water is clean for drinking. Since they don't die, I believe them, but I do not drink their water myself."

"Why don't they just boil the water before drinking?" John asks.

"Actually, I don't know what they do before they drink the water. My guess is that they do not boil it. It would cost too much for firewood or charcoal. But they let the water sit in the sun. Maybe that helps to purify it a little."

John looks at Jamina, who just shrugs her shoulders.

"To tell you the truth," the headman continues, "many of those villagers walk all the way to our village to get water for drinking."

John is quite intrigued by it all. "These two springs could be used as a major source to build a dam or two and provide running water for much of this cluster of villages. But, I know, the government has no money. They need foreign aid for that—including, perhaps, for paying the engineers!"

John and Jamina want to go to the next village where there is some swamp gardening going on, and thank the headman before taking him back to where they had met him. On the way, Jamina leans over to John. "Don't forget to give the headman a tip."

"How much should I give him?"

"Give him sixty." By that Jamina meant 60,000 kalas, which is equivalent to fifteen US dollars. John looks at her. "Is that enough?"

"That's plenty."

John places the folded money in the palm of the headman's hand as they exit the vehicle.

"Headman, thank you very much. I hope we have not taken too much of your time."

The headman smiles and bows to Jamina. He then bows to John and says, "Thank you, sir. Thank you, madam. God bless both of you."

At the next village, less than a mile away from where they drop off the headman, they go down to an area where farmers are planting a variety of vegetables and swamp rice.

Jamina points to the group of people working on the rice. "You see those farmers in the middle of that swamp? They are working with their bare feet. And you know what? There are sometimes snakes in there—poisonous snakes."

"What do you mean?" John asks. "Do you mean snakes that can kill you?"

"Yes," Jamina replies. "But there is one blessing. The snakes are not so poisonous that you will die immediately. It can take several days. So you have time to go see a professional. I'm sure you know that many of these people, though, don't go to a doctor and use their own native herbs instead. Most of the time, the herbs seem to work. Anyway, as you know, snakes are afraid of people, so the incidence of snake bites is not high. I think the snakes are themselves running away from us."

"Strangely, I am more afraid of snakes now than when I was growing up. I always hated snakes, though. I did not differentiate between poisonous and non-poisonous snakes. In the US, some people allow their kids to keep snakes as pets. Not I. As for herbal medicines to address snake bites, I never believed they worked in spite of what our local people used to say when I was growing up."

John and Jamina walk around, looking at the farmers. Then Jamina says, "I constantly wonder why the scientists in our universities do not do more serious research on those herbal medicines."

"Those guys are simply not imaginative. That's the only answer I can think of. Once I asked the same question to one of those scientists, soon after I read that Western scientists were stealing our traditional knowledge and native plants and then had the guts to go and patent them. The scientist told me they needed research grants and that his university had no money to support the kind of research that was needed. So I told him, jokingly, that maybe he should go find himself a drug company in Europe or America to support him. I never heard from him again. Sooner or later, I'll track him down."

John stops to focus on the view. There are three men and two women working together in the rice field. They seem to be clearing weeds and checking the rice plants, which have blossomed beautifully. John realizes that it should soon be harvest time for this crop. He turns away as if to move on.

"My African friends who are scientists say that when the Africans do joint research with scientists from the industrial countries, those industrial country scientists find a way to steal all the credit. Poor miserable Africans, we don't seem to be able to win anything, not even credit for our labors!"

Jamina just looks at him and smiles.

They soon notice that the women are coming out of the farm towards them. They wait.

"Hello," John says to the ladies. "How do you do? So you are finished working?"

"Yes," one of them says, "we go cook now."

"Where do you live?"

"Over there," she says, pointing to a cluster of huts built of dirt and corrugated iron sheets.

"So you are from this village," Jamina says.

"Yes. Where you come from?"

"Lamongwe."

"You come to find somebody?"

"No, we just came to see you working," Jamina responds.

Both ladies smile and the one who had not spoken asks, "Well, you like it?"

"I do."

"Your man likes it, too?"

"Yes."

As they walk back to their vehicle, John suddenly stops and stares straight at Jamina.

"I hope I have not bored you today. I have a lot of questions I want to ask you. But I decided that it would be better to do so when we go to the restaurant tomorrow."

"No, John, you have not bored me. This was a good idea, this trip to the countryside."

"You are so pretty and kind."

"Thank you."

They decide to drop by a market, since Jamina says the fruits here can be better and cheaper than in Lamongwe. John is not surprised. As they near the market, John notices how it spreads. He remarks in a sarcastic tone, "At least these people are forced to use the outdoors to display their wares. In Lamongwe, they have buildings but the people still display their merchandise outside. It makes traffic near the markets so congested."

Jamina, rather surprised, smiles. "John, when was the last time you went into a market in Lamongwe?"

"Not since my early teens."

"Well, they are dark and dingy and muddy. Of course, I understand your feelings. In addition to the traffic, street trading adds to the squalor of the city. The solution is to build bigger, brighter, and more sensibly designed markets and then compel the traders to stay in them. Then the government can organize a publicity campaign asking people to buy only from those who sell inside and not to patronize those who sell outside the markets."

"That is a brilliant idea. If it works, it may be the beginning of an onslaught against street trading in general. It won't be easy to achieve results. I have a suspicion that to build enough of these markets, the government will want foreign aid."

"Well, you should know."

They drive off towards Lamongwe.

The next day, John collects Jamina and they go to a Chinese restaurant. After ordering, John asks, "Jamina, you seem so devoted to your teaching. Do you also want to raise children of your own someday?"

"Yes, why do you ask?"

"Jamina, you are very pretty, you are brilliant and educated, and you have a very pleasant personality. I am sure that men have been after you. So, I am honestly interested to find out if you are opposed to getting married. Maybe you are looking for Mr. Right. I have a stake in your answer, you know. But if I embarrass you, don't answer."

"I'm not embarrassed. The answer to your question is yes, men have been after me, and I am interested in marriage and raising children of my own. But if it does not happen, I am not going to be distraught about it. After all, I almost became a nun."

"Why didn't you?"

"I was not sure why I wanted to do it. I like to have positive reasons before I do something as major as that. In retrospect, I suspect I was fascinated by the nuns who I admired for their kindness. They were also teachers."

"Yes, it's a very sensible approach," John says, nodding, "to have good reasons to pursue a career. Most of us don't really have good reasons, except perhaps we liked the subject matter when compared to the alternatives."

"I like this restaurant very much," Jamina says, looking around. "I think we need a good Thai restaurant here as well. Can you believe we have no Thai restaurant? I am crazy about Thai food. When I travel to Europe or America, that's mainly what I eat."

"Do you travel much?" John inquires.

"Every summer for the last ten years I have visited Europe or else the US or Canada."

Jamina pauses as they enjoy the food. John is quiet, also. So, she continues.

"You see, I have Nigasilian friends in many countries, so I have home bases from which I can organize trips. When you live in Nigasilia, you run crazy if you cannot go away for a few weeks every year."

John cannot help but smile. "So how do the majority of people in this country maintain their sanity?"

"That's a good question," Jamina says thoughtfully. "Studies have shown that Africans, in spite of all their problems, are happy—on average, that is. When people get frustrated around here, they go dancing. But honestly, I think that people without knowledge of other places don't get bored as much we do. Maybe that's why you people in public policy should be wary. Television and the Internet are allowing people who do not travel to see and hear about what is going on in faraway places. More and more of our people are traveling. Then, of course, there are the diasporans, including the illegal ones. So perhaps more people are going to become insane around here."

John seems amused. "Should we start training psychiatrists?" They take a couple of bites and he asks, "Would you want to become a paramount chief like your dad?"

"No, I'm not crazy about that archaic institution. It is undemocratic. We have over sixty such chiefs in this country. That's like having sixty monarchs. Yes, chiefs are elected, but you must come from a crowning house before you are eligible to run. We have superimposed upon chieftaincy all these modern constructs like mayors, district councils, and chairmen of district councils, and we are really struggling to clarify how they all fit together. We need a serious national debate in this country on the future of chieftaincy."

"I couldn't agree with you more. As someone said once to me, the chiefs are guardians of the traditions of the people. So they cannot possibly disappear in one fell swoop. If we wanted that in this country we should have done so at the time of independence."

"I think you are right. But as we modernize, we will still have the problem of how they fit into the evolving structures. My dad believes chiefs are still valuable. But he does not doubt that over time the institution will disappear."

John interrupts. "Do you want dessert? If not, do you mind if we take a walk on the beach?"

"No, thank you, I don't want dessert. I like walking on the beach. Let's go," Jamina says, with a broad smile.

John pays the check. Getting to the beach from the restaurant is just a matter of crossing the road. It is the same Lumpimo Beach as near the Bokubo Hotel. This middle area of the three-mile stretch is always busy, since there are a number of small bars and diners along the road, on the same side as the beach. But the access to the beach is not blocked by the entertainment houses. There would be public uproar if that became a risk.

As they hit the beach, John asks, "Your mother is Muslim, right?"

"Yes, and she is very devout. She has twice visited Mecca."

"But your dad is Catholic?"

"Yes."

"Does your mother usually fast during Ramadan?"

"Yes, as long as I can remember."

"But why did you decide to become Catholic?"

"I simply grew up as one. I can't tell you how it all started. I was too young, obviously."

"Well, I am Anglican."

"I know."

"How?"

"I asked Mahdu."

"Of course. So tell me, what kind of boyfriends did you have in the past?"

"I have had only two somewhat serious boyfriends. The others were just special friends."

"So, why didn't you marry one of the two somewhat serious ones?"

"Oh, those men, they were not serious enough. They were too anxious to have sex. When I told one that I had no intention of having sex before marriage, he almost flipped."

"Why? Did he think you were unusual?"

"Maybe. John, I almost became a nun. If every man I meet wants me to have sex before marriage, then I will never marry. I'm very serious. My mother never had sex before she got married."

John was quite familiar with this topic. Elizabeth used to tell him how their mother would remind her not to have sex before marriage, because once the boys had it with a girl, they would move on. Moreover, their mother used to remind Elizabeth that if a girl became pregnant while in school, she was expelled. John was always protective of Elizabeth. The boy had to be doing well in school. If not, John was determined to harass him. Fortunately, he was never put to the test, because Elizabeth was herself very conservative and strict about the boys she wanted to encourage.

"Mahdu told me you have a brother in America. Is he Christian or Muslim?"

"Yes, Jamehun. That boy is nothing—a non-believer."

"He is then very rare. There are not many Nigasilians who are non-believers. How did he come to that point?"

"I wish I knew the answer, because my parents keep asking me the same thing. I tell them he must have come under the influence of the wrong group in America."

"I suppose that's as good an answer as any."

So far, they have been enjoying the waves and all the other activities on the beach. They watch a couple of teams of fishermen pulling their nets to shore, boys playing soccer, people drinking at bars at the edge of the beach, and quite a few people, including some Caucasians, taking walks. John stops, gazing at the boys playing soccer. Jamina doesn't understand what is so interesting about that. John notices the look on her face.

"Oh, I want to see how they score. I have never seen a goal being scored on these miniature goal posts."

The width of the goal is about three feet and the height only about two feet. John has been seeing these goals in parks where the boys play pick-up soccer, but he has never seen a goal being scored. There is no goalie, but it is easy for one of the defenders to just stand in front of the goal and block any shot.

"I have not either, but I have not cared to watch."

"You are right, let's go."

They turn to walk back to the restaurant. As they do, John asks, "Do you swim?"

"Yes, but only in a pool."

"You know, I never learnt how to swim properly. I took a few lessons but gave up. I convinced myself that I did not have the time. Now I regret it. It's such a pleasant way to exercise. It is better than jogging, in my view."

As they approach the restaurant, John asks, "Have you transacted any business with the Chinese here in Nigasilia—catering, custom-made furniture, construction?"

"No," Jamina responds, "but I have seen some of the construction work they have done. If I have to do any major construction in the near future, I'll go to them. They are reasonable in price and their finishing touches seem much better than what most of our own people do."

John is genuinely surprised. "Do you think it is a matter of skill or of discipline?"

"I think it is a combination of both. But this is only my view. Some of my friends insist that there are excellent Nigasilian builders and that they would rather go to them than any foreign construction firm. They say we must patronize our own."

"But who built your house?"

"My house was built by a Lebanese construction firm."

"How do they compare with the Chinese?"

"Oh, I don't think I can generalize. But, as you know, the Lebanese were here long before the Chinese."

"Yes, you're right."

John is anxious to book another date with Jamina. He enjoys her company very much. "What are you doing next weekend?"

"On Saturday, I'll play squash in the early afternoon and go to a birthday party in the evening. On Sunday, I'll go to church and then play squash in the afternoon."

"Whose birthday party?"

"One of my best girlfriends turns thirty-three this coming Thursday. She is just using the occasion to have a party."

"Can I come with you?"

Jamina obliges. She enjoys his company and is pleased he asked. She was too shy to take the initiative.

"Sure, you can be my date. I was just going to go alone, otherwise."

When John drops Jamina at her place, he walks her to the door.

"Thanks, Jamina, I really enjoy being with you. It's like I have known you for a long time. It's hard to explain, but I am not embarrassed to say it. I love your company."

"Thanks, John. I have enjoyed every minute with you."

He kisses her on both cheeks.

On Saturday, when Jamina and John arrive at the hall where Jamina's friend, Vivienne, is holding her party, they are almost the first to arrive. The only other guests are the representative of the United Nations Development Programme and his wife. Vivienne's fiancé, Santie, is of course also there.

Jamina introduces John to Vivienne. Vivienne has a small frame and a lovely shape, with an upright stance as if she is trying to be taller. She has a smallish but broad face and big eyes with long eyelashes. She fixes her stare straight into the eyes of the person she is addressing, as if eye contact reassures her that the other side is truly interested in what she is saying.

"John, welcome. It's my great pleasure to meet you. You have made me jealous, taking my friend away from me so many days now."

"Oh, sorry about that. Now I will have to find a way to pay for my sin."

As Jamina suddenly gets distracted by Santie, Vivienne says, "Jamina enjoys your company and that makes me happy, too. Anyway, let me get the waiters to serve you something." She turns around to make sure Jamina is not in a position to hear and then whispers to John, "I hope you will dance with Jamina. I don't want her to go home without dancing, and she likes you, I know."

Jamina steps back. "Oh, Vivienne, let me quickly introduce John to our UNDP friends."

Jamina knows the UNDP representative and his wife and introduces them to John. The UNDP man is eager to talk to the president's son.

"John, I have heard a lot about you already," Ishan Chand says. "I gather you have been busy, setting up what is a completely new department."

"Yes, I have to set up the office while at the same time I have to begin doing the substantive work."

"Are you able to get the people you want?"

"So far, I have been able to get one young PhD economist who came home after being away for many years. We also already have one research assistant and two secretaries. I am currently negotiating with two Africans in the US and one in the UK to take sabbatical leave and come spend a year with me. So, we are making some progress. And you, how are you finding your stay here?"

"My work here is fascinating, actually. We have quite a few things we are funding here, in diverse sectors of the economy. I basically just manage the office and see that projects are implemented as programmed."

"Do you have to travel a lot around the country?"

"I do. We bring in the experts and consultants to do much of the specialized technical work. But we need to introduce them to the country and assist them with logistics. So I need to know the country and the people. Also, we need to make sure our experts do what they are supposed to do."

People have begun to stream in. Jamina and Vivienne step out to the main hall and walk together as Vivienne greets her guests. After Vivienne greets everyone, Jamina walks quietly back and sits next to John, who has just scheduled a meeting with the UNDP representative.

"Sorry, dear date, I deserted you for my dear friend. She wanted me to be by her side."

John jokes, "I'm surprised Santie did not feel left out."

"Oh, he's used to that. He sometimes says we act like twins."

John laughs. "This is a nice hall. How long does a party like this last?"

"Why do you ask?"

"No particular reason. Just that a party like this can last a long time. I don't mind, though, if the company is good."

"Well, this one will not last too long. Vivienne plans to have the food served soon, cut the cake, and have a couple of toasts, and then she will open the floor for dancing. I plan to leave early. I'm an early bird no matter how great the company."

The party is well organized, the guests blend in very well, and the food is plentiful and sumptuous. It is a buffet, which starts with fruit salad and regular salad. Then, for the main meal, the choices are a stew with mixed chicken and beef, fish in fillet cuts with sauce on the side, and a lamb stew. These are served with rice cooked in two different styles as well as boiled potatoes and mixed vegetables. For dessert there are three different kinds of cakes.

After everyone has had something to eat, Vivienne thanks everyone for coming. Then she says, in a very excited tone, "Well, the floor is open. Please get up and dance a little. There is still plenty of food and drinks. Please don't be shy and don't leave any of that food for me."

As soon as Vivienne makes the announcement, John turns to Jamina. "May I have the pleasure of dancing with you?"

John and Jamina end up staying on the dance floor for three numbers. All three are long African pieces from three different countries. The two of them dance apart for the first two. Then, for the third, John wants to hold Jamina's hands and dance close. Vivienne looks at Jamina and gives a smile of approval, to which Jamina responds with a gentle smile and mouths: *Thank you.*

Since Vivienne's party, John and Jamina have been talking to each other on the telephone regularly, almost every day, in fact. They have also been on two more dates in the center of town, basically just to see each other, take a walk, have something to eat, and be in each other's company. Today they have a date to see an outdoor art exhibition not too far away from the Chinese restaurant where they had lunched the other day; they will then go sightseeing up some hills in Lamongwe.

"Jamina," John asks, "is it just me or are good Nigasilian sculptures becoming harder and harder to find?"

"No, John, it's not just you. The artists today are both less patient and less skilled, on average, than they used to be. Unfortunately, the highly skilled and patient ones are being drowned out by a whole slew of mediocre artists. So you have to spend more time looking to find the good ones. You also have to be careful about the wood they use. With staining it is a challenge to discern what you are getting. I notice that some of the best sculptures are found in the hotels, but those hotels overcharge tremendously. Those who are keen collectors know how to locate the best artists. The Nigasilian sculpture market is truly international. If you find a hundred excellent ones, at least 80 percent will be from other African countries."

The art exhibition is one of paintings, oil and watercolor mainly. Most of the paintings are straightforward depictions of everyday life and nature, nothing particularly sophisticated or elaborate. No Kandinsky or Pollock among these artists.

John says to Jamina, "It's amazing that most of these people haven't gone to any formal school to learn their trade. They have simply decided to paint and develop their skills through practice and experimentation."

"Yes, but many of them go through apprenticeships with older painters. We have also begun to teach and study art in our colleges and universities. But a number of African countries are far ahead of us. God only knows what will happen now that your mother is gone. The so-called Ministry of Tourism and Cultural Affairs is simply not interested."

John does not quite agree. "I was under the impression that Sanjo Manray is one of the enlightened ministers."

Jamina decides to be generous. "That may well be true, but he cannot do it alone. He needs to have people in his ministry who understand these things. Most of the senior people in that ministry have never been to a decent art museum or art exhibition anywhere in the world. When they go abroad, they are more interested in shopping. They don't have a clue about what goes on in the artistic world."

John nods in agreement. "Yes, that's a shame. But that sort of promotion and sponsorship should not wait for government. We need artistic societies that can organize the artists and the art festivals, educate the public about local art, and foster schools, workshops, and studios. The one aspect that will be a hurdle is how to generate incentives for creativity in the absence of serious art collectors. We will need to leapfrog the local market and link up with the international art world. When I settle down I will see who I can encourage to take up these challenges. You know, we economists have found that a place that is pleasant to live in and visit also has an advantage in attracting capital and talent."

"That makes sense to me. Well, then, I would suggest you start with the university art lecturers and the operators of local art galleries. You can begin to develop a true network that way. We could use a real art museum in this country. We really have none. Can you imagine that, in today's world?"

They leave the art exhibition and head for a mountainous area to do some sightseeing. By himself, John does not usually feel like doing things like this. But he is happy just being with Jamina. Jamina, too, is very comfortable with John. She wants to take the opportunity to show John the things that irritate her about the country, as well as help him understand why her cousin, Kontana, is excited that John is here to help. As they drive up, Jamina points to the diminishing vegetation on the hillsides and the thick clusters of small houses of tin and wood dotting the landscape.

"John, someone has to do something about this. We, in the Conservation Society, have made all kinds of efforts. These hills are going to start sliding down someday. When we have to dig out bodies from beneath mudslides during the heavy rains, maybe then the government will listen."

John does not need much convincing; he sees the problem as well and has been reading about it in the newspapers for some time now, even before he came to stay. "These hills are in the general catchment area for the two major dams of the city."

"Yes, these hills are all part of the riparian zone. That vegetation is essential. It improves water quality by filtering runoff from the catchment. That vegetation traps and absorbs pollutants before they enter the water. The water people know all that, and they have been pressuring the government to do something. The Nigasilian Energy and Water Company is a state enterprise, and even *it* has not convinced the government to act. What are we waiting for now?"

John is also frustrated. "The Energy and Water Company people complain they are struggling with the costs of fuels and chemicals, the poor payment of bills, workers' inefficiency, illegally connected pipes, lack of power supply, etcetera. These are not difficult problems to solve. They don't have to wait for the World Bank to tell them they should raise tariffs. All right, they may need some money for investment, because right now they cannot even lay proper pipes in areas where new houses are being built and they need more water pressure. Now, we are talking about the capital city. This place is a joke, really! It's not a country. Take workers' inefficiency. The workers, for example, have to distribute bills, read meters, and mend leaking pipes around this city. On any given day, the workers come up with all kinds of reasons why they cannot perform those tasks efficiently, from lack of transport to lack of materials and equipment. So, you see, the whole system is a mess. I think privatization would help. But I will not get support for that, I know."

"I agree. But going back to the problem of these hills, why is the government so afraid of doing something? They are all squatters. The government can break down these shanties and stop the cutting of trees; in fact, they need a replanting campaign. I know all the excuses the government gives, but I don't believe any of them. If they send the army and the police to clear all these hills and have the areas guarded, none of these people will dare riot or come back."

"Maybe government can succeed by doing so. But they are afraid that they will simply be shifting the problem of overcrowding to some other part of the city and they don't want to be accused of driving the people out."

Jamina can do little more than sigh. "I guess we are stuck."

They head down from the hillsides to the center of the city for a late lunch. As they get out of their vehicle, the stench is unusually nasty. The sewage system of the central business district has burst and the sewage is seeping onto the street. They cannot park here or even eat in such a neighborhood. So they decide to drive to another restaurant some distance away. The central business district is the only area of this city with a centralized sewer, and the authorities cannot even do a good job of maintaining such a small system. Jamina and John agree that, given the level of efficiency of public services, no one can be certain how long it will take the authorities to clean up the mess.

As they prepare to park at the other restaurant, two young men walk up and offer to guard their vehicle so that no one vandalizes it. This is quite normal in Lamongwe. Given the lack of respect for other people's property, and so much pedestrian traffic in the city, people might touch, lean on, and even slide some sharp instrument across your vehicle. But that is not the only threat you face. Those boys who offer to guard your car could scratch your vehicle in revenge if you refuse. John never bothers to weigh the risks. The tip these boys want is small, the equivalent of around fifty cents in the US. So, when John does not have his chauffeur around, he simply accepts the offer.

As the waiter hands them the menu, John says, "You know, I came here for the first time in early February with two director generals. I like it. It is simple, no fuss, Nigasilian, and fast."

"Yes, you are right. Unfortunately, I go to Nigasilian restaurants only for the company. I don't go for the food, because I can do at least as well myself and I have a wonderful cook at home."

John smiles. "I guess when I settle down I shall also try to get a first-rate cook. Anyway, Jamina, I have thoroughly enjoyed being with you today. I don't mean to embarrass you, but I love you and I think of you every day. I hope you enjoy being with me the way I enjoy being with you."

"Yes, I very much enjoy being with you, John."

Drumming up all the courage he can muster, but still looking rather shy and slightly timid, John smiles at Jamina and says, "Jamina, I would like to ask if you would accept my request that we go steady."

Jamina smiles. "You mean you want me to leave all my other boy-friends and just date you?"

"Yes," says John, "if you think it's worth the pain."

Jamina keeps quiet for a moment. "Well, none of the others is worth the effort. So your answer is yes," she says.

"Thanks, dear," John says. "Thank you."

They look at each other and smile sweetly, absorbing the moment with the ultimate relish, like trying to enjoy the full effect of a great wine as it is swirled in the mouth and swallowed slowly so as not to have it rushed past the back of the tongue.

As they walk to his vehicle, John reaches for Jamina's hand and she gives it to him in a gentle way. They have never held hands before.

When they reach her house, Jamina says, "You can come in for a minute."

He steps in, closes the door, and embraces her passionately. It is as if they have each been waiting for this moment. Each one can feel the other is in love.

Chapter 6

The first Sunday in April, John calls in the early afternoon, before 1:00 p.m., inviting Jamina for dinner at his father's place the following Wednesday. His father is anxious to meet her. John will pick her up at her house. It will be just the three of them.

Right now, it is 1:00, and John is relaxed and on his way to his driver's house to see him and meet his family. It is a gesture that John knows can be highly appreciated in Nigasilian society. He told them not to prepare anything, but they have bought some beer for him, which they have struggled to keep cool with ice they bought from a small supermarket not very far away.

Samura introduces John to his wife, Yeynoh, and their son and two daughters; all three children are still in primary school. He also is introduced to two friends who are visiting. They knew that Samura's boss was coming to visit, and wanted to meet the president's son.

Samura and family live in a small, three-bedroom, one-story house, built modestly with concrete and a corrugated iron roof, about three miles, as the crow flies, from John's house. The kitchen, toilet, and bathroom facilities are all outside the main house. They use firewood and charcoal for cooking. It's a house built by someone who expects the building to be torn down, in the not-too-distant future, to be replaced with a modern construct. John's driver and family are, in a sense, helping to preserve the land from intruders and illegal occupiers. They have brought some chairs and everyone is sitting outside, in the yard, at the front of the house. It's a nice area in general with a good tarmac road and a sidewalk that is not full of people and their wares.

After the introductions, Samura says, "Doctor, thank you for coming. So this is where I lay my head at night."

Yeynoh says, with a broad smile covering her face, and her teeth prominently displayed, "Doctor, thank you for your kindness to Samura. God will bless you and your family. Hey, Samura said your madam died. I'm sorry to hear that. God will help you take care of the children. You talk to them in America?"

"Yeynoh, thank you. Your man is also a good man. He is very serious and works hard. Yes, I talk to my children all the time. They like Nigasilia, you know. They like to come for holiday here. I hope your children are trying hard in school."

"Yes, sir, thank God. I have my small market to help Samura. Hey, it's not easy. Things are hard in Nigasilia."

"Doctor," one of the young men butts in, "Pa Samura says you have come to help your father make things better for us. We hope your father will go around and visit the people to see how they are suffering."

"He does," John says, rather defensively.

"Oh, well, near here, he just passes with his many vehicles. They stop traffic and they rush past us."

"Well, he cannot visit everybody. Sometimes he has to depend on people to tell him how the common man is suffering. But I can tell you that my father knows that life is not easy for the common people. He knows. You know, before he became president he was just an ordinary citizen, going around just like you and me. He also has relatives who are suffering. My friend, there is nothing my father does not know about the common man's suffering."

"I believe you, Doctor, but still, maybe your father should come and talk to us face-to-face, you know, so we will feel better that he knows about our suffering."

"Okay, my friend, I shall tell him."

On Monday morning as John enters his office, his cell phone rings.

"Rabena, hi, what's up?"

"There is a permanent secretary that wants to talk to you badly. He is around and would like to talk to you after he meets with the VP."

"Okay, do you have any idea what he wants?"

"Yes, he is fighting with his minister, one of the VP boys."

The permanent secretary is the most senior administrative officer in a ministry. Within the hour, Abu Contey walks in and introduces himself to John. He is the permanent secretary in the Ministry of Works, Housing, and Infrastructure.

"Welcome, Abu, it's my pleasure to meet you. How can I help you?"

"Dr. Bijunga, I just came from a meeting in the VP's office. My minister was also there. My minister is trying to push me out of the ministry."

"Why?"

"Because we quarreled. Sir, since he came, I had never seen such corruption before. No one is perfect but he is just too much. Sir, he is diverting a lot of construction and building materials to his own private use. He is now on his second house and he has only been there for three years. He had no house before he became minister."

John pulls out one of his log notebooks, turns to a clean page, and writes, "Private use of public property."

"Sir, the man is also terrible when it comes to subcontracting. If you don't give him a good bribe you don't get the job. The contractors don't worry; they simply add it on to the cost. But you have to pay up front. That means you can bribe him and still not get the job."

John writes in his logbook, "Accepting bribes."

Then he turns to Abu and asks, "So, why does he want you out?"

"Because I told him that all the people in the office are saying he eats too much. I told him they will start leaking information to the press. Then he told me to shut up. I lost my temper and told him he was a stupid fool."

"Oh, that's serious. I thought people in your position have been trained never to lose your tempers with the politicians."

"That is true, Doc, but I lost a lot of sleep thinking about how I could stop that man, because he was getting worse every day."

"So what do you want me to do?"

"I don't mind a transfer to another ministry, but I don't want a bad report in my file."

"How many years more do you have?"

"Ten. I am only fifty."

"So you want me to talk to the VP?"

"And to your father, also, because the VP seems to favor the minister."

"Okay, I'll see what I can do."

Abu leaves and John telephones his father and relates his meeting with Abu. The president tells him that, yes, he and the VP are going to discuss the issue that afternoon at 2:00.

As the VP walks into his office, the president asks, "So, Mr. VP, what is this big problem between Maigo Bang and Abu Contey?"

"They do not like each other. But also Maigo says that Abu accused him of being too corrupt and acting like a stupid fool."

"So what kind of corruption is Abu talking about?"

"Abu said, in our meeting this morning, that the minister was diverting government materials to the building of his house and that he was taking bribes for subcontracting."

"So, what did the minister say?"

"He says it's all a lie."

"What do you think?"

"To tell you the truth, I will not say that any of our ministers is clean, but in this country small bits of corruption here and there are not considered a crime. Still, there is an understanding that you should not overdo things."

The president gets up from his chair as if to stretch his legs.

"But Kamake, we have to change that attitude and let all our ministers know that we will no longer tolerate these violations. I have vowed that this government will have zero tolerance towards corruption. Then we set up an anti-corruption agency. You agree with me, I would assume, that our actions must reflect our words. So, please, don't let anyone get the impression that corruption here and there is not a crime."

"You know I agree with you. I was just describing the general attitude in this country."

"What do we do with Abu now?"

"I think we should transfer him to another ministry."

"And what do we do about his accusations? There must have been good reasons for him to say what he said to the minister. Maigo is an excellent engineer and he is doing a decent job in that ministry. But I will not encourage corruption even by him."

"Okay, I shall talk to him about it."

"I will transfer Abu to the Ministry of Tourism and Culture. The permanent secretary in that ministry is very good but he has been there for a long time now and is overdue for a transfer."

When Jamina walks into John's office a little after 4 p.m. later that Monday, John greets her warmly. "How were things at school today?"

"Do you subscribe to your school's diasporan alumni association?" she asks.

All the secondary schools in Nigasilia have diasporan alumni associations. Typically, one covers North America and another one is based in Europe.

"Yes, I do subscribe to their charity work and make significant contributions of books and money; but in all honesty, I am not as active a member as some of my schoolmates."

"Well, every year without fail, we receive three types of donations from our associations in North America and Europe. One donation is directed to school construction and maintenance, the second one is intended for supplementing teachers' salaries, and the third is meant for student scholarships. That does not include the book donations they also make for the library, which they ship as frequently as two or three times a year. They also gave us all the computers we are using. Anyway, two people who came from the US and the UK brought some of the money this past week. So, our head teacher made the announcement to the teachers today. Of course, everyone was happy."

"So what are you constructing now?" John asks.

"Actually, this year we want mainly to repair some broken windows. There are so many of them. The kids break some and street people break others."

Jamina asks John how his day has been.

John narrates his meeting with Abu Contey, to which Jamina responds, "Good, we need those types of perm secs," referring to the permanent secretary position.

"The rest of my day has been so-so. I had a meeting with the minister of finance to discuss my budget. I realize deep down that I will not get everything I want, but I need to try my best anyway. So far, the minister has been very cooperative. After a certain point, I may have to take control of the appeal process vis-à-vis the donors. I also worked on that address I told you about that I have to give to the Labor Union Congress. I want to encourage the unions to take greater interest in fostering education and skills training, and to do outreach to the young people. Unfortunately, that kind of talk does not get to the vast majority of workers in our country. The majority of workers here are not in labor unions, and not because they are so-called white-collar employees. In this country, it is because they are in the informal sector or in enterprises that the labor unions have simply ignored. This means that I have to find a way to communicate with those people.

Petty traders, money changers, domestic servants, farmers, market women, small shopkeepers, tailors, potters, porters, self-employed artisans and craftsmen, food preparers, cooks, caterers, hair dressers, barbers, cobblers, small-scale repairmen . . . Many of the associations that these groups have formed are a far cry from labor unions. I want to find out a few things from them and I also would like to motivate them to help themselves and put pressure on the authorities."

Jamina steps closer to John with a frown on her face. "Why? Do you want to enter politics in a serious way?"

"Enter politics? You mean run for Parliament or become a minister? No, no, no. The way things are going, I may not even last in this advisory post. No, I just want to shake up this system, get the masses excited, and have them scare the real political leaders into doing the right thing. I want to encourage mass movements, the sort of thing that radicals in a vibrant civil society would do."

"Isn't it easier to just talk to your dad?"

"Jamina, I don't see how that approach will work here. Our political leaders, including my father, have to believe that the people will rise up and overthrow them if they do not act to improve the lives of the average person."

"I'm afraid you are right, as far as your objectives are concerned. We do need the change. But as far as provoking social movements, because that's what you are trying to do, isn't it, how will your father think of it when he realizes what you are doing?"

"Well, I guess we shall find out sooner or later."

Before they leave, John decides to introduce Jamina to Rabena, and when they reach her office, the president's confidential secretary jumps from her desk. "Jamina, it's so good to meet you. I don't know how I have missed you before. I have heard so much about you. You are the biology teacher whose students do so well in the certificate exams, and you are the chief's daughter who is so active in the Conservation Society. When Minister Kontana told me that he had introduced you to John and that you were going out together, I told John I had to meet you. My daughter is one of your admirers."

"Mrs. Karam, I have heard a lot of good things about you, too, and I am very pleased to meet you."

"Call me Rabena; that's good enough."

"One of these days we can have lunch or dinner together, as you like. I hope your daughter is doing all right in university. John told me about her."

"Yes, she is doing quite well. Let me give you my cell phone number."

They exchange numbers and promise to get in touch.

Jamina promised to be at Vivienne's around 5:30, before Vivienne and Santie go out tonight. Vivienne lives with her parents, not too far from Jamina's house. Vivienne's parents are in and sitting with the other two on the veranda. They greet Jamina, ask her how she is doing, and then they decide to leave the three young people and go inside and watch television.

Santie turns to Jamina and says, "The earrings you gave to Vivienne are beautiful. Where did you buy them?"

Jamina smiles. "Actually, I bought them in London last summer. I was going to give them to Vivienne as a Christmas present. But then I saw this beautiful piece of cloth that was relatively new in Nigasilia. So I decided to give her that for Christmas and save the earrings for her birthday. I did not want to spoil her by giving her two nice presents for Christmas!"

Vivienne goes inside and brings out a big Oxford Dictionary of English. "Well, this is what Santie gave me."

"A dictionary!"

"Yes," says Vivienne. "I have been complaining that I could use one. Mine is very old and worn. Poor Santie had to order it, since there was no one coming from abroad that could bring it for him. He refuses to tell me how much the postage cost. He paid to have it sent by courier."

"You see, Jamina," Santie interjects. "You see the price we pay to show our love?"

"It seems more like we pay for not having any decent bookshops or post office," Jamina counters.

They all three laugh and then Jamina turns to Vivienne, shrugging her shoulders. "So our friend Yokito did not get the transfer he thought he was due."

Vivienne, who has a bachelor's degree with honors in geography from the University of Nigasilia, works at the Customs Department; Yokito is a colleague of hers.

Vivienne's smile fades. "No, I'm afraid Yokito has lost out. I have been telling him that he is too greedy and selfish. In fact, he is a fool, if you ask me, and does not look far ahead. When his boss gives him an assignment, he does not often go and properly thank his boss. Now he has lost the opportunity to be transferred to one of the biggest money-making branches. Yokito's reputation has spread and that's it; he will only be left with the dregs unless he changes. Now he has to hope that this does not affect his promotion."

At Customs, as in many other departments in Nigasilian public service, when your boss assigns you to tasks in which the opportunity to exact or receive bribes is great, you are expected to share the booty with your boss. If you gain a reputation for not doing that, your boss will assign you to tasks where the opportunity to receive bribes is minimal.

"John was laughing at you the other day," Jamina says. "He says he sees these signs all over Customs imploring us to be patriotic, and to not practice corruption. He thinks we should remove all such signs until there is hope that they will have any effect."

"And when will that be?" Santie asks.

Jamina was emphatic in her response. "Never!"

"That's what I thought," Santie says, "since there is corruption everywhere in this world."

Jamina gives him a stern look. "Santie, I hope you are joking. You know what people are talking about. They are not saying eliminate corruption everywhere. But we can reduce it drastically and eliminate it completely in some important cases."

Santie, with a wave of his hand, responds cynically. "You may be right, but I don't believe it. How can we, with such low salaries?"

Santie grew up in a household struck by misfortune. The only surviving child of his parents, he lost two siblings at very young ages, one at only two years old and the other at five, both from preventable illnesses—typhoid and amoebic dysentery—combined in one case with diarrhea and the other with malaria. He was the oldest of his siblings. His dad had a tough time in the civil service, because he tried to fight corruption and was, therefore, disliked by most of his coworkers, who called him, derisively, "Mr. Clean." Santie studied agronomy at the University of Nigasilia before taking a master's degree in agricultural economics at Michigan State University in the US. He holds a senior professional position at the Ministry of Agriculture in Nigasilia.

After a short pause, Jamina presses her point. "John says there are ways, including raising salaries and making government more efficient. But he says economic policy as a whole will have to be done much better in this country."

Vivienne interjects. "Do you think he will succeed in improving economic policy? At my party, I asked him how he was doing in his job. 'Not very well,' he said. 'People here don't want to change.' Then he said it would take too long for him to explain."

Jamina does not feel like going on with the discussion. "Well, Vivienne, I think I have hinted to you already some of the problems he is having. He is faced with a challenge and he has to deal with it."

Santie asks Jamina, "Are you looking forward to dinner with John's father on Wednesday? Whose idea was that?"

"It was John's idea. He said his dad knows my parents very well but that the president has not seen me since I was a little girl. John said his dad remembers me as very shy and studious."

Santie, in a more agreeable frame of mind, cheerfully adds, "Well, it should be a nice evening for you. I tell you, honestly, I had never met John before the birthday party, but I found him a really pleasant person. He just has to be patient with us here in Nigasilia. He can't hold us to those high international standards to which he has become accustomed."

Jamina responds with a taint of sarcasm. "I'll tell him." She glances at her watch and knows it's time to leave.

In addition to a teacher's meeting after school on Tuesday, Jamina is very busy with exams and grading papers, so John does not want to disturb her too much. But he still asks if he could drop by in the evening and just read at her place and do some drafting as well, while she does her work. He will bring his laptop. They can also watch the news together. Jamina asks if she can prepare a light supper for the two of them. She has a cook but she assures him she will make something delicious herself. John accepts the offer with pleasure.

When there is no traffic, it takes him about twenty minutes to reach his destination. With rush-hour traffic, it could be more than twice as long. The traffic in the city is just getting worse. A major problem is the behavior of the taxi and private bus drivers. These drivers disobey traffic laws at will. They stop anywhere their passengers beckon and will often not move far enough to the curbside of the road, or the shoulder, forcing vehicles behind them to wait. The narrow Lamongwe streets and the pedestrian traffic just make matters worse. To add to the aggravation, a large proportion of vehicles in the city are old. Breakdowns occur often and disrupt traffic flow. Some of the vehicles should clearly not be on the road. But corruption is rife in that area.

John is not late as far as Jamina is concerned. She says they might as well eat first and then they can work afterwards. She has prepared fried shrimp in a simple sauce of tomato, onion, pepper, and garlic. She toasts some bread and they begin their meal.

During the meal, Jamina asks if John has spoken to his boys anytime this week, since he has been so busy. "No," John says, "but I have sent them e-mails and they are doing fine." She asks if she should bring anything for his dad tomorrow and he says no, it is not necessary, especially since she will be going with him.

The two finish their meal, and John goes to watch the news. Jamina is about to go into one of the bedrooms, where she has a desk for working, but first she goes to the couch where John is sitting, and they kiss. John gently pulls her toward him and tightly embraces her.

The next day, John and Jamina arrive on time at the president's place. A servant promptly takes their orders. As they wait for the old man to get ready and come down, John gets up, looks absent-mindedly around, and then beckons to Jamina. "Grab your drink and let me show you the library."

"Does your dad find any time to read?" Jamina asks. "I see books on all kinds of subjects. Who orders the books?"

"Well, he reads on the weekends but, as you suspect, he does not spend as much time reading as he would like. As for ordering the books, a librarian from the Library of Lamongwe comes here once every two weeks to take care of that."

When they return to the living room, the president enters and says to Jamina, "Welcome to the Presidential Hut. John has spoken so much about you. I know your father very well. He is one of our more able chiefs. Your mother I also know well. I knew you when you were much younger. I would not have recognized you now if I had run into you on the street."

"Thank you, Mr. President, it is my great pleasure and honor to meet you. I hope I can live up to the picture that John has painted of me."

John puts his hand on her shoulders. "You will."

The president invites them to the table. As they sit, he says to Jamina, "I know this is Easter exams week for you. I hope I am not distracting you with this dinner."

"No, Mr. President. I'm used to the pressure around these times, so I have found ways to organize myself enough to give me time for relaxation."

The president is interrupted as the waiter brings the oysters to start the meal. "I hope you teachers are being patient with us. We realize that things are not easy, with crowding in the classroom, inadequate facilities, and low teachers' salaries. We are doing our best and will try to do better. As a science teacher, it must be especially strenuous for you to work without a good lab. What is the situation regarding computers?"

"We are counting on alumni associations in the diaspora to help us in this area; in fact, they have already started to do so."

"Good. Please let them know we are unable to do more because we don't have the resources; it is not because we do not care."

"Sure, Mr. President, I will do so."

Jamina does not understand why a country like Nigasilia that is so rich in natural resources cannot generate the resources required for something as important as good-quality education. Anyway, there is no point bringing this up here. She is sure the president hears the same thing from a lot of people all the time.

John then says, "I showed Jamina the library. She was very impressed."

"Thank you," the president says. "For that library alone it is great to be the president. Unfortunately, I don't get the time to read as much as I would like to. Anytime you want to come and read, tell John to bring you. Or you can come by yourself. Just tell John to call the gate to tell them that you are coming."

"Thank you, Mr. President."

The waiter collects the dishes and goes to bring in the main dish, which is a combination of chicken and shrimp in a peanut butter sauce. The peanut butter sauce is one of the classic Nigasilian sauces that go well with any meat or fish. It is usually served with rice. The side vegetable this evening is steamed spinach.

As the waiter does the rounds, there is a moment of silence. The president does his best to keep the conversation going.

"The schools are going to have two weeks of vacation. I am sure teachers and students alike are looking forward to that. What are you two doing for Easter?"

John sees an opportunity to jump in. "I'm going with Jamina to her church and then on Easter Monday we will go to a picnic organized by her church members. At which beach is it again, Jamina?"

"It will be at Kutianbo Beach."

The president's face lights up. "That's my favorite. I'm sure you will have a good time. John probably has not been there for ages."

"That's right, Dad."

John glances at Jamina and she glances back with a questioning look on her face. John is thinking of the conversation he had with her about wanting to stir up the people. His dad notices, but thinks they are just experiencing romantic sparks. So he says nothing and restrains himself from smiling.

Then John says, "Dad, here's an issue I have been meaning to raise with you for some time now. Some of the ordinary people I have been talking to think that you should find a way to communicate more directly and informally with the general population of the country."

"You mean like these so-called town meetings that American politicians like?"

"Yes, Dad, I mean town meetings, but with one important difference. From what I sense, the youth of this country want both open and closed meetings. Anybody can come to the open meetings. But the closed meetings will be held for particular groups; for instance, market women, drivers, union members, and teachers. That way, you will be able to get a different perspective of their trials and tribulations. The community will not want a small group of educated people to dominate such meetings. The people are grumbling because their expectations were high when you took over. You will be able to hear firsthand what they are complaining about, and they will hear from you directly about your problems and what you are trying to achieve. I am sympathetic with their concerns. I don't think that the government is communicating enough with the people. In fact, many of the people believe that the government is not really interested in what they think or even know about their suffering."

"So you have been hearing all these things yourself from the people, or have you been reading about all this in the newspapers?"

"Both, Dad, both. At another level, Kontana, Manray, and Frah are also informing me about what people are saying to them."

"Well, so far you haven't told me anything and I see you or talk to you every day. Anyway, you are right, John. The substantive ministers and I should talk more directly to the people. To tell you the truth, I have myself been thinking it is strange that we do not have a news conference tradition in which the president answers questions directly from the press. It is almost as if we are afraid of the press. Hence we create this post of minister of information to shield us. I shall consider this suggestion. People around here get nervous about radical changes, so I have to be very cautious."

Shaking his head, John has to restrain himself. He really wants his dad to just go ahead and ask his ministers to do it. He is boiling inside. *He will never get voluntary support, damn it.*

The president can see his son's anger. But he looks directly at Jamina and says, "I'm amazed that these Nigasilian young men have let a beautiful and intelligent lady like you stay single."

"Maybe I am to blame. Like most women, I guess, I am trying to find the right man."

The old man does not want to embarrass his son or Jamina by pursuing the subject any further. They are finished with their meal. So, he invites them to the living room.

Jamina asks, as they sit, "Mr. President, what is the hardest thing about being president?"

"That is a difficult question. But in a sense the answer is obvious. The electorate thinks you should have a painless solution to all the problems of the country, and every one of the most active members of your political party thinks you must find a good-paying job for him or her in the public sector."

"Yes, even those of us not involved in politics can sense all of that."

The president looks as if he has remembered something he was eager to say.

"Incidentally, Jamina, we are beginning to pay some attention to the concerns of the Conservation Society, especially logging in the interior and the deforestation of the hills around Lamongwe. So, I hope we will be able to take actions that you and the other society members will approve of. I want to assure you that the ideas and the concerns of the Conservation Society are not falling on deaf ears. You will just have to be patient with us."

"We will try, Mr. President."

"But Dad, what I hear is that the political leadership of the country does not really care about issues like deforestation, the diminishing vegetation on the Lamongwe hillsides, or the environmental destruction by the mining companies."

John is merely trying to provoke his dad to act.

"John, who has been spreading that kind of wicked rumor?"

"What does it matter?"

The president does not answer but stays quiet, so John decides to rub it in.

"People just look at the evidence and it is there. The government is guilty as charged. The political leadership should act to prove the rumor wrong."

Jamina is becoming uncomfortable. The president does not want to go on with the topic and is delighted when he sees Jamina indicating to John that it is time to go. The few seconds of silence are long for the president.

"Dad, thanks again. I think I should take this young lady home."

The president gets up, with both hands outstretched. "Jamina, I have enjoyed meeting you. I hope I see you again soon."

"Thank you, Mr. President. This has been a wonderful evening, and please don't forget to thank the cook for me."

As they drive home, John says, "I can see that Dad likes you; in fact, I assure you, he was very impressed."

"Well, he is a very kind man. But you gave him a hard time."

"I agree, but I don't want to accept that after all my complaints about leadership in Nigasilia, my dad, my great dad, may not be the leader I'm waiting for. I am not able to accept that."

"Then why don't you try to become the leader yourself, if you think you have all the answers."

"Well, of course, I don't have all the answers. But more to the general point, I can see that I will have to make compromises with a lot of people for whom I have no respect. I may also have to accept a lot of policy compromises I don't want to make."

"No, you can tell people what you stand for and then let them decide if they want you on your own terms."

John nods repeatedly, as if in a trance. "You are right, you are right."

When they arrive at Jamina's home, John says, "Darling, you are my bedrock already. Sleep well. I love you."

They kiss, and then Jamina says, "I love you, too, dear."

On Friday, John goes to deliver the dinner speech at the annual Nigasilian Labor Union Congress, which is a two-day event. He has not attended any of the two-day sessions but he has been briefed by the secretary general. After an excellent dinner, John is introduced and he takes the podium. The dress is either black tie or traditional costume. John is in black tie. The speech, by tradition, is to be kept short.

"Dear ladies and gentlemen, thank you for a delicious dinner and excellent conversation. I am honored to have been invited to give this speech. I have already been told that your Annual Labor Congress events have gone extremely well so far. So, at this juncture, towards the very end, I have to make sure that the good news continues. But, of course, you have invited me to help you appreciate the challenges that you face in these difficult times and suggest ways that you can meet those challenges. That means that some of what I say will imply hard work for you. But that is nothing new. The labor movement, worldwide and historically, has always been about facing challenges and finding ways to overcome them. So, in the midst of all this lovely food and wine, I am forced to bring you down to earth, to the Nigasilian reality, but hopefully in a positive way.

"I begin with the obvious. The labor movement in Nigasilia has left out the majority of the labor force. Of course, it is clear why. The labor movement here started, in colonial days, as a movement of people who worked in large foreign enterprises, which invariably meant the mining companies and the large retail and trading establishments. The only exception is the motor drivers' union. But even there, I gather that that union operates virtually independently of the core labor union movement that organizes this congress. I believe that part of the problem is because the labor union congress still thinks of itself as addressing issues related to negotiating wages, salaries, pensions, and working conditions with big companies. The motor drivers' union is, of course, concerned with negotiating with the government as the government tries to control taxi fares and transport fees for private wagons and buses, as well as petrol prices, which are still officially controlled. All of this is not bad. But this is a developing, and may I say poor, country. The labor union movement should broaden its objectives and think about the welfare of all working people, a loose term for all workers, excluding the top executives and managers.

"So, the first message I would like to deliver is that the labor movement in Nigasilia should also become the voice of those workers in the informal sectors of this country. This means the small farmers, the petty traders, money changers, domestic servants, market women, small shopkeepers, tailors, potters, porters, self-employed artisans and craftsmen, food preparers, cooks, caterers, hair dressers, barbers, cobblers, small-scale repairmen, and so on. I have observed that all of these groups have associations, or what we economists call 'clusters,' where they discuss their problems and their disputes and try to come up with solutions and joint action. I want to encourage the labor union movement to invite the leaders of these associations and clusters together and begin the process of incorporating them into the movement.

"What kind of issues will this process find itself having to address? Let me give a few here. First and foremost, labor's biggest problems today are illiteracy and lack of basic general education among the mass of Nigasilians. You need to work with the authorities to find a solution. Adult education programs will, no doubt, be key here.

"Second, the country is in dire need of a sound technical and vocational education and training program. The labor movement needs to put concerted pressure on government to do something to make this happen soon. A thorough analysis is needed and a comprehensive program put in place. There are many countries around the world, particularly in East Asia and Europe that can help us.

"Third, the attitudes of our working people have got to change. In modern societies, people cannot systematically absent themselves to attend lengthy weddings, funerals, and all sorts of celebrations during working hours. If you want to be in the modern world, then you must find a way to adapt to your culture. Also, although we do not want to encourage the exploitation of our people, those in charge of labor policies must be cognizant of what others are doing. Hence the degree of freedom and flexibility that the top management of companies will have with respect to hiring and firing, overtime pay, minimum wage, leave, treatment of unions, and the hiring of foreigners at all levels of a company must be similar to what the leading countries of the world are doing. Our labor union movement should be willing to adapt.

"Finally, the labor union movement must instill into our workers a determination to aim for high quality in their work and to take pride in that search. I have, for example, been amazed at the low quality of what we call 'finishing' in many types of work, especially artistic and artisanal work. The labor union movement should find a way to instill pride in our working people, so that the aim for high quality in workmanship becomes an obsession rather than a pain. I have seen such pride in many developing countries, particularly in East Asia, and that is why they are leaving us far behind."

On Saturday, John and Jamina decide first to go to a chimpanzee sanctuary. Once they arrive, Jamina says, "You know, a few years ago, Nigasilians used to visit this sanctuary to see the albino chimp. But it is dead now. The sanctuary is making forward progress every year, bringing in orphaned and captured chimps. But God alone knows how many Nigasilians now come. The elites are the worst. They hardly show up."

"I bet you that even for something like this, we depend on foreign aid."

"Yes, we do—both for money and personnel."

"Is the Conservation Society promoting a zoo in this country? Or are you satisfied with national parks and sanctuaries?"

"We focus on national parks and sanctuaries. But I think a zoo is a lovely idea, especially in Lamongwe. The school children will appreciate it and it will give families one more thing to do. There are not many activities here for parents to enjoy with their children. We have gone backwards in this country. We have no real zoo, no amusement parks, no presentable movie houses, and no concert halls or theaters. That's why the elite prefer to take their children abroad when they want to give them a treat and expose them to modern living. Even a young person like me can see that the past twenty years have been nothing but backward movement. It really hits you when you go abroad and see how deprived our people are. You are the economist, John. Can it all be explained by poverty?"

"A lot of the deterioration in our lifestyle cannot be explained by declining incomes. It's almost like we are going through a dark age. Sure, the declining income aggravates the situation, but it is more than that. We need something to reinvigorate us, to revive our creativity and our keenness to copy the best in others up to the limit of our economic capability. There is no doubt that the cultural and political leaders are partly to blame for this predicament."

Jamina and John leave the sanctuary and drive to visit some hillside villages not too far away. "There you go," says John, as he recognizes the gardens and the terrain. Even he can remember these. The gardens of rice and vegetables are beautiful to see. The houses are less so; without exception, they are in a state of disrepair. Pointing at the cluster of houses, John says, "*That* can be explained by declining incomes."

"What are you talking about?" Jamina asks.

"The houses; look how decrepit most of them are. This is a beautiful area. Why don't the people with money come and buy it all, renovate and refurbish these ones, if possible, and knock them down and build new ones when the old ones cannot be saved?"

"Where will the current owners go and what will they do for a living? What will happen to the agricultural activity here?"

This is not the same neighborhood that Jamina was complaining about as harmful to the riparian zone. This is a very different and historic neighborhood. But many of the descendants of those who built it in the nineteenth and early twentieth centuries now reside abroad, their parents and grandparents having gone as students to study and become doctors and engineers. It is not clear why so many of the original expatriates did not return. Now their descendants don't really know Nigasilia and so do not come to their ancestral homes to rebuild neighborhoods like this one. The descendants of those same families who were left behind have fallen on hard times and are in no position to rebuild the affected neighborhoods.

John, after some reflection, remarks, "Yes, there are issues indeed. As the economists will say in their boring language, 'What you are observing is the equilibrium solution to Jamina's dilemma—beautiful agricultural farms and decrepit buildings in these beautiful hills.' So, there it is, nothing more to be said."

They drive farther out into the country towards a village famous for its baskets. The baskets come from several villages around but the weavers traditionally send all their baskets to be sold in this particular village, close to the main highway.

John is relaxed as he gazes at the winding route, hilly on one side and downhill toward a river or valley on the other. The hilly side is always on the right of them as they drive away from Lamongwe. The vegetation is luscious and green. Where the green is sparse, there are exposed granite rocks, some of which have been partly broken up by daring construction types for use in architectural or engineering enterprises. Nearer to the road are adornments of large and tall cotton trees, some of them many centuries old, with wide spans of branches that street traders exploit for the shade they provide. Otherwise, those folks must satisfy themselves under the mango trees that line the route, although long stretches of emptiness in between leave the passersby at the mercy of the sun's rays. On the left side of the route, huge areas of mangrove swampland are used for farming. But much of it is allowed to be covered by the mangrove trees that grow naturally in the swamps. People cut down the trees and use them as firewood, mainly for regular cooking or baking. Those trees are truly beloved by the natives, for they burn slowly and emit immense heat with their flames.

When they reach the village, John sees that the main road is not lined with baskets and traders. The people gaze at them but no one says anything until a young man walks up and says, "Hello, sir. Hello, madam. Are you from Lamongwe?"

"Yes," answers John. "Why?"

"The way you are looking around."

"You live here?"

"Yes, sir."

"What do you do?"

"I help my father in the farm."

"Do you go to school?"

"No, sir, I don't go to school anymore. I used to go but I left after primary school, because my father had no money to pay for me to go."

"I see. So, where are all the baskets?"

"You did not see them on the road, sir?"

"Are those all?"

"Well, they sold some of them today already, but not too many."

"Is there someone in your village who makes the baskets?"

"Yes, sir, let me bring him to you."

The young man soon returns with an older gentleman and introduces him to John.

"Old man, tell me, the people don't have more baskets to sell?"

"Oh, some people now send their baskets to Lamongwe by transport. Traders also come here and buy them. But sir, we don't make many baskets like before. People don't buy like before."

"Do you know why?"

"I think now they like to use plastic bags, onion bags, and rice bags. Also, people use bags that come from abroad. They are cheap. The people say our baskets are too dear and are not so easy to carry. So they use our baskets for special ceremonies."

John tips both men and goes back towards the main road. They look at the baskets and Jamina buys one after beating down the price a little from the original offer.

Then they set off on their return trip to Lamongwe.

On Easter day after service, John takes Jamina to his house. It has never been convenient before to bring her but Jamina is anxious to see the place. John shows her the house and she gets to meet his cook, houseboy, and daytime security guard. At night, two security guards will come on duty. John's household staff members have all heard about her and are delighted to meet her.

"You are the houseboy?" Jamina asks.

"Yes, madam."

"So what do you do when the master is not there?"

The boy giggles. "Sometimes I work in the garden, sometimes I clean the yard, sometimes I wash clothes for the master."

"But your plants don't look good."

"No? I try."

"I think you should hedge them a little, you know what I mean?"

"Yes, madam."

"And you, Security Guard, you are not wearing your uniform. Where is it?"

"Oh, madam, when I was coming this morning I fell in dirty water. These clothes I am wearing I keep here for emergency."

"Well, tell your office to give you an extra uniform for emergencies."

"Oh, I have another, but I left it at home."

"Well, tell your company to give you one more, you hear? Two uniforms are not enough."

"Yes, madam."

"Okay, you two be good now."

They both simply grin with their teeth and say nothing.

"Are you two happy here?"

"Yes, madam, very happy. Doctor is very kind."

Jamina goes in to meet the cook next. "You are Sabrina, eh?"

Sabrina, with a smile, says, "Yes."

"Your master is very proud of you. Where did you work before?"

"Oh, you know, I started to work in some Lebanese restaurant. Then I went to work for Bokubo Hotel for many years. I was deputy chef before I left. I was too tired to deal with all the people I worked with. Too much headache. Those waiters especially were a problem. Now I do my own catering. Someone in the president's office who remembered me from Bokubo told me of this job and said the man was looking for someone with experience. So I decided to come. I still run the catering business. I have good help with the catering."

"So, are you happy? Do you want something changed?"

"Well, Doctor is kind, but it is not easy. Many times I prepare something delicious for him but he does not feel like eating it because he ate somewhere else at lunchtime and is not hungry. I want him to be telling me his plans. Look, I can make a good light meal for the evening when he is going to have a heavy meal during the day. You see, lady, the freezer is not always good and I don't like to keep food in there for more than two or three days. I want Doctor to eat freshly cooked meals anyway."

"Is that all?"

"Oh, I would also like to have some cookbooks so that I can prepare more Chinese, French, and Italian dishes. Now, I call up the cook at the President's Hut to get ideas from him. I know him, for long time now. He is a kind man but I don't like to bother him so much."

"Okay, Sabrina, I will try to get you some cookbooks. I will also tell Doctor to tell you his plans. But he will not know every day. Sometimes people just ask him to go to lunch so they can talk business."

"Thank you. I understand."

Jamina decides to have lunch here with John, as if to sample the woman's cooking and to encourage her to continue her good work.

On Easter Monday, John and Jamina drive out to Kutianbo to join the picnic organized by Jamina's church. Many participants come on two buses hired by the church. But some people have their own vehicles. That way they can leave when they want to and perhaps sightsee in the neighborhood. All those who drive themselves are asked to make a small contribution to the church. Everyone brings their own food and drinks. Stephen and Betty Mongo from the Lamongwe Golf Club are there, as are Vivienne and Santie. None of those four belong to the church but they have come for Jamina's sake. They have coordinated their efforts and have organized a potluck. John brings wine, water, and beer; Jamina brings the food. They also bring folding chairs to sit on as well as beach towels.

The chief organizers arrived early to make sure their party has an excellent spot and adequate space on the beach. Everything works out smoothly. After greetings and compliments around, the mini-group of six checks its supplies and makes sure that each one has a drink and some food to start. Santie turns to John and asks, "John, when was the last time you did this sort of thing?"

"Lord, I can't even remember. Since I was a boy, I guess. I can't even remember the last Easter I spent in Nigasilia."

"But this is nice, right? They don't have beaches like this in America."

"This pristine, they don't. There is too much development and overuse of the beaches in America."

Kutianbo Beach, despite its golden sand and lovely view, has no toilet facilities. If you must go, then you either go into the bushes not too far away, in the water, or to someone's house close to the beach. John looks around and adds, "I wonder what it would take for the headman to organize the village to put a toilet here. They can charge a small fee for use."

Santie laughs. "That demands too much organization for these people. You have to collect money for the construction. Then you have to make sure the toilet is properly policed, so that nonpaying people, especially the local villagers, do not slide in here and misuse the facilities. You have to keep the facilities clean. And then you have to decide what to do with the money collected, such as maintenance. Most of these village headmen cannot organize their people to do anything approaching that level of complexity. People will not want to contribute to the original investment because they cannot see the direct benefit. You will have to call on the central government to do it. Not even the district councils containing these sorts of villages are organized enough to decide on priorities. Outside of obvious things, the central government tends to decide their priorities and then give them targeted funds. All these villages do is list projects they would like financed. We need time, but we will get there. There is no need to rush."

John does not agree with that kind of attitude. "Well, I guess Kutianbo Beach will just have to wait for normal development, right? Once there are hotels, bars, playgrounds, and restaurants here, there will be bathrooms for sure. Maybe that's how it should be. What a place!"

Santie plays the game but is more patronizing. "Yes, why build a fancy road when there is such light traffic? I, for one, love this state of underdevelopment. It stays very pretty. This is the only time of year when you get such a crowd here."

Santie is very proud of Nigasilia, having returned after two years of studying in the US. John has met other Nigasilians like this who get very defensive when those who have stayed abroad are critical of certain standards in Nigasilia.

John turns around as if to butt in on the conversation of the others, but decides to just listen. Stephen Mongo is in the middle of narrating a recent experience he'd had on one of the beaches frequented by Western tourists.

"So I took a second look to see if this was the right person. And it was. Here she was with a very short skirt and a shirt with a very low neck. Then she kept on bending over, as if she was looking for something in the sand. And several of these foreign men were close by, just staring at her. So I said to her, 'You, girl, go home. What are you doing here?' And you know what she said to me? 'Why? Do I make you feel good? Do you want some?' That girl cannot be more than seventeen. As I said, I know her mother, a very quiet woman struggling to send her children to school, with nobody to help her."

Betty Mongo is in the teasing mood. "You should have said yes to find out what she would say."

Stephen plays the game, too. "I did say yes, but I won't tell you what happened next."

Vivienne laughs loudly. "Sure you did."

Stephen suddenly puts on a straight face. "I just told her I was going to tell her mother and then walked away. And I did go to her mother the following day."

Vivienne has seen these cases before. "Maybe you did not tell her mother something she, the mother, did not know. Many of these mothers are under stress and can't support their families, especially when there is not a responsible man around to help. If their children bring home money, they don't ask how the children got it. It does not matter whether they stole, begged, or did something worse."

John turns to Jamina and asks quietly, "What brought that discussion?"

"They heard you and Santie talking about the lack of toilets and so Betty said one of the reasons she loves this beach is that foreigners don't frequent here because of the lack of facilities, and so one does not see prostitutes hanging around."

John takes a couple of steps in Betty's direction. "Betty, you were telling me about your diasporan friend and the problems she is having buying land; I should start looking around for land, too, in case I get serious about staying here."

"Let me tell you, John, that particular woman can be really funny. Since she came for Easter she has been going around with an umbrella to shield herself from the sun. So I said to her, 'You rub on all this sunscreen stuff. Why do you need an umbrella?' So she says to me, 'You people, your sun is wicked here. Maybe it's this global warming thing.'"

Everyone except Jamina finds this funny.

"Don't laugh. She may be right," Jamina insists.

Betty nods as if to agree and continues with her story. "Anyway, she bought this piece of land. When she hired someone to start putting up pillars to fence the property, a gang of boys came and uprooted them. They said the true owner sent them to do that. That true owner happens to be someone different from the person who sold the land to my friend. That, of course, is the boys' story, which is their master's story. To cut a long story short, the case ends up in court. This woman has her documents, including the survey of the land. The other party also has produced a legal document, including a survey. You would think the authorities would first of all find out if the surveys are of the same land. The court has even gone to the land in dispute. Now, all the Ministry of Lands and Country Planning has to do is check the two documents and their records and give the court its findings. But the ministry will not move. They are waiting to be bribed. But then the court also does not press for movement. Everyone keeps telling her she should go give some handshake to the judge as well. This thing has been going on for a year now. The woman says she is not going to bribe anyone, because if you bribe once, they can just keep dragging on the case to get more. But now she does not know what to do."

John becomes angry. "I think my dad should ask the minister to look into the case. But there is the question of principle. It should not require connections and bribery to have such matters resolved by our government and the courts. This is simply outrageous."

John suddenly remembers Mahdu Kontana telling him when John was here for his mother's funeral that the minister of lands and country planning is very corrupt. He is determined now to find out more about what goes on in that ministry.

Santie, in his usual lackadaisical manner, laughs it off. "Welcome to Nigasilia."

John and Jamina glance at each other and shake their heads in disgust.

"If we do not find a way to make our legal system more efficient, we will not be able to make progress in our economic development," John says. "So it's high on my list."

All six decide to take a walk on the beach and mingle with others in the picnic party. Jamina, Vivienne, and Betty approach a group of women, all of whom they know well. John and Santie decide to go watch a group of young men playing soccer some distance away. And Stephen finds a friend of his who beckons to him to come have a chat.

After chatting with the group of women, Betty, Vivienne, and Jamina decide to continue strolling on the beach in the opposite direction from where John and Santie are watching the soccer players. Betty turns to Jamina.

"Jamina, I really believe you two are made for each other. John strikes me as a very considerate person who does not simply think of himself. I am also fascinated by how he is always thinking about ways Nigasilia can improve. Maybe he will get the president to do something."

"Well, thank you, Betty. I love the man, too. But I am worried that he may be too impatient with us. I'm sure you are surprised to hear me say that, because I am always the one complaining about how rotten things are in Nigasilia. Well, John is far worse than I am. He wants to shake up the whole system. He has been here for less than four months and he is already anxious to see changes."

"Good for him," says Vivienne. "It's about time we had someone like that around here. You two will be not only great partners but a great team to help energize people to get up and act."

"Yes, but you and I know that it will take a long time to change things around here in a significant way."

"And you think John does not know that?" Betty says. "He knows. I'm sure he knows. But if he does not push and push hard, the process will not begin."

They continue their stroll, enjoying the sound of the waves as the water approaches the beach.

As for John and Santie, after watching the soccer players with some delight, they head back to the main gathering. As they do so, they are approached by a group of young men.

"Dr. Bijunga," starts one of the gentlemen, "we are members of Jamina's church and have heard that you and she are now boyfriend and girlfriend. We are very pleased. But we wanted to ask you how you see things here in Nigasilia. You think things will improve?"

"I don't know if they will, but they could, if we all work hard and cooperate with each other."

"You know, you are not the first to say this. Many people in this country feel the same way. But then, why don't we cooperate?"

A second gentleman offers his perspective. "I don't think it is that simple. We have too much corruption and also the big countries are doing a lot of things that harm us. Our commodity prices are being held down and these big countries take our minerals and do not compensate us adequately."

A third gentleman cannot resist joining in. "But why are we so weak? The minerals are our own; we don't have to sell if the prices are not what we want."

The second gentleman is provoked enough to ask, "Then what about our commodity prices? Who controls them?"

John does not really want to get into a deep discussion here, but he feels it is his obligation to say something, at least as a sign of respect.

"Markets determine the prices, for the most part. It is not perfect, but it is the market. You know, you gentlemen raise a lot of interesting issues, but we have no time to discuss them now. We should enjoy our picnic. Ask Jamina to arrange a meeting in my office sometime; I would like to discuss these issues with you. But I leave you with one thought. Nigasilia has very little influence in world markets. When we negotiate mineral arrangements, we are often dealing with companies that have excellent staff, data, and resources. Many other small countries in other parts of the world have done well under similar circumstances. What we Nigasilians should do is learn from the experiences of those countries. We should find out how they operate, what they are doing right, what they have done wrong, and what they have learnt from their mistakes. The plain truth is that everyone out there who deals with us is pursuing their own self-interests. We have to find a way to deal with them while making sure they do not exploit us."

Together, they walk back to the picnic area. Soon people begin to collect their things. Those who came with the buses have to be alert so they do not get left behind.

Chapter 7

When John was back in the office after Easter, he called Mahdu to see if there was someone at the Ministry of Lands and Country Planning who would be willing to reveal the corruption going on at the ministry. Mahdu jumped at the opportunity and put John in contact with a deputy director, who agreed to meet John in his office that Friday.

Just before the man is due in his office, John pulls out the logbook in which he is making notes on corrupt practices and places it on his desk.

"Welcome, Mr. Kokola, welcome. Thanks for coming. Your first name is Winston, right?"

"Yes, Doctor."

"Well, I think Minister Kontana has told you already that we are worried about the things we hear are going on in your ministry. Who would you say are the big culprits?"

"The minister, Mansa Sanara, the deputy minister, and the director."

"Oh, so the big men. What kind of things do you know firsthand?"

"Many things, Dr. Bijunga. For example, if you want to register or sell a big piece of land, say like eight to ten town lots, for instance, the minister says he has to sign. Before he does you have to see him. When you do he will insist that you give up some of the land, maybe two town lots. If you refuse, he won't sign."

John writes in his logbook "Extortion and blackmail." He then asks, "Is he the first minister to behave like that?"

"Yes and no. In such a situation, the previous ministers I worked with found a way to get money from the landowner or buyer. But this is the first one I know who not only wants money but land also."

"What does he do with the land?"

"He sells it or gives it away. So far he has given land to two of his girlfriends."

"Do the other two people do the same?"

"No, sir, they usually simply want money to approve or sign documents, or to pass on the relevant documents for the minister's signature."

"But don't all you senior people do the same?"

Winston smiles. "Yes and no. We don't usually ask. The lawyers of the buyer or the seller will give us something to speed up the process. It is part of their performance to move things. Their clients know that. Everyone knows that."

"So you all accept bribes but only the biggest people extort."

Winston shrugs. "You could say that, Doctor. Everyone knows this. The salaries are low and we must live."

"Did you know that the president has said he is going to enforce a zero-tolerance policy?"

"Yes, but petty corruption, no one can stop it in Nigasilia."

The president has called a meeting with the VP; the minister of education, Budayo Kontine; the minister of finance and development, Tubo Bangar; and John. John has written a paper to argue that if the country is going to accelerate its development and reduce poverty quickly it must take a comprehensive look at education and training.

The president starts the discussion. "Gentlemen, as you can see, the chief economist is arguing that the education commission report was unsatisfactory, focusing only on trying to explain in broad terms why the school certificate results have been dropping. Even that problem they did not tackle well, according to John, but we will not get into that here. John is arguing that we should focus especially on trying to improve our literacy level and rates, our math and science achievements at all levels, and our vocational and technical education and training."

John was critical of the commission's report because it recommended that kids spend an extra year in secondary school, thereby increasing the total years of schooling before tertiary education. The report did not make any specific suggestions with regard to teacher training, pay and incentives; facilities in the schools; or the role of the parents' support at home. Thus the report made no suggestions as to how to improve the situation.

Budayo Kontine responds first. "Mr. President, let me say, first of all, that we agree that the commission's report was not as exhaustive as it could have been. But the commission was looking at short-term responses only. The other problems, the commission figured, are of a long-term nature and are being addressed by the ministry. And that is true. In fact, we are addressing those issues right now. But they will take a long time to fix."

The VP interrupts. "Okay, so what about the issues that John is bringing up on math, science, and TVET?"

Budayo folds his hands and looks at each of the others in turn. "Well, when it comes to TVET, we have also begun serious work. I'm surprised that John's paper did not acknowledge that. We are currently doing a thorough review of the national TVET policy. We are going to address the overall governance issues, facilities, and the question of finance, especially for the trainees—private as well as public finance."

The president asks, "What is your time frame?"

"Six months."

"That is too long. Just for setting out the work program? Three months are enough."

"Okay, Mr. President."

"Yes, you are right, Budayo," John says, "I should have mentioned that you are addressing the various areas. My paper, as you can see, tries to offer suggestions in each of these areas. And I am also deeply concerned with implementation—the processes, rules, and the organization to ensure implementation."

"Yes, and we will take your suggestions into consideration."

"So what about our math and science problems?" the president asks.

The minister of education leans back and folds his hands. "I agree with most of what John is suggesting, though his ideas are not new. But I am not so sure about insisting that all students attain a minimum standard in mathematics before they are allowed to pass from one grade to another."

"Budayo, I am trying to counter the fear of math with the fear of failing. Too many of our children come to school with the attitude that they cannot learn math. They have to be born with a certain gift for math, many of them think. Otherwise, they believe, they cannot learn. My observation is that many of them are encouraged in that attitude by their parents and sometimes by the teachers as well. So we need to change the attitudes of the parents, the students, and the teachers."

The president asks, "Finance and Development, what do you think?"

"I like the suggestion," Tubo responds. "It seems like an appropriate incentive."

The president turns to the VP and gives a big smile. "So, Mr. VP, what do you think?"

"I think it is a good suggestion. We should try it. But we should be realistic in setting the minimum standard."

"Yes," the president says, "and we should also avoid the problem of people thinking that the minimum is good enough. We don't want the minimum target to become the maximum for even the best kids."

"Okay," Budayo replies, "we will work with our university lecturers and school teachers of math to implement this one."

In the middle of the meeting, John remembers he was planning on calling his cousin Borbor. He calls as soon as he gets to his office. He inquires if there is any news from Alfred, to which Borbor says no. In any event, John is interested in finding out about procurement and subcontracting procedures in various government and public sector departments. At the same time, a visit to the education department would help him find out a little more about Alfred, who has disappeared with no further contact with his family back in Nigasilia. Alfred never married but he has a son with a young lady who has since married and lives with her husband in the UK. The son is also in the UK, but neither Borbor nor the Bijungas have seen Alfred's son for many years. John is sure he would not even recognize him now if he bumped into him.

Borbor has arranged for him and John to talk to the chief procurement officer at the Ministry of Education. They agree to meet in John's office, after working hours, on Monday. The procurement officer is a bit nervous about the meeting.

"John, please meet Shekou," Borbor says as he presents the guest.

"Shekou, you are not in charge of subcontracting, only procurement, no?"

"Yes, Dr. Bijunga. I used to be in charge of subcontracting, especially for big construction projects. But Minister Kontine transferred me to help develop the procurements, since I have been through all the relevant training and have many years of experience doing both procurement and subcontracting."

"When did he transfer you?"

"Soon after he came to the ministry. He brought someone from outside the civil service to replace me. I found out later that the person was his close relative."

John is suddenly confused. Why did Borbor bring Shekou here? What is he supposed to ask next? What does all this have to do with Alfred? John turns to Borbor.

Borbor looks at Shekou. "Shekou, tell Dr. Bijunga how Alfred got his contract."

Shekou explains that some of the contractors were giving the minister huge fees to secure contracts for new schools, playgrounds, and repairs, much of it financed by foreign aid money. Alfred had applied several times but had not been given any contract. Then an old friend of Alfred's, who works for the ministry and knows two or three contractors who had given the minister money as bribes for contracts without securing the contracts, got all the details and gave Alfred the information. Alfred found a way to see the minister in his office and threatened to tell his uncle, the president, if he did not receive a contract. Unfortunately for the minister, that same friend held a senior position in the accounts section of the ministry and gave Alfred much information of other malfeasance.

"What other information did she have?" John asked.

Shekou replied, "Well, for example, the minister would organize ordinary social private parties in his house, include some foreign diplomat or diplomats, and then bill the whole thing as official, when it was just a social gathering among friends. What I am saying here is that the parties would not be in honor of the diplomat or diplomats. Because if they are, yes, the minister is permitted to treat the parties as official business. Even worse, he would go abroad on the pretense of attending a conference on education and training. He would then take one of his assistant secretaries who would attend the meetings and draft the report. He would simply show up for the opening and closing sessions and then go about his private business. Then he would stay in expensive hotels, and claim huge entertainment allowances with receipts that were in fact for the entertainment of friends and relatives. These receipts and claims were all bunched with similar documents and no one in the office dared to isolate them and expose the minister."

John takes his logbook and writes: "Embezzlement of public funds" and "Accepting bribes."

"So how did Alfred use this information?"

"He simply gave a few examples to the minister to prove that he knows."

"So how do you get on with the minister yourself?"

"Not very well, but I am due for retirement in six months, so I am not worried."

"So you yourself have never in your career taken bribes?"

"I have taken gifts to help people, including helping them complete bids and procurement requests, but not when I am in charge of the decision. Sir, I am not perfect, but I am sensible and cautious."

John does not know what to make of all this yet. Right now, he is embarrassed that his cousin Alfred twisted arms to get a contract.

Sanjo Manray, the minister of Tourism and Cultural Affairs, has been working on a paper on tourism promotion and development in cooperation with John. The paper is almost complete and Sanjo and John go for a quick bite, in celebration, to a cafeteria in the middle of town. They both order kebbe, fried chicken legs, and Coke.

As they sit, Sanjo, in great excitement, pulls out his notes that he has brought with him. "So, John, you have been a real asset to us on this paper. Thanks for your technical help. As we agreed, we have four big main sections. Section one will be on the current institutional and organizational arrangements for tourism development and promotion in Nigasilia. Section two will discuss the challenges facing Nigasilia in tourism development—challenges such as human capital; infrastructure; institutions, public policy and regulations; and public awareness of the nature of tourism potential in Nigasilia and the importance to the economy. Section three will be a discussion of ways to promote cooperation and joint action, involving the public and private sectors, for tourism development and promotion. Section four will elaborate on other actions by both the public and private sectors to further progress toward realizing Nigasilia's potential in tourism."

"Sanjo, with regards to cooperation and joint action involving the public and private sectors, do you think you will be able to work with Sitenne?"

Kweko Sitenne is the minister of local government. Sitenne is bound to be involved directly or indirectly with government projects in tourism promotion and development in the bulk of the tourist sites in the interior of the country, especially the many islands and forest reserves.

"Well, I have to prepare for that fight," Sanjo says. "But if I have a way to take him out soon, I will. The man is so corrupt."

"So let's take him out, if he will be a nuisance to you. There must be someone in his ministry who can give us information."

"Just talk to the local government people, the chiefs, the headmen, and the business people in those up-country areas. When this man visits, if they don't bring out some real stocks, he does not support their projects."

"I'll remember to log that one when I get to my office," John says. "But to deal with him we have to find people who are willing to talk."

"Oh, people will talk, once they know he's under siege and cannot seek revenge."

Summer soon rolls around and John's sons are about to come visit. By telephone and e-mail, John and his boys have been in constant communication. But the boys have not seen their father for some five months. They are as anxious to see him as he is to see them. John worries about how he will keep them busy and happy. Coming to visit for four to six weeks is one thing. But now they will be coming for almost three months. In addition to that, he has to work. How will he balance work and play? The boys are, of course, older than before, which might be a plus but also a minus. They could be more creative, be left to explore the place on their own, and make friends more readily. But they could also become more easily bored, or find that the boys and girls their ages are far less aware of aspects of modern living that they take for granted.

John is now convinced that it would be a terrible idea to confine the boys only to children of the elites. He does not want to raise sons who look down on other people. They are ready for more exposure to the reality of Nigasilia. He wants them to see the poverty, the misery, and the plights of the ordinary person in Nigasilia; it might stir their imaginations and inspire them to help ameliorate poverty. They should learn that the human condition varies immensely from place to place. He would like his boys to ask why some people are so poor, and why they seem incapable of improving their lives. The boys go to church regularly and they pray for the poor. John always tells them that prayer is not enough. Human beings have to act in purposeful and decisive ways to make a difference and effect change.

But in the US, neither John nor his sons mix with the poor. John simply makes tax-deductible contributions. He does not even follow up on whether those programs successfully alleviate poverty. Here, in Nigasilia, the poor are highly visible. The boys cannot simply go to neighborhoods where the poor are hardly seen. In Nigasilia, the poor are everywhere, right in your face. You do not have the luxury of complete ignorance.

The children arrive in early June. They are brought home with John's private vehicle and arrive almost three hours later, not too long after John himself gets home. He opens the door himself and all three embrace. For a while, nothing is said. Then John says, "Look at you two."

"Hi, Daddy," the boys say.

"Hi, fellows. You look well, very well. You are even taller. Great to see you. How were your flights? I assume you had no problems at the airport?"

"You know, Dad," William says, "they took us to the VIP lounge. Everyone was looking at us. There were no other kids there."

The driver and one of the servants bring in the luggage and John specifies where to drop them.

"Did you like the lounge?"

"Yes," says William. "They gave us some ginger ale to drink while we waited for them to bring our luggage."

"Let me show you to your room and you can take a shower and change," John suggests. "I'll show you where the fridge is now so you can have something to drink. We will be having dinner soon. I'll show you around afterwards."

Soon after they ready themselves, John introduces the boys to Sabrina, the cook. Then, as they sit down for a simple dinner of rice with chicken in peanut oil stew, with lettuce-and-tomato salad on the side, Donald asks, "Daddy, are you happy? Do the people like and appreciate what you are doing?"

"Yes, I'm happy," John says, with an expressionless look on his face. "But Nigasilia is a difficult place for someone like me. I am here to help the people make good decisions so the country can move forward and become developed like the US. That means I have to tell them to work hard, cooperate amongst themselves, not steal or waste money, and spend enough on education and training. I also have to make sure they encourage business people both in Nigasilia and abroad to invest their money here."

"But what is hard about that? Why do they need you to come tell them? Why don't they just do it all?"

John still does not know how to explain to his boys, in language they can understand, that as far as the *doing* is concerned, the devil is in the details.

"Well, Donald, the government says they do not have enough money to spend on education. They also say the business people just want to make quick profits here and take their money out and invest somewhere else."

William asks, "Does Grandpa like what you are telling them to do?"

"Yes, he does."

"Good. Is he all right?"

"Yes, Grandpa is all right. You and Donald will be coming to the office with me in the morning to see him. He cannot wait to see you two."

"You know, Daddy," Donald says, "our teachers have been telling us about poverty in Africa and we have told them that you have come to Nigasilia to help the people. My social studies teacher told me a few days ago that he was in the Peace Corps many years ago. Do you know about the Peace Corps?"

"Yes, I know. These are US citizens sent by the US government to help, especially as teachers, in the small towns of Africa. You will have a lot of opportunities to see the poverty here. But you already saw a lot of it in the past. I hope you told your teachers what you have seen."

"Yes, but you told us that poverty is worse now. You said that the worst areas were too dangerous for us to see."

"Yes, I did." John pauses. "Anyway, I will see what I can do to give you a better picture. But Nigasilia has many beautiful things that you should tell your teachers about, too. It is not all bad and gloomy."

William wants to talk about Jamina. "Daddy, are we going to meet Ms. Tamba?"

"Yes, of course, she can't wait to meet you. She will come to the office tomorrow. You will like her."

John had told his sons about this beautiful school teacher, Jamina Tamba, who has been very kind to him. He did not say she was his girlfriend but the boys suspect she is.

"Did you know her before?" William asks.

"No, I had never met her until Minister Kontana introduced me to her. They are cousins."

"So have you been going out with her a lot?" William glances at Donald to make sure his brother does not think he is asking too many questions.

"Yes, but she is a very busy woman. As I have told you, she is a teacher of biology and has several other interests. When you meet her, you can ask her about what she does. She is a very sweet person."

Donald decides to interrupt. "Daddy, can we go and see the house now, or do you have work to do?"

"I made sure I would have no homework tonight. I have missed you boys too much and wanted just to be with you until you decide to go to bed. But don't tire yourself out; we have the whole summer together. Apart from wanting to see how the poor really live, what else are you interested in? I shall show you a few things that tourists like to see when they come, including a beautiful island, Waititi. Ms. Tamba will come with us on that trip. She knows the area very well. Her parents live not far from there."

"What about the beaches?" Donald asks.

"Of course we will go to some beaches. I have not forgotten the mountains, either."

After the tour of the house, Donald says, "I did not expect the entertainment room would be so large."

"Yes, Donald, when they build these houses, they expect their senior officials to routinely entertain a lot of important people."

"Have you entertained anyone?"

"No, I have been too busy to think of that. But I will start doing so soon."

The boys wake up rather early the next day. John asks if that was one consequence of the discipline of boarding school, and both simply shrug their shoulders and smile. The plan for the day is for the boys to meet Jamina and visit their grandfather. Jamina had suggested that John take them to see their grandfather in the morning and that she would drop by John's office so they could all four have lunch together.

When they arrive at the president's office, Rabena is there. The boys had met her very briefly on their last visit to Nigasilia.

"Hello, Mrs. Karam," they both say cheerfully.

"Well, hello, boys. Oh, it's so lovely to see you two. We have been expecting you. And look how you have both grown. How is school?"

"Fine," both reply.

"That's good, I'm sure your father is very proud. Well, your grandpa has been expecting you. He said I should send you in immediately. Fortunately, he has no one with him now."

Rabena buzzes the president. "The boys are here."

"Bring them in, bring them in, thank you."

As John and the boys walk in, the president jumps up from his desk and embraces them. All four struggle to maintain their composure and they all know why; everyone is thinking about Grandma.

The president turns away and looks up at the ceiling, saying in his mind, *God, please give me courage.*

"You boys are looking well," he says. "The school must be taking good care of you. I hope you are still doing well at your studies."

"Yes, sir, we are doing very well," Donald replies.

"Grandpa, you look well, too," William says, and both boys approach a window to take in a view of the city. In Lamongwe, the tallest buildings are only about ten to sixteen stories high. The boys can see City Hall, the Anglican cathedral, and the Lamongwe port, where ships are either docked or waiting to dock. The boys are more interested, though, in the throngs of people perambulating the streets. They are particularly fascinated by those carrying loads on their heads.

After a few moments, the president, who has been quietly looking out the window with the boys, says, "Isn't that colorful?"

"Yes," Donald replies. "But does the noise not disturb you?"

"Oh, I don't hear it anymore. Or rather, I don't let it disturb me."

John next takes the boys to his office. He has his own private office with an area for his secretary, plus three small decent-sized offices for his staff, together with a conference room, which he shares with other small departmental units.

John currently has only two economists and two research assistants working with him, in addition to three secretaries, including his own. He introduces them to his boys as he takes them around. As the three of them enter the conference room, the boys look at each other in great surprise. "Daddy, your office is not small like you said," Donald protests.

"Yes, but when my office is fully developed, I will need more space. Most ministries have their own buildings or floors."

"Do you see Grandpa every day?" William asks.

"No, not every day, but we talk every day."

As they return to John's private office, his secretary signals to him that Jamina is here.

"Okay, boys, Ms. Tamba is waiting for us."

When they enter the room, Jamina embraces them both. "You must be Donald and you William. How was the trip to Nigasilia? I'm sure your grandpa was excited to see you."

"Hi, Ms. Tamba, nice to meet you," they each say in turn, with broad, genuine smiles.

"Well, I am happy to meet you, too. Your dad has told me so much about you. He is very proud of you both."

When they sit down to eat at Miatta Place, where John and Jamina had dined after the art exhibition, Donald asks Jamina, "Ms. Tamba, do you enjoy teaching? Are the kids here troublesome in school?"

"Oh, I enjoy teaching very much," Jamina says. "Maybe your dad has already told you, I teach biology in a secondary school for girls. They are like students everywhere, I guess. Some of them misbehave but most are respectful. They know that education is important to their future."

William joins in. "My dad says that teachers in Nigasilia don't get paid very well and that the classes are crowded."

Jamina laughs. "Yes, your dad is right. But, you know, teachers everywhere do not get paid well, even in America. But America is a rich country, so even when teachers are not paid well, they can still survive on their salaries."

Donald interjects. "But my dad says that you are lucky and your grandfather left you money, so you do not suffer like the others."

Jamina glances at John. "Yes, Donald, that's true. But I don't have a lot of money, just enough to allow me to be happy and not mind the low salaries."

They continue to eat and then Jamina says, "I know you boys love the beach and your dad will take you there many times. But when he is very busy, just call me and I shall pick you up and take you. How is the food? You boys ordered like experts. What's your favorite?"

"My favorite is the peanut sauce with fish," Donald replies.

"Only with fish?" Jamina asks.

"Oh, I like it with shrimp and chicken, also."

"What about you, William?"

"I like shrimp or lobster cooked as stew in peanut oil."

"I see. Well, those are two delicious dishes. I shall have both prepared for you sometime. Do you like curry?"

"Oh, yes," Donald answers enthusiastically, with William shaking his head in agreement.

"Okay, I shall have some curry prepared for you, too."

"So, Ms. Tamba intends to stuff you boys. You know, she has a very good cook, but she is an excellent cook as well."

Jamina wants to let the boys walk around in the busiest part of the commercial district. She knows from talking to John that this is something he has never done with the boys before. As they step out of the restaurant, four young boys, no doubt in their twenties, approach them. Two of the beggars are in wheelchairs, being pushed by the two others, even though the boys could manipulate the chairs on their own. John's boys do not know what is going on until John hands some cash to the beggars. Donald asks, "Are there many beggars in Lamongwe?"

"Yes, Donald," John replies, "too many. And you know what? It is because most of them did not pay attention in school and now do not want to work. Some of them come from areas where there is plenty of farmland available to them as part of their family land. But they all want to come to Lamongwe and live"

Donald protests. "But the boys in the wheelchair, they cannot work on the farm."

"True, but they can go to school. We have schools for the handicapped and they can even go to normal schools if they want. Here in Nigasilia, almost all handicapped people think they are helpless, especially those who come from very poor homes. Even the parents encourage them to beg."

Jamina wants John to be more sympathetic. "Donald," she says, "some of the children in this country who come from poor parents find it hard to stay in school. Their parents are not educated enough to help them in any serious way, like making sure they do their homework. The parents also do not have money to buy books for the children or to pay their school fees. You know, we do not have free secondary schools. The poor children also have a lot of domestic chores at home and so are not able to devote enough time to their studies. Moreover, they frequently lack electricity to study. This may be because the parents are trying to cut down on bills. More often, it is because the parents cannot afford generators or fuel for generators to supply electricity when there are blackouts, which occur more often than not."

"Oh, that is sad. Daddy, is what you are doing going to help?"

"Yes, Donald, it will help a little. Elementary school is free. We want to try giving them free materials, like notebooks and pens and pencils.

Then in secondary school we want to help them with textbooks. In addition, the government controls school fees in all public schools. So we try to keep the fees fairly low."

"That is good," Donald responds.

John continues. "Anyway, we want to find a way to help young men like those beggars get training so that they can become painters, electricians, plumbers—things like that."

"Okay," Donald says absent-mindedly, because he and William are staring at an area where the street traders have spread their wares all over the sidewalk. They whisper to Jamina and she and they cross the street to the other side to watch the activity. John tags along. As the four of them approach the traders, many ask in loud voices what they are looking for. Jamina simply says, "Sorry, we do not want to buy. Anything. We are just showing these two boys around. They came from America for the holidays." The traders leave them alone and go on to address other passersby.

When they arrive at their grandfather's residence later that evening, the boys want to tour the house again. So Grandpa takes them on a tour himself. They are particularly fascinated with the library. They go to both floors and look at the books to see if they can recognize any. They shrug their shoulders repeatedly as if to say, Oh, well, don't know this one.

Towards the end of the tour, William says, "Grandpa, you are living in this big house all by yourself. Why didn't you ask Daddy to come stay with you?"

"Well, William," the president replies, glancing at John, "your dad is an important man here. So he will begin to have many people over who come for dinner or simply to visit him. It is important that he has a place where these people can feel comfortable. Many would not feel comfortable visiting your dad if he were staying at the president's place."

As they all settle down to have dinner, the boys ask many questions: How many hours does Grandpa have to work every day? Does he have to read a lot of documents? Does he take vacation? Does he travel to many countries around the world? Does he enjoy being president? Does he watch soccer matches? Does he have time to watch television?

The president is quite impressed. The boys sound mature for their years. At times, they remind him of professional journalists. To the question of whether he enjoys being president, the boys are not quite satisfied with his answer of yes. They want more.

Donald says, "One of my teachers said that he does not know why anyone would want to be president. He said it is a hard job."

The president smiles. "Yes, it is a hard job, but if you do it well, you can help many people, and you can help your country to become better for all those who live in it. That is what makes me happy and what I enjoy about the job."

Then Donald asks, "Grandpa, but how are you going to make the country better for them? Today we saw four young men begging. Daddy said it was because they did not have enough education. Ms. Tamba said that it was because they have poor parents and so did not have enough opportunities. What do you think, Grandpa?"

"Well, Donald, you have the answer in your question. We will try to give them better education and training and to encourage them to go where they can find work."

"Grandpa, one of my teachers said that Africans were poor even though Africa is rich in natural resources. Then one of my friends said that Africans must be lazy or stupid. Daddy said that Grandma used to say that Africans *act* stupidly. Do you agree?"

"Did you ask your father whether he agreed with Grandma?"

"No, because Dad says that Grandma was always right."

"Well, my boy, no one is always right. Take it from your grandpa."

"So, what do you think?"

"I think the Africans have not been given a chance to show what they are capable of. The Africans are only now beginning to find themselves. Did your teachers teach you about slavery and colonialism?"

"Yes, Grandpa, a little, especially in our history class," Donald says.

"Good. So keep an open mind and you will find out, as you grow older, why Africans are so poor, despite the natural gifts. It is a very difficult subject. I expect your daddy to help teach you, if he can only stop being mad at us Africans for not acting more boldly."

John has been listening intently. He is very proud of his sons but feels like moving to a lighter subject for his father's sake.

"Grandpa, Donald has not brought any piano books with him tonight but he can play off memory the first movement of Mozart's Piano Sonata in C. Do you want him to?"

"Oh, good. Donald, if you are not feeling ready, you do not have to, you know."

"It's okay, Grandpa, I have played that piece enough. It won't be perfect, but I'll try."

They finish their dinner of yam-and-lamb curry, with vanilla ice cream for dessert, and move to the living room. Donald gives a very good rendition of the piece.

John and Jamina take the boys several times to Lumpimo Beach and Kutianbo Beach. Today, June 15, Jamina decides to take them to another of the most beautiful beaches, Bonta Beach. There are two islands that can be seen from Bonta; one of them is several miles away, and although residents live on it, Jamina does not feel comfortable crossing with the boys. The smaller of the two islands is only a couple of hundred yards away from one end of the beach, and one could hire small boats to make the crossing. Jamina looks for a safe boat and the boys feel confident enough to take it. The boat is small but with a modern outboard engine. There is no one on the island. It makes for a beautiful walk among the plants and small creatures.

"Are there snakes here?" William asks as they get off the boat.

"Well, William," Jamina replies, "I don't know of anyone who has seen any snake here. The island, as you can see, is small. The vegetation is very diverse and not too thick. You have fruit trees like cashew, mangoes, and cocoa, and flowers like bougainvillea, yellow bells, and orchids."

Donald asks, "Are there monkeys? Because even Lamongwe has monkeys up the hills."

"Yes, you are right about monkeys in Lamongwe, but we do not have any here. Incidentally, if you look down the slopes here you can see some large turtles. They grow to more than three feet long. As you can see, huge rocks border the island, just like what you find near the beach area."

After exploring the island they cross back to the main beach, where men are building boats on a rocky area. Donald and William are fascinated by them.

"So what do these men do with the boats?" Donald asks.

"Oh, they sell them. Some of them will be used as fishing boats, some as sailing boats, and some will become equipped with engines."

"Are the boats expensive?"

"You know, Donald, I know really nothing about that. But these men are very skilled and they will build any kind of boat you want out of natural materials they can find in Nigasilia. You just have to find your own sails and engines. They can make paddles for your rowing boats as long as you do not want them too sophisticated."

Although it is a Monday afternoon, quite a few people are out, including some Caucasians from Europe or America. The beach is some thirty miles away from central Nigasilia, along the Atlantic coast but away from the estuary. There are a couple of fair-sized restaurants and bars just bordering the beach, mainly to serve visitors. Jamina and the boys have a nice lunch of fish and chips at one of the restaurants and then go back on the beach to play.

William asks Jamina as they walk, "Ms. Tamba, did you know my grandma?"

"No, William, but she was very popular in Nigasilia. She even came to my school once on Prize-Giving Day. That's when we give prizes to the kids who have done well in school. She not only awarded the prizes but gave a speech. The children loved her."

"What did she talk about?" Donald asks.

"She addressed the girls directly. She said they should continue to improve in their educational achievements. She said that in Nigasilia, girls and women have equal opportunities with boys and men, so the girls can achieve anything they want. They just have to work hard."

"Did the girls like her speech?" Donald asks.

"Yes, especially the senior girls. You know, we women teachers have been telling our students the same thing. So it was good for them to hear the president's wife say those things, too."

"Oh, that must have been nice," Donald says.

William asks, "Did the girls clap a lot for her?"

"Yes, they just clapped and clapped."

It is Friday, June 22. Among other things, John has been working over the last couple of weeks with the Ministry of Trade and Industry on the review of the country's export promotion plan, which has been in place for two years now. They are preparing a workshop, National Export Strategy: Progress in Implementation, and will soon send out the invitations to about a hundred stakeholders from the government, business, and the university. John drops by Mahdu's office for a brief meeting.

"So, John, I gather from my cousin that the kids are really having fun. It looks like Jamina is also having a great time with them."

"Yes, indeed, they have all been having fun. You forgot their grandfather also. The boys have spent two Sundays alone at his place. Jamina has taken them to the Lamongwe Museum and the chimpanzee sanctuary, and to the beach a number of times."

"Good to hear. Now, to business. For the first day of the workshop, when we have the full discussions, I think we have the program completed. For the second day, my staff is in the process of consulting with the producers and the exporters on how we should organize the breakout sessions."

"Okay, that makes sense. If I may ask, what have your staff and you been finding out on the implementation problems in your discussions with the producers and the exporters? I know we shall get the full details at the workshop. But I'm just curious."

"The picture is not good. The exporters and producers have been drawing our attention to many problems, particularly in the areas of quality management, export packaging, cooperation between government and businesses, and cooperation among the producers themselves. The exporters have been frank about not developing export competence fast enough. Hence, progress in export diversification and increasing the country's market share in traditional exports will be slow."

"I'm not surprised. We can see it in the trade statistics of the central bank and Statistics Nigasilia. Well, in my presentation, I am going to stress that the successful implementation of the export strategy requires substantial supporting policies from the authorities to improve the macroeconomic environment, reduce the cost of doing business, and improve the enabling environment for innovation in business."

"What about the financial sector people? What are you going to say to them? You are covering that too in your presentation, right?"

"Yes, of course. I will remind them that the financial sector, via increased efficiency, competition, and innovation, can assist in implementing the export strategy by increasing access to finance and reducing the cost of that finance for producers and exporters."

Mahdu slams his fist into the palm of his hand. "I think we are ready to go."

It is the second Saturday in July. John, Jamina, and the boys plan to go watch a soccer match between two of the national soccer association teams in Nigasilia. John has never taken his boys to a soccer match in Nigasilia. Today's game is big; it is a good match to take them to for the first time. When they collect Jamina she smiles at the boys. "Are you looking forward to the match today?"

Donald says, "Yes, we are. Do you usually go to soccer matches?"

"At most once a year, when they play the knock-out championship match, and only if my parents decide to go. They usually are able to get tickets for the comfortable seats in the covered stands, since my father is a chief."

"Daddy, is that where we are going to sit?" William asks.

"Yes, William."

Donald then turns to Jamina. "Ms. Tamba, did Daddy tell you that he has not been to an association match in Nigasilia since he left high school?"

Jamina giggles quietly. "No, Donald, I do not remember him telling me."

"Yes, Donald," John says, "I have not been to a professional soccer match anywhere since I left high school. In the US, I have been to professional basketball and baseball games, golf tournaments, and American football matches. But I can't play any of those, while I can play soccer. Isn't that interesting?"

Jamina sits back once they reach their seats. "Funny, I have not asked you this, but did you play soccer in college?"

"I did, but only for fun. I did not try out to play for my university. I did not want that kind of a commitment, not to any sports."

The boys get really into the match. These are the two leading teams of the first division, even though the season is still young. The regular soccer season lasts from the first week in April until the first week in

September. There are all sorts of tournaments after that, until the end of November. The team in blue is in first place, while the team in yellow is in second place.

The game gets going just as the experts predicted in the newspaper commentaries. The ball possession is evenly matched, but the team in blue has more chances to score. Then, to the surprise of the fans, judging from the reaction of the crowd, the yellow team scores first, thirty minutes into the game. And so it remains for the first half.

At half time, as they sip water, Donald says, "You know, I think that the two defenders of the blue team were trying to play an offside trap. I don't think they noticed that the third defender was a little bit behind them way on the other side of the field. So they did not properly cover the yellow striker close to them. When the ball was passed to the striker, he just took off straight for the goal."

"You are right, Donald," John interjects, "but still the striker had to blast his shot on goal from some distance. If he had tried to get too close to the goalie, those defenders would have caught him."

"Yes," William says, "and did you see the way the ball just curved?"

"I did," Jamina says, "and that fooled the goalie. I wonder if he really tried to curve the ball or if it was just good luck."

As they drive home from the soccer match, which ended in a one-one tie, Donald says to his dad, "Dad, you used to tell us that you did not like going to soccer matches here because people fight too much during the matches. You said that the players fight and the spectators fight also. But the match was very orderly today."

John does not quite know how to respond. "Did you enjoy the match?"

"Yes."

"Did any player argue with the referee?"

"No."

"So there was no need to fight. The association has also been punishing teams if their players cause any confusion and especially if they get thrown out by the referee."

"But the supporters of the teams could still fight, even if the players are behaving themselves."

"That's true. So they did not need to fight today. We were lucky."

Jamina intercedes. "Donald, yes, it is true that in some games they do fight, but usually nowadays it is the spectators that fight, because when players fight they get red cards. I'm sorry we did not take you on a tour to show you where most of the policemen sit below the covered stand. Usually there will also be plainclothes policemen who sit in the stadium to observe the behavior of the crowd. Nowadays, because of the police presence, and the severe punishment for disruption of games, very few people, I should say, take the risk of starting a fight."

John takes the next four weekdays off and spends time driving the boys around and walking the streets with them, just to give them a better sense of places they had not been before. The boys are appalled at what they see. Away from the center of the city, people walk out of their houses and dump trash in the gutters. When a gutter becomes blocked, the water simply overflows and runs down the streets until it finds another gutter empty enough. People urinate in the streets. Garbage piles up on sidewalks because the public garbage bins fill up faster than the authorities can handle. Everywhere in the city, thousands of young men just stand around with no clear objective or direction. All over the city, boys hawk handfuls of goods. John explains to the boys that thousands of people have no place to sleep, and make do with market stalls, deserted buildings, and street corners.

Most of the streets in Lamongwe are in disrepair; many have never been paved. The boys wonder why people build their houses on streets that are barely motorable. Vehicles break down everywhere and sometimes the owners try to repair their vehicles right in the middle of the road. On several occasions, John's sons watch such vehicles being dismantled, the useful parts extracted. John tells them that those parts would be sold or used by the dismantler in another vehicle that he has somehow obtained. Traveling to other towns and villages, not too far from Lamongwe, within a thirty-mile radius, the boys see more of the same. But in the countryside, with bush and grassland nearby, hardly any garbage collects along the main streets. Of course, the poverty is no less than in Lamongwe. Even in the middle of the day, the village huts are dark, with few windows to let in the sun.

On July 20, as soon as he arrives at work, John walks into the office of one of his economists who has been working with the two research assistants and a couple of staff members of the central bank on the issue of access to finance for small and medium enterprises.

The Chamber of Commerce, the labor union movement, and the government are all complaining that the banks are not lending to small and medium enterprises, or SMEs as they call them, and for the small amounts the banks lend to SMEs the banks are accused of charging high interest and service fees. So the president has asked John and the central bank governor to come up with answers to the criticisms. SMEs are important in creating jobs. Also, the elections are coming up soon and the president needs the support of those who see this issue as important.

Some people complain that the banks are too conservative and are unwilling to devote resources into understanding the SMEs and to develop appropriate ways to lend to them. Others say that the banks legitimately find it too risky to lend to the SMEs, and that the cost of administering and servicing the loans are also high. Still others argue that a major problem is that the Nigasilian legal system plus government and central bank regulations make it difficult for banks to lend except to the government or big businesses. John is of the view that all three perspectives have some element of the truth. The objective of the study is to find out how these factors operate and what policies can be put in place by government, the central bank, the banks, and the SMEs themselves to make it possible for SMEs to receive more loans from banks without the high cost to the enterprises and high risks to the banks.

"Songo, how is the project going?" John asks.

"Oh, quite well, actually. Right now we are still collecting data. From the banks, for example, we are collecting information on how they lend, on their clients, on their interest rates and service charges, on the sources of their funds, on their activities to develop their markets in Nigasilia, on their decision-making procedures in lending and investing, and on the problems that they see in operating in the SME loan market."

"Are you getting good cooperation?"

"Oh, yes."

"What about the SMEs? Have you started collecting information from them?"

"Yes, and that one is also working well. So far we have been getting 100 percent cooperation in the sample."

A few days later, as John gets ready to leave his house for the office, Jamina calls him. "John, have you heard the news about Fisherman's Bay?"

"No, what news?"

"There was serious flooding there last night and five children drowned in their sleep."

The Fisherman's Bay community is one of the worst living environments in Lamongwe. On the big estuary of the Kelora River, the reclaimed land emerged from trash and various debris deposited by residents over many decades. Soon, hundreds of poor people who could afford nowhere else to stay in Lamongwe constructed shacks on the land and turned it into a residential area. Despite repeated appeals, and even official attempts to evict them, the residents refuse to leave the area. No government, local or national, has been willing to evict them by force.

On his way to the office, John cannot resist going to the area to witness, firsthand, what is going on. There are many hundreds of people there, just standing and talking about the disaster.

When John arrives at the office, he goes to speak to his father. "Dad, I am sure you have heard the news about Fisherman's Bay."

"Yes, why?"

"I stopped by there to see for myself and to hear what people are saying."

"So, what did you see and hear?"

"People were crying, repeating that it was a horrible sight to watch the bodies of the five children who died. Many of the people were nasty in their comments. Some said they didn't understand why anyone wanted to live in such a nasty and dangerous place. Many others said that if we had a good government it would have cleared the place a long time ago."

"John, each time there is some problem in that area, people say the same thing. Usually, it is not this bad. Normally, if I may use that word, the people there simply quarrel, fight, and injure themselves."

"Dad, when will you insist that the place be cleared—by the city, by the state police, or by the army?"

"John, while you were sitting in America, we tried to clear the place several times. But the people there want to be in Lamongwe and we have no place anywhere else to put them."

"So where does that leave us, Dad?"

"Right now, I don't know, John. We have to let people be, to give them autonomy and to give them opportunity. We should leave them alone as long as they are law-abiding. Most of these people have no education, no skills, and no steady jobs. They can go somewhere else in this country and do better. But they want to stay here, in Lamongwe, even if it means living in Fisherman's Bay. I have to keep the big picture in my focus. Let's improve education and training and try to attract businesses. Apart from that, let people make their own choices. If we try to move those people out by force, there will be only chaos and disorder in this place. Even some of those people saying the nasty things you heard will then turn on us and accuse us of despotism and cruelty."

"But even on public health grounds those people should be removed from that place. Fisherman's Bay is surely the worst case."

"I'm not so sure, John."

Towards the end of the summer vacation, only a few days before the boys are due back to school, John decides to take them to visit a favorite Nigasilian island of his, Waititi, near Jamina's parents' town of Wombono, some 170 miles away from Lamongwe. It would have been great to combine the tour with a visit to Jamina's parents. Unfortunately, a three-day regional chiefs' conference had been organized at the same time, some eighty miles away from Wombono, and Jamina's parents are in attendance. John, Jamina, and the boys will still stay at the house during their visit to the neighborhood. After all, it is Jamina's second home. They spend two days and three nights in Wombono. On one of those days, Jamina takes John and the boys to Waititi, some thirty miles away.

John is surprised to find out that United Nations and NGO types love camping on the island. The island has a wildlife sanctuary and the densest population of primates on the planet. Some of the chimpanzees there are very rare. There are also some 150 bird species on the island. Jamina informs John that the island is rich in biodiversity and that a major aim of the ongoing conservation efforts is to preserve that biodiversity. The boys marvel at all the natural beauty.

There are a few persons around from that area of Nigasilia, for whom this is home, and they benefit economically from the freshwater fish, the plants, and even some of the wildlife that they can hunt for food without serious threat to the stocks involved. As they take it all in, Jamina turns and looks at John as he watches the tourists. From the expression on his face, Jamina knows what John is about to ask. So, she simply answers the question. "Yes, John," she says, "you hardly ever see Nigasilian visitors here, except for a few scientists."

To John, it is even worse than that. "A place with such excellent tourism potential is not attracting normal tourists because of the un-derdeveloped infrastructure. Even the camp is makeshift. Only people with a scout mentality and those used to dealing with refugees in de-serted places would want to come here for a visit."

Then, laughing, he looks at Jamina and says, "The conservationists will really have nothing to worry about for a long time."

"Well, like they say, every cloud has a silver lining. Just look at your boys. They are really taking it all in."

John turns to them and says, "Boys, isn't this just stunning?"

"Yes, Dad," Donald says. "Ms. Tamba, I hope your society is able to prevent people from destroying this place."

"We will protect it, Donald, one way or the other, even if we have to protest in the streets. But we will not have to, because all the countries that are helping us in our development are also interested in maintaining this sanctuary. So you will see it anytime you want when you come to Nigasilia."

John glances at Jamina and moves closer so they can hold hands. The boys look at each other and smile.

Chapter 8

The largest university in the country, the University of Nigasilia, had asked John if he could deliver the address at the commencement ceremony toward the end of October. John decides that the occasion provides him an excellent platform from which to incite the youth, mainly the educated youth, to organize a movement dedicated to pressuring his father and all those in charge to act resolutely in the pursuit of good economic policies and curbing corruption.

As far as John is concerned, the history of Nigasilia demonstrates that poor governance cannot be handled simply by changing the government. Poor leadership and saboteurs of good policies survive and prosper irrespective of the government in power. John strongly believes that radical action is needed and he is determined to sow the seeds for the required mobilization process. This commencement address will be the perfect opportunity for those seeds to be planted; maybe they will fall on fertile land. John prepares his address to be as provocative as possible without raising too many eyebrows. It is a test of his resolve.

On commencement day, John is there in his full academic attire. After the usual formalities, John is introduced and he steps onto the podium. The resplendent panorama in front of and behind him is captivating. The president of Nigasilia is not present, as he happens to be on a short trip abroad, though the vice president is in the audience.

John turns his head left, right, and behind to recognize the dignitaries sitting on the stage. He closes his eyes for a split second. And then he plunges into his speech with fervor.

"Mr. Vice President, honorable ministers and members of Parliament, Vice Chancellor, distinguished guests, members of the university staff, graduating students, it gives me great honor and pleasure to stand before you this afternoon, on this auspicious occasion, to deliver the commencement address."

He begins by praising the faculty for their work under difficult economic circumstances that have left libraries, laboratories, and other facilities at the university lagging behind those in the modern world. "It is encouraging," he continues, "that despite such severe constraints your students hold their own in the major universities of the world when they do post-graduate studies abroad."

John has additional words of praise for the students. "You should be commended for your determination to persevere under these circumstances. I remember when every Nigasilian student who attended this university received a scholarship that included a monthly allowance for expenditures such as clothing and entertainment. Now, only a few of you have scholarships of any kind. Each summer I've come home on vacation I have visited the university, for one reason or another. And I have seen the hostels where you reside and the dining room where you eat. The economic conditions of Nigasilia have forced you to live and study under severe hardship. The question before us is: what can we, as a nation, do to make things better for future generations of students."

This brings John to the central message of his address. He looks around to be sure everyone is listening.

"I hope the rest of you here today will bear with me if I speak directly to the graduating students. It is their day and they deserve the privilege.

"More than four decades ago, our fathers and grandfathers bargained for independence from our colonial masters. There was euphoria. The prevailing view at the time was that we had broken the chains. Those chains had limited our education, deprived us of basic human and democratic rights, and restrained our development. It seemed then that a new dawn had emerged. We could develop our infrastructure, educate and train our people, modernize our agriculture, industrialize, and widen our economic relationships beyond the confines of the colonial master's domain.

"Four decades later, what kind of a Nigasilian world will you, the young graduates of this august university, be entering as professionals? Some will regard that world as brighter than the one our fathers and grandfathers inherited at independence. We can now vote for our leaders. Literacy rates are higher, even if still much lower than hoped for. We have more professionals of our own, relative to the population, than at independence—doctors, engineers, scientists, economists, lawyers; just name it. Our paved roads are several hundred miles greater than bequeathed us by our colonial master. Yes, we have made progress in some objective sense. Yet our lot is worse off than at independence. Why?

"One plain fact is that our population is much greater than at independence. Another, and more important, reason is that most of the rest of the world has advanced far ahead of us in every sphere of relevance to the well-being of the human race. We are now part of the inner city, as Americans would say, the slums of the global community. We have fallen behind. Globalization has bypassed us. We are technologically several generations behind the majority of nations outside this continent; our standards of health, education, and nutrition are lagging behind the industrial countries, Latin America, and virtually all of Asia, and the distance between us and those ahead of us has widened since independence. Independence gave us freedom to make choices in governing ourselves. The evidence, by any measure you choose, is that we have failed. We have scored an F. And we have no one to blame but ourselves and our leaders.

"Just think of your particular group of graduates. What fraction of you is graduating in science, engineering, or telecommunications? The answer, certainly, is not very encouraging. And you are not to blame. The school system never prepared you to be otherwise. Our school system is not tuned in to the idea that this is a developing country and that there are certain skills required if we want to be on the high road to economic development.

"Many of your classmates in school dropped out or failed without graduating from secondary school. Where are they now, the dropouts? They are probably walking the streets looking for odd jobs or trying to acquire certain skills to become painters, carpenters, masons, tailors, blacksmiths, electricians, plumbers, and mechanics. Will they master these skills? Highly unlikely. The system of skills development is antiquated in this country. Our leaders have paid little attention to the issue. They have been satisfied with an informal system of training that is primitive, to say the least. The formal technical institutes are underfunded, lacking in equipment and qualified instructors, and treated like irrelevant stepchildren of the education system. Moreover, most of the young people who drop out of secondary school need additional basic education before they can be subjected to the rigors of formal technical and vocational training. The majority of them are barely literate."

John pauses. The silence is petrifying. He himself is really down in spirit. So he swallows and sips water that has been placed at the stand.

"The plain truth is that what your parents and grandparents have built for you so far is a land of misery—Misery Land. It is a land of corrupt and inept public officials, social elites that for the most part are unenlightened, and a mass population that is ignorant and fatalistic. It is a land of filth, dirt, and poverty. It is a land of poor infrastructure and technologically backward people. You have to go out there and begin the process of radical reform."

John pauses again. He opens his eyes and raises his head. He thinks of his father. But he does not care. He thinks of his mother. She would have approved of what he is saying. To his audience, the pause seems long; some turn around to see if others are also wondering what's going on.

"My dear young graduates, economic development is not like aging. It does not happen merely as a function of time. This country can remain backward for the next two hundred years in the absence of resolute action to promote development. If Nigasilians want to progress and progress fast, they must act and act tenaciously. You represent the future; the ball will soon be in your court. Of course, many of you may have already decided to escape this place. But I know that most of you, even when you decide to go abroad for further education or to make your fortunes, will still harbor a deep desire to return home someday. At the very least, you will be saddened by the misery in your land of birth. Hence, you do have a stake in this country's progress. Some of you may also want to go into politics and the civil service. Do so, if you like, but please don't see that as an opportunity to steal government resources. If you do, I hope the others, I am advising here, will find a way to exterminate you, like we do with the pests and insects that spread debilitating diseases."

John is like a man ready for dueling. He swallows to calm himself.

"So what kind of actions can you young people take? Let me suggest one general approach that has worked historically. But it requires a lot of details that I cannot specify here and should leave, anyway, to your imagination, since you have to manage the process. What I mean to say is that you need *social movements* that are tenacious in achieving their objectives. Such objectives, in this case, I would suggest, would include ensuring good policies from our political leaders as well as clean and efficient government. Take to the streets, write in the newspapers, and educate the electorate. Don't be satisfied with the government telling you what it is trying to do. Judge the government by what it actually does and the economic growth and development it is achieving. Insist on results and accept no excuses."

The audience now becomes noisy, murmuring. It is not clear to John what they are saying. He does not care, but it causes him to stop and wait for them to quiet down. Then he continues, speaking slightly louder.

"What this means is that you need to decide on the criteria by which to assess your government, and you must collect the data from the government to use as weapons—yes, my friends, weapons. You must force your government to be transparent in all its major activities. Work with experts in civil society and in business. Your social movements should include intellectual persons from the universities as well as persons from business. They should comprise persons from all walks of life and all corners of this country. And, of course, women as well as men should be prominent. Your social movements should communicate with the bilateral donors and the multilateral financial institutions that give aid and advice, may I say even comfort, to your government. Insist that these foreign governments and organizations consult with the leaders of your movements. In these activities, take no prisoners—be militant and aggressive in your actions, and don't ever take no for an answer. But do not—I repeat do not—be violent, and please, no riots!"

There is more mumbling. In Nigasilia, mass protests, whatever their origin or objectives, often end in riots and looting, as the rabble-rousers use them as opportunities to steal. After the audience quiets down, John continues, speaking more softly, with both hands firmly on the podium.

"My dear young people, you have no other choice. Your Nigasilian governments have shown little inclination to pursue economic development in the resolute manner that is necessary to lift us from our backward and wretched Misery Land. And the aid donors have shown no courage in cutting off aid when the government is wasting money. Of course, the aid donors sometimes try to control the government. That approach does not work, either. The point I want to make is simple. Take charge through well-organized social movements or you are doomed to exile, or else to misery if you stay in Nigasilia, even if you participate in corruption.

"My dear young graduates, your social movements will require enormous cooperation and mobilization. To enhance the prospects for success, they must be underpinned by formidable organizing principles. In this country, it is clearly high time for an age of true enlightenment, and we should use internal debates to encourage the development of homegrown ideas on public policy, which in turn will drive the kind of social movements that I am promoting here today. The idea of enlightenment is to encourage reflection on issues so that ideas emerge. Yes, of course, ideas without implementation are useless and so you will certainly need to go beyond the debates. You need, too, the action part of the social movements.

"I am here stressing the importance of debates only because one of our major shortcomings in this country is that, compared with many other countries, especially outside this continent, little formal discussion takes place on public policy. Political platforms, for example, contain bland statements and promises about democracy, multiculturalism, cultural activities, and economic development, while political campaigns are devoid of serious discussions on the burning issues.

"One consequence is that individual choices in voting are dominated by ethnic, regional, and sectarian sentiments, and voters end up with no objective benchmarks against which to assess the performance of their leaders. Indeed, a major consequence of the absence of discussion is that the notion of leadership is itself not well understood. Formal discussions will encourage a general consensus on the problems and the possible ways in which the country can address them. Your discussions should benefit as much as possible from the available global stock of knowledge; for example, include experts, whether foreigners or Africans in the diaspora.

"Of importance also to your movements will be outreach involving education and enlightenment of the masses of this, our beloved, country. Motivate the masses to participate intelligently in politics and give them the capacity to identify good political and community leaders. The masses must be not only bodies but also minds supporting your social movements.

"And when you address the masses, I want you to get them to understand, without insulting or talking down to them, that in the modern world there are things that influence how people perceive you, and whether they respect you and are willing to deal with you or simply want to leave you alone. In today's world, such perception will affect whether serious investors want to come to this country. This perception is shaped by your respect for other people's properties and space, including being quiet at certain hours of the night; your degree of cleanliness; attention to detail in work and play; whether you are able to keep a promise and avoid petty crime; your pride in autonomy; and your ability to take responsibility for your actions.

"My dear young friends, because we have not learnt as a nation to be efficient in the use of our resources, we have not been able to generate income to ensure that we can increase our per capita consumption and at the same time increase our per capita investment in equipment and knowledge. So now we find ourselves beggars in the world. We beg both for consumption and for investment. Well, the first lesson a good leader should impart to the citizens, if the citizens don't know it themselves, is that the world owes us nothing and has no obligation to deposit anything in our begging bowls. Moreover, people with any pride don't take pleasure in begging. But it is obvious that we take such pleasure. One of the first things our leaders do after they take office is go around begging to wealthy nations. Let us encourage foreign investment but let us do our best to reduce and soon eliminate our aid dependence. No aid-dependent country gets much respect in this modern world. Such a country does not even have the freedom to speak out on issues without worrying about what its aid donors will think and do. My friends, just think—is that not a worse condition than being subjected to colonialism? It is voluntary subservience. We have the right to be free and we throw away the keys to our freedom with our bad policies.

"Nigasilians are very proud of the riches and the beauty of their country, and they should be. But all the riches and the beauty only create opportunities, which we can exploit. We can earn foreign exchange and create jobs in activities as diverse as agriculture, industry, mining, tourism, and fishing. We can even export mineral water if we put our minds to it. I am amazed that our leaders are not ashamed to have so many of our citizens become émigrés, when we have so much job-creating potential here. To add insult to injury, those who are left behind cannot, on average, survive without the remittances received from those émigrés. Isn't it crystal clear that we are doing something wrong? Well, my dear young friends, you have chosen leaders to fix the problem. Hold them accountable. Accept no excuses.

"I told myself, when preparing this speech, that I would try to be brief, and I shall be. But there is one last thing I should say. I have asked you, the educated youth, to rise up and take charge in pressuring your leaders to do a better job in governing our beloved country. In taking charge, I would not advise you to take the approach that seems attractive to many amongst you. I have heard it said that things would be better if only those under fifty were in total political control of the country. Be wary of the under-fifties. They are hungry. We in Nigasilia are not blessed, as is the case in advanced countries, where many young people can count on millions of dollars, or some other hard currency, of endowed wealth. The young here basically have none. So when they capture a high position in government at an early age, they see it as an opportunity to accumulate wealth quickly. That is why so many of you young people become so corrupt when you are suddenly catapulted into high office. That is not good for the country. That will not take us out of Misery Land."

There is loud applause, with some in the audience, including the graduating students, beginning to stand.

"So there you are. There is your challenge. Good luck and I wish all of you the best in your varied endeavors."

The speech receives a standing ovation. As John makes his way to the reception afterwards, the VP, who seems to be in a hurry to leave, approaches him. "John, I did not know you were such a revolutionary. Did your father see a draft of the speech?"

"No, I did not have it completely drafted before he left."

"Well, well. Anyway, I have to run. I have another function to attend. I'll see you in the office."

At the reception, three of the distinguished guests at the commencement and one of the professors at the university walk up to John and congratulate him for a very brave speech. Then one of them says, "Dr. Bijunga, I was struck by the fact that in your speech, you failed to address all the ways that the outside world is adversely affecting economic development in Nigasilia. Don't you believe that our economic development has been deterred by the International Monetary Fund and World Bank conditionalities, by international commodity markets, and by the multinationals? Also, aren't there still lingering effects of slavery and colonialism?"

John agrees with the gentleman that slavery and colonialism have had long-term negative effects. "Where I differ from a lot of people around here," John says, "is that I believe we should treat the adverse influences of slavery and colonialism the same way we treat inheritance, endowment, or genes, and move on from there. If we are being bullied to institute bad policies, then you should ask yourself why we have to listen to these outsiders and why these outsiders want us to institute bad policies. In addition, why don't they do the same to all those who are making progress in other continents? My friends, stop blaming outsiders for our incompetence. We have enough autonomy to do something about our current condition."

The following day, October 31, all the newspapers cover John's speech in their front pages. Overwhelmingly they are pleased that the failures of Nigasilia were highlighted. But some also argue that John let the IMF, World Bank, the multinationals, and the commodity markets off the hook. Then there are a few who wonder if John is right to be encouraging the youth to make explicit demands of the government. One of the leading newspapers suggests that John may, in fact, be wishing for some kind of revolution.

Two concerned cabinet members who immediately want to talk to John individually the day after the commencement speech are the vice president and Mahdu Kontana. The VP sends a message to John to drop by his office that morning.

When John enters his office, the VP gives him a fatherly sort of smile and says, "John, I didn't realize you were that frustrated with what's going on around here. Yes, we have problems, and yes, there are people who don't want us to do the right thing because it is against their own selfish interest. But you can't deny that we are trying our best. We are faced with enormous difficulties. The world is making things hard on us and we inherited a mess from previous governments. So what is this trumpet call to the youth to form social movements? What really are you asking them to do? I can tell you that those students are already in line at the government offices looking for work. They are also looking at the private sector. But the truth is that since independence, most of those European companies that used to be steady employers with great benefits have left. Maybe as a nation we are to blame, but not this government. We are even trying hard to attract some of those sound employers back. So what will a protest accomplish?"

John stares at the VP. "I don't agree that we are trying as hard as we can. If we were, our economy would have been experiencing far more rapid growth on average, and high growth every year. We would not wait for growth to depend on the vagaries of the weather and the international commodity markets. Look at our agriculture. It is basically stagnant and technologically backward. We are not doing anything to diversify our economy. Look at our tourism; we have such fantastic potential, and yet we are close to zero because of our lack of infra-structure, our customary land tenure system, and our hopeless labor force. I could go on and on."

"Yes, John, you are right, we should do better. And we are going to try harder to do better. But why are you inciting the youth to cause confusion for us?"

"Because I want to make sure there are no detractors thwarting the success of this 'trying hard,' as you put it. I want the youth to watch carefully the actions of all of you who have been selected by the people to govern this country and for you, the governors, to know that the youth are watching and that they will judge the government by its performance, by the results of its actions, and not by its repeated statements of what it is trying to do. I want to motivate you."

"In short, John, you are raising the stakes. Well, I hope you can contain the youth. There are lots of rowdy ones among them. Oh, not the ones you addressed yesterday, but all those dropouts and un-educated ones to which you alluded in your address. But let me tell you, if there is any trouble we will deal with them. Please pass the word along that we will tolerate no rowdiness. We will bring out the police and the army in full force. And we will not be afraid to shoot."

John does not believe that his dad will allow the youth to be shot unless they are a threat to people's lives. "Sir, I am not encouraging the youth to cause mayhem or bloodshed. I only want peaceful dem-onstrations, when such action is deemed necessary. I also want the government to open lines of communication, so that the youth will have a better sense of what is going on and the government can hear their concerns and frustrations firsthand. Moreover, I want gov-ernment programs in technical and vocational education and training to be expanded. I want the youth to insist on results, not big talk and propaganda."

John looks at his watch and knows that Kontana will soon be at his office waiting for him. The VP notices John eyeing his watch.

"I don't want to hold you up. I have told you what I wanted to say. So, unless you have something else to add, please feel free to leave."

"Thank you, VP, thank you."

John hurries back to his office, where Kontana soon drops in. "John," he says, as if wondering aloud, "are you sure that asking young people to challenge the leaders is the appropriate strategy to produce action from the government? What exactly do you expect the graduates to do? What is this social movement idea? Who are the enemies that the movements will be fighting against? I thought you and I had an understanding. Your role was to be instrumental in getting your dad to take charge, to stop behaving as if he is weak."

John folds his hands, unfolds them, crosses his legs, uncrosses them, and then looks straight at Kontana. "Yes, you are right. I was supposed to convince my dad to be stronger in his leadership and to implement policies and to not cave in to serious opposition from interest groups. I will have to ask him why he is not taking charge in his leadership style. My dad likes to build consensus. But then he should influence the direction and the content of the consensus. I don't believe that most of those who govern this country care about the rapid transformation to become developed. They care only about their power, position, and perquisites. My dad behaves as if he does not know this."

John would prefer that someone like Mahdu Kontana see his speech as an attempt to help weed out persons working against his father's attempt to implement sound policies for economic development. But Mahdu now surprises him with a question.

"John, are you sure that your dad is not like those others you criticize and despise? Okay, take out the perquisites. I don't think your dad is as corrupt as the others. I'm assuming that the ability to get away with corruption is among the perquisites."

"It surely is." John pauses and Kontana says nothing. He wants an answer from John.

"Kontana, you just set me thinking. I've always thought my dad put country first. The only problem I have, and I am being open now, is that I am still not fully convinced that my dad is the kind of leader that we want in Nigasilia. He is not forceful and resolute enough."

"So there you have it, John. Do your best to find out if he is the right kind of leader, and if he is not, how you could help him become such a leader."

John is surprised at the line Kontana is taking. He wants to be sure he is not misunderstanding.

"What do you mean?"

"As far as I know, you have spent a lot of time studying the literature on leadership and you have been researching the role of leadership in successful developing countries, particularly those in East Asia."

"Well, I shall keep talking to my dad about his leadership style, my view on what a good leader needs to do in this country, and what people like those in the Chamber of Commerce are saying about his leadership."

"Okay, fine, I am sure you will. But in the meanwhile I just don't understand what you are trying to do, inciting the youth to demonstrate."

"Kontana, my father needs some push from below. When the people prove that they will not tolerate certain outcomes, the political leaders in this country, including my dad, will begin to fear that the people will rise up unless the people see results. The government will also stop issuing meaningless documents and making elaborate speeches about what they are trying to accomplish—they will know that they will not be allowed any excuse. Without loud, clear, and militant support from below, my father will not be bold in his actions or succeed in whatever he is trying to do."

John pauses to avoid monopolizing the discussion. But Kontana sees that he is not finished. So he signals to John to continue.

"There are saboteurs in this system, and I mean it. The way things are now, they will always win and my dad will continuously have to explain to the population why the government is not achieving its objectives. That state of affairs is totally unacceptable; in fact, it is deplorable. I cannot sit by and allow it to happen. We need powerful weapons to counter these powerful saboteurs."

"John, if you believe in what you are saying, then you should uncover these saboteurs so we can shame them and remove them from office. Otherwise people could retort that just because someone doesn't agree with your dad, that does not mean they are saboteurs. How do we know those opponents are not right? That's why your dad is in search of consensus. On that, even I agree. The challenge is how we arrive at consensus, putting the country first, of course."

There is a brief moment of silence and then John responds. "Well, take for instance the case of procurement. We brought experts from abroad to help us write a first-rate procurement law. Then we have been training our public servants as diligently as we can on the procurement procedures and on the interpretation of the law itself. On the face of it, the public servants in the central and local governments, as well as the state enterprises, seem to be following the procedures as earnestly as possible. Yet when you look at the results, nothing has changed. Contracts are given to builders who disappear with some of the funds or leave the jobs unfinished or, still worse, do such shabby jobs that we have to condemn the work and begin all over again. Materials are way below the expected quality, and services for which we contract get done late, and typically poorly. But none of the personnel responsible for the procurements get fired or even reprimanded. And, of course, the ones who do the lousy work, the suppliers and the contractors, are still in the system and benefit from further government contracts and procurements. If we insist on results, we can change all this."

"John, you leave me dumbfounded because you have a point, a great point," Kontana concedes. "But your strategy can't work here. We have too many hooligans and too many uneducated people. They will be hard to control if demonstrations and protests begin. We see it throughout Africa and we have a history here, too. It is a risky strategy.

But I understand where you are coming from; nothing else has worked so far. Let's pray that the youth will be orderly when they respond to your call. If there is mayhem, property will be destroyed and there will be many casualties. Let's continue to keep in touch. I'll be interested to find out how your father reacts to your talk on the leadership issues and what you intend to do. Remember, we are together on these issues. I'm here to help and support you. I'm sure your father will talk to you about your speech the moment he returns from his trip. That will be a good opportunity to start the dialogue."

Kontana turns to leave. But John is still not satisfied.

"Kontana, why was my father chosen to lead the party?"

"Because the party faithful thought he had the best chance of leading our party to victory."

"Why did the party want to win?"

"Well, we had an agenda. But to tell you the truth, most of the party members were just anxious to get the other party out. They felt they were too tribalistic."

"That is, they were keeping all the goodies, the perquisites, for a few."

"Yes."

"So it wasn't about the country. It was all about power, position, and perquisites."

"Yes, but then a few of us thought if we had the power and the positions we would develop the country while the other party would not. As I said, we had an agenda."

"But that is going nowhere. The country is not moving forward."

"Well, not as fast as we had hoped. But things would have been far worse with the other party. At least our party *wants* to move the country forward. Perhaps, in terms of achievements, we are moving too slowly for people like you and me. John, we need to continue to push as hard as we can. But we also need to be realistic."

☯

On the following Saturday, November 3, Jamina and John throw a small dinner party at Jamina's house. They invite Yingyi, the Chinese gentleman who sat next to John on the plane when he was coming home for his mother's funeral. Yingyi seems to be enjoying himself in Nigasilia. But in another six months or so he will be going back to China to work for one of their industrial firms, in the finance division. Also invited are Betty and Stephen Mongo, Vivienne and Santie, as well as Malika Kaykai, Tarik Day, and Raboya Bami from the Chamber of Commerce.

John's speech is on everyone's mind. But they know that once they broach that subject it will dominate the rest of the party. So, even without planning, everyone stays away from it for a while. First, everyone wants to talk to Yingyi. The Nigasilians admire the achievements of China, with their high rates of economic growth, rapid transformation, and impressive export volumes and values. But they hardly ever get to socialize with the Chinese who are working in Nigasilia, interacting with them primarily at the business level. Neither the Chinese nor the Nigasilians make serious effort to reach out to each other at the social level.

It is an informal buffet dinner, although waiters serve drinks and hors d'oeuvres before the main meal. As people relax and enjoy the evening, the conversation becomes quite lively.

Jamina, for example, tells Yingyi, "Everyone who's been to Shanghai tells me that it is a beautiful city. I hope I get the opportunity to go there someday. I also want to tour Beijing and visit the Great Wall."

"Well, I hope you get to see all of those," Yingyi replies. "But China has many other interesting places to visit. Of course, if you only start with those two cities, that would be good, too. The part of the Great Wall not too far from Beijing is very popular with the tourists."

Then Santie joins the conversation. "I hope you are having a good time here."

"Yes," says Yingyi. "Your people are very friendly. When they come to the hotel, they like to ask us about China. Many of them tell me they would like to visit someday. That is good."

Malika Kaykai jumps in next. "We have been trying to make contact with your Chamber of Commerce. Your people have agreed to meet with us. We want to assure your people that if you are having any problems, we will be happy to help you. We also will be able to learn something from you. As you know, we would like to explore joint ventures. Although we don't have a lot of money, if we pool resources we can think of something to do together. John Bijunga, here, has been discussing some ideas with us and he thinks that we should explore joint ventures in tourism. He says it's not farfetched to have not only the business relationships but also to have Chinese people coming to Nigasilia on vacation. So, we can jointly invest in hotels, campsites, ferry boats, and buses, and we can organize trips to some of our beautiful islands, mountains, forest reserves, wildlife reserves, and sanctuaries. What do you think?"

"I agree," replies Yingyi. "You should continue your conversations with our Chamber of Commerce executive members. A number of senior members are interested. I will leave Nigasilia soon but I can help you to meet some of the important people. I know for sure that some of them are looking for ways to enhance cooperation with Nigasilia. There are business people in China also who are looking for possibilities all over Africa."

"Your English is very good," Vivienne says. "Where did you learn to speak it so well?"

"I started to learn English in China, in school, and then I did graduate studies in the US."

Vivienne asks if Yingyi has been able to do much traveling in Nigasilia.

"Oh no, I have traveled only a little. Maybe I will try to do some more before I go back. I don't know if I will have another chance to come to Nigasilia again. But it is such a beautiful country."

The conversation turns to John's commencement speech. Tarik Day asks, "John, how did your colleagues in the cabinet take your speech at the university?"

"Oh," John replies, "they understand my frustrations and what I am trying to do. They are all concerned, though, but for different reasons. Some are worried that the young people will start something that could boil over and cause a breakdown of law and order. Others are concerned that I want to stir up the population to put undue pressure on the government. Then there are the others who believe it is a good idea to encourage the educated youth to become keener watchdogs of public servants. But even this last group hopes that no trouble comes out of it all."

"I find myself in sympathy with that last group," Day admits.

Santie looks concerned. "If the students come to you to ask your advice on what they should do, what will you tell them?"

"Honestly, I don't know," John replies. "But if the youth want change, they will have to do some thinking about what to do without me holding their hands all the time. I will, of course, offer them advice and suggestions. Look, when you talk to the young people of this country, they are usually very forthright and confident about what they want—education, training, jobs, and decent wages and salaries. They just don't know how to get what they want. All they see are obstacles. They will tell you they have a government that should find the means to those ends. I don't think that's a bad approach for the youth to take. If the sitting government doesn't have the answers, it should step aside and let another group of leaders take over. My own concern is that whatever movements these youth decide on should be truly national, involving men and women from all walks of life and from all four corners of this country."

Vivienne interrupts. "How would such a movement be different from a political party?"

"The members of the movement would not be in the business of seeking political office," John replies. "Yes, they would be acting politically. In fact, if they ask my advice, I would tell them to know what they are fighting for. What are their aims and goals? Also, they should not give the impression that they want to bring down the government. Rather, they should want only to see governance improve."

Raboya Bami joins the fray. "Have you been able to talk to the president since the speech?"

"He returned yesterday and called me this afternoon. He wants to talk tomorrow evening. When he called he said nothing much, just that it was important that we have dinner together."

"Do you think he will be happy with your speech?" Bami asks.

"It all depends on how he interpreted it. Anyway, if he is not happy with it, his view will likely be that I am mistaken. He would not presume I am trying to cause mischief or provoke an insurrection."

Stephen and Betty Mongo have been quiet until now. "John," Stephen begins, "some of the people at the golf club wonder whether your father will think the speech was unwise."

"In fact," Betty adds, "some are afraid that these young people in Nigasilia will not be able to handle serious protests without becoming violent."

"I'm not too afraid, as long as the college-educated youth control the movement. And I really don't see how a coherent social movement focusing on good economic governance can get off the ground if that movement is not led by the college-educated youth. I'm not talking about protests against food prices now. I have great confidence that my approach makes sense. Someone needs to stir up the enlightened masses to put pressure on those governing to act in ways that are good for the rapid economic development of the country."

Betty asks John, "What about the newspapers? Have they not tried to contact you for interviews? They blasted the story all over their pages. They are anticipating an official reaction from the president. They want to know how the president feels about his son delivering such an inflammatory speech."

"Yes, three of the papers have contacted me for interviews. But I have turned them all down."

Stephen is sympathetic with John's approach. "The youth will want to make specific demands on the government. And for that, they will need your guidance."

Chapter 9

John has not seen his father since the president returned from his recent trip abroad. The president had traveled to both the US and the UK. In the former, he visited the UN in New York, and had discussions in Washington at the White House. In the UK he had a number of meetings with some members of the cabinet, including the prime minister at No. 10 Downing Street.

All in all, the president had a very successful trip. The US promised to help with the organizational costs of the next elections and to have the US Agency for International Development help search for an economic expert to beef up the analytical team in the Ministry of Finance, at least for a three-year period. USAID also promised to finance two experts in the National Statistics Department, officially called Statistics Nigasilia.

In the UK, the Department for International Development, DFID, offered to increase assistance in budget formulation and management and in agricultural extension services. In return, the Nigasilian president promised both countries that his government would focus on private sector development, continue the progress to firmly implement democratic institutions and processes in the country, and move even more resolutely to control corruption.

At the start of their private dinner, the president says, "John, the commencement address worries me. As you might imagine, my concern is not with you wanting better governance. My concern is that, in your speech, you say that the youth of this country should organize social movements as a means to pressure the government to achieve better, indeed satisfactory, results. Do you intend that to be an attempt to coerce the government to accede to specific demands? Who will decide the specific nature of these achievements and determine when the effort made by the government is satisfactory?"

"To begin with, I really believe the people of this country deserve to be given specific targets for a number of socio-economic variables, in addition to clear goals for economic growth. I mean, for example, variables such as infant mortality, adult literacy rates, and average years of schooling for adult Nigasilians. The government will then be free to decide how it achieves these targets. My department will be quite happy to help establish the targets as well as assist with the policies that will be necessary to achieve those targets. The way I see it, this approach will prove that you are doing your best to make life in this country much better for the common people."

"So what happens if we do not meet the targets?"

"Then the cabinet must be reshuffled and some of the ministers must go."

"Who decides who goes?"

"The president, of course, will decide."

"What if the president does not want to make any changes in his cabinet?"

"Then the president will have demonstrated that he wants to keep an incompetent team. So he must resign and we would have new elections."

The president is not amused. He says in an abrasive tone, "What if the president refuses to resign?"

John is adamant, the tension visible in his eyes. "The social movements would be left with no other choice but to demonstrate until the president resigns or agrees to change the cabinet. If the president changes the cabinet, he must explain his reasoning: why he has made these changes, how and why he expects things to improve, and the time frame for each improvement."

The president leans back in his chair. "What a grand plan. But it is too rigid. How do we keep the targets realistic? What will be the process of negotiations in setting the targets?"

"This whole thing, Dad, is like having an incentive contract. If you do not like the idea of being subjected to pressure from the youth, I would recommend a national council on socio-economic governance with representatives from the government, Parliament, civil society, and business. This council could even be recognized in the constitution. The exact structure and decision-making procedure can be debated and I would be willing to give my views at such a debate. This council would recommend the socio-economic targets for the government. Parliament would approve the targets, and the government would agree to implement policies to achieve them. If the government does not reach any target, then it must come up with convincing evidence to the council and Parliament that any deficiency in performance was due to factors that the government could not have counterbalanced or otherwise prevented."

The president is quiet for a while, his hand covering his mouth. "But if this were all to your grand plan, why did you not just tell me this or bring it up in cabinet for discussion? Why ask the students to pressure the government? You encourage them to take charge, take no prisoners, and accept no excuses. This is all tough language, John. And now you tell me about an incentive contract. Why can't the national council be an advisory body, making recommendations to Parliament and the government to achieve certain socio-economic targets? There is no need for recommendations to be given the status of a contract."

John raises his voice. "If the targets are not considered part of a contract, the targets will be meaningless and the council powerless. All those people in our system who I want desperately to defang will still be running around with all their venom intact, ensuring the impotence of our fragile system. And if the national council is only an advisory body, we do not need to have Parliament represented in it."

"John, what people are you talking about that you want to defang? And if these enemies are so powerful, what makes you think they will want you to introduce a mechanism that diminishes their power?"

"Dad, I know you would like to make this country develop much faster than it is. Indeed, I would like to believe that you want the rapid economic transformation process to begin now. But so far, you have been unable to introduce the kinds of policies that will achieve such a grand objective. So I have come to the conclusion that you must be facing some opposition. I cannot point to any person or group of persons that are obstructing you, although I have my suspicions. In any event, I believe that if the government can get active and visible pressure from below, you will be able to rapidly transform the economic management of this country. The collective social action of the youth, especially the educated youth, is one such pressure."

John looks at his dad, who seems uncertain how to respond. John finds the courage to continue.

"Dad, you are the president. You can simply say you want to create a national council, and then nominate a small group to come up with recommendations for its specific structure, composition, and terms of reference."

The president refuses to yield. "John, all I see is you trying to incite the youth to revolt. And that's what many other people see as well."

John is ready for the heat. He remembers his conversation with Kontana about leadership and his dad's ability to be the right leader for this country. He wants to explode but he must stay respectful; he is talking not only to the president but to his father.

"Dad, you are governor of a system that is not working. It is failing to deliver the goods to the public, to the ordinary citizens. This is happening in spite of your brilliant mind and your concern for the people of this country. It is failing because you have surrounded yourself primarily, even if unwittingly, with ministers, senior civil servants, and state enterprise managers who have no interest in any policies that threaten their economic, bureaucratic, and political self-interests. You don't know how to get rid of these people. In fact, you may not even be able to separate the wolves from the lambs, the snakes from the mice. Dad, you need help to get rid of these people or to force them to change for the better. You need help from below. Some people I talk to doubt your ability as a leader. I have not known how to react because I cannot find the facts to show these skeptics that they are wrong."

"I could use some help, John, but not from immature revolutionary-minded citizens," the president insists. "Let me consider this idea. If I find merit in it, I shall bring it up in cabinet. It would be interesting to have some kind of advisory committee, comprising civil society and the business community, the Chamber of Commerce types, to make recommendations to us on appropriate socio-economic targets. We can then count on the support of those groups when it comes time to implement the targets that they have established. But we don't want targets treated like elements of a contract. We have enough conditionality coming from those who give us aid. This is a democracy; there are enough incentives there. We don't need any more to do our job."

"Dad, think about it, really think about it. You need to show greater leadership than you are showing now. It is not enough to say that you are where you are because the country cannot find a better leader. If I were in your shoes, I would not be happy with that. I love you, Dad; I do. But think about this proposition. Modify it anyway you want but come out with something that will make you look and act like a strong leader who is interested in the economic welfare of the citizens of Nigasilia."

"Why do you say all this, John? What evidence do you have that people are dissatisfied with what we are doing? And if that's true, why are the newspapers not more vocal?"

John wants to be respectful but he cannot help hitting back. "Dad, are the newspapers expressing praise for what you are doing? If you want an honest and correct answer to your question, I would suggest you invite an international research firm with pertinent skills to do a survey of Nigasilian public opinion. But you probably will want aid for that, too!"

The president appears weary but John is not finished. "And elections are coming up next year. Many people give the opposition a fighting chance. They say that despite all your talk and promises, they cannot think of one way in which their lives have improved, though they can think of several aspects of their living conditions that are now far worse. The disorganization of the opposition might help you. But would you want to win only because the opposition behaves as if it doesn't want to win either?"

"John, you've made your point. There is nothing more to be said."

The following day, the president requests a meeting with the vice president to talk about John's commencement address. When the VP arrives, the president asks, "Kamake, you were there when John was delivering his speech. What kind of reception did he get?"

"He got a standing ovation, but hardly any response during the delivery. The speech was too somber to have elicited much clapping before its conclusion. I had to leave soon after and did not attend the reception. But as I walked out, a couple of people on their way to the reception told me they were surprised he was so critical when his father has been president for some four years. They also felt he had ignored the role of external factors in explaining our poor performance. But on the whole, they agreed with him that we should look mainly at ourselves for our failure to move forward."

"What is your own opinion of the speech?"

"I thought the speech showed tremendous sympathy for the plight of the common people as well as deep commitment to improving governance in this country. What I did not like was that his words were unnecessarily provocative. He was calling on the youth to demonstrate their displeasure by holding us to performance targets."

"How do you think we should respond?"

"We should not publicly say anything one way or the other," the VP advises. "If we have to, we can simply say that we admire and agree with Dr. Bijunga's concerns. We should emphasize that the last government left the finances and other assets of this country in shambles and that Nigasilians should be happy that we came in when we did; things would have been far worse today, otherwise."

The president demurs. "But John has heard many people complain that they have not seen any improvements since we came into power."

"People will say that, of course; they expected us to make life rosy for them in four years. We have to find a way to get them to take responsibility for their individual predicaments."

"John is afraid that the disaffection of the youth is growing," the president says. "They might begin to organize demonstrations against us. Worse still, he is afraid that if the opposition is able to organize itself, it could actually unseat us in the coming elections."

"I am determined to make sure the opposition is not able to do that," the VP says.

The president, sensing something dire in his colleague's tone, responds, "Well, I hope we will play by the rules. I must warn you in advance that I will not let our friendship deter me from rebuking you publicly if you blatantly violate the democratic process. We have to continue the path of civility."

The VP replies calmly. "Sure. I meant only that we will campaign hard and counter every lie. But Samuel, I want to advise you not to underestimate the dirty tricks of the opposition. They are willing to break the law but want to cry foul when we clamp down on them."

The president returns to the order of business. "Anyway, I would like your opinion on a suggestion of John's. He thinks we could counter some of the criticisms if we create a kind of national council on socio-economic governance that would set targets on economic growth and welfare variables. John's department can take leadership in identifying useful socio-economic targets and helping us design policies to attain them. The national council will comprise persons from civil society and business and perhaps from Parliament and the government as well. My view is that if we decide on such a council, it should be advisory."

The vice president folds both hands on his lap, taking time to choose his words carefully. "I think it is a good suggestion, especially if we think of the council as strictly advisory. But I would suggest that we wait until after the elections, which I am positive we shall win, before we implement this idea. I would not want to give the opposition any opportunity to point to shortfalls in our progress."

"All right, Kamake," the president says, "I understand the logic of your argument and I respect your judgment. But even if we decide today to institute this national council, by the time we decide on its structure, composition, and terms of reference, let alone its budget, the elections will have come and gone. By the time we finish this process, it would be logistically impossible for the council to produce anything of substance before the April elections, which are barely five months away. So, I shall present this idea for further discussion in cabinet. I will let John, the minister of finance, and the minister of trade and industry work closely on this one. You have many other things on your plate, and with elections coming up I would like you to pay serious attention to our campaign strategy." The president pauses. "As usual your views have been very helpful. Let me not hold you up any longer."

It is almost lunchtime for Rabena when the president buzzes her in. When she enters his office, he asks her to sit down and make herself at ease. He notices the look on her face, so he quickly says, "Oh, there is nothing the matter, nothing grave. I just want to have your opinion on some political issues. You go to church, to the market, you have women's groups . . . What do the people think about this government?"

Rabena sits back and appears genuinely relaxed. "Mr. President," she says, "the people like you, but they think you have too many corrupt people around who do not care about the ordinary person."

The president puts Rabena on the spot. "Do they name these people who they think are corrupt?"

Rabena resists the temptation to provide names. "Mr. President," she replies, "the people I talk to know that I work for you, so they don't call names when I am around. But people are also afraid of mentioning names because those who might overhear them could be relatives or friends of a person they mention. People are afraid to call names."

The president obliges. "Yes, of course, I can understand that. But what do people criticize, generally?"

Rabena hesitates. The president is patient and willing to give her time to phrase her response. They usually talk about family, world affairs, social events, religion, and television programs; they even gossip about the relationships and careers of their mutual connections. But they never engage in this kind of political discussion. Rabena finds herself trying to respond to the president while at the same time wondering why he is suddenly, today, asking these questions. Is he nervous about the upcoming elections?

"Mr. President," Rabena responds, "people say that things are hard and they are constantly wishing for relief. Of course, you have those who talk about the filth, the traffic, the lack of electricity, the poor state of our health facilities, the water problems, and the bad roads. But the majority of people worry about the cost of living and their low incomes. Most people have to find someone to lean on for support. That makes them unhappy."

The president probes further. "Do the people blame anyone but themselves for their condition? Don't they give us some credit for the progress we have made on infrastructure, especially the roads?"

"They say the government is not doing anything to help them. They are angry about transport costs and school fees, which they think government can do something about. Mr. President, most of these people live in Lamongwe. They do not care too much about the roads going up-country. And to be honest, electricity and water situations have not really changed over the last four years, and jobs are not any easier to get than before. Many also say they do not get paid on time. Teachers, for example, are often not paid for several months. Many have to fall back on private lessons, or even sell snacks to students. But this means more spending by parents. Worse still, those who cannot afford the lessons lose out."

"So what do they say we have done right?"

"Mr. President, they never say much about what you are doing right. The one thing they say is that your government seems less corrupt than the last, and that there are more small foreign investors beginning to come in because of that. My judgment is that they believe you should have moved faster to alleviate their hardship, and that you should have achieved more by now."

The president wants to know about the response to John's speech. "Rabena, since my son delivered his speech, the people you meet, are they discussing that speech?"

"Mr. President, people commend your son for his concern. They say they were sure that you had consented to his speech; otherwise he would not have delivered it. Many of them, though, do not understand what he wants the young people to do."

"You have been very helpful, Rabena. That's all I wanted to ask you."

Rabena returns to her desk, pleased that the president consulted her in that way. She decides to call Jamina to schedule a lunch for Saturday.

On Tuesday morning, the president invites Kontana to his office. "Kontana, I wanted to talk to you because you are close to John and straightforward. What was your take on John's commencement speech?"

"It was a good speech in emphasizing that, as a nation, we have failed to meet the challenge of independence. The speech made no compromise over the question of who is to blame. We are to blame for our failure. My own worry, and I have told John so, is that I do not feel there was need to call on the youth to organize social movements to pressure the political leaders. I don't trust these young people's ability to ensure that things stay orderly. I felt John should not have pursued that path. He can always talk to you if he is not happy about how you are managing things. He should have simply left the general message to the young men and women that we as a nation should organize ourselves to govern better."

The president picks up on Kontana's intimation. "So do you think I manage well?"

Kontana skirts the issue. "People say there are persons in the cabinet, individuals within the ranks of the senior civil service, and certain heads of public enterprises and autonomous agencies who are corrupt and inept. The people express their dismay that you have not done anything to punish these officials."

The president, a little impatient, asks, "So if the people have such information, why are they not letting me know? Why don't I see anything in the newspapers that such information is out there?"

"Mr. President, that is a good question. Maybe you should address the public to the effect that you have heard rumors about certain senior public servants and that you will leave a whistle-blower box at certain locations for people to provide names and evidence. John and Rabena are the only two people in public service I would trust in the early stages to have access to the boxes."

The president really doesn't like the idea, but he does not want to be that frank with Mahdu Kontana for fear of embarrassing him.

234 • Dancing With Trouble

"But won't the people wonder why I am doing this only now? Won't they wonder why officials close to me haven't briefed me, warned me, until now? I find your suggestion intriguing, but I'm afraid it might expose us to ridicule. Anyway, let me think about it."

Rabena and Jamina choose to eat in the center of town. There are usually too many people in the beach area on the weekends and they do not want many interruptions. In fact, sometimes people ask you to join them, not even considering that you might want your privacy.

Rabena and Jamina sit down and order two popular Nigasilian dishes. Each orders a different sauce with rice. One sauce is made with the leaves of the sweet potato plant and the other is made with the leaves of the cassava plant. They both love the dishes cooked with smoked fish and a smattering of beef and pigs' feet. In Nigasilia, this sort of meal is cooked mainly in palm oil. Both Rabena and Jamina know this place, called Lady Jane, very well. It is not too far from Miatta's Place, and its Nigasilian cooking is generally thought to be better.

"So, what has been happening to you?" Rabena asks. "I haven't seen you for a few days now."

"Oh, I have been very busy at school and with the Conservation Society. What about you?"

"Things have been very busy. There have been all kinds of international delegations coming. The only relief I get is when the president travels. Even then, I have to keep track of all the events he will have to attend to the moment he returns. But it's not a problem; it's nothing new."

"Have you heard from your daughter since she went to Cornell?"

"Oh, yes. She is fine. She says that it is beginning to get cold. Poor girl! But she is well prepared. She has bought enough warm clothing."

Rabena then grows serious. "Jamina, advise John to be careful with some of those cabinet ministers. They all appear to warm up to him because his father is the president. Tell him to be careful with the ones he sees always hanging around the vice president or those who address him as Professor. Those are the ones who are jealous of him."

"I tell you, John is aware. He once said to me, laughing, that many who call him Professor are trying to tell him that he is living in the clouds and should come down to earth. John tells me all the time that we in Nigasilia have an anti-intellectual tradition and so people try to make fun of serious intellectuals. He says this disdain of intellectual activity is why intellectual mediocrity usually wins. In fact, he says that when intellectual mediocrity combines with political connections, it always wins. Anyway, thanks for alerting me. I will let him know that he should be careful."

Rabena clarifies further. "Everyone in the party believes we are going to win the next election. The VP is anxious to firm up his base before President Bijunga's second term ends. So he encourages all these wheeler-dealer types." Rabena hesitates. "Also, please advise John to be careful with these young people. He has to make sure they don't cause any trouble. To tell you the truth, it is the president I worry about."

The following day, John and Jamina spend the afternoon together. When Jamina tells him about her lunch with Rabena, John's reaction is simple: "Those rascals, yes, I have known for a long time that they are among those I would like to see toppled from their offices. They are always hanging around the VP, which makes me a bit wary about the man."

"But they are members of the cabinet. There is nothing wrong with them hanging around the VP, no?"

"I don't know; I really don't."

"Do you think the VP likes you?"

"No, but I don't think he dislikes me, either. I do think he is afraid because my dad is listening to me and will continue to do so."

On the social movement idea, John says, "There are all these well-educated people in civil society and business who spend a good part of their day complaining about the lack of electricity, the water situation, the filth, the corruption, and the poor roads. Yet some of them find a way to join the manipulators of the system for their own benefit, including scheming for public sector jobs and contracts. Then there are those who try to stay outside 'the system,' as they call it. Instead of raising their voices in anger, the members of this group fool themselves that they can stay autonomous. Well, very soon they will find out the obvious: they can only run so far from the dominant system. Realistically, to live in this country, you either join the system or you fight it."

As Jamina and John enjoy a post-lunch walk on the beach, they watch three groups of people pulling in the fishing nets. Bringing in a net is always a slow and painful process. But by the time John and Jamina observe them, they are almost done. Then there are the traders who wait to buy and resell and, of course, the odd individuals like John and Jamina who happen to be passing by. Here on Lumpimo Beach, this routine is repeated every day, from the afternoon to evening. Jamina and John watch the first net being pulled up and the contents emptied out. There is not much edible, just lots of jellyfish, for which the locals have no use and simply dump back in the water. The fishermen are deeply disappointed. Jamina and John watch the second and third nets drawn in. The results are the same.

"The fish on these shores are disappearing," Jamina says. "The big trawlers are, indeed, taking everything."

They return to their vehicle and drive to Vivienne's. Jamina had promised to drop by; yesterday, Vivienne had shared the news that she and Santie had decided to get married in January. They figure that the event has to take place in January or early February. Otherwise, they might have to wait until after May at the earliest. Elections will be in April and the campaign period will be tense. Moreover, Easter will fall at the end of March; that means that part of February and the whole of March will be off-limits for weddings, given Lent. They will have the engagement in December. Vivienne has asked Jamina to be her maid of honor.

Vivienne offers John and Jamina drinks. When she returns, Jamina asks Vivienne if she knows the date of the engagement.

"No," replies Vivienne, "Santie has to arrange two or three dates with his parents and then I will talk to my parents and see which is most convenient for them. Santie's side has to find a spokesman to lead the group here. So, in a sense, the spokesman controls the schedule."

"Yes, of course," Jamina responds. She turns to John. "John, do you know what we are talking about? Do you remember how these things are done?"

John confesses that he doesn't. "To tell you the truth, only in theory. I have never observed one myself."

"Not even when you were growing up?"

"Yes, not even then."

"Wow, that's strange."

"I agree."

Jamina explains. "On the day Vivienne and Santie get engaged, you will accompany me here and observe the ceremony. We will shut the door and then the party from the bridegroom's side will arrive at the set time. Accompanying the adults in the visitors' party will be a young girl carrying a colorful calabash on her head. Inside the calabash will be a variety of gifts. First, since the two to be married are Christians, there will be a Bible. Then there will be an engagement ring, a dowry, and a piece of cloth, which is normally about six yards. The dowry these days is always cash and is meant to be symbolic. In addition, inside the calabash there will be a selection of cooking ingredients and sewing items. Typically these are needle and thread, salt, sugar, spicy black peppercorns, ground red pepper, kola nuts, and a small amount of sweet oil. Finally, there will be a selection of coins—kala coins, not foreign coins."

John shakes his head. "Where will Santie be all this time?"

"Santie will not be in the party," Jamina responds. "He will be waiting at home with friends and family for the news that everything went well."

"I see."

"Anyway," Jamina says, "then the visiting party will knock at the door. A spokesman from Vivienne's side will ask what the visitors want and why they think they can find it there. A little later the door will be opened to them. That only happens after the visitors plead that they are looking for a beautiful rose, which they have spotted in this luscious garden. Once the future bridegroom's party enters, they will be presented with a few ladies, young as well as old, one at a time. They will be asked each time if this is the rose they mean. On each such occasion, the visitors will say no and add a few words as to how the rose they want is different. Then, finally, Vivienne will be brought out, and, of course, she will be the rose they have come seeking. Then there will be joyful celebrations and dancing, speeches, and the presentation of the calabash. Vivienne's side will also have gifts for the bridegroom's party and some words in response to the visitors. The gifts of the hosts will include a bottle of rum, a bottle of gin, and some cloth, enough for a fancy shirt."

Awed by the details of the ceremony, John turns to Vivienne. "Are your parents very pleased? Do they know the parents of Santie?"

Vivienne, in her lively manner, says, "These are my parents. If they did not know Santie's parents, they would have sent an investigation team over to check those people out. My parents are too conservative for their own good."

"I like that," John says. "A marriage is a union not only of the two people who get married, but of the two families."

John takes Jamina's hands and pulls her toward him. They embrace as if no one else is present.

On Monday, November 12, John comes to his father's office for a meeting on foreign aid. There will be an aid donors' coordination meeting in the first full week of December, in London, and the president wants John to be part of the delegation, which will be led by the minister of finance and development, Tubo Bangar. The vice president has also been invited to join the three of them at this meeting in the president's office. The minister has drafted a speech to be delivered at the London meeting. Even though John and his staff have commented on the speech, and the minister has taken some of their comments on board, John is really not happy with the general tone.

The speech calls for more aid and pleads to the donors to reduce the delays in the delivery of committed aid flows. John insists that the speech does not build a convincing case that aid money should be directed toward areas where it would make the greatest contribution to the growth of Nigasilia, like education and infrastructure, and away from activities preferred by donors, like decentralization, civil service reform, and logistics for elections. Worst of all, there is nothing in the speech on what Nigasilia plans to do to reduce aid dependence in the near future. In fact, the speech leaves no doubt that such aid dependence will grow over the foreseeable future.

"I just don't understand," John begins, "why we Nigasilians, with our country so rich in natural resources, are not ashamed to beg. We cannot even try to show that we think of such begging as only temporary. It is as if we are stupid, lazy, and incompetent."

Minister Bangar jumps in. "John, we do not have the ability to reduce our aid dependence. We do not have the income, the savings, or the tax revenue, given our huge demand for development finance.

Moreover, this meeting in London will be about the amount and nature of aid—not about aid dependence."

John, blazing mad, considers walking out of the meeting. "Yes, I agree the meeting is not about aid dependence. Yet we must assure our donors that this routine begging will end. Remember, gentlemen, that if we manage our natural resources more efficiently, stop stealing and wasting government resources, focus on the basics in our development strategy, and do what it really takes to attract serious foreign investors, we can increase our investment, productivity, per capita income, saving rate, and tax revenue with far less foreign aid, and we can grow out of foreign aid quickly. But just look around. What serious investor wants to come here? If I were minister of finance and development, I would not enjoy going around the world with my begging bowl pretending I am somebody just because I hold a big position in this miserable God-forsaken country. To tell you the truth, I am not keen on going if that is the speech we are going to deliver."

The president beckons the others to stay quiet. "John," the president says, "do not go to the London meeting. You feel too strongly." The president turns to the vice president and the minister. "Gentlemen, there is nothing more to discuss. Bangar, I am sure if you need any more assistance from John, he will give it to you. I know my son. He has said his piece and it is in good faith."

John and Tubo Bangar had arranged to have lunch the following day and they decide to go to a Lebanese restaurant away from the center of the city, on one of the beautiful hills. After ordering, Tubo says, "So your dad let you off the hook."

"Yes, I hope you will forgive me."

Half-jokingly, Tubo says, "No, you owe me lunch. Not today, some other time."

"So, I have information on three of the boys. The two left are Tureno and Sitenne. I get some information on Tureno tomorrow, when I visit my aunt. Manray is getting information on Sitenne."

"Great. Two of Manray's staff actually came a few days ago and got some data on project requests by the different districts, the recommendations by the minister of local government, and our recommendations. You know we keep all that data here. I did not ask my people to show me what they gave them. But they seemed to have provided the information very quickly and without asking for any special approval. So I assumed it was not anything highly confidential or difficult to collate."

"Do you also keep data on the initial requests by the different villages and towns in the districts?"

"I'm not sure, but if we want it we can get the information from the districts. They are supposed to keep all that information and we have a right on grounds of development planning to request it from them. The minister cannot tamper with it unless his senior professional staff is in cahoots with him."

"Okay. Anyway, Manray and I will be continuing our discussion soon. What Manray found out was that the minister does not report to the districts what projects he sends forward to your department. He only reports back to them what has been approved after the president signs."

"How did he find out this?"

"Well, we want to know if there is some relationship between the success in getting their projects approved and so-called gifts they give the minister of local government. So Manray, who knows so many of the top district officers, called around and asked if they were given reasons why some of their projects were approved and the others not. They each said no. Then he asked if they knew what projects were actually sent forward to the Ministry of Finance and Development. And again they said no."

"Hmm. If your shop needs the help of my people, as you and Manray continue with this investigation, just go ahead and use them. I will instruct them accordingly, especially before I travel."

"Thanks. We will call for enhanced audits of the five ministers, since we know where to look and what to look for. But when I present the evidence, those guys will not want to go through the pain."

"Why not?"

"Because we can make them a good offer. If they simply resign in exchange for light punishment—that is, taking the resignation itself as a punishment—they will not be prosecuted and risk going to jail. If they insist on being thoroughly investigated and all the evidence of the whistle-blowers is officially obtained in a court of law, they would not only be fired but would be sent to jail."

The next day, Wednesday, John drops by to see Auntie Marie on his way home. He has been anxious to actually see her and find out how she is doing. But his cousin Safie has also arranged for him to meet Kadija, a senior registered nurse at General Hospital, and her husband, Wilfred, a pharmacist, working with the largest drugstore chain in the country. Kadija and Safie have been friends since high school days. Auntie Marie and Safie are sitting on the porch chatting when John arrives.

"John," Auntie Marie says as she gets up to embrace John.

"Well, Auntie, I see Dr. Mondeh has been taking good care of you."

"Yes, John, now you can tell Lizzie that you are sure I am making progress."

"Safie, you look well, too."

"Thank you, John. I don't let too many things bother me these days. How is the family—the boys, I mean?"

"Oh, they are well."

Kadija and Wilfred are soon at the gate and Safie gets them and introduces them to John. Auntie Marie knows them already. Kadija gets a beer each for everyone, including Auntie Marie, but mineral water for John, which is his wish.

"Kadija and Wilfred, thanks for coming. I am trying to talk informally to people around who are not simply government bureaucrats, to give me different perspectives on what is going on around here."

John does not want to say directly that he is investigating corruption because he is not sure how willingly Kadija and Wilfred will reveal information.

"My father is trying hard to improve medical facilities. But we don't seem to be making progress in the quality of medical care. When I look at the budget I see a lot of money coming from foreign aid that is spent on health facilities. And yet, if you talk to the doctors, they keep telling you there are not enough drugs, the facilities are not improving, and the pay remains low. My dad is very concerned and, as chief economist, I need to worry about it, too."

"You should talk to the medical people."

"Yes, Wilfred, I intend to talk to the doctors, the nurses, and the pharmacists, as well as the non-medical personnel. I also will talk one-on-one with the minister of health for his perspective. In cabinet, we discuss these issues, but I have been meaning to talk to him over lunch or dinner. What do the medical people think about him, the minster?"

Kadija and Wilfred look at each other and then turn and look at Safie. All three laugh.

"He is not a serious man," Wilfred says.

"What do you mean?"

Wilfred looks at Safie and Kadija.

Safie then says, "Dr. Bijunga . . ."

"Call me John; it's okay."

"John, the man has no shame. You know, General Hospital orders most of the drugs for the government hospitals. In fact, we order through Wilfred's company. The minister and some of the doctors steal the drugs for themselves. The doctors take the drugs for their private patients. In the case of the minister, I really don't know what he does with his own."

"So is he the most corrupt minister you have seen?"

"I have not seen any honest one yet. The one before this was the worst."

"Is it only medicines these people steal?"

"No. This present one has taken for his private use two new refrigerators that were bought for keeping medicines and has registered under his name two SUVs bought for us by one of the aid donors. One of those SUVs he drives himself as his private vehicle. I don't know what he has done with the other one. Look, John, there are so many other corrupt things the man is doing. Just go talk to some of the nonmedical personnel. They will tell you."

John thinks he has enough to work on. He will fill in his logbook as soon as he can.

The following Tuesday, November 20, John and Sanjo Manray meet in a restaurant for lunch. They have been brainstorming on how to put together a corruption case against Kweko Sitenne, the minister of local government. Sanjo has been doing most of the legwork. But he now wants John and his economists to do some statistical analysis for the case.

John wastes no time. "Sanjo, we might have to depend a lot on the whistle-blowers for this one."

"What do you mean?"

"On the statistical analysis, we will have a huge problem, what we economists call an identification problem."

"What is that?" Sanjo asks, in a tone reflecting astonishment.

"Okay, let me try my best to explain. Look at what we have and what we are trying to do. The villages and towns in a district present projects for financing to the district office. The district office examines the projects and helps the villages and towns formulate the requests coherently. The requests are then sent to the Ministry of Local Government, which does further vetting to improve the presentation of the projects and then passes all or some of the requests to the Ministry of Finance and Development. Finance and Development orders the projects in some way, using criteria that we don't need to get into here, and hands their report to the president. The president finally decides on the projects to be approved for financing. So far so good?"

"Yes, John, so far so good."

"Now, you are telling me that the people you have spoken to in the villages and towns have told you that all they know about are the first stage and the last stage of this scenario. In other words, from the time they submit their projects they are in the dark and only see the president's approval list. Am I right?"

"Yes, indeed." Sanjo shakes his head as he waits for John to tell him the problem.

"You are saying that your staff has informed you that the local government minister does not pass on all the projects that come from the districts to Finance and Development. You are saying that he seems to favor localities that give him a lot of presents—animals, land, cloth—when he visits them."

"Yes."

"You have collected data on the gifts and we now have information from Finance and Development on what they received in the past three years from the Ministry of Local Government."

"Yes."

"You feel that, for some localities, the Ministry of Local Government deliberately suppressed some of their best projects and did not pass them on to Finance and Development. That way their projects also suffered in the rankings by Finance and Development."

"Yes, John."

John continues. "So now we want to see if there is a correlation between the value of gifts received and the quality of projects passed on, or even the fraction of projects passed on, from Local Government to Finance and Development, taking into account other factors that could influence the passing-on decision."

"Yes," Manray says. "So you think your economists will uncover the role of the gifts?"

"It is very difficult to be certain. But if we find a strong correlation, after controlling for factors that appear reasonable, we will have a good case. Already you are telling me that you have lined up some whistle-blowers who will attest to the fact that the minister deliberately sabotaged certain localities based on their leaders. Hence, this statistical analysis is only part of our case."

Chapter 10

Santie and Vivienne get married on January 5, 2002. The wedding party is out taking pictures and everyone is waiting for the bride and bridegroom to get to the hall so the big party can begin. John is observing everyone as if he wants to compose an essay, when four youths approach him.

A young lady speaks first. "Dr. Bijunga, good day, sir. My name is Marie Santana. I hope you are enjoying the wedding." She looks around at her friends. They are fidgeting, rubbing their hands and tapping their feet.

John is taken aback, though it is nothing unusual in Nigasilia for strangers who recognize you to greet you so warmly. "Good day to you, Marie. Yes, I enjoyed the ceremony."

"My friends and I want to talk to you about this social movement that you brought up. Of the four of us here, only one was among the graduates, but the rest of us have felt as if you were addressing us as well."

"Well, I'm glad to hear that. The response has been even better than I could have asked for."

Marie continues. "Dr. Bijunga, we want to hear your views on our plans to form a social movement of the sort you discussed in your speech."

John looks at each one of them, wondering why these kids would pick a time like this to discuss such a serious subject.

The young people are a bit nervous because of the serious look on John's face. They are delighted to hear him say, in a pleasant tone, "All right, let us go outside, away from this noise, and let me hear your plans."

The five walk out to some vacant seats outside, somewhat removed from the main flock of merrymakers.

"Gosh," John says, "do these disc jockeys have to play the music that loud? No one is dancing yet. Don't they want people to have civilized conversations?"

The youths look at each other and say nothing; the loudness of the music is just fine with them.

One of the young men speaks up next. "Dr. Bijunga, my name is Moduba Maquita. We are calling our movement Society for the Total Reform of Nigasilian Governance, or STRONG for short. We want good jobs and good pay, yes. But we also want to help our people. We want to see illiteracy reduced in this country. We want to see corruption reduced also. We want to draw up a manifesto and present it to the government. Then we want to organize a mass demonstration with placards that call attention to the Nigasilian people's suffering and their need for relief. We want to demand that the government sit down with us and discuss how it intends to improve the lot of the ordinary people in this country. In fact, we would like to sit down with the president, or at least with the vice president."

"Dr. Bijunga," the second young man jumps in, "my name is Dungu Etter. We plan to set up local branches of STRONG throughout this country. The local branches will do most of the mobilization and the outreach to the population, like you encouraged in your speech. Although we will focus on the young people, we shall also try to appeal to the older people. We believe it is important that the older people support us as well. Then we want to organize workshops, where we discuss issues that bother our people about the way our governments behave and govern our country. We would very much appreciate your advice and leadership, if you have the time."

"Dr. Bijunga, I am Fiatuh Jallowa. We are also concerned about the upcoming elections. We want them to be free and fair. We hope to see equal and fair treatment of all parties during the campaign. For instance, members of the cabinet, especially the vice president, are going about campaigning right now. But they insist they are only making visits as part of their normal course of duty. When the electoral commission announced that elections would be held on April 20th, it also announced that campaigning should not begin until February 1. But I tell you, Dr. Bijunga, everybody knows that the government party, your party, has already started to campaign. We think that is unfair and we intend to lodge a formal protest to the president, and to the chairman of the NEC."

John is shocked to hear that members of his party may be using official trips for the purposes of campaigning. He restrains himself, though, because the young people could be mistaken.

John smiles at each one. He then asks each person to tell him about her or himself. Other than Fiatuh Jallowa, the young people come from very poor families and are the first in their immediate families to graduate from university. All four were born outside of Lamongwe, but as their parents came to Lamongwe when they were very young, they did some primary schooling and all of their secondary schooling here. All four had siblings that died before the age of five from either cholera, measles, or typhoid. The mother of Moduba died during childbirth. Each of them has at least four living siblings. Most of those siblings have very little education, although three of them are currently at university; of the three, two are younger brothers of Fiatuh. They are all in their early twenties and none of them is married or has children. As for their university education, Marie Santana has a degree in English, Fiatuh has her degree in accounting, Moduba received his degree in geography, and Dungu got his degree in sociology. They are all gainfully employed, in the private business sector and the international NGO sector. All four know the bride and groom very well, through church or school alumni associations or extended family connections.

John shakes his head in amazement. "I'm proud of you all for your educational achievements and for what you have done so far in pursuing this social movement idea. I think what you are doing is fine. Your plans are sensible. I shall be very happy to talk to you about your workshops and manifesto. But you will need to tread carefully. Don't go preaching dogma. I would rather you allow people, both within STRONG and those who participate in your workshops, to express their views and make suggestions. STRONG can then come up with some kind of consensus as to the problems it wants the government to address. Look for people who can talk about experiences in other places, especially from countries that have done far better than we have."

John stops to see if the young people want to speak, but they are waiting for John to volunteer more suggestions.

"A problem I see for you is that it is not easy to organize such workshops without money. It would be great if you are able to get international NGOs to help. But without explicit government support for what you are doing, it may not be easy to get such assistance. So, for the time being, you will have to make the sacrifices yourselves. As you mobilize more people to your cause, the burden on each individual will be lighter. Draft your demands for the government. You don't have the technical capability to make suggestions about how the government should go about solving the problems—at least not yet. If your movement attracts technical experts in each of the areas you address, maybe then you will be in a position to suggest solutions."

Fiatuh Jallowa asks, "So, Dr. Bijunga, you like the manifesto idea, am I right?"

"The idea is a good one if you can be precise about the specific areas that you would like the government to improve. You can come up with as many such areas as you like. But let them be important areas, each affecting a broad segment of the population. You should also suggest that the government outline, in each case, what it plans to do and that it spell out some measurable yearly or biannual benchmarks against which to assess progress. It is a good idea to insist, as you suggest, that the government recognize your movement."

"What about demonstrations? Do you think they are a good idea?" Fiatuh asks.

"Yes, if they are orderly. I would rather think of them as marches, though. You should make sure you have large numbers when you organize these marches. And the more national the representation of the marchers, the greater the impression will be on the political leaders. Moreover, don't conduct illegal marches; if the police want to refuse you permits, come and talk to me. Try your best not to lose control of STRONG. Don't allow rabble-rousers to penetrate it. If you do, the movement will lose credibility."

The wedding party has arrived and the members are about to get out of their limousines and enter the hall, so John and the four young adults quickly return to their tables. The master of ceremony picks up his microphone, beckons to the disc jockey to stop the music, and calls out selected family members and sponsors who wish to dance down the aisle. After the dancers reach the MC, they turn around and return to their various tables. When that segment of the celebration is over, the MC stops the music again to announce the entrance of the newlyweds and the rest of the wedding party. Everyone stands. As the wedding party enters, the disc jockey starts the music and the newlyweds and the rest of the wedding party begin to dance, as they proceed down the aisle toward their table. The newlyweds take their seats at the high table and the party proceeds with prayer, the cutting of the cake, the meal, and the toasts. This is all followed by dancing, snacks, and more drinks.

When the dancing and the merriment reach their apogee, the music suddenly stops. The MC announces it is time for those with gifts to bring them up to the newlyweds. As the line begins to form, John wonders how this tradition emerged.

Earlier, in church, he had observed a related ritual. The newlyweds were each given a big tray. Then, while chanting religious folk tunes, the people in the congregation and the choir came up to the couple and deposited money in one or both of the trays. Towards the end of the church service, the person who attracted the greater amount was announced the winner.

At the time, John had turned to the guest sitting next to him. "To whom does all that money go?"

"It goes to the priest and the church."

"But three priests officiated. Do they share it four ways, with one part going to the church? On top of that, the offertory was meant for the church. I think this money goes to the priests."

"I believe you are right, sir."

"In which case, I suspect the priest of the church will keep most of the money. After all, he gets to count it first."

The man said nothing in response. Luckily, the organ was by then playing loudly.

Now, in the reception, as a number of guests line up to bring their gifts up to the bride and groom, John walks out of the reception hall to get some fresh air. He notices that leftover food on guests' plates is being poured into plastic containers and handed to some boys outside on the street. The boys are casually and somewhat raggedly dressed. They are clearly not among the wedding guests, but they do not look unusual in any other respect. He turns to one of the guests outside to make sure that his suspicion is correct, because the reality seems painful. "What do those boys want to do with all that leftover food?"

"They are going to eat it all themselves," the guest replies.

John nods solemnly, but cannot stop thinking of what Fiatuh Jallowa told him about the VP. So he returns to the party and walks straight up to her as she chats with her friends.

"Fiatuh, can I have a quick word with you?"

They walk outside again, after Fiatuh says good-bye to her friends.

"Sorry I had to distract you from the party," John says.

"Dr. Bijunga, it's no problem. I was going to leave soon anyway. I have to do some accounting work for my father this evening."

"Oh, what does your father do?"

"He runs a security company, Complete Security."

"I've heard of that company."

"My father is part owner."

"Anyway, what I wanted to ask you was who told you about the VP's trip. When was it, where, and did they tell you what he did?"

"Oh, I witnessed most of it myself. I think it was the second Saturday in December. Yes, it was December 8. Anyway, it was at Newtown. My father, two of our senior security staff, and I were visiting our office at Watabom, which oversees the security operations of all the small towns in that neighborhood. Our business is picking up fast in that area and we are determined to dominate the market there."

Watabom is just twenty-five miles from Lamongwe. Newtown is just three miles from Watabom travelling eastward. John stays quiet, because he wants Fiatuh to finish her story.

"So when we heard that the VP was coming to Newtown and he was going to have a rally with some of the youth there, the others in our team wanted to see what was going on. We all know the soccer field where he was holding the rally."

"From the time I was growing up that soccer field was already there. Anyway, what happened?"

"We were lucky we arrived just at about the same time the VP was arriving. They were playing music. There were two pickup trucks which accompanied him, with several young people sitting in the trucks. Then there were two police vehicles, with about, maybe, ten policemen. The VP came in an SUV that did not look very official. There was also a loud speaker. He came down and used the loud speaker. Then as he was speaking another big truck came with a lot of T-shirts with your party's colors and logo, which they distributed there. My father and the other people in our team think there were around five hundred young people there, almost all of them boys. Some of them must have come from some distance away for so many of them to be there. I wondered why they were willing to come. I saw all of them going home with T-shirts."

"So it was a rally, just like a political campaign rally. What did the VP say in his speech?"

"The VP said a lot of things about the country, about how the present government was doing its best to improve the lives of the common people, and about how concerned your party is about the youth of Nigasilia. Then he said that if the opposition party wins the coming elections the youth will suffer far more than they are suffering now."

"Was that it?"

"Oh, I forgot to mention that they also served some snacks in small packages. I saw only the Coke, water and other soft drinks."

"What about kala?"

"No, I did not see them distribute any money. But I am not really sure."

"Okay, thanks, I appreciate your time. Good luck with STRONG."

"Thanks, Dr. Bijunga."

On the Tuesday following the wedding, the vice president calls John to his office. The VP has heard from cabinet ministers who are worried about John's objectives to have so-called corrupt and inept public officials run out of public service. These cabinet ministers had friends at the wedding reception who overheard the youths talking amongst themselves after their conversation with John.

"John," the VP begins, "I gather you recently gave advice to some young people who are setting up an organization that would give the government ultimatums based on your social movement idea. I have also noticed you have become very friendly with the minister of finance and development; I hear you have advised him to audit certain ministries and transactions of the government. Is this correct?"

John is delighted that the VP has heard these things. "Mr. Vice President," John replies, "I don't know exactly what you have been told, but everything you just said is true. The youths described their plans to me and asked for my advice, which I gave to them. Every piece of advice was consistent with my commencement speech and the conversations I have had with you. I told them to eschew violence and to prevent rabble-rousers from taking over their organization."

"What is this about auditing certain ministries?"

"I want the Ministries of Education, Lands and Country Planning, Local Government, Health, and Works, Housing and Infrastructure audited, focusing on the five ministers. I also would like to see the Customs Department, Ports Authority, and National Revenue Authority undergo the same scrutiny, but these can wait. I am now focusing on the ministers. We need to help implement the zero tolerance of corruption policy of this government and I would hope that you would be one of those pleased at the prospect of making sure everyone is abiding by the rules."

The ministers involved are all boys in the VP camp, the ones who call John "Professor" as a sign of contempt, and who tell their staff that they are not interested in any advice coming from John's department. John, Mahdu Kontana, Dumomo Frah, Sanjo Manray and Tubo Bangar have been collecting preliminary evidence and lining up the whistle-blowers, to ease the job of the Ministry of Finance and Development in organizing the audits if necessary.

"John, I was one of those who ardently pushed for the zero-tolerance policy to be put in our party's agenda."

After a brief pause, John, looking straight at the VP, says, "Mr. VP, since you have shared what you have heard about me, may I tell you what I have heard about you?"

The VP is clearly shaken. "Go ahead, John."

"I heard that you went on a trip a few days ago and organized a rally in an open field under the pretense that you had gone to open the field so the youths could play football. Mr. Vice President, if that is not political campaigning, I don't know what is. And you know that campaigning is not yet allowed." Then John, without waiting for the VP to react, tells what Fiatuh had told him.

The VP is surprised that John has all that information in such detail. He cannot hide his embarrassment. "So I got carried away. I am dedicated to my party."

"Mr. Vice President, where did all that money come from? And I mean for the gifts, the fuel, the tips to the boys who accompanied you, and for the trucks, which you most likely rented, except if they were government trucks, which would be another problem for the party."

"John, the vice president is entitled to official travel and entertainment allowances. Also, the party T-shirts are financed by the party."

"The money did not come from your office budget. It came out of miscellaneous expenditure on emergency travel and supplies."

"So that's what you and the minister of finance and development have been doing."

"Yes, we are trying to keep everybody transparent, aboveboard, and properly accountable; remember we have zero tolerance for corruption, which you support."

"Your minister friend gets on my nerves. He thinks he is the pope."

"If you pick a fight with him, you will be picking a fight with me as well."

"John, be sensible. You have a future in this party. If I win the nomination when your father's second term ends, I would consider you very seriously as a vice-presidential choice. Don't waste your time defending that fellow."

"I appreciate your confidence, but unless things change around here, I would not be interested in continuing as a member of this party after my father leaves office."

After a brief moment of silence, John continues. "Mr. Vice President, since you are interested in the youth, here is a piece of advice. The next time you address them, please carefully explain what our government intends to do and when. Tell them what we plan to do to improve the teaching of science and mathematics and to alleviate the overcrowding in the classroom. Second, there is the big area of technical and vocational education and training; we need to rebuild the formal system almost from scratch. Please tell the young people what we plan to do and when. Third, we have serious issues in the area of organized sports. Football and track and field activities are disorganized and our standards have gone down; that's why our performance at the international level has been woeful. The young people are tired of watching their national team lose in football, or their representation at the Olympic Games confined to two or three bad athletes accompanied by a dozen or more officials who go along for the ride."

"All right, John, I think we have had enough for today."

Later that day, the VP calls on the president. "My worry is that John is too innocent about the reality in this country. In the process he may be undermining you, his own father. He could also damage the prospects of the party in the coming elections."

"Kamake, I don't think John is as innocent as you say. Anyway, he has been open about his criticism. I think, in fact, the people will credit me for allowing my son to speak so freely about what is going on. As far as I know, and tell me if I am wrong, John has not even one time blamed me or this government as being directly responsible for the ills of this country."

"Don't you think people will begin to ask what we have done to cure those ills?"

"If we cannot answer that question in our favor, then maybe we deserve to lose the election. So, let's think about the answer. You are spearheading our strategy. Go do some thinking so that we can have a coherent answer. Is that all you want to talk to me about?"

"No, I also want to talk about your minister of finance and development. You have to be careful with Tubo. He is spreading word that we are misclassifying certain expenditures. Now he and your son seem to be ganging up on us, calling for special auditing of certain ministries and statutory bodies."

"Well, Kamake, are we misclassifying certain expenditures? If the ministries and statutory bodies are specially audited, nothing out of the ordinary would be discovered if they have been clean, so what is the problem?"

"These are sensitive times. Elections are coming up. We do not want the newspapers going around printing that we are doing special audits."

"Kamake, I would not worry about that if I were you. But I would worry about giving people the impression that we have begun our campaign before the official date designated by the electoral commission. I am sure you will use your good judgment to prevent any questions as to our deep commitment to maintaining the principles of equal treatment of, and fairness to, all parties throughout this election."

The VP is taken aback but he is determined not to be on the defensive.

"You are right, Samuel. I shall caution our people not to violate such a paramount principle in our drive towards having a peaceful election."

Returning to his office, the vice president immediately telephones the minister of finance. "Tubo, can I talk to you for a few minutes?"

"Yes, VP."

"Have you been going around telling people that I am getting you to misclassify my expenditures? What is all that about? What expenditure did I tell you, the minister of finance, how to classify? We have rules for classifying expenditures. And you are supposed to know the rules and even more so your professional staff. So why would I instruct you on what to do? Also, what is this enhanced audit of five ministries that you are supposed to be steering?"

Tubo listens without interruption then says, "Sir, John was the only person I told about your misclassification, because it is a misclassification. If you now want the right classification, please send me a memo. As you know, I wondered about your classification, but I did not bring it up to the president because I did not feel like embarrassing you."

"Tubo wait. What do you mean?"

"Well, you went and talked to the youth in Newtown, and you told me that it was to give a presentation to the youth, to inspire them and get them to compete without disorder and fighting in their matches. But some people say that you went there to promote our party and that the way you conducted yourself you were actually campaigning. As regards the audits, John has raised doubts about certain transactions within the five ministries concerned and, indeed, their decision-making processes. He and I have discussed his concerns and I believe they merit serious investigation. You have a choice. We can move on, inform the president about what we plan to do, and do it quietly. Otherwise, we can have a cabinet meeting on the issue."

"Why can't you just drop the whole thing?"

"I would rather resign. And when I resign I shall tell the whole world why I did."

Two days later, the five ministers who could be audited drop by to see John. John and his minister friends have been accumulating evidence against the five ministers, and whistle-blowers have been lined up to give evidence in case there is an exhaustive inquiry. Following telephone conversations with each of the ministers, John sent them details of his evidence against them. He gave them the choice of resigning or having him send the information to whomsoever he chooses, including the president. Hence, they asked him for an audience.

Of the five ministers, the minister of health, Sambana Tureno, is the greatest disappointment as far as John is concerned. This fifty-year-old man is a medical doctor, having specialized in gynecology and obstetrics. Everyone thinks of him as brilliant. But somewhere along the way he lost his sense of responsibility. His wife is also a doctor but they are now estranged because he has fathered a child with a lady in her thirties. He has one child with his wife, a beautiful daughter, who is in university studying biology. Tureno's family has been steeped in politics since independence. But his father, who was a minister in a previous government, left office to avoid corruption charges. John is surprised that the brilliant Tureno learnt nothing from his father's experience.

The other major disappointment is the works, housing, and infrastructure minister, Maigo Bang, no relation to Nathan Bang, the schoolmate of John who is married to the German lady. A trained civil engineer and a silent partner in a successful engineering consultancy firm, the fifty-two-year-old has known John for some time. On one occasion, when John was on a visit to Nigasilia, he met Maigo at a friend's reception. Among other subjects that came up was the ways in which high-level corruption in Nigasilia manifests itself. Maigo volunteered information on his engineering firm's experience with such corruption. At that time, Maigo explained how they had lost bids for government contracts purely because of corruption. Now, being on the other side of the bidding process, it appears that Maigo is practicing exactly what he had condemned.

The other three ministers belong to a group of individuals that John is highly suspicious of when it comes to handing out ministerial posts. They are below the age of fifty, have no real money to begin with, and come from relatively unknown families—hence no reputation to protect. The minister of local government, Kweko Sitenne, and the minister of lands and country planning, Mansa Sanara, both had illiterate parents, who combined peasant farming with small-scale market trading. Sitenne, who grew up in Lamongwe, recently told John that he used to study under streetlights, because the one-room house in the compound where he lived had no electricity. Those were the days when electricity supply in Lamongwe was much better than it has been for the last two decades.

The minister of education, Budayo Kontine, was somewhat luckier. His mother was an elementary school teacher. But he was born out of wedlock and still doesn't know his father. His mother came from a very poor family. At least she was literate and paid attention to Budayo's education. Budayo has a doctorate in educational psychology and taught for a short time at the university level before entering politics. John has been told that Budayo goes around bragging that he will become rich sooner rather than later.

Jamina dropped in just before the ministers were due to come. John liked the coincidence and so did not try to send Jamina away. When the ministers enter, John greets them. "Gentlemen, I hope you do not mind Jamina being around."

"Look, John, have her around," Budayo responds. "If you don't mind her here, we don't. Right, fellows?"

The minister of education gets down to the problem quickly. "John, what do you want from us?"

None of the men is sitting down. John is leaning rather casually against his desk. Budayo has both hands folded behind his back, head raised high, feet astride. His anger is visible, his eyes wildly open. The others are pacing as if to calm themselves.

"All I am asking is for an audit and an investigation of the charges I have accumulated against you. I believe that you gentlemen will want your names cleared if you are innocent. Otherwise, we will make sure that the newspapers have the necessary information."

There is silence. John decides to break the tension.

"The question is, are you clean? There are plenty of hungry people out there waiting for your jobs. So, it's a simple bargain that we need to strike. The president will order an investigation into your performance. If illegal activities are uncovered, they will be made public and you will be fired. If nothing comes out of the investigation, your stars will shine. My own view, for what it is worth, is that if you are guilty of corruption you should resign. There is no need to drag the party and the country through a traumatic process when you know you are guilty. But worse than that, if you do not resign on the basis of the limited evidence that I will present, and we have to do a formal investigation, including audits, you will be prosecuted in the courts and you could end up in jail, in addition to losing your jobs. I would like you to know that I have more evidence that I will present in the cabinet paper. Also, we have a line of whistle-blowers whose evidence will come at the trials, if we go ahead with those."

The health minister interjects. "In the meanwhile, we are innocent until proven guilty, right?"

"Of course," John replies.

The minister of lands and country planning is boiling inside. "John, did we do anything against you for you to hate us?"

"I have come to believe that you are doing things that make the common people hate us all. Your actions keep our country backward so that I cannot raise my head in the global community and say with pride that I am of Nigasilian origin. My country is considered close to dirt in the world out there, thanks to poor governance by people like you. In my view, poor leadership in Africa should be considered a capital crime. Prove me wrong. Show me that you have been honest and good leaders in your ministries."

The minister of health has had enough. "Okay, so let the audits and investigations proceed, if the president wants them. Then we shall go from there. I don't care, at the end of the day, what you, John, think of me. As far as I am concerned, you can go to hell."

John does not want the incident to boil over into a physical confrontation. So he remains still, but bursts out nevertheless.

"*You* will go to hell," John replies. "What have you done with all the money you and your collaborators earned selling stocks of medicines in the black market? Those medicines were supposed to be sold at subsidized prices to the poor. Now the poor people are mostly given prescriptions and asked to go buy the medicines in the market. You and your collaborators have stolen refrigerators ordered for health services. You have given contracts to your friends to build clinics in small towns. Many of these have not been built or have been built so poorly that they have had to be condemned. You are using health department SUVs, many of them acquired through foreign aid, for your private use. Where do you think *you* will end up?"

"That's it; I have had enough," Maigo bursts out in anger, and he and the others barge out of the room.

John turns to Jamina. "Well, how did it all go?"

"Better than I expected. I can see that you wanted me to be here to limit the vileness of the language."

"Yes, I did not want us heaping insults at each other. I think as far as that goes, I succeeded. But we are all playing games. These guys are not afraid of being exposed for what they have done. They expect the VP to find a way to protect them. But they also know that the information I have is real and powerful and that I can use it when and where I want to. The more the general public finds out, the less able the VP will be to protect them. That will make them careful in their future behavior, even if I am not able to force them to resign right now."

"I see your point."

"But I have to find a way not to lose this battle. If I do, I will lose heart, because the four of us have spent so much time trying to put together the evidence against these fellows and to line up whistle-blowers. If I lose this battle, my fear is that I may start to lose heart. The hill would seem too difficult to climb. I fear that I may simply wake up one day and say to hell with it all."

"You are giving up already, John? You knew from the outset that this was a high mountain to climb."

"Yes, but not Everest. I don't have enough energy or patience for that climb. Sometimes I feel like screaming."

"Really, my dear, screaming?" Jamina places her hands over her ears and opens her mouth. They burst out laughing. They are both thinking of the famous late nineteenth-century painting of Edvard Munch.

"It's a hard climb," Jamina admits, "but it is not a nightmare. Stay with Everest."

John and Jamina are hungry and decide to have dinner in a Lebanese restaurant close to Jamina's place. Official campaigning begins February 1, some three weeks away, and John is already worried. As they settle down to dinner, he says to Jamina, "You know, the VP's office has become the command center for the upcoming elections. My dad has given the VP charge of organizing our campaign strategy and I am not so sure that the VP is planning on operating according to rules of the Election Commission and the law in general."

"What do you mean?"

"Well, I don't want our party to harass the opposition at their rallies. We also have a huge amount of money in the budget for so-called logistics. The bulk of that money is purportedly for financing operations at polling stations, transporting equipment, and for security. But much of it could be diverted to 'helping' our campaign," John says rather sarcastically, signaling the quotation marks as he mentions the word 'helping.' "The plain truth is that I don't trust the VP. He has been too long in politics in this country. All those types are dirty players. But the truth is I don't have firsthand evidence yet of what the VP is planning."

"John, you have been away too long. This is Nigasilia. Both parties will have their rabble-rousers organized to interrupt the other's rallies. There will be fighting; many people will get seriously hurt. That's how we practice democracy here. We have all come to accept that. What we try to control is the extent of the fighting and the casualties. Over time, I am sure things will improve. But for now, that's our country."

"I do realize that with education, rising per capita incomes, and greater maturity in the practice of democracy, things will improve. Yet, even with our low incomes and low education, I don't like that history you just repeated. We can do better. I also know my dad is determined to stop that rut. I need to find a way to help him achieve that. I would like to help make sure that my dad achieves his objective of having his party set a good example. We call ourselves the Nigasilian Progressive Party. We should live up to our name. We can set the tone. If we do not disrupt the opposition party in their campaigning, the opposition will itself behave better. In fact, if we set a good example, the people will support a clampdown by the police if the opposition misbehaves."

"So, have you discussed all this with your father?"

"Yes."

"And what did he say?"

"He said he was going to do everything possible to prevent violence. But he also said that the opposition believes in violence. I asked him if using the police was not enough. That's where he becomes fuzzy. He thinks the opposition will taunt the police until they use clubs on them and then the opposition will complain of police brutality. So he says we should also line up our militants to confront those of the opposition. But he is adamant that we should not provoke the violence. For him, our militants are nothing but a deterrent."

"Is that not a reasonable approach?"

"No, because we may not—indeed, we will not—be able to control our militants. You see, we have rabble-rousers inside the cabinet and they will goad our militants into aggressive actions against the opposition."

John becomes fidgety, scratching his head. He is clearly tired of arguing. Jamina says nothing, just looking at him. John decides to change the subject. "Were Vivienne and Santie able to come to an agreement on the house they want to rent?"

"Yes, they had to talk to the owner who lives in the UK, because the agent here was not sure the owner was willing to come down that much. You know, those people have not had good experience with tenants. The last one not only was slow in paying the rent and left with three months unpaid, but also caused severe property damage. Those poor people have had to spend thousands of pounds in repairs. You know, renting a house has become a pain in this country. If you build a nice modern house, the only tenants worth considering are staffs of embassies, major international NGOs, and multinational firms. Even among those, one sometimes gets reckless tenants."

"So you do not plan to be a landlady yourself?"

"No. If I have money I shall find other forms of investment."

Jamina pauses and smiles at John. "My mother is asking me if there is anything special you want to eat when you visit. I have told her that you are easygoing and will eat whatever they normally eat. But she still called me this morning. I have been forgetting to ask you. So, do you want anything special?"

"Yes, I want deer meat."

"Venison? Are you serious?"

"I can't remember the last time I had venison in Nigasilia."

"Wow, I'll ask her. But I can't promise. Deer are not native to that part of Nigasilia. My dad hunts, but when he does, those aren't one of the animals he brings back. Anyway, if you are really serious they will get it for you."

"No, I am not serious. But here's a serious request. I would like fish stew, using freshwater fish."

"*That*, they can get for you."

The next day is very busy for John. Apart from his normal work, representatives from STRONG made an appointment to see him and discuss their activities and achievements so far. Seven STRONG members arrive at John's office in the late afternoon. Three of them, Fiatuh Jallowa, Marie Santana, and Moduba Maquita, he had met already at the wedding of Vivienne and Santie. The other four, a woman and three men, are introduced to him for the first time. Gabie Manray, the nephew of the minister of tourism and cultural affairs and the young man leading the team, starts the discussion.

"Dr. Bijunga, we are very grateful that you have agreed to see us. We thought it would be good for us to get your reactions on what we have accomplished and what we plan to do. As we indicated in our brief discussion at the wedding, we have decided to form an association. We want it to be run efficiently. Hence we have gone through the trouble of forming an executive committee, of which I am the chairman. We are still struggling over the constitution. So far, we have simply drafted objectives and procedures so that we can operate in an orderly manner."

John, folding his hands in front of him and leaning back in his chair, inquires about the background of the four new STRONG members. They all have bachelor degrees. Gabie Manray has his degree in chemistry; Bobbo Sabu, nephew of Raboya Bami of the Chamber of Commerce, studied history. The other two are Mamia Bayan, a young lady who studied economics, and Basie Belonga, who studied political science. Interestingly, they are all secondary school teachers at the moment, though none plans to remain in teaching much longer. They are all in their mid-twenties. Mamia Bayan comes from the chiefdom of Jamina's father, and Basie Belonga is the son of a well-known medical doctor in Nigasilia.

John unfolds his hands and grabs the arms of his chair. "Very interesting; I am pleased to meet you. I am happy to see that all of you setting the pace here are good examples for the youth."

"Dr. Bijunga," Mamia Bayan says, "most of our work depends on volunteers but we collect membership contributions and have a bank account. Our treasurer is one of our older members and is a chartered accountant. Already we have organized town meetings where we have raised issues with the people to fully understand their main concerns. We have also discussed with the people what they would like to see the government do, how they think we should petition the government, and how the government should be held accountable."

Basie Belonga jumps in. "People are unhappy with the way our democracy is working. They say we have elections but we end up with poor leaders. They don't understand what is wrong with us. They say the politicians don't seem to care about the people who elected them. People tend to agree with your advice in the commencement speech. They want annual explicit targets set and a way to punish the government for not meeting those targets. We are going to draft a manifesto, as you already know. In that manifesto, we will state that all the Nigasilian governments have failed to significantly improve the lives of the people since independence."

Basie pauses, as if expecting John to say something. But John does not know what the young people want him to say.

Mamia Bayan takes over again. "Then we are going to follow your leadership and state that we believe the governments have failed because of poor economic policies, traceable mainly to poor political leadership and corruption. Dr. Bijunga, what kind of indicators should we list and what kind of targets should we have and how do we put pressure on the government to meet those targets? We plan to ask for a meeting with the president in which we will present him with a copy of our manifesto. But it is to Parliament that we want to organize a big march to make a formal presentation, with journalists present."

John looks rather pensive and is uncertain how to respond appropriately. But he knows he must say something encouraging to his visitors, who are looking to him for leadership.

"What you need are socio-economic indicators of the sort used in the Human Development Report of the United Nations Development Programme. In addition, you must say something about economic growth and real per capita income. Real per capita income growth is the most important socio-economic variable, as it helps improve the others."

Bobbo Sabu, the vice chairman, turns to John. "Dr. Bijunga, we are also concerned with the upcoming elections. We want the whole process to be free and fair—that is, the campaigning, the voting, and the ballot counting. We want to demand that STRONG be allowed to have election observers at the polling stations and at the tabulation exercise. If we are denied, we plan to demonstrate. We shall make our demands at the State House, at the Parliament, and with the National Election Commission. We have already sent letters to all the major embassies and international organizations represented in Nigasilia, spelling out our demands and asking for assistance in pressuring the government to accede. We do not want the reporting of the campaigns over the government radio and television stations to be biased toward the government party. We do not want government funds being used to finance the campaigns of the government party members. We do not want ballot stuffing on polling day."

Bobbo stops talking and they all now look at John with great expectation.

"Well," John begins, "I have nothing but praise for what you have been doing. I just hope that you are doing your best to have wide representation of educated youth from all over the country. Be impeccable in your actions. Don't encourage any type of corruption in your organization. Shun violence. That will be the biggest challenge that you face if you organize protests. There is an enormous population of uneducated and disaffected youth in this country. Don't give them an excuse to riot and loot. If you want to protest, get the police to assist you in maintaining order and don't tolerate any youth who are likely to demonstrate disorderly behavior."

The young people wonder why John is ignoring their demand to be observers. What John is saying, he has said to them before. Why is he going in circles? They are turning and looking at each other, and John suddenly realizes that he has not responded appropriately.

"As far as the elections are concerned, don't be too upset if you are not extended observer status. Make a list of your concerns and present them to the international observers. If you have any evidence of wrongdoing or foul play before or during the elections, collate the facts as you see them and present them to the international observers."

The young people do not comment. John knows he has just said what the youth did not want to hear, and decides to steer their talk in another direction. "How are the chiefs and village headmen reacting to your activities?"

"So far, they have been courteous," Bobbo says. "They think of us as not bad as long as the respected young people in their towns and villages welcome us. But they have, without exception, told us not to 'bring trouble.' They have informants keeping track of our movements. We have decided to stay away from local government issues. That way, the chiefs and headmen think we are on their side in trying to get the central government to improve the lot of their people. We also have let them know that, as a group, we do not favor any party. We stay officially neutral. Each individual in our organization decides which political party he or she wants to support. We do not encourage partisan debates in our meetings."

"Good," John says. "What about the female youth? How active are they in your organization?"

Fiatuh Jallowa speaks first. "Well, in terms of participation in workshops, women are not very active outside of Lamongwe. But things are improving in the bigger towns. Three out of the nine executive members of STRONG are women, including me and Marie Santana, whom you met at the wedding. I am the program coordinator, which is the busiest portfolio. I can do it because I work with my father, as I told you at the wedding. I help keep the books for the company. I want to ultimately complete my chartered accountancy. As our chairman told you, I do not keep the books of STRONG. We thought it would be good to have a full-fledged chartered accountant do it, since we are involved in fund-raising and need to build our reputation."

Gabie Manray steps in. "Dr. Bijunga, to add to that, STRONG itself, I believe, will be a small organization, even if most of the young people end up participating in our programs. The reason I believe so is that the educated youth of this country will be restricted by their jobs. If you work for the government or state enterprises, for example, it will be hard to actively participate in our group."

John agrees. "Many employers will dissuade their workers from participating in what they will no doubt see as camouflaged political activity."

"Exactly, sir."

"How do you raise funds apart from membership fees?"

"Many small businesses, especially those owned by foreigners, are willing to help us," Gabie explains. "But normally they want to do so without letting anyone know about it. Three of them even lend us their old vehicles when we ask, although we travel mainly by regular public transport. In addition, we go around to the older Nigasilians, especially those who lived abroad for a number of years. Many of them are willing to support us. We give them evidence of our income and expenditures, so they know we keep accounts. That is why we have a middle-aged chartered accountant as our treasurer, and we have opened a bank account as well."

"I see that you are doing the right things. Well, that pleases me. Now you have to make sure that things do not degenerate. You plan to pressure government to improve its governance. Hence, you must be a good example yourself."

At home that night, John finds it difficult to go to sleep. He is excited at the prospect of the upcoming trip tomorrow with Jamina to see her parents. He was disappointed he was not able to meet them over the summer.

Then he starts thinking about all the troubling issues in his life here in Nigasilia. His work in the office is progressing reasonably well, although he would like to have achieved more by now. If he was trying to do research for a book on the nature of poor governance in Nigasilia, then he would be doing a wonderful job. But he is here to propel the Nigasilians to improve governance. And there it is not easy to move fast. Maybe he should be more proactive in encouraging open discussions and debate at the national level on what it takes to improve governance. John is particularly worried about implementation. So they can establish rules and design policies, but how should they organize themselves to implement the rules and the policies? How can implementation be assured? Economists talk about incentives and about compensating those who will lose out once the right rules and policies are instituted. But what incentives do you give those who are simply afraid to give up their privileged positions?

John also worries that too many of his party members may not really care how they win the next election, so long as people do not get hurt in riots and clashes. What can he do to ensure a civilized and fair election process?

Then his thoughts turn to STRONG. John wonders whether he really knows what those young people are doing. How much should John encourage them? Are they going to use his name in begging for money or in convincing other youth to join them? What if others who are not as educated or committed to good governance use these workshops to start a riot? Can the sensible members control them? The STRONG membership is small and the potential hooligan group is so large.

As John thinks about all these issues, he slowly dozes off. After a while he begins to dream. He sees a beautiful lady in a lovely pink dress. She beckons for him to sit near her. Then he notices that he is in his house in Arlington, Virginia, and that the lady is Cecilia, his first wife.

"Cecilia? Is that you?"

Cecilia begins to speak. "John, you look unhappy. Why? Our sons are doing well. Jamina is beautiful. She has the qualities of gentleness, patience, and understanding that will make her a great mother to the boys. And she will support you the same way I did. Go ahead, John,; ask her to marry you. I want you to be happy. Go on; live your life. There is no reason for you to be so unhappy, no reason at all."

Chapter 11

It's a long drive to Jamina's parents' town. John sleeps for most of the first hour. When he opens his eyes, he caresses Jamina's hand gently. He suddenly releases it, embarrassed that the driver may be watching via his rearview mirror. He gazes out the window and retreats into a reflective mood. He enjoys driving through the countryside. The terrain, as always, delights him but there are just too many destitute people along these two-lane roads.

"It is as if no one thinks that the traffic is going to demand wider roads. It's a small country with a small population; all this talk of African unity will not change that. Of course, if only these idiots who run the country could get their act together, Nigasilia could be a place where people around the world come for holidays, or even where they reside in order to avoid heavy taxes on their earnings elsewhere. Look at all those places in the Middle East and the Caribbean to which people rush. What do they have? Nigasilia has everything except desert. And who needs desert, except when petroleum or minerals are underground?"

Jamina has been listening. "Yes, dear, you are right."

"I am right about what?"

"Nigasilia can be a magnet for retirees and can entice people who want to use it as a tax shelter."

"Well, I hope that does not include criminals."

"You mean drug traffickers?"

"Yes, and money launderers, too."

After a little less than four hours on the road, they reach their destination. Jamina's mother steps outside and hugs Jamina and then John. "Welcome, welcome. I hope the drive was not too difficult." The fifty-eight-year-old fair-skinned lady smiles just like Jamina, who in turn looks just like her. Mrs. Tamba is also small in body and speaks with a hoarse tone, leaving the impression that she is straining her voice when she speaks. She was once a school teacher like Jamina. Born in the north of Nigasilia, quite some distance from Wombono chiefdom, she worked in Lamongwe after her education at a teacher's training college. She met her husband in that city through the friendship of the two families. Her father was a very successful businessman and his lawyer was Chief Tamba's father.

"We did have to slow down in a few places because of these podas that were stopping to pick people up or drop them off," Jamina responds. "You know, we actually saw the long side door of one of the vehicles fall off. The assistant simply got off, picked up the door, and hung it again, and they were on their way. Things are deteriorating, Mamma. It's as simple as that."

"Yes, I agree."

"Where is Papa?"

"He is out; he'll return soon. Let's go in. I'll get the boys to bring your bags in. John, I'm pleased to meet you. We were so sorry to miss you when you and your boys came to this area. I hope they are doing fine."

"Yes, Mrs. Tamba, they are doing fine. I was also sorry to miss you both then. I am very happy to meet you."

Jamina gently butts in. "Mamma, I brought some fish and shrimps for you in the cooler. Let them not forget to return the cooler to the vehicle. It is John's and he uses it when he travels."

"John, how is work?"

"Not bad, Mrs. Tamba. You know, things are not easy around here. But I am adjusting. I have no alternative but to adjust."

"Well, don't adjust too much. We want you to help make things better. I'm sure your father will support you. You will find out when you talk to the people around here that everyone is complaining. My husband is tired of saying to people that the present government is doing its best and that it found things in a terrible state when it took over."

"Yes, my daddy tries his best to support me. But I try not to complain to him about every problem I have. As for the complaints of the people, he hears about them, too. He is sure that he is doing his best and hopes the people will come to appreciate his efforts in due course. He is determined to improve the situation."

They move from the living room to the veranda for some fresh air. Not long after, Chief Jawana Tamba comes home and embraces Jamina warmly.

"John, I am pleased to meet you. Sorry about missing you last time. The timing of the conference was just unfortunate for me."

"Chief, I understand. I am delighted to meet you, too."

"I hope everything is going well. Jamina talks about you all the time. She says you work very hard. How are the boys? I hope they enjoyed their summer stay here."

"Chief, things are moving, although I hope they will move much faster. My sons had a wonderful time when they were here. Your daughter she has been so good to me. She is like a rock to me, my biggest supporter."

When they settle down on the veranda, Chief Tamba asks, "So, John, what do you want to see move faster?"

"Chief, in two words, economic governance. And by that I mean not only improving the policy design but even more importantly, the implementation of the policies."

"So then what do we need?"

"Leadership and cooperation, Chief."

"Yes, we all talk about leadership and that's what elections are all about, deciding on the leadership of the country. How do you think we are doing in that area?"

"Well, my father is the leader, so maybe I should be careful what I say here. But really, when I talk about leadership I am talking about the top leadership in all areas of our society—government, business, and civil society organizations. We need to have rules, processes, and organizational arrangements that enable us to give power only to those who want change and are able to initiate and manage change throughout the society for the economic development of the country as a whole. Of course, we all have to agree on the change we want and that is where cooperation among citizens and the leadership intersect."

"Yes, we can benefit from a consensus on the change that we want and how to get the change implemented. I agree with that."

"I guess what I am trying to say is that I think we have the capacity to do much better in our economic development. But then we need to give power to those who will make the changes that will result in the kind of sustained growth and economic transformation that I believe we can attain."

Jamina interrupts. "Papa, can I be excused? I want to have a word with Mamma."

"Sure, Jamina, go chat with Mamma."

As Jamina leaves, John continues. "Chief, the hurdles I see are enormous. First, we must agree on the changes we want to see. Second, we must identify the kinds of people who will be capable of managing the process. Third, we must have a selection process that ensures that it is those capable people who are given power. Finally, we must have a system of authority, transparency, and accountability, which will ensure that those people have the incentive to do their best when given the power."

"Where do you see the biggest obstacle?"

"In my view, it is the selection process."

"What else is a problem in the system, or is the whole system faulty?"

"I think our system of accountability is not adequate to convince power holders to act in the public interest."

"You know, John, I have been a part of the inner discussions on local government reform and decentralization in this country. Some of these issues you are raising have come up in those discussions as well. There are many people in this country who think like you. The answer is always something about having more democracy and greater decentralization as well as a more efficient legal system."

"It is very important that we reform our legal and law enforcement institutions, including finding ways to drastically reduce corruption. As for democracy, that's a big one. Democracy has its virtues, and as our education and per capita incomes increase we will make progress in that area, because people will demand more rights as they become better educated. But for resolute and rapid economic progress, increasing democracy is neither necessary nor sufficient. So let's fight for democracy. But let's not base that fight on what democracy will do for economic development."

"Where does that leave us, John?"

John senses the tension in the chief's voice. They must avoid going in circles. So many discussions among the elite in Nigasilia do just that.

"The people must find a way to pressure any government they have to improve economic governance in concrete ways, and with solid results."

"I have been told that an organization called STRONG has been formed to act on your advice. We are all here waiting to see what happens."

In the kitchen, the two women talk while John and Chief Tamba are having their serious analyses.

"Mamma, you are looking well; relaxed, too."

"I have had nothing to worry about, thank God for that. So, Jamina, are you and John getting on all right?"

"Why, you don't believe me when I tell you so over the phone?"

"Is he serious about you?"

"Yes."

"How do you know?"

"He has sent Mahdu to test me. John is careful, you know. He does not want me to turn him down."

"What did you tell Mahdu?"

"I said I had to ask my parents."

"Jamina, I don't believe you! You know we will support you on any choice you make."

"Yes, Mamma, I know. But I wanted to think a little. John is not going to stay long here in Nigasilia. He is not going to change things the way he wants to. So he will have to leave or else go insane."

"Then you can go with him to America. You can come home as often as you like."

"I don't know if I want to live in America. In fact, I am sure I don't want to leave Nigasilia. I am happy here. I go abroad every year and return. I am useful here and enjoy the social life as well. But I love John, I love him very much, and I would like to say yes to him if he asks me."

"Jamina, the only thing you will lose by going to America will be your work here. You can come home every year."

"I would be deserting children who need me. They don't need me in America."

After a pause, Mrs. Tamba says, "Well, the school will just have to find a suitable replacement."

"Or I can marry John and he can return to America and I can stay here. We shall see each other every Christmas and summer."

"Jamina, you are going to be pregnant and have children. The children will need the two of you."

"No, I can take care of them here, in Nigasilia. John has his two boys. He can worry about them."

"Well, I don't know what to say, Jamina."

"Mamma, I understand how you feel. As you might imagine, I have a problem with it, too."

Samatu, the cook, calls out to Mrs. Tamba that the meal is ready and the four soon settle down to dinner. As they pass the first dish around, Jamina says, "Papa, each time I talk to Mamma, she tells me you have been very busy."

"Yes, Jamina, this is true, for all kinds of reasons. Our people have been busy putting together requests for project financing from the central government and we have to cost and prioritize the projects. Then there is the usual barrage of cases that come to my court—bush disputes, marriage disputes, theft, assault. On top of that, I have been asked to participate in a panel to investigate rights to chieftaincy in one of our neighboring chiefdoms. To crown it all, as you know, the general elections are just around the corner. I have had to participate in selecting the candidate for our party, our symbol bearer. Too many people want to enter Parliament, and for party unity you have to listen to them all and build a good case for the candidate you select. I know that people are going to listen to me. But if I show any sign of partiality in the process, I will lose respect and my candidate could lose at the general election."

"So, how do you think your candidate is going to do this time?"

"I believe he will win. You know him, Banbey Tokemato."

"Yes, his wife teaches elementary school in Lamongwe. I did not know he was interested in politics. He is supposed to be a quiet man. I know only his wife, though."

John compliments the food. "Mrs. Tamba, this is so good. I hope it was not a problem getting the fish."

"Thank you, John. We eat freshwater fish around here all the time. So it was not difficult. I just wanted one without too much bone. I hope you like it."

"Yes, thank you."

John then turns to the chief. "Chief, do you see any political campaigning around here already?"

"Honestly, no, I am not aware of any campaigning here, John. But the opposition is accusing our party of having started campaigning in some parts of the country. For us, there is no point. The opposition is weak and we will win even if we do not campaign."

John decides, after a brief moment of reflection, to ask a difficult question. "Chief, some people argue that we should ban chiefs from having explicit political affiliations with political parties. What is your own view?"

"John, it is a complex question. I know you ask it because the candidate the chief supports in the general elections usually wins. But the chiefs in this country often shift their allegiances from one party to another from one election to another. So you can find a chief for Party A today and for Party B in the next election. And sometimes you wonder whether the people do not influence the chiefs as much as the chiefs influence the people."

Mrs. Tamba interjects. "John, my husband knows what he is talking about. He used to favor the United Party. It was Mahdu Kontana, our nephew, and your father who convinced my husband to join the Progressive Party."

Jamina adds, "John, Mahdu told me your father attracted him to the Progressive Party."

"I see. I knew he fell out with the United Party. I am happy he decided to join my dad."

"I was, too, even before I met you, John. Your dad was very much liked as a lawyer. He was considered honest and straightforward, and everyone knew the interest of his clients was primary for him. His fees were also considered reasonable."

"Chief, do you get the feeling around here that the people are happy with him?" John asks. "I guess if they are overwhelmingly in favor of the government party the answer must be yes."

The chief is direct in his response. "No, John, the answer is not yes. But they do not trust the opposition at all. They say the opposition is full of rats. They are not happy with government in general. John, if you look at our schools, our hospitals, and our roads you will see why. Our water supply situation is also awful and we have no electricity around here, except what a few of us produce with our generators. That's why we are asking for fiscal decentralization, so that we can improve our infrastructure and attract more business."

"Maybe you are right, Chief. But you are currently allowed to raise taxes to spend on local projects. Still, you don't, because your ability to raise taxes is limited. The tax base is not there. It may be better for people to put pressure on the central government to improve infrastructure and basic services all over the country, given the advantage of the central government to perform that task. After that, one can proceed with greater fiscal decentralization, because all communities will then have the foundation on which to attract business. Indeed, communities will then engage in healthy competition among themselves. In fact, they will learn a lot about governance from each other."

"Yes, John, I understand. But so far we have not succeeded in pressuring the central government to do what it should do."

"All right, Chief, I hear you. I shall tell my colleagues in the cabinet, and my dad especially, that we should do better."

The chief turns to Jamina. "Jamina, you have been so quiet. How are things? Mahdu tells me that you and John go everywhere. John, you must have some magic, because my daughter used to say that young Nigasilian men are not serious."

"In truth, the only real complaint I have is with the school situation," Jamina says. "We are getting short of science teachers. Fewer people are graduating in science and most of those who graduate do not feel like going into teaching or teaching here. I would like to do a master's degree, but I do not plan to leave my teaching job in Nigasilia.

You can't imagine how important it is for those girls to see a woman in science."

Mrs. Tamba is eyeing John to see his reaction. But John only shows that restrained, calm smile of admiration that he seems to always have when Jamina is speaking.

John already knows deep down that Jamina does not want to leave her teaching job. But he does not want to address that problem until Jamina agrees to marry him.

Mrs. Tamba asks, "John, are you not proud of her? She is so committed!"

"Yes, Mrs. Tamba, I am. I think Jamina is an excellent role model in more ways than one. Chief, she is the one who has the magic. She motivates me to be a serious man."

"In that case, you both have magic." They all laugh.

Mrs. Tamba takes a deep breath. "I gather you want to go sight-seeing tomorrow. Then on Monday, the chief has invited some of the elders to come here to meet you. John, it is really for you, since they all know Jamina. On Tuesday, I gather John wants to see a little bit of economic activity in the surrounding villages—farming, fishing, wood and water collecting, and selling in the markets. That will be a busy day. On Wednesday, some groups want to sing and dance for you, right in this compound. John, Jamina told me you would enjoy that."

In every Nigasilian chiefdom, organized cultural groups of performers entertain with singing and dancing. They help maintain the local traditions that go back several centuries. They are all part of what westerners call traditional music and dancing.

Mrs. Tamba turns to Jamina. "Jamina, did I forget anything?"

"No, Mamma, you have it all correct. We leave on Thursday, as you know."

After they retire to their room, Mrs. Tamba tells Chief Tamba that John has an interest in asking Jamina to marry him. "But you just heard what she said about not wanting to leave Nigasilia. She believes

John will go back to America because he is not going to get those in government to do what he wants them to do, or at least not as quickly as he wants."

"My dear, don't let that worry you. I know John's father. That man will find a way to keep his son in Nigasilia. Also, you heard John. He has tremendous love, admiration, and respect for his father. When I put those two observations together, I will bet you anything that John will stay in Nigasilia, at worst until his dad's term ends. By then he will have understood the ropes sufficiently to make him want to stay for good."

"All right, Jawana, you are usually right."

"I am not promising that it will be easy, though. So let's pray for them and for us because we want our daughter to be happy and to get married and have children. She will make a wonderful mother."

John and Jamina enjoy the holiday very much—the landscape, the sociability of the people, and the squaring off on difficult subjects, like the future of chieftaincy in Nigasilia, fiscal decentralization, and the leadership problem in the country. John can go on and on discussing these subjects but even he will often feel he is being too serious. Jamina will often wink at him to change the subject or simply intercede and change the subject herself.

Easily the most relaxing part of the vacation occurs on Tuesday, when they go around observing economic activities. The very first farm they go to is being cultivated by a man and his three sons.

In the majority of Nigasilia, the land is not really owned freehold by the farmer. It is all extended family land in most areas of the country. The individual farmer is simply allocated land, to use for as long as the family allows via their decision-making procedures. But leasing, pledging, and even renting of land is allowed by the individual.

The majority of farmers tend to farm several small parcels of land, sometimes called fields. This phenomenon is known as fragmentation. It can be the result of inheritance by the family of pieces of land not adjacent to each other. It can also result from the attempt of the individual farmers to get different types of land suitable for different types of crops.

Most of the farmers are mainly subsistence farmers. They sell less than 50 percent of what they produce, the rest being for their own household consumption. Hence, they typically want to grow several different types of crops. Sometimes a single farmer could have up to ten fields, with the average field no more than one acre. A farmer could grow fifteen or more crops in all his fields. But the average tends to be eight or nine crops.

Of course there are large-scale farmers, too, with several acres of land in one or two fields. Such farmers are commercial farmers. They may cultivate foodstuffs like rice or peanuts, or they could grow coffee, cocoa, palm trees for palm oil, and other crops, for local sales but especially for exports. Large-scale farmers are in the minority.

John is visiting this farmer with a young man in the chief's household. Jamina has decided to stay home and visit with her mother.

John watches the farmer and his young coworkers. All their implements are simple tools, just like those of other Nigasilian small farmers in the country. It bothers John that Nigasilian technology in farming is so backward. He has heard agriculturalists say that they cannot use the tractor efficiently because of the soil and terrain. But then, how come no one comes up with something to use apart from primitive tools like the hoe and pickax? The country seems to be stuck using what is produced somewhere else or confined to Stone Age technology. Farmers hardly use fertilizer, because it is imported and they can't afford it. But why is that the end of the story? Can the country not do something about it?

The farmer gets the feeling that these two visitors want to talk to him, although he does not know who John is. He has already recognized the young man from the chief's household, and the man introduces John as Dr. John Bijunga, the president's son.

"Doctor, I'm happy to meet you."

"Well, I'm happy to meet you, too. So, is this all the farm you have, or do you have any other fields? How big is this farm anyway? It looks big; you are a lucky man. So what do you grow? Are those your relatives, or just helpers?"

"Doctor, there are only six acres here," the farmer says as he smiles with pride. "I have three other farms. My wife has a small one also, making four other farms. Four of my children farm my other three farms and one child helps my wife. The boys you see here are also my children."

John is astonished. "How many children do you have?"

"Only ten," the farmer says, beaming.

"You are a lucky man. Your wife must be very strong." John knows there must be at least another woman, but he does not want to ask bluntly.

"No, Doctor. Three women. But my first wife died."

"Oh, I'm sorry. One of your wives farms; what does the other one do?"

"She is a trader. She sells fish and other things for cooking. She goes to the marketplace every day. She also cooks and sells food."

"I see. So, how many crops do you grow in this field?"

"Only about eight, including cassava, yam, sweet potato, and groundnut. In the rainy season, I grow some corn here, too. The other things we grow include okra, pepper, and two or three vegetable leaves for cooking. Most of the leaves we eat are from my woman's farm."

The other high point of the week is the cultural show. The singing and dancing are sometimes rapturous, sometimes celestial, and sometimes sensual. Jamina and John are in each other's arms as they watch. At the end of each number, they kiss. The performers get a kick out of that. Out in the countryside, such effusive kissing is highly unusual. Once, after six young girls dance bare-breasted, Jamina and John kiss, and the dancers and the audience all clap, shouting, "Yes, one more time." John and Jamina oblige with just enough of a romantic touch to show they are truly in love, without seriously violating custom.

Back in Lamongwe, the following Monday, during recess time at school, Jamina's cell phone rings. She looks at the number and it is Mahdu Kontana. "Hello, dear cousin," she answers.

"Jamina, I heard your trip was fabulous. John has told me all about it. So, did you talk to your parents about John? Do they approve?"

"Yes, Mahdu, they will support my choice."

"Then you will say yes to John, if he asks?"

"Mahdu, I don't want to live in America. If he accepts that condition, then he can ask me and I will say yes."

"He knows your condition already. He says you made it known."

"But still, make sure he knows I am serious."

"I will. He plans to ask you very soon."

"I hope he knows that I follow tradition. He will have to write to my parents, asking for their permission."

"Jamina, he is not a foreigner; he knows."

"Yes, but some of these Westernized Nigasilian girls are throwing that tradition out the window."

"John knows you, Jamina."

So the week flows by, too slowly for John. Despite all the signals Jamina gives him, he is still not sure that she will say yes to his proposal. He thinks her instincts to become a nun and her commitment to her students will make her unsure about marriage, especially with someone who prefers to live abroad. He and Jamina see each other on Wednesday when they both dine at Vivienne's house. Then on

Thursday, Jamina invites him to watch television and have dinner at her house. Finally, today, Saturday, February 2, they will dine at the Indochinese restaurant not too far from Jamina's.

From the moment they enter the restaurant, Jamina notices that John has a rather distant, pensive look on his face. Once they've selected a table and settle back into their chairs to look over the menu, Jamina asks, "My dear, did something happen at work today?"

"Why?"

"You seem far away and your eyes are so serious."

"I guess I am surprised to find this restaurant here. You and I have been hoping for a Thai restaurant to come to Lamongwe and when one comes it takes me months to find out."

"John, that look has nothing to do with that! Someone gave you a hard time at the office."

"Jamina, I want to marry you."

"Before or after we eat?" She smiles.

"Jamina, be serious. Don't bother to tell me you don't want to leave Nigasilia. I know that. We will worry about that when the time comes."

"No, John, you have to be sure in your mind that you accept my decision."

"I have. The only thing I have not decided is the kind of adjustment I will have to make. But I promise you, I will honor your wish. I love you too much to give you up when your reason for wanting to stay is so laudable. Now, will you marry me?"

"Yes, John, I will."

John smiles approvingly. "I know I have to write your father for permission to marry you. Once I receive your father's reply, we can then plan the engagement. Stephen Mongo will be my spokesman. He knows what to do."

"Do your boys know that you want to give them a stepmother?"

"Jamina, they love you. They may be children but they know I could marry again."

"My parents, Kontana, and I have to find a suitable date when we can have the engagement. Stephen will also be consulted. I think I will be the one with the greatest constraint, because I will not want to miss school for too many days. Don't send a lot of money for the dowry. Stephen will know that, of course. For us the dowry is symbolic. Then you must send a cow as well. This will be your present to the elders and close friends of the family. The cow will be eaten that same day. The affair will start early afternoon. At the time of the wedding, my dad will take care of the food and drinks for the celebrations in the village as well as here in Lamongwe. First we will celebrate here in Lamongwe. Then a few days later we will celebrate at my parents' place."

The two focus on their meal of lobster and rice until John breaks the silence.

"So when will you want the wedding?"

"Not before June."

John pulls out a small diary from his bag. Because of the small denominations of Nigasilian currency and the fact that almost all transactions are in cash, Nigasilian men often carry small bags that rival women's handbags.

"Saturday, June 15, looks perfect."

"Wow, you really mean business, don't you? I will let you know for sure in a day or two. I know your boys will attend, but don't you want your brother and sister here as well?"

"Well, of course. What about your brother? Can he come?"

"I will have to give him enough notice."

"You have more than five months."

Jamina agrees that this should be enough time. "In the letter to my parents, you just want to say in plain language that you and I have been dating each other since early March of last year, and you have come to realize that you would like to spend the rest of your life with me and to have children of our own. Say you have asked me and I have expressed the same desire. But the two of us want the blessings of my parents, and this letter is asking for such blessings and support. If you want to embellish the letter, you can state the qualities that you see in me that will make me an excellent wife and mother. Then give the credit for these qualities to their upbringing. Say that interacting with them has confirmed that opinion. Don't forget to give a solemn pledge that you will do all within your power to make me a very happy woman and that neither they nor I will regret the union."

John already drafted the letter; after all, he was not unaware of the tradition. But as soon as he gets home, he goes to his computer and does one more edit. Early on Monday, he sends the letter, addressed to both parents, by courier.

All the ministers are present on Wednesday, February 13, when the president opens the meeting.

"So, honorable ministers, what we have in front of us is a set of allegations of corrupt practices by five of you, our honorable ministers. The chief economist is arguing that corruption at the highest level is a major reason for our slow economic development. Hence, we owe it to our country to remove from office corrupt political leaders.

"The chief economist has worked in cooperation with four other ministers and a good lineup of whistle-blowers, who will testify if we have to go to trial. As you can see from the exhaustive report, he has grouped the charges into six categories; namely, private use of public property, accepting bribes, graft, extortion and blackmail, embezzlement of public funds, and abuse of power.

"You also have to remember that this government is committed to zero tolerance when it comes to corruption. So I am not going to entertain any discussion about the level or gravity of the corruption. At this level, corruption is corruption and the ministers must go. If the case goes to trial, then the judge or judges can worry about the severity of the corruption and thus the nature of the punishment.

"Now, the chief economist is recommending that we allow the ministers to resign if they agree that they have been corrupt. If they dispute the charges, then a thorough investigation should be conducted and the five ministers brought to justice, including fines and possible imprisonment. I would like to know how you all feel."

There is complete silence and then Kontana says, "Mr. President, you are the leader, you should decide. It is very difficult for us, being ordinary ministers and colleagues of the accused ministers. Still, the paper by the chief economist includes detailed examples of the corrupt practices, as well as statements from these whistle-blowers. Without further investigation, including cross-examining the accused, we cannot conclude that these ministers are guilty. But the minsters know. So they can agree to resign, if they are guilty. Otherwise, they will put the country through agony, including expense of an inquiry and trial."

No one else seems ready to say anything. So the president says, "Okay, I shall let you all know within two days what I have decided to do. But since we are all here, I would like the VP to give his views on the matter."

The VP looks relaxed. "Mr. President, I don't know of any public official who has not at one time or another done something that could be interpreted as corrupt. Yes, I know these allegations are very serious and hence should be treated seriously. I also know that we are committed to zero tolerance of corruption. Ultimately, if the ministers do not accept guilt, we will have to investigate. But I think to do any investigation now would be disastrous for this party, given the elections are just round the corner. Once we begin the investigations, knowledge of it would be widespread. In fact, the findings would be exaggerated, and rumors and facts would be intermingled. The opposition party would seize the opportunity to brand the current government as replete with corrupt ministers. This would give tremendous political leverage to the opposition and force the government into the defensive. I will bet you that almost everyone sitting here would be branded as corrupt."

The president turns to John. "So, Chief Economist, what do you think?"

"I think we should go ahead with the investigations now, unless the ministers accept their guilt and resign. The opposition will not use it against us, because they do not have a clean record themselves. If I were sitting in your chair, Mr. President, I would use this as a signal to all that we take seriously, in this party, the control of corruption at the highest level."

Tubo Bangar speaks first. "Mr. President, I support John completely."

Sanjo Manray agrees. "So do I, Mr. President."

Dumomo Frah adds, "And I, too."

"Does anybody else want to speak?" the president asks. It is clear that no one does.

"What about the accused ministers? Do they want to speak?"

"Yes, Mr. President," Sambana Tureno responds. "We are innocent until proven guilty. That's our view, all five of us." The other four ministers shake their heads in agreement.

"Okay, my friends, that's it. I shall send around a short memo tomorrow telling you of my decision. The choice is investigate now or wait until after the election, as a minimum, as the VP recommends."

The following day, the president sends around a one-page memo to the cabinet ministers announcing that he would postpone the decision on having a detailed inquiry of the allegations until after the coming elections. In John's opinion, this was a major victory for the VP, who would no doubt try to come up with other reasons for not conducting the inquiry once the elections are over. If need be, John believes that he should confront his dad on this one. But he thinks it is not wise to do so yet. In fact, he realizes, this might be a good opportunity to let the VP ruin his standing with the president.

❤

John has an important date today at Jamina's high school, where he is to answer questions of the students. He is very impressed at the knowledge, sensitivity, and keen interest of the girls. They are concerned about violence in election campaigns, government corruption, overcrowding in classrooms, serious scholarship shortages for university, the high costs of textbooks, limited computer facilities in secondary schools, government arrears in paying teachers, the low level of salaries in the country in the face of rising prices of consumer goods, grave electricity shortages, the high costs of transport in getting to and from school, and the lack of jobs for college graduates. They want to know if the government is fully aware of the suffering of the ordinary person and, if so, if the government is considering steps to alleviate these problems.

John knew these would be the sort of questions the girls would ask. They are the same concerns of their parents. He has to leave them optimistic without giving them false hopes. He assures them that the government knows about all these problems and is working to alleviate them all. But, he says, the problems are difficult and big results will be slow in coming. John struggles to keep his answers simple.

"If I may do so, girls, let me summarize my response to your concerns. First, we need to find ways to educate our young people for the modern world. That means that we should emphasize mathematics and science in our schools and we should modernize our technical institutes to provide modern technical and vocational training for those who do not go on to universities. Second, we need to attract investors. For that, we need a well-educated and skilled population of workers, we need decent infrastructure, we need an efficient government that does not frustrate businesses, and we need towns and cities where educated and sophisticated people would like to live. This is the kind of environment that we are trying to create. It is not easy. Not everyone in government understands that we can do better than we are doing now. And that is very sad and disappointing. We have to educate those people. But I also want you to appreciate, because it is the reality, that our government faces serious constraints. Still, we can do better than we are doing now. I am sure about that. The citizens of Nigasilia, including you young people, must let our government know that you want them to do better. Let them know you expect more from them, because you know they can do better. Tell them I told you so."

A representative of the school then rises to give a vote of thanks to John. She reads from a drafted statement.

"Dear Dr. Bijunga, we, the girls of this school, are very grateful to you that, in spite of your very busy schedule, you made time to come talk to us today. You have answered all our questions and have left us with many things to think about. You have made us aware that we can act and that we must act to change certain things important to our future.

"Dr. Bijunga, you have inspired us to work hard in school. You have been very firm and straightforward that if we want to really get ahead, we should pay attention to our math and science. Other subjects are important, but in the world in which we live, those who are good in math and science have an advantage. You say we should not be afraid of math and science. We can be good in them if we are serious, determined, and apply ourselves.

"Dr. Bijunga, you want us to pay attention to what our political leaders are doing and to find a way to let them know when we are not satisfied. You told us to not be passive, to not just accept what our leaders do as if we have no choice. We are used to saying in this country, 'Well, that is the system.' What you have told us today is that we should put pressure on the leaders to change the system, because the system we have is rotten.

"Dr. Bijunga, we, the students of this school, hope that more people like you will be leaders in this country to help give our people ideas to make this country a better place. Thank you, sir, and God bless you."

The girls clap and cheer. John is beaming as he clenches both fists in celebration. But inside he is depressed, because he is not sure that the government will be able to deliver. In his mind, the governance of Nigasilia is in the hands of too many thieves and incompetent leaders. It is not easy to weed out the worst of the pack. The citizens will just have to work with the hand they have been dealt by a fundamentally defective system.

The next day, John receives a letter by courier. It is Jamina's parents' response. Jamina's parents thank John for his kind words, writing:

> *You have demonstrated to us that you are a true gentleman of the highest order. And when we put that together with your brilliant mind, we could not have asked for a better son-in-law. Having known both of your parents, we are not at all surprised. What would have surprised us is if you were less of a gentleman than you are. We have enjoyed every moment with you and we have seen the joy you bring to our daughter, confirming what she repeats to us almost daily via telephone. Yes, John, it gives us enormous pleasure to give our full support and blessings to the potential union between you and our daughter. We have utmost faith that you will be happy together. And we hope you give us grandchildren soon, as many as you both wish.*

John finishes the letter and telephones Jamina immediately. "Can I drop by around seven? I have something to show you."

"Sure, Vivienne and Santie are dropping by around the same time. They have not seen me since we came back from my parents'."

"That's fine, I'll not stay long."

When John arrives, he has a boyish smile on his face, prompting Jamina to ask, "What are you up to?"

"I have a love letter for you," John says as he hands her the letter.

Vivienne and Santie drop by as Jamina finishes reading the letter. John takes his leave and Santie walks with him to the door.

Vivienne draws Jamina aside and whispers, "Jamina, I think I am pregnant already."

"But you have been married for less than two months."

"Yes, but during the first month Santie wanted it all the time."

Jamina cracks up. "Congratulations, I hope you are right. I also have news for you. My parents just replied to John giving their blessings to the marriage."

"Well, my dear, congratulations. Of course, there was no doubt they would, but it is still good news."

"Yes, and they wrote a very pleasant note."

Vivienne cannot resist. "Jamina, do you think John will bring his two boys to live here once he settles down with you? I think you will be a great mother to them."

"Oh, I am looking forward to being a mother to them. But I should leave John and the boys to decide where they will live. If John asks my opinion I shall give it to him."

"What will you advise him to do?"

"I will tell him that I am thrilled to be a mother to the boys but that he should think of their schooling as a separate issue. They can continue boarding school in America, he can transfer them to Europe, because that is closer, or he can bring them here to go to school. People do go to secondary school here and then go to university abroad. The boys are also Americans, so that will be of some advantage if they later want to attend college in the States."

"I think transferring them to Britain or bringing them here is better. America is too far away. They are still schoolboys."

"You may be right, Vivienne. But I think the boys should have a say in the decision as well, don't you think?"

Santie pokes his head into the room. "So when is the engagement?"

Vivienne snaps at him. "Santie, they just agreed to marry. Fixing the engagement will take time. You know that."

"For normal people, that's true. But these two are superhuman. I figured they had all that planned out by now."

Jamina smiles. "Santie, when we fix a date, you will know."

When John gets to the office on Monday morning, February 18, a member of his staff walks up to him and says, "Dr. Bijunga, have you seen today's *Tribune*?"

"No, why do you ask?"

"Here, look at the headline."

John takes the paper and is shocked. The headline reads: *Is the Vice President Protecting Ministers from Corruption Charges?*

The article contains the allegations that John had detailed in his report on the corruption of the five ministers. John reads quickly through the newspaper article and is amazed at the details. It even reports the vice president's remarks as if the journalist had read a transcript of the meeting.

John has no doubt that whosoever wrote the newspaper article had seen his cabinet paper. One of the ministers must have leaked it. To him, there are three suspects: Sanjo Manray, Dumomo Frah, and Mahdu Kontana. All three are adamant in fighting corruption.

John finishes reading the article and then decides to make a call. "Kontana, I am sure you have seen the article in the *Tribune*."

"Yes, I have. I am not unhappy about it. Are you?"

"I am not sure. Do you have any idea who leaked my paper?"

"I don't know who leaked it."

"Do you think your friends could have done it?"

"Sanjo and Dumomo? I am not at liberty to even think they could have done it. They are more than friends to me, John."

"Yes, I know, I am sorry for asking. I will let the president and the VP worry about it."

"Good man."

John is more confused than upset. He has lost control of the situation, though the president's hand will now be forced.

After Mahdu Kontana ends his conversation with John, his mind wanders and he replays the events in his head.

The day the president sent the memo around saying he wanted to postpone the decision, Kontana was raving mad and knew that Dumomo Frah and Sanjo Manray would be mad as well. So he called them up and they agreed to meet in his office that very day to decide what to do. They did not want to discuss the matter over the phone.

Sanjo Manray spoke first. "I think we have only one option. We have to find a way to get it to the press."

"But how?" Mahdu Kontana asked.

Dumomo Frah proposed placing 5000 kala each—the equivalent of about $1.25—in two small envelopes. He would fold half of a regular printing paper and put it in a third envelope, with no money, and then seal all three envelopes. Mahdu's secretary would put each envelope inside a big brown envelope and seal all three. Then each would pick up an envelope and take it home to open it. The chosen one who opened the envelope without any kala would then decide.

It is the closest they could come to choosing the short end of the stick, since anonymity was important. Whosoever was the chosen one to leak the story, including John's cabinet paper, to the press, would decide whether to go ahead with the idea. If he decided to proceed, he should do it at a time and with a newspaper of his own choosing, revealing nothing to anyone.

Kontana slumps comfortably into his chair, pleased. He was not the chosen one to do the leaking. That's all he knows. He does not even know if one of those two was, in fact, the origin of the story. Many other people had access to the cabinet paper and the vice president has many people in and outside the cabinet who would like to see him shamed.

At midday, Jamina telephones. "John, there is a lot of excitement around here about an article in the *Tribune*. You must have seen it. Where did they get all that information? Is it from your cabinet paper?"

"I'm afraid so."

"Will your colleagues think you gave the newspaper the information?"

"No, Jamina, that's the last thing they will think. None of them will believe I want to undercut my father in such a blatant way."

"So what is your father going to do now?"

"What I always wanted him to do; that is, proceed with the investigations if the ministers do not accept guilt and resign."

"That's it?"

"Yes. My dad wanted an investigation anyway because he saw my evidence and believed the allegations were founded on solid inquiries. But the vice president, who was opposed to an investigation, knows how to manage election campaigns and my dad did not feel like discouraging him yet. My father was stuck between Scylla and Charybdis, a rock and a hard place. This leak gets him off the hook. He can now say that we can no longer delay an investigation, and the VP will not be able to argue against that. Someone, I'm not sure who, may have to publicly respond to the article. That said, I would like to know who leaked my paper."

"Do you suspect anyone?"

"Yes, three people; your cousin and his two minister friends."

"How will you find out if you are right?"

"I don't know. Do you have any suggestions?"

"Don't ask any of them if he is the one."

"Why not?"

"Because your very asking will be a sign of disrespect. An insult."

It's time for Jamina to return to her class. No sooner had Jamina hung up than the president calls. He wants John to drop by his home in the evening. The president hangs up, just as the VP calls, and asks if John can stop by after lunch.

"John," the VP says as John enters his office, "I am positive that the leak came from inside the cabinet. Now, this initiative has been yours. You know my argument has been that the opposition could use it against us. What has happened is worse. Now the press is accusing me of shielding corrupt ministers. So, what do I do now?"

John quickly decides that this is no time for revenge. He can get what he wants without humiliating the VP.

"I am sure my father will want to respond through the minister of information. But I can get him to agree that you should address the nation on radio and television. The speech will be approved by the president. I can work on the draft with you, if you wish. It has to be delivered as immediately as possible. In order to give you and Dad time to prepare the speech, I would suggest the day after tomorrow at the latest. I suggest we tell the nation that the newspaper did not have all its facts right and that the government has been discussing how to investigate the allegations mentioned in the newspaper. 'In fact,' your speech can say, 'the newspaper got its information from a cabinet paper that was evidently leaked.' We can say that the cabinet had finished its discussions and that the president was to decide the timing and nature of the investigation. We can add that there was no question that an investigation would take place and that the Anti-Corruption Commission would participate in that investigation. Moreover, if we wish, we can be stronger and say that the president, in fact, has since decided that the investigation will begin by, say, February 25, and will take no more than six weeks."

The VP does not waste time. "All right, John, let's proceed that way."

At dinner that evening, the president broaches the topic in his usual direct manner soon after he and John sit down to eat.

"John, during that cabinet discussion of your paper, your anger was visible, especially when the VP was talking. You had accumulated more evidence than I had ever seen supporting an accusation of corruption. Now here were people, including my VP friend, who wanted to halt your crusade. I can understand you being annoyed and disappointed. Well, your friends have started the process of helping you get rid of the most corrupt ministers. You will succeed. I will accelerate the process. But there is an important implication for you, John. None of those ministers is a Thomas Becket. But *you* have to do penance, too."

"What do you mean?"

"Well, John, just as you are trying to mobilize the educated youth to fight from the bottom for change, so some people, including your friends in the cabinet, are trying to convince you of their support in the fight for change from the top. You can't leave them for your wonderful America and your ivory tower position. That, John, will be your penance, helping to push the engine here with us rather than writing academic papers and attending all those wonderful cultural events in America. But look at things from your friends' position. You are the son of the president and you are passionate in the fight for good governance. John, that is unique in Africa. The sons of presidents are usually at the forefront of the corrupt gang. Not only do you have leverage with the president but you also have the right mind and character. This is how they see things. God has given you to them, as we say in Nigasilia. They will not let you go without a fight."

John does not really want to talk about his future in Nigasilia now. He wants to understand how the system facilitates leaks. "So who do you think among those friends of mine spilled the beans?"

"I don't know. But it is not our finance man. Tubo Bangar is not that type. He is too cautious and conservative."

"So you think there must have been a conspiracy."

"Yes, John, that's how we do things here. There is always a conspiracy. And usually the conspirators do not even know who actually did the damage. All they know is that one of them is guilty."

"Doesn't it bother anyone?" Then John smiles sheepishly. "As for the penance, I would rather not think about it yet."

His father stays silent, so he continues. "Jamina also does not want me to leave Nigasilia, because she wants to stay and help her country. Now these citizens, whoever they are, do not want me to go because they want me to help in the fight for good governance. So that's two strikes against my going. Are you going to deliver the third?"

"I'll try, John, I'll try."

"Now, if you can so easily identify the leading suspects, can't other people, like the VP, for example?"

"Yes, of course. But so what? They cannot ask the suspects or request an investigation. Around here we don't investigate leaks. People will think we are just acting and they would not take us seriously. Then on top of that, no one will cooperate with any investigator. You see, people expect these kinds of leaks. But this one was unusual in one very important way. It did not say that an investigation on corrupt practices was being postponed until after the elections. It said that the VP was protecting certain ministers. This was not a simple leak. It was designed to hurt the VP. That makes it unusual."

"So won't people be interested in knowing who hates the VP that much?"

"Maybe, yes. But generally people are not particularly interested in identifying the whistle-blowers. You deprive them of an important topic in their parties and clubs. Of course, the last thing they want is prosecution in some court of law. That is simply socially unacceptable. That's why no one will cooperate in an investigation."

"So how do you plan to respond to the newspaper?"

"I will discuss it with the minister of information. He could write a letter to the newspaper, saying that no one is covering up any corruption and that we are still discussing in cabinet the document that has been leaked. Alternatively, the minister can simply call a press briefing and read a statement prepared by the government."

"You know, I have perhaps spoken to the VP too soon. I suggested to him that it may be a good idea for him to go on radio and television and say something to that effect. I even volunteered to help him with the speech."

"All right, let's move along that path. You will clear the speech with me, right?"

"Of course, Dad."

The next day, John drafts the short statement for the VP, who then takes it for approval by the president. The following day, soon after the evening news, the vice president delivers the speech.

"My dear men and women, it is with great sadness and humility that I find myself here this evening having to defend myself against one of the most blatant and wrongful accusations that has ever been made against me during my public service in this country.

"One of our newspapers in this country, which we have come to admire for its high standards of journalism, has become a victim of some malicious person; indeed, someone unprincipled enough to leak a confidential cabinet paper. As a result, the *Tribune* has fallen to a new low and chosen to malign my reputation with unfounded accusation. Yes, five cabinet ministers have been accused of actions that could be interpreted as corrupt enough to warrant serious disciplinary action. Following a cabinet paper, there has been some cabinet discussion of the matter. The focus of the discussion was the timing and the nature of the inquiry into the allegations. There was no question about the need for an investigation. The issues were when the investigation should be conducted, and who will do the investigating. In the cabinet meeting, I stated that, given the present preoccupation with the elections on top of the enormous business of running this country, and given the breadth of the charges and hence the enormity of the required investigation, it would be wise to postpone the inquiry until after the elections. In fact, I have come to believe that it would be better to do so, to ensure the process is not tainted by the elections. Because, as you might expect, those who are in opposition to this government will try to twist everything that happens during the investigations, distorting some facts and accusing the government of trying to cover up for its cabinet members. Is this what the newspaper considers my protection of the accused? I call it ensuring that the investigation will be complete and fair to all parties. The president, our great leader, saw the rationality of this line of reasoning and decided to postpone further consideration of the whole matter until after the forthcoming elections.

"Dear fellow Nigasilians, I trust in your good judgment and fairness. Good night, and best wishes to you all."

The speech was considered a good one by the next day's papers. Even the *Tribune* wrote in its editorial page: "We do not regret having brought the matter to the attention of the public. But we are willing to give the vice president the benefit of the doubt that he was not trying to protect the ministers from being sacked or the government from criticism, but was only worried about the timing of the inquiry if fairness is to be assured."

It is February 21, the day after the speech. The VP has asked the five ministers to come see him in his office to discuss the next steps, sometime in mid-afternoon. As he reflects that morning, he believes that, in light of his speech, the prospects of his party winning the elections may have improved, but at the cost of the careers of his best henchmen and foot soldiers. He is annoyed at the actions of the five ministers. What fools they have been, in spite of their education.

When the five ministers enter, they look somber. Maigo Bang speaks on their behalf.

"Mr. VP, we truly are sorry for putting you through such trouble. No doubt we have made mistakes, but we do not think that we have been so corrupt to be disgraced. We would like you to arrange a meeting with the president, so we can apologize to him. The president has had no complaints with us or about us. We really don't understand why his son is so against us. It must be those four ministers who put him up to it."

The VP is now shaking with anger. "You people still don't understand. You are all brilliant academically and yet you do not see that John wants you people out of the government because he knows that the president, his father, is committed to his policy of zero tolerance. That commitment was a big part of our campaign. Also, John believes our corruption at the highest levels hurts our economic development. You people don't even know how to steal small. And you have been very selfish in your stealing. It's all been about you, for yourselves, not for the party."

The VP stops for a moment. He is tapping his feet, irritated. The ministers dare not move. "Look," the VP continues, "if it comes to it, I am not going to argue against having an inquiry. If we go through the pain of having an inquiry, then the president will not be able to protect you from prosecution. If he does, the newspapers will destroy his reputation. Why would he want to protect you? So you people have a clear choice, unless you like being in prison. If you are guilty of corruption as charged in John's paper, you have to resign."

"Mr. VP," Sambana Tureno says, "if we offer to resign, will they drop all charges?"

"No, they simply won't bring formal charges."

"So there will be no legal charges?"

"Yes, Sambana. There will be no legal charges. And so you can then go about your business and do whatever you like. But the president must agree to the arrangement. It would be a kind of plea bargain. You won't plead guilty or confess to corruption. You would resign for personal reasons. The newspapers will speculate, of course. We cannot control that."

Maigo Bang butts in, speaking in a soft monotone. "Can you please, Mr. VP, speak to the president, so that we can take that option?"

After the five ministers leave, the VP telephones the president to request that they meet on Monday. The president asks if the VP wants John or anyone else to be there. The VP requests that they meet alone.

When they meet, the VP is clearly in low spirits. It takes him some minutes to regain his composure.

"Samuel, I fully realize that you are committed to the zero-tolerance policy and on that I support you. I also appreciate John's fervor on this issue because of his strong belief that corruption at the highest levels hurts our economic development. My one disappointment has been with the five ministers being accused of corruption. I have taken them under my wing, because they are dedicated to our cause. They are willing to roll up their sleeves and work for the victory of our party. So, I have been on their side. But a mentor should not condone his protégés when they are not behaving themselves. So, I have spoken to them. They will resign their ministerial posts. What I want to ask of you is that you permit them to resign for personal reasons and not prosecute them further. The newspapers and the public at large won't criticize you for it. Everyone will know of the corruption charges. Everyone will assume that you pushed them out. People will understand that the investigations and the prosecution will be costly. So they won't mind."

"Strictly speaking, they should be fined, their assets should be seized, and they should serve some jail time. In freeing them from all that, the minimum I can ask for, and I really mean the minimum, is that they also give up their membership of our party. Kamake, I am doing this because you have asked me. I was otherwise ready to pursue them to the limit of the law."

"I understand your position. They will send the resignation letter, from government and our party, within the week."

John, Jamina, and her parents, in collaboration with Mahdu Kontana, have been getting everything arranged for the engagement ceremony and celebrations in Wombono. The engagement has been set for April 6.

The president has decided he will drive up to the provincial capital some thirty miles away from Wombono on April 5. There is an official Presidential Rest House there. He will attend the ceremony on April 6 and drive back to Lamongwe the next day.

Soon it is April 6 and everyone is in a cheerful mood for what turns out to be a dignified and elegant engagement ceremony. Jamina is dressed in a long, flowing, white embroidered gown with matching head gear. John has on a gray safari suit in long sleeves and matching cap. In the olden days, in Jamina's region of Nigasilia, this ceremony was deemed the wedding in accordance with customary law. The couple would go home together and consummate the arrangement. But the modern educated people think of this ceremony as merely an engagement. Jamina, on top of that, is a devout Catholic. So when they return to Lamongwe, she will not be residing with John. She will not even sleep in the same room with John at her parents' house. All of that will wait until after the Christian wedding, which has been set for June 22.

When the ceremony begins, Stephen Mongo, the spokesman for John, addresses the parents of Jamina and the assembled relatives and guests. He states that John is requesting the hand of Jamina in marriage. He expresses the deep love that John has for Jamina and assures them that John has promised to take good care of her and to treat her with respect and dignity.

Mahdu Kontana, the spokesman for Jamina's side, responds. He stresses that Jamina has been well brought up and that they are giving her away expecting that she will be loved, respected, and treated well. If there is any trouble, John is free to return her to her parents or any other close relative if the parents are not around. They do not expect John to be violent to her in any way. If he violates this trust, then it would be considered an assault on the whole family and he would have a big case on his hands. The spokesman emphasizes that the family is consenting because they have come to know John and to respect him. They have great hope and expectation that he will be a wonderful companion and husband to their daughter.

The spokesman for John then presents the dowry. This is only a token, he stresses, because no value can possibly be placed on the woman and the love that the man has for her. Both parents of Jamina accept the dowry. In return, the spokesman of Jamina hands a present to the other spokesman as a token for the appreciation of the respect that the visitors have demonstrated for the family of Jamina and the trouble the visitors have taken in traveling a long distance. Then Jamina's father takes her hand. He approaches the center of the room at the same time that John, accompanied by Stephen Mongo, does the same, coming from the other side. Then her father places her hand in the outstretched hands of John and says, "Well, I hope you two are happy together." There are cheers and clapping as they take seats that have been placed for them in the middle of the gathering in the garden.

An elderly woman, respected in the community, walks up and says, "Jamina, in our tradition, I would talk to you about married life and how you should behave towards your husband. But you are a modern girl. So I will leave that for your priest to do. Anyway, I wish you well. Behave yourself, respect your husband, and try not to be too jealous. I pray that God will bless you with healthy children." John and Jamina embrace the old lady.

An elder gentleman, also respected in the community, similarly walks up to the couple, looks at John, and says, "I also would, in our tradition, talk to you, my boy, about how to behave and make your wife happy and your marriage a successful one. But I also will leave that for the priest. In the meanwhile, I will say this to you. This woman comes from a good home. You should respect her and love her. I have known her since she was a little girl. She is one of the best women you will ever find. Don't ever be cruel to her. I pray that God will be with you both every day." John and Jamina embrace the old man as well.

John and Jamina proceed to exchange engagement rings. A young girl presents a small fanciful ceremonial basket to the elderly woman and man. The woman opens the basket and the man takes the ring wrapped in a white cloth and puts it on Jamina's finger. Then she covers the basket and gives it to the man, who opens the basket for the woman to take the other ring, which is not wrapped, to place on John's finger. Both John and Jamina then kiss each other and the two elderly persons. Everyone in attendance screams, "Hurrah!"

And then the celebrations begin.

Chapter 12

Elections are just around the corner. Deep down, John is not worried. His work has allowed him to get a good sense of what is likely to happen. His father and his party will win. The opposition is disorganized. The people still remember it as the party that took corruption to unprecedented heights, encouraged political thuggery, was very tribalistic, and through its disastrous governance pushed the abyss of misery in the country down to a new depth. John is disappointed that they will not win because of the positive achievements of his father's party. But for his father's sake, he will take the victory any way they can get it, apart from triggering unfair competition or rigging the votes.

The election campaign started in earnest on February 1. John does not agree with much of the process that has been implanted in Nigasilia. Citizens cannot register to vote anytime they choose. They have to register only within a certain narrow window in the calendar year. If one is out of the country during that period, sick, or otherwise unable to register, that's it. It is not a matter of registering before a certain date in order to have your name on the register for a particular election. You simply cannot register at all to vote outside of the specified dates fixed by the National Election Commission. That period by law is merely twenty-one days. In addition, you have to register for each general election. The old register, in effect, is hurled out and a new one opened. On top of that, you must register in the ward in which you reside and hence will vote. So you cannot simply register anywhere in your town, district, or province. It must be in your ward, which could be a small subsection of your town or district.

As he is driven to the office Tuesday morning, April 9, John mutters, "Why can't the old registration card be good until an individual decides to change address? It is like being guilty until proven innocent. You must prove at each round of election that you are still alive and still reside in the same ward. They even put up a preliminary list of the voters after the twenty-one days and allow persons in the ward to object to a name on that list on the grounds that the person does not reside there. What kind of fraud are we afraid of to have designed such a system? Is it double registration? Is it voting for someone who previously registered and is now dead or out of the country? You could die or leave the country between the registration and the elections. There is enough time for either occurrence. So many people find the system burdensome and yet they do not change it. Why? I bet many of the elites in this country are able to manipulate the system." John pauses to reflect. Then he continues, muttering a bit louder than before.

"You know, maybe the system has some logic. We lack adequate picture identification. We have too many people with similar names. The majority of people outside the main towns don't even have proper addresses. Then, of course, our level of computerization is abominable. Let's face it, we are a backward country. But this idea of twenty-one days for registration, they should at least change that. Then they can begin to chip away at the other constraints. The ID cards are the easiest. We are already committed to having those. As for names, maybe everyone should have four names. Even three names may not be enough to make sure we don't have duplication." He pauses again. He's not done.

"But when people vote they place dye on their thumbs anyway. I suppose they do not trust the dye. But how can you begin to trust when the evidence is so strong that the people are, indeed, untrustworthy?" John puffs air out of his mouth in frustration at the traffic.

"Or take this idea of restricting the length of campaigns. Why is campaigning officially confined to a certain period? Is that because our campaigns are usually so disruptive to public order? That makes sense, I suppose. If we are going to fight, let's shorten the period so we do not waste too much money on security or kill too many people. It is these campaign rallies. They are rowdy and the politicians say nothing. You don't hear a word from the party or the candidates about what they intend to do for the people when they get elected."

The driver, Samura Sonenge, interjects. "Sir, you are right. But the people don't go to the rallies to listen to the candidates. They go for what they can get. Sir, you know, right now, the same people go to the rallies of the two parties. They simply change their colors. They go get the T-shirt of the party and dance for it. We don't know how these people will vote when the elections come. The people say that they have to eat before the elections because we, the ordinary man, may not get anything from these people again once they are in power."

"But do the people know where the politicians get the money for the rallies?"

"Sir, the people know. Some of the politicians are rich and some are spending money they have stolen. Many of the party supporters live abroad. Those diasporans give a lot of money to the parties, because they think that they can get jobs if their party wins. You know, many of those diasporans are working too hard abroad, and they have no power or opportunities there to steal big money. So they want to come and get political jobs here or get top jobs in the civil service or the state enterprises."

John smiles; he has heard all this before. It is the general talk among Nigasilian diasporans everywhere, especially those that do not have any political connections in Nigasilia.

The driver looks at John via his rearview mirror, catches John's eye, and observes his smile. "Sir, I actually know someone very well who has given a lot of money to the two parties. . . . Yes, both of them."

When John arrives at the office, he learns from a colleague that some fifty miles north of Lamongwe, a rally by the government party was disrupted by the opposition thugs; one of the vice president's henchmen, the chief party organizer in that area, was beaten up. The man was in critical condition at a hospital in Lamongwe where he had to be rushed after first aid had been administered. Almost simultaneously, there was a road accident in which two of the opposition-party highflyers got killed. Their car veered off the road at high speed and rammed into an electricity pole. The opposition is crying foul play. They had been returning from a rally in which heckling youths, supposedly supporters of the government party, were disrupting the proceedings. There had been skirmishes quite close to where the car was parked and the police had to intervene.

The evidence of sabotage, though, seems weak, among other reasons because the tire popped quite some distance away from the scene. A survivor of the crash, in a statement to the police, said that the driver was going too fast. Still, the opposition is vowing revenge. John telephones his father and suggests that the minister of information call the press and say something to reduce the tension.

John sends for three of the newspapers. They are littered with bad news. The headquarters of the opposition in two districts have been ransacked and one of them actually burned down. It seems as if the police have been focusing more on protecting the properties and offices of the government party than those of the opposition. John phones the VP and advises him to remind the interior minister and the head of the police to act in a fair manner. Aid donors will be watching. John knows that will certainly get the attention of the VP. For John, that is probably the only virtue of aid dependence. He tells the VP, "We are going to win the elections. We don't need to harass the opposition." John is struggling to stay civil. Just because the country's per capita income and average educational level are both low does not mean that the people should behave like animals.

John picks up his cell phone and dials. "Hi, Dad. With all this violence going on, I would advise that you call the police chief and let him know that the police should protect all the parliamentarians, ours as well as the opposition's, equally. Then, if the violence does not stop, maybe you should go on radio and television and tell the people that you are willing to bring out the army if any violence erupts again, that you would not spare any hooligans no matter their party affiliation."

"Okay, John. I agree with you. I shall talk to the police chief and let's see what happens after that."

John hardly recovers from his frustration when he receives a phone call from Stephen Mongo.

"John, do you know that the central bank governor is going around leaning on senior commercial bankers to contribute to the government party's election effort?"

"No, why would he do that? You people should just ignore him."

"Maybe we should, John. But he is a big man and we don't know how to do it."

"Stephen, do nothing. The man is acting like an idiot. I'll find a way to get him to stop."

"I think he is also pressuring the Chamber of Commerce. In fact, I know that for sure."

John calls the minister of finance and development immediately. "Tubo, do you know that the governor is soliciting contributions for our party from the commercial bankers and the Chamber of Commerce?"

"We are not that desperate for money."

"Then why don't you let him know that."

"John, if you have heard something, you talk to him. Please. He is a VP man. That's how he got that job. If I talk to him he will simply ignore me and tell the VP that I am working against the interest of our party."

John proceeds to call the governor, Victor Kunongo. "Governor, John Bijunga here. How are you?"

"Hello, Dr. Bijunga, what can I do for you?"

"Governor, I see you are a serious Progressive Party man. I did not know that you were so committed."

"What do you mean?"

"Well, I am hearing gossip that you are soliciting money from the commercial bankers and the Chamber of Commerce. I'm sure you don't want such a rumor spreading around. You know the papers are busy looking for all the gossip they can find. We don't need another big story now, I'm sure you will agree."

"Yes, I agree with you. I certainly do not want lies circulating. Look, all I said to these people was that our party has been working hard for businesses, and they should show their appreciation."

"You never told them to make financial contributions?"

"No. But they are big people and they probably misinterpreted what I meant."

"You see, this is what I mean. Say nothing more to them. If they mention financial contribution to our party tell them you don't want to discuss such a sensitive topic with them, because you do not want rumors spreading that the governor of the Bank of Nigasilia has been going around campaigning for the government party."

"I will cease any activity that would raise such a suspicion."

Soon after lunch, the VP telephones John and asks if he could drop by before going home. When he arrives, they greet each other and the vice president says, with a warm smile, "Congratulations on the engagement. Your father told me everything went very well. I think the whole of Nigasilia must be looking forward to this wedding. I called you because I have not been able to really talk to you about the elections since the campaign started. You know, John, at the end of the day, no normal person enjoys violence. When normal people are violent it usually reflects their fears or they are simply responding in kind to what they see as violence against them. I have not encouraged violence. But perhaps I should do more to discourage it. Your father has been a wise friend to me in that regard. He is always cautioning me against coming down to the level of the opposition."

"VP, I myself think that we have to find a way as a nation to reduce violence in politics, especially during election campaigns. We economists believe that our low incomes and education have something to do with it. But that is only true in a relative sense, that is, when compared to richer countries. I believe that in an absolute sense we can still have much less violence than we have now. Thank God, so far no one has actually died as a direct consequence of these campaigns. I hear that even our man who was seriously injured is now going to recover soon."

"That brings me to another subject, John. This STRONG group has written a letter addressed to the president. Have you seen it?"

"No."

"That's surprising. I thought they would have consulted you before they sent it to the president. Anyway, your father has not read his copy yet. It just came at lunchtime. They are asking to have representation as election observers at polling stations of their choosing and at the tabulation of the votes. Now, John, this is a group that, as far as I know, has no legal status. They are only in the process of formation and right now operate like a youth club. Those particular youth are threatening to march to Parliament and the State House if we do not respond to them within a week. Is this a joke? We are having serious local and international observers at our elections. Why would these young people think they should be recognized within that elite group? Why don't they continue to focus on their organization, properly register STRONG, and then approach government with any suggestions they have? Where is this manifesto that they were working on? After they are properly registered, we will at least entertain them and listen to their demands. But now they spring this on us?"

"Do they have an address on the letter?"

"No, they say they will send a delegation for their answer next week Tuesday. That's just four days from the elections. They threaten to march on the eighteenth if we turn them down."

"Well, this is precipitous action on their part. It makes no sense to give them observer status now. I would advise that you alert the police to get ready in case they decide to march. Then get the army on alert in case their march encourages looters. But tell the army to go slow on live ammunition, if they have to intercede. They should arm themselves with tear gas. So that's preparing for the worst. In terms of preparing for the best, I would suggest that you and the president invite me to any meeting with them. Then, with both of you sitting there, allow me to answer the STRONG representatives on your behalf, if you don't mind. The youth won't mind. They are good Africans; they know the spokesman is allowed to answer for the chiefs, with the chiefs sitting right there."

"Well, John, it will be up to your father, of course. But when he asks my opinion I will suggest that he accepts your proposal."

In the meanwhile, as soon as he ended his telephone conversation with John, the president had summoned the chief of police of Nigasilia, Alimam Jallowa, to his office.

"Alimam, remember, we agreed that we would not tolerate any violence during this election and that we would do anything necessary to prevent violence. You were supposed to train your people and to do preliminary investigations that would help you anticipate potential sources of violence. You were supposed to protect all politicians campaigning. With all what is going on, you have failed so far. Alimam, if you embarrass me and the nation, I will have no alternative but to relieve you of your job."

The police chief stood in an erect military position all the time the president was addressing him. "Your Excellency, my teams in certain localities have failed me. I am already making changes and disciplining them. If there is more serious violence, I will not wait for you to sack me, sir. But for small skirmishes, I will beg your forgiveness; those are impossible to prevent one 100 percent of the time. What we aim to achieve is to stop them as they start, arrest the culprits, and lock them up without bail until trial. Once the word gets around that we are that strict, you will see, sir, even the skirmishes will stop."

"Okay, Chief, right now you have my confidence."

"Thank you, Your Excellency."

Jamina and John are headed for the Indochinese restaurant tonight. He lets Jamina worry about the order. She is always right as far as he is concerned. She knows his taste and the menu.

After completing the order, Jamina says, "Vivienne is pregnant. She confirmed that today."

"Wow, that's great. Do they care whether it's a boy or a girl?"

"For the first child, does anybody care?"

"How many children do they want?"

"Three. That's what Vivienne wants. So that's what they will get, God willing."

"How many do you want?"

"Two. That way I'll have four."

"I understand. To tell you the truth, I am not so sure that I want you giving birth in this country. Too many women die during childbirth here. And at your age, we have to be cautious."

"It's usually the very poor ones, John, that die from childbirth."

"Well, I still would not want to take the risk with you. As soon as we get married we are going to the US for our honeymoon. Then we shall hook you up with my group of doctors. We shall plan our life so that you have your first child around August or September of the following year. We want to be sure that you are on holidays here and can be in America for the delivery."

Jamina laughs. "John, I thought having lived in America for so long you would have realized that the modern woman does not tolerate you men trying to control them like little infants with no minds. Also, I have not yet decided that I want to go to America for our honeymoon. I suppose I have a say in the matter, right?"

"Yes, you have. Sorry, Jamina, I get too excited about these things. You know I love and respect you. So we will decide together. Don't mind me."

John looks dejected, so Jamina sympathetically asks, "How did Donald's recital go?"

"His music teacher says it went extremely well. He thinks Donald can become a classical pianist if he wants. But I don't think Donald himself or I want him to go in that direction. He can be more useful in other areas."

"Yes, I can understand that."

"So, has your mother recovered from the engagement ceremony?"

"Yes. I spoke with her today, in fact. She is relieved, of course, that she did not forget anything. That is what she usually worries about. She does not mind doing a ton of things. But she hates forgetting one little thing. So, if I turn out to be a perfectionist in our social life you will know where I get it from."

"Oh, I don't mind that, because then I don't have to worry about anything."

"Right you are. Except that I may be asking you to help me do this and that. Then we'll see how relaxed you will be."

"I can't win, can I?"

Jamina smiles and taps John's hand. "I have got to go back to my routine. I am feeling fat and lazy. I have not played squash for some time now. Come with me on Saturday to the club and watch me play, will you?"

"Of course, my dear. After all, I will hardly see you next week. It's the last week before the elections on Saturday and my father wants me to go to two rallies with him. I hate those events. They are not campaigns. They are more like parties. And I will have to pretend that I am enjoying them. If there is trouble and I get beaten up, make sure they fly me out immediately. My father knows doctors in the UK."

"John, there is no violence at rallies of the presidential candidates. It's when these underlings campaign that hoodlums feel at liberty to disrupt the proceedings. When the presidential candidates are there, the police protection alone scares them. So I am not worried, and you shouldn't be either."

Early the next day, the VP walks into the president's office for a meeting that had been pre-arranged to review progress in the campaign. Before getting to the main agenda, the president raises the issue of the STRONG demands. "Kamake, what do we do about this group? I talked to John last night and he said that they never consulted him. I guess they figure that they can handle matters themselves and do not need big brother anymore."

"Yes, that must be it."

"John thought it may not be a bad idea for us to meet them. He would also like to attend the meeting. He suggested that after a few introductory remarks by me, he jumps in and convinces them that their demand for observer status is neither reasonable nor necessary. But I don't like that approach. This group has no status yet in Nigasilia. Why should I meet with their representatives? I think only John should meet them. If they are not happy with that and want to march, we will not give them permission, unless they have registered properly by then as one of our civil society organizations."

"When I spoke to John earlier in the day, he did not mention your opening remarks. He was going to be the only one speaking to them with the two of us just present. On reflection, I think your suggestion is preferable."

Six days later, the STRONG representatives arrive calmly for their appointment. They had called the day before asking if it was all right for them to come by at 10:00 a.m. and had been assured that they would be given a hearing at that time. They were told to be no more than four.

Moments after they arrive, John walks into the small conference room where they have been waiting. They all smile at him immediately. The four young people are Gabie Manray, Fiatuh Jallowa, Bobbo Sabu, and Marie Santana. All four stand up and in unison exclaim, "Dr. Bijunga, good morning."

"Good morning. It is good to see you all here." They reintroduce themselves and John continues. "The president and the vice president cannot see you because they are very busy this morning on some important matters of state. But they have discussed your request and I will speak with full authority from them. I assume you have completed the necessary registration of your organization with the Ministry of Social Welfare?"

"No, sir," Gabie Manray, the leader, responds. "We plan to do so next month. We have asked a young lawyer to assist us with the legal registration."

"Then how are you different from a group who walks off the street and tells us that they belong to a youth club that is concerned about democracy in this country and would like to be given observer status in the upcoming elections? If we grant you such a status, I hope you can see the risk we run. Look, even once you are properly registered, we will not necessarily agree to give you such a status. We would want to know what expertise and interests you bring to the table. We already have international organizations, bilateral aid donors, and highly reputable international and domestic civil society organizations coming to act as observers. Don't be in a rush. Register your organization. Continue your workshops and earn respect through that process. Then work on your manifesto if you are still interested in pursuing that route. This insistence on being an observer in the coming elections is a digression that you don't need."

"Dr. Bijunga, can we just discuss among ourselves a little?"

A few minutes later, John returns, and Gabie Manray speaks again. "Thank you very much, Dr. Bijunga, for agreeing to talk to us. As you know, we have a lot of respect for you and we do appreciate your advice. So we will give up our main idea for coming here. Thank you again. Please apologize to the president and the vice president. We did not intend to waste their time."

"I thank you, also, for acting in a mature manner," John replies. "I shall relay your message."

Soon after he had returned from the engagement, John received a call from David Simpson, the brother of his late wife, Cecilia. David had been assigned to cover the elections in Nigasilia for his paper. The paper knows about his connections to John but does not think that will pose any ethical problems.

John makes no attempt to help David through the formalities of entering the country. It is important to both of them that David be treated as would any other reporter from the US coming to Nigasilia. Once in Nigasilia, David has a busy schedule. He has naturally been in touch with the US Embassy, the Nigasilian Association of Journalists, the Ministry of Information, and the general secretaries of the two major political parties. But he did ask John if he could arrange an interview with the president.

David is interested in talking to a broad sample of voters—educated and non-educated, blue collar and white, high income and low, male and female, Lamongwian and non-Lamongwian. He is curious to know why people vote the way they do, what motivates them to vote one way rather than another. He is keen to observe the voting—the lines, the orderliness of the voting, and the spirit and demeanor of voters. Finally, he intends to talk to the observers, especially the international observers, and hear their views of what has unfolded.

The evening of the second day of his seven-day visit, David has dinner with John and Jamina at Jamina's house. As they begin their meal, Jamina asks David, "Has your newspaper always had this kind of interest in Nigasilia or does this reflect your personal influence?"

"Actually, the paper's interest in Africa has been strong for the past thirty years. There are a few countries that they keep track of, mainly the largest ones in each region. Typically, they follow events like elections and civil wars. Occasionally they will research themes, such as corruption, activities of non-governmental organizations, that sort of thing. Since I covered Nigasilia for the NGO study, they have kept Nigasilia as one of my countries."

"Well, I hope you enjoy your visit. Unfortunately, John was telling me that you will not have much time for visiting our beautiful sites, particularly forests, hills, and islands. I hope you have another opportunity to come here soon."

"Well, from what I have been hearing, I might have that opportunity soon."

Jamina knows that David is referring to a possible marriage, and all three laugh.

"I hope we will have the opportunity to read your article," Jamina says. "We can always download it, I hope."

"Yes, of course," David responds. After a slight pause he says, "This is a delicious meal. I love shrimp but this sauce that you people make is so good."

"Actually, it's very basic. It includes onions and peppers, tomatoes, tomato paste, and spices. Anyone can make it. You can use olive oil, peanut oil . . . just about any kind of light oil as you like. Tonight the cook used olive oil."

"So what are you doing tomorrow?" John asks David.

"I'll go around interviewing people on the streets and then I'll try to interview a couple of the national election commissioners as well as the leader of the opposition."

"Where will you be on Election Day?"

"I'm going up to Bogoba."

"Great," Jamina says, "that's not too far from my parents. Sorry your schedule is so busy that I cannot get people of the town to show you the larger neighborhood."

In the days preceding the election, David would stop people at random on the street, tell them that he was from the US to cover the Nigasilian elections, and ask them questions. He conducted interviews of some sixty people, one-third of them in Lamongwe and all of them randomly selected from ordinary people walking on the streets. They all voted strictly along party lines; apart from the presidential candidates, most of them did not even know the names of the Parliament members of their constituency for whom they were going to vote. They were all worried about jobs, corruption, and tribalism, in that order. David asked one high school dropout in Lamongwe, "How will people get jobs without education?"

The fellow responded, "The government should give us the education."

"How?"

"Free schools, free books, free materials, and transport money."

"Is that all?"

The boy laughed.

Interestingly, the majority of the answers from the ordinary people were in the same mode.

David asked to interview a representative of the Chamber of Commerce. The Chamber asked someone to talk to him on the Chamber's behalf, a dealer in a vehicle sales agency. David asked the dealer about the ordinary people, especially the youth, complaining about jobs. David explained that the youth were saying their jobs were influencing their vote. The dealer laughed. "I don't believe it. Neither party is better than the other one in providing jobs for the community. It's all tribalistic and corruption talk. They feel they will get jobs if one party goes in rather than the other because of favoritism. My friend, the politicians who run this country don't know how to create jobs the way you and I want to create jobs."

"What do you mean?"

"Look, everybody knows that if we want to put the youth to work, we need infrastructure, education, and training of the youths, discipline of the workers, and efficiency in the public sector's provision of services. Taxation is not bad, in practice. The taxation people are really poor at collection, and you can bribe them to reduce your effective taxation, so they can set any rate they like. We don't care."

On Election Day, David was particularly impressed by the orderly lines and the presence and vigilance of the police. He approached a group of women standing in one of the lines in Bogoba, the second largest town in Nigasilia some 160 miles from Lamongwe, and one of the three towns he would visit in the interior during his trip.

"How long have you ladies been standing in line?"

"For about two hours."

"Isn't that long?"

"No, we will be voting in a few minutes. This is nothing. The lines used to be longer, but now we have more polling stations, so the longest we stand will be about two and a half hours."

"Is the line always as orderly as it looks?"

"Yes, we don't fight or quarrel, and if an old man or woman comes, we usually allow them to cut in front of us."

David has dinner one night at a Nigasilian restaurant with Mahdu Kontana, Dumomo Frah, and Sanjo Manray. The dinner takes place on the last night before David is to leave. That evening, as they settle with their first course, Sanjo Manray looks straight at David and says, "You know, David, our governments in Nigasilia are always sensitive to what foreign reporters and diplomats write or say about us. We are always afraid that they will say things that will discourage foreign investors or tourists. I hope you have not found anything that will lead you to write something discouraging."

"Actually, Minister, I doubt I will write anything that will make tourists and investors more eager to come. But I believe people will look at Nigasilia more closely than before. Remember, I have come simply to observe elements of the democratic process. I have not investigated your economic policies at all. As far as democracy goes, I find that you are making tremendous strides. The impression left on me, and all observers that I interviewed, is that the elections were orderly and fair. There were enough polling stations so that lines were not discouragingly long, and those manning the polls had been well trained. Voters seemed relaxed. I realize that I observed the actual voting only in Bogoba. But I spoke to the international observers of many polling stations around the country. I realize that the opposition is saying that in the counting, a higher percentage of ballots were disqualified in the areas in which they were favored. But the international observers disagree and contend that, statistically, it is not an accurate accusation. This, of course, remains to be fully verified."

"I believe that having the ballots counted at the polling stations in which they were cast helped quite a bit," Sanjo says. "At least this is the general conclusion we have drawn. Before this election, we used to transport all the boxes to some central place in each district. That led to all kinds of fraud. Boxes disappeared and there was evidence of stuffing boxes. But now I think we have drastically reduced the chances of those kinds of things happening."

"John told me this is your second visit to Nigasilia," Dumomo Frah says. "Did you see any difference?"

"Actually, no, I did not see major differences. Things are not any worse or better than I observed the last time I was here, which was in 1997. Well, there are more Chinese here than before. But I don't suppose that was the kind of thing to which you were referring?"

"No. I meant the way the place looks in general and the impression of economic activity around."

"In Lamongwe itself, there are a few more modern-looking houses. But they are more than counterbalanced by a greater number of tin shacks. I have not been able to enjoy the beaches and the hills as much as I did the first time I was here. I also want to see some of your wildlife and forest reserves. I will have to come with my wife, if not my children as well, and spend some time with John. You seem to have a very beautiful country."

The very next day, it's time for David to return to the US. John lets his driver use his private vehicle to take David to the airport. But enough time is allowed for David to drop by John's office on his way. John has a surprise for him. He was able to arrange for David to have a quick word with his father.

When they enter his office, the president asks David, "Is this your first experience with elections in Africa?"

"I'm afraid so, Mr. President."

"Well, I hope we did well."

"Yes, Mr. President, it was orderly, and I was impressed. To tell you the truth, I did not know what to expect. As you know, the news about African elections is not usually good. So what did you do this time that you think worked?"

"Well, let me say, to start, that it was not perfect. Early in the game, there was violence. So, I had to let everyone know by my words as well as my actions that I was very serious about ensuring an election process free of violence, intimidation, and rigging. For this, three things were essential. First, the police had to do their work with vigilance and efficiency. Second, the international and local observers had to be seen observing, and they had to have the logistics and the access to be effective observers. Third, the National Election Commission had to be competent at doing what they were supposed to do, starting with the registration process."

"I gather you are confident that you are going to win. Did that help?"

"What do you mean?"

"Well, this confidence could have made your party people believe without a lot of persuasion that they did not need to cheat or to engage in violence to come out victorious."

The president throws up his hands and smiles calmly.

"Look, you have a point that I can't deny. But Nigasilians, I am sure, also believed that I was very serious, whatever their political affiliation. Deep down they knew I would not tolerate violence or cheating."

"Well, I am glad to hear that. I am also happy that, as far as the elections are concerned, I can write without any reservations that it was a resounding success. Good luck, Mr. President, in your second five-year term."

Two days into the counting—normally four to five days pass before the results are announced—the president asks John to come and see him in his office.

"John, it is obvious that we are going to win. I am trying to have my cabinet in place no more than a couple of days after the NEC announces the official results."

"I think that's a good idea."

"John, I want you to be the minister of finance and development. I will incorporate your current department into the new ministry. It will become the Economic Analysis Department. I don't think we shall have any problems with parliamentary approval. It is all clearly logical."

"Yes, the reorganization is logical. But what will happen to Tubo Bangar? I don't want him to think that I maneuvered him out of a job. Have you spoken to him?"

"No, I wanted to be sure that you would accept my offer first. I will offer Tubo the Ministry of Health. That is an important ministry.

Our primary health care is not improving, women are dying from childbirth, and our public health facilities have deteriorated seriously over the last two decades. I need someone committed to good governance in that ministry. Tubo has done a decent job in Finance. I like him and think he is the right man for that job, even though he is not a doctor."

"Oh, I have no doubt things will improve under him. But you might have to give him a free hand to discipline people at all levels."

"Yes, John, I know. I agree."

"When are you going to talk to him? Jamina and I are planning a party the Saturday after this one and I want to invite him."

"I'll talk to him first thing tomorrow."

"Good. Thanks, Dad. I am very pleased with the offer."

"Well, you deserve it."

The following day, as soon as he is finished talking to the president, Tubo drops by John's office and greets him warmly. "Congratulations, man. Your dad just told me that you finally agreed to become a minister. I am happy that you are taking over. I was afraid that the VP would engineer something to get me out of this ministry. I wonder why they decided to send me to Health. I think that it is an important ministry. But for some reason it seems so difficult."

"Well, if anyone can change that reputation, you can. My dad himself came up with the suggestion. He recognizes that it is a difficult ministry and he has enormous confidence in you."

Four days after the polls, the results of the elections are officially announced. John's father won 58 percent of the votes, so there is no need for a runoff. The president is disappointed. He wanted to win at least 60 percent. The government party did better in Parliament, winning some 62 percent of the seats. The opposition won 30 percent, while some minor parties and independents won the remaining 8 percent.

On the first Saturday in May, John and Jamina throw a dinner party at John's house. Invited are John's four cabinet friends and their spouses. The five Chamber of Commerce people, on whom John has come to depend, attend as well: Baba Tey, Paul Sutu, Malika Kaykai, Tarik Day, and Raboya Bami. Then there are the leading friends, Vivienne and Santie, and Stephen and Betty Mongo. They decide to include Rabena as well. Rabena has been complaining to John that she never gets to see Jamina because John monopolizes all her free time. John feels sorry for Rabena because her daughter is now in the US and so she must be feeling quite lonely.

This is more than a normal gathering of friends. There is good reason to celebrate. There is, first of all, the engagement of Jamina and John. Apart from Mahdu Kontana, Stephen Mongo, and Vivienne and Santie, the others were not present at the formal gathering and they want to drink a toast to their friends. Then there is the victory of the government party. They are all pleased because they admire the president and are happy for John. Finally, John is becoming a true insider in politics as a minister. They figure that must be good news to all who want to see improved governance in Nigasilia.

Soon after the first drinks are served, Rabena rises to her feet. "Ladies and gentlemen, I would like to propose a toast to two wonderful people who must have been made for each other, Jamina and John. I, for one, can't wait for the big day to come. Cheers to Jamina and John." The guests all raise their glasses and say "Cheers!"

John asks everyone to fill up their glasses at the drinks table, while the waiters place the hors d'oeuvres on the main serving table. Jamina looks around to make sure everyone is fine. She catches Stephen Mongo's eyes and he asks her, "Jamina, what will you and John do with two houses when you get married?"

Jamina laughs. "We will keep both and toss coins to know where we sleep each night."

"I think that's a neat idea myself," Betty jokes.

"Well, you know, my house is mine, so we will keep it. I will let John decide if he wants to keep this government house. I actually like its simplicity. Maybe I'll convince him to come live with me in my house and then we shall come here whenever we want to be very romantic, because in my house I'll be cold. It is too sacred."

The Mongos burst out laughing.

A waiter soon comes around collecting the used plates. The main course is about to be served. Baba Tey gets up and says, "I would like to propose a toast to the Progressive Party for its victory. Of course, I will not tell you for whom I voted." Everyone laughs. "More seriously, I want to commend the government party for doing its utmost to limit the fighting during the campaign and for running a fair and clean election. Nigasilia has turned the corner in its democratic journey."

John shouts, "Hear, hear!"

Baba Tey continues. "I wish the government all the best and hope it succeeds in making Nigasilia a good place for ordinary people and businessmen alike. Cheers!"

Everyone raises their glass again and drinks heartily.

John turns to Sanjo Manray. "Manray, I think you have to reply to that one."

Manray agrees. "Well, Baba, thank you for your well wishes. The government of Nigasilia has to work for all the people. The government cannot succeed unless it has the overwhelming support of the people. Of course, we count businessmen and businesswomen as part of the people, too. So thank you, Baba, and I hope you all will do your own bit in helping us to succeed as a nation, no matter what party you voted for."

People approach the table in small batches for the main course, in the midst of laughter and lively conversation. Everyone is having fun and John and Jamina do their best to circulate. When the main course is over, the waiters collect the dishes; everyone knows that dessert and coffee or tea is about to be served. Kontana slides over to Dumomo Frah, and whispers something in his ears. Dumomo then bangs his knife gently against his glass to call everyone to attention. "Ladies and gentlemen, I want to propose a special toast to John. Even though he is the son of the president, you would not know it from his behavior. This man has his country at heart and he loves his father. Well, many of us love John, too." Everyone cheers.

Dumomo continues. "As you know, John is now minister of finance and development. For those of us who were worried that John would soon run away and leave us here, his decision to accept this offer is a signal that he is in this fight all the way. So, I would like to propose a toast to the health of our dear friend and wish him all the best in his new assignment. To John, the minister of finance and development! Cheers!"

After they all take their sips, John says, "Let's serve dessert, can we?"

Everyone gets up and heads for the table. When all return to their seats, John walks to the center of the room. "Thank you all for the toast, and Dumomo, I thank you for your kind words. You know, when I decided to come here, I knew it was not going to be easy. What I did not fully reckon at the time was that there were committed people who were determined to walk with my dad across the forest to help clear the path. You, my friends, and especially the four cabinet members here, are among those good people. I thank you for your support. When one has been away for a long time and returns to assist in the governance of this our beloved country, he or she needs friends. If I did not appreciate that before, I certainly do now. So thank you. I hope we will continue the walk together."

Everyone claps. Santie, who likes to tease John, says, "John, we will walk with you through the forest. But you have to remember that the implements we are holding have been affected by the environment here. We can't brush off grass or blow dirt off as rapidly and efficiently as you can. So you just have to be patient with us."

"You mean I am not already patient?"

"You are trying, but you have some way to go."

There are, of course, serious discussions, too. For example, Dumomo Frah, always on the serious side, walks up to Tubo Bangar who is chatting with Kontana and asks, "How are you going to turn things around in the Ministry of Health? No one seems to be able to do a good job in that ministry. The World Health Organization thinks we could have a serious health crisis in this country in the next few years unless we act now."

"I have actually given a lot of thought to exactly that question. It seems to me that the answer is easy and not so easy at the same time. Simply put, we need to walk the walk. Yes, it's all about implementation. We have been voicing a lot of excellent objectives. For example, we have been talking about focusing on primary health care. To that end, we have talked about improving services and educating citizens about immunization, sanitation, hygiene, and safe drinking water. But when it comes to implementation we have shown insufficient commitment, and our delivery has been woeful to say the least. Much of the problem has to do with corruption, of course. So we must address that. But a lot of it also has to do with poor administration and a weak analytical basis for decision making."

"I can only wish you luck. It is a very important area. If you succeed, we shall begin to see our standing rise in the Human Development Report of the UN. Anyway, with you at the helm, I am optimistic."

Since their meeting at the State House, the STRONG youth have followed John's advice to the letter. They soon completed the necessary registration. By the end of the first week in May, they had brought two drafts of their manifesto to John for comments. Today, the second Wednesday in May, the STRONG representatives arrive at John's office with what they think is a draft that John can approve. The manifesto is important in their overall strategy and they do not want to issue it without John's approval.

The manifesto is titled "Holding Government Accountable for the Socio-Economic Welfare of Citizens." It calls on all civil society organizations in Nigasilia to unite behind a set of indicators by which to judge government performance. This unified civil society movement will demand that government annually publish data on specific socio-economic variables. John, in his advice to them, had insisted that the relevant socio-economic variables contained in the manifesto satisfy three basic criteria. First, they should be widely acceptable by the various socio-economic groups in the country. Second, they should be readily quantifiable. Third, they should matter greatly in the sense that progress in those variables clearly indicates progress in the general socio-economic welfare of the population at large. John also advised the group to keep the number of variables small, certainly no more than ten. The group's decided list of variables were infant mortality, death from childbirth, life expectancy, literacy rates, average years of schooling, proportion of population with access to safe drinking water, electricity production, proportion of population with access to electricity, and real income per capita.

The final draft of the manifesto, which they have come to discuss today, demands that the data published must be validated by some internationally credible organization. The unified civil society movement must then meet each year and vote on whether it considers the progress being made by the government satisfactory. The movement must hold a news conference and issue a press release as well. If the progress is judged unsatisfactory for three years in a row then the movement must do everything in its power to bring down the government.

John thinks that the last part of the manifesto should be modified. "I think the decision to change the government should be based on performance over a four-year period. Of course, the annual assessments should take place. That is fine. But our governments have five-year terms. If the government fails over its first four years, then all you need to do is organize to see it defeated in the next election. You can achieve your goal without threatening public order, since you will not have to march to bring down a sitting government before its term ends."

It does not take the STRONG representatives any time at all to accept the suggestion. They are anxious to have John's support and do not want to challenge him on details that do not contravene their major objectives. They reason that it is enough that John agrees with the general principles and approach. They can live with that, at least until they gain more credibility and stature with the populace at large. That part of the manifesto will be changed to read: "If the performance of the government over a four-year period is judged unsatisfactory, the unified civil society movement will do everything in its power to have that government and the associated political party defeated in the next election."

The STRONG representatives explain to John that they intend to publish the manifesto as a small pamphlet and sell it to the general public to raise modest funds. They will send copies to the government, through the office of the minister of social welfare. They will also send copies to several news media. Most importantly, they will now approach several relevant civil society organizations to discuss the next steps in the implementation of the manifesto.

"Okay, my friends," John admonishes the group as they are about to leave, "stay calm and sensible. Continue earnestly with your workshops and sensitization programs. If you run into serious problems in reaching an agreement within the unified civil society movement, do not hesitate to come and see me. I wish you all the best."

Two days later, John and Jamina have dinner with the president. The old man had not seen Jamina for some weeks now and so asked John to bring her over. When they enter the Hut, the president embraces Jamina. "I see John has been hiding you. You shouldn't let him do that, Jamina. How are the wedding preparations coming along?"

"Things are moving, Mr. President. My mother is coming to Lamongwe tomorrow for a few days, just to be in tune with what we are doing down here. In Wombono, of course, she is taking care of things. But she has a lot of help there, and that celebration will not be as huge as it will be here. Anyway, John and I have arranged the hall, we have contracted a caterer and a disc jockey, and John will take care of the drinks. We have already started sending out the invitations. We are luckier than many people in Lamongwe, because the people we are inviting have all got proper addresses."

"John was saying that you want to go to the US for a short honeymoon."

"Dad, we are still discussing that," John butts in.

Jamina thinks John may be a bit embarrassed and tries to help him. "Sir, I think John wants to give me a proper tour of Washington. I am interested in doing a master's degree in the US or UK and if I am married to John, the US is logical. But I am not sure yet whether I want to go anywhere outside Nigasilia for our honeymoon."

The president glances at John and decides not to comment.

Then John, looking rather serious, says, "Dad, I am more concerned about introducing her to an obstetrician so that she doesn't have to deliver any baby here in Nigasilia. She has a 10 percent chance of dying from childbirth if she delivers here."

With a frown on his face, John's dad asks, "Is that right, John?"

"That's what the statistics say."

Jamina smiles. "I told him that those statistics apply to the poor in this country. The well-to-do have their private doctors, nourish themselves properly, and go to the only decent private hospital we have to deliver their babies."

"I guess you are right, Jamina," the president says. "But that also means we should try and work towards having more than one decent hospital, doesn't it? Anyway, for the time being, John may have to shield this from the press. If they pick up that you've gone to the States to deliver your child, they might exploit this information."

John is defensive. "We'll be paying for it from our own private funds. I think that is permissible."

The president is not happy with the line of conversation. "And your father, Jamina, he is well, I hope."

"Yes, sir, he is doing very well. He has a lot of nitty-gritty tasks to perform. But I came to the conclusion some time ago that chiefs enjoy those tasks. I think that unless you want to perform those tasks you do not have the temperament to be chief. Many of those tasks seem dull to me."

"Jamina, you may be right. But one problem that he was very instrumental in resolving for us was anything but dull—mediating in a chieftaincy dispute in a neighboring chiefdom."

"Oh, yes, my mother kept me abreast on that one. I am glad it is all over now. I guess you two will share notes when he comes for the wedding."

"Yes, in other words I asked John to tell you that I have invited your father for a one-on-one meeting at the State House when he is here. I will send an official car to pick him up at your house. You also got my note from John inviting you, your brother, and your parents for the get-together of the two families at my residence, right?"

"Yes, Mr. President."

"You and John will bring everyone that night. I don't want my son to have to remind me that I should not use an official vehicle for what is a private family affair. You know him, Jamina."

"Yes, sir, I do."

While they move from the dining room table to the living room, Jamina says, "Mr. President, did John tell you that he spoke to the girls in my school? They asked him all sorts of questions, indicating that they want to see government improve their lives."

The president, hoping this is not another difficult topic, responds. "Yes, he did."

"Did he also tell you he advised the kids to let their leaders know that they want the government to do better?"

"Yes, Jamina, not only did he tell me but he told me with the biggest smile across his face. I guess after mobilizing the college-educated youth, now he wants to go to the secondary school level. Well, we are not yet ready to indict him for inciting insurrection."

"Mr. President, you should have seen how excited those girls were over your son."

John interjects. "Were you jealous?"

"I was just very surprised. I have never seen a speaker in the assembly rouse them that much. They are still having long conversations about him with me, Mr. President. Many of them are saying they will come and wait on the streets near the church to see us on our wedding day."

"Jamina, that just shows how well liked you are in the school. The appreciation for your commitment to the girls must show up in many different ways. John told me that he almost had to sign a bond that he will not persuade you to live in America before you would accede to his request to marry you."

Jamina taps John on his shoulder and smiles. "Don't mind him, Mr. President. He exaggerates."

But the president suddenly lights up. "No, if that's what you did, I am happy. I myself have much more use for John here in Nigasilia than in the US. Any offer you can make him to stay here that he cannot refuse is a good offer to me. I support you."

John and Jamina glance at each other and smile.

"John, you mentioned to me some time ago that the boys' schooling would be a major dilemma for you. Have you thought it through yet?"

"I am averse to bringing them here, because the facilities are inadequate. I realize that students do survive here and go abroad to leading universities. But those who are able do so are a small minority. The boys are used to decent libraries, computer facilities, laboratories, and real bathrooms. The adjustment would be traumatic for them. So for me, the effective choice has been between American and British boarding schools. The advantage of British boarding schools is proximity to Nigasilia. But the boys are used to the American system and David and Frances are around in case of emergencies. So far, though, I have been ignoring the problem of money. But it is a real one. I may have to apply for financial aid. My savings are limited. I don't want to sell my house in Arlington. If money becomes a real concern, then I may have to rethink the whole strategy."

The president realizes that this could complicate John's decision to stay. But he is not quite mentally prepared to accept that reality as yet.

"So you have thought seriously about the problem. I'm sure you will make the decision that will be best for the boys and for you as well."

John cannot avoid bringing up, even in a muted form, the most important thing that will influence his decision on whether to stay in Nigasilia: whether he would be able to get the majority of the leadership in Nigasilia to resolutely pursue sound economic and political governance.

"You see, Dad, if Nigasilia had been serious about development like Singapore, I would not have been faced with such a miserable choice four decades after independence. I would simply have brought the boys here."

"Well, we are not Singapore, John. We are not. Do you still intend to argue for this national council on socio-economic governance?"

"You, and especially the VP, had left me with the impression that you would not mind further discussions of the idea after the elections. I am willing to give up the grand notion of a national council as well as the idea of tying targets and benchmarks to the survival of a regime. What I would suggest, then, is to specify minimum targets that we commit ourselves to meeting. As to the variables, I would suggest the same ones as the STRONG kids will outline in their manifesto, a copy of which you will receive. I helped them in the choice of the variables and I believe that those variables are adequate to use in assessing progress. We can decide the targets we want to set and try our utmost as a government to meet those targets. You will discover that how we perform with respect to those variables will be a reflection of the quality of our economic governance as a whole."

"I am willing to go along with that approach, though when we come to specify quantitative targets, I predict with certainty that you and I will struggle. You will want to improve everything at lightning speed. I will, in contrast, insist on our being realistic."

John does not agree. "Dad, stop repeating this mantra that we are not East Asians, that the world is a tougher place now than when the East Asians were achieving their fast rate of growth. If we make the necessary adaptations, given the resources that we have, we can grow our economies in today's world as fast as they grew theirs in yesterday's world."

"Yes, John, I know the sermon. As you work around here, you will find that you have to adjust a little. But your ambition is good. You might end up inspiring us all to do much better than we had dreamt."

Chapter 13

From the president's house, the couple heads to Jamina's.

"I am impressed how much he trusts and respects you," Jamina says. "He always wants to discuss complex issues of state with you, what you call governance issues."

"Well, they are governance issues. But you forget how much he frustrates me. I keep wondering who on earth has planted these ideas in his head. He is in effect telling me that we cannot jump the fence to get to the other side because we are not as capable of jumping as those on the other side. And worse still, the fence, he says, is higher now than when those on the other side had to jump. So, either because of our incapability or the fact that the fence is higher now, we must get those on the other side to chip off some of the fence before we can attempt to jump. Well, I have news for my dad. It costs something to do the chipping and those on the other side have limits as to how much of that cost they want to bear. I need to find a way to convince the old man that we will need to jump the fence in the absence of any chipping. Have you been following me, Jamina? You look perplexed."

"Why are you going in circles? If you do find out who has planted ideas into your dad's head, what will you do?"

"Shield him from those peddlers of wicked ideas, who only prevent our people from achieving their capabilities."

"But you are being unfair, John."

"What do you mean?"

"The people you call peddlers may be only trying to help since they have observed that we are not making serious attempts to jump. They would like to see us on the other side. Ugh, here I go using your fence analogy."

"Yes, you may be right, Jamina. I really should not be concerned about the peddlers. My frustration, I guess, is that I seem to return to the same question all the time. Namely, how do I convince people here, including my dad, to do what they need to do?"

"You don't think you are making progress?"

"No, Jamina. I think, in fact, I have come full circle. I have gone round a hill and still not climbed it. All I have achieved is viewing the hill from all sides. I now know that the hill is high, but it is lower than Everest. So there is hope. But what do I do now? I am not sure I have gained any insight as to where to start the climb."

"It seems to me that in going round the hill you have succeeded in climbing a few feet. You engineered the firing of five corrupt ministers. You were one of those who helped make the last elections almost violence-free and the process free and fair. You have motivated a group of youth to start a serious social movement. And you have convinced your father to think about specific socio-economic variables to target. The only thing now is that he might be less ambitious than you."

"But given how far down we are, we need to move faster. How do I continue the fight for rapid change? No one around here seems to be as anxious as I am to move fast, to run. So I have to walk? What a pain. The best I can do, perhaps, is to get them to walk faster. But we don't have the luxury of walking. We have to run or completely lose sight of the rest of the world."

"What if we lose sight of them? We will be living too and probably more happily than those far ahead of us on some journey to God-knows-where."

"You see, that's the kind of attitude that I fear among Nigasilians."

"Okay, John, you have a point. Since I met you I have been telling you the many ways that I have been unhappy with governance in this country. But the plain truth is this: you will never get the leaders of this country to move as fast as you want them to move. The way I see it, if you cannot adjust to that reality, you will be an unhappy man here. You should go back to America."

John stares at her with a horrified look. Jamina gives him a gentle smile.

"Moving back won't disturb our marriage unless you insist that I go with you. I will visit you during Christmas and you will visit me during summer, because your summer holidays are much longer. I can come to America for one year to do a master's degree soon after we wed. I can apply to start the September of any year you wish to return. So don't take me into account when you consider whether you want to stay."

"I will disappoint my dad if I leave before his term ends."

"So that's your choice, John: your happiness or your father's happiness. I don't think you will be able to have both, unless you change."

In the middle of his sleep, John suddenly sees a figure in pink. John has no idea where he is. He cannot recognize anything around him. But there is a celestial quality that frightens him.

"Cecilia, you are dead. Why don't you rest in peace?"

"John, the boys, let them continue school in the US. David and Frances will help. I will tell them to do so, and they will listen to me. They will do as I say. John, those boys are Americans and they are your sons at the same time. Remember what you used to tell me? 'Cecilia, don't make this sound like a problem in advanced calculus.' They can be Americans and your sons at the same time. You see, John, if you decide to stay and help your country, your sons will understand. Do you know how many competent Nigasilians would have loved to be in your position? Don't be too frustrated that they don't move as fast as you want them to. Keep trying. They will move faster than they would have otherwise."

John wakes up startled. "Yes," he mutters, "they will move faster, but I will still have to lower my standards. And I can't; no, I can't. I will go crazy. This is Misery Land. I cannot encourage these people to remain the way they are."

Jamina's mother, Fatima, arrives from Wombono on Tuesday, May 14, to spend a few days with Jamina and to help with the wedding arrangements.

"I find it really great that so many women have gone into catering," Fatima says. "When we were getting married, all the cooking had to be done by our parents' friends or relatives. I remember in those days we used to have enormous pots to prepare the food over wood or charcoal fire. I don't even see those kinds of pots anymore. In this country, they probably have melted all of them down to use for something else. I like this country; nothing goes to waste."

"Yes, we recycle everything."

"These caterers, so many have good training. I remember when they could find regular work only in hotels and restaurants. Now they not only set up their own restaurants, but if they have money, they can have a profitable business as caterers as well."

"I think that all these Nigasilians who have spent time abroad and are coming home on visits or even permanently have done a lot to develop small businesses of various kinds."

"You think so? Well, it sounds logical."

"We are taking the wedding program to the printers this Friday. I'll show you the draft tomorrow. John and I have already discussed all the details of the design with the printers. We want it to look artistic and elegant."

"Good, that will give the printers enough time."

"Oh, yes. All they really need is a week." Jamina pauses. "You know, when we first met, John asked me how come I grew up as a Christian.

I told him I didn't have a good answer. Perhaps it had to do with going to a Catholic school and having one Catholic parent."

"We also got married in a church. My parents did not mind. They were more concerned about my staying Muslim. Jawana assured them of that. It is easier for a Muslim to attend church than the other way around. When you go to church, you can just sit down quietly. When the parishioners get up to sing or pray, you get up and say nothing. When they kneel to pray, you can simply sit, put your head down, close your eyes if you like, and say any prayer quietly in your heart. So no one knows that you are not participating unless they specifically focus on you. It is much more difficult to stay invisible in a mosque, where the act of praying is far more demonstrative."

"One of the great blessings in this country is that Muslims and Christians get on so well with each other."

"Yes, thank God. In fact, the vast majority of families here seem to include both Christians and Muslims. Indeed, that is why we participate actively in each other's religious holiday celebrations. For whatever reason, the Muslims in this country have never tried to impose Sharia law, not even in districts that they dominate. In turn, the right to marry up to four women, if you are a Muslim, is recognized."

"And you can do even better if you marry by native law and custom. You can have as many women as you can afford."

They both laugh.

"John keeps saying that Nigasilia is Misery Land. I will have to tell him that there is one crucial misery we have been spared—sectarian conflict. I think those are worse than tribal or clan conflicts. With sectarianism, people invoke God or some infallible prophet to legitimate their fervor. For tribal or class conflict, they can do no better than claim the need to defend their customs and traditions or birthright. Those do not have the same mystical powers as God or a prophet."

"That's true."

They pause and Jamina brings some fruits for dessert. "You know, Mamma, since I have been conscious, I can't remember Papa ever attending a Muslim wedding ceremony. He always goes only to the celebrations afterwards. But I know of cases where people go and just stand and observe."

"Yes, and he has done that, too. He simply hasn't done that recently. In fact, he hardly attends weddings these days." They recall a story Fatima told Jamina many years ago and laugh heartily.

Jamina's dad was invited to a Muslim wedding by a lady who used to be his girlfriend. Both Fatima and Jawana went to the wedding. They were not married yet, but since Fatima is a Muslim, Jawana wanted her to accompany him. When they entered the mosque, Jawana stood in the back with Fatima. She did not immediately notice because the ceremony started as soon as they arrived. When Fatima finally noticed him, she said to Jawana, "Do you realize that you are the only man standing here?" Jawana turned around and noticed that he was in the middle of all the women. He gently veered his way to where the men were standing. After the event was over, Fatima did not dare laugh at him.

"You know your papa still talks about that incident. Did I tell you that the poor lady died in a road accident only a few years after the wedding?"

"You did. Where is the man now?"

"He lives in the US and I heard that he remarried. But I don't know if he has any children."

"Have you ever worried about Papa having girlfriends since you've been married?"

Mrs. Tamba sits back in her chair, folds her hands across her lap, tilts her head, and winks at Jamina. "Why? Do you know any that he has?"

"No," Jamina says, raising her hands, "I am just curious because all these Nigasilian women say that you have to watch these married Nigasilian men. They are never satisfied with only their wives."

"Well, Jamina, you are the biologist. Haven't you told me that a man could impregnate in one month as many women as the number of children that a very healthy woman can have in all her life? Maybe nature has tilted the scales in favor of men's philandering." They both laugh.

"But I have also told you that humans are not only biological animals but social animals as well. We women have our own power, too. We select our men for certain qualities, including the willingness to invest in parenthood."

"Some of the women don't seem to obey that rule. Look at all these young girls with babies and no father in sight."

"Certain types of behavior are simply not permissible, no matter what your biological instincts are prompting you to do. Well, I certainly will try."

"You are not worried about John, are you?"

Jamina shrugs and shakes her head. "No, I'm not worried about John."

Her mother smiles approvingly.

On Thursday, early evening, John is getting ready to drop by Jamina's when he receives a call from David.

"Hi, John, how are you?"

"I'm well, David. Thanks again for your decision to attend the wedding."

"Well, as I told you in my e-mail, Frances is looking forward to visiting Nigasilia. You know she has never been anywhere in Africa before."

"Yes, I know. Don't raise her expectations too high now. But we shall try to point her to a few beautiful spots."

"That would be good. John, part of my motivation in calling you is that I heard from mutual friends that you drafted what they thought was a well-written book entitled *How Aid Underdevelops Africa*, but that you have decided not to pursue publishing it. Is that true?"

"Yes and no, David. I actually did most of the drafting of that book before I came to stay. Well, for one thing, I have this latent fear that, if I publish it, the bums will not understand; they will hate me. But more importantly, to tell you the truth, I believe my work here in Nigasilia will give me an opportunity to strengthen the book, as I will acquire a deeper understanding of the underlying reasons why Africans find it so difficult to break their dependence on aid."

"I guess I understand. But on your fear of being hated, who are the bums—those who take the drugs or those who distribute them?"

"Both. Both the addicts and the pushers will hate me."

They laugh heartily. But then John adds, "Actually, there is a related problem. When you stop giving the drug to the addict, you have to decide if you do so gradually or rapidly. I prefer the rapid solution because of my fears that the gradual option will not work with this Nigasilian addict. This addict will find a way to hang on. I am trying to better understand why. My fear is that if you stop the dope in one fell swoop, you have to deal with the withdrawal. As a practical matter, I must now find a solution to the withdrawal problem. I must determine the optimal pace of getting this addict off the dope. This would be of relevance to other countries, I'm sure."

"I can only wish you luck, John. But whatever you do, please publish that book soon. And don't make it too technical. Policy makers must understand it, too."

"I agree. But how did you hear about the book?"

"The chairman of your department, Wilkinson, e-mailed me after he read my article on the visit to inquire about you and Nigasilia. So, I called and told him you seemed happy. He asked if I had met the new woman in your life. He sounded as if he wishes you would return."

"Well, that's good to hear."

"So how is the new job?"

"So far, so good, I would say. But I am only cautiously optimistic. I worry that I am in a tug of war. I have to quickly build a momentum for rapid change or else I have to leave this place before I get changed for the worse. To tell you the truth, the main reasons why I have decided to give it a go around here are that my dad is the president, he is not corrupt, and he demonstrates enough flexibility to give me a slight glimmer of hope."

"But then what happens when your dad's term ends?"

"That question is going to weigh heavily on my mind over the next year or so. Right now, I am leaning towards leaving this place no later than the next presidential elections. I don't see anyone in the party that I would want to serve under."

"So, what about you? Wouldn't you want to be president?"

"I have only casually considered that. And I immediately saw an obvious reality. The majority of the king makers in our party will not support me, given my views on economic and political governance. They will not want me. They know, from watching and listening to me, that I will be very strict about the kinds of rules we establish and in enforcing those rules. The degree to which I will compromise will be limited."

Mrs. Fatima Tamba welcomes John with a big hug.

"Sorry I am late. David called."

"There is nothing the matter, I hope," Jamina inquires.

"No, nothing is the matter. He just wanted to ask me how I was adjusting to my new political position. Mrs. Tamba, this David is the brother of my late wife."

"Oh, he is the one who is also helping you out with your boys."

"Yes."

"He is coming for the wedding, right?"

"Oh, yes. And he is coming with his wife. Their two children will be away at camp while they are here."

"Yes, we read about such things only in magazines."

"I am thinking of encouraging some coaches to organize camps around here. They may need sponsors. I will have to see if I can find some for them."

Jamina interjects. "That sounds like a good idea. When did you think of that?"

"When I was debating with myself what my boys will do here every summer."

"So, I guess necessity can be the mother of invention."

"Well, let's wait for the dream to become a reality before we begin to celebrate. But I am optimistic about the potential use of such camps. Many diasporans come during the summer. Then there are the foreigners whose kids visit them over the summer as well. If those two groups have a demand for camps, then someone will find it profitable to organize camps, especially here in Lamongwe. I just have to open their eyes about the possibilities, the prospects for real profit."

"Dear, I assume that you are eating with us, right?"

"Mrs. Tamba, your daughter knows that when I come to her house I am expecting her to feed me."

"Yes, John, I was just teasing you. Let's go eat."

The food, leg of lamb and couscous, cooked Mediterranean style, arrives almost immediately once they sit at the table. As they start eating, John asks, "Mrs. Tamba, do you believe dreams have any significance?"

"What do you mean?"

"Oh, like reflecting your state of mind, foretelling something, whatever."

Jamina narrows her eyes. "Why do you ask? Have you been having dreams lately that you do not understand?"

"I dream a lot and they almost always seem to reflect my state of mind. But some people say that dreams have deep meaning and often foreshadow something; a sign, as it were."

Jamina looks at John rather seriously. "What have you been dreaming that makes you look so worried?"

"I'm not worried. Do I look worried? I just want to hear what your mamma has to say first. Anyway, to ease your mind, it is not anything alarming."

"Here in Nigasilia, John, people have all kinds of beliefs about certain kinds of dreams," Mrs. Tamba says. "For instance, they say if you laugh in your dream, then something sad will happen in the near future that will make you cry. In contrast, if you cry in your dream, then something will happen that will bring joy and happiness to you. Also, they attach special significance to dreams involving fish. They say if the fish is charcoal-dried, it is a bad omen. But if the fish is fresh, that's good. Then, to top it all, they say that if you dream that someone is getting married, then that is a real bad omen for that person, while the opposite is true if you dream that the person dies."

"Have many people had experiences that support these beliefs?"

"It's a good question, John. But people still believe, so maybe that answers your question."

"Jamina, if you dream that I get married, don't tell me." They all laugh.

John tells them the dreams he's had, in which Cecilia tells him to marry Jamina and not worry about his boys. Mrs. Tamba does not quite know how to react in an appropriate way, since the human subjects in the dreams are so dear and private to John. Jamina knows that her mom does not want to dwell on the matter of John's future in Nigasilia.

"John, how are your boys doing?" Mrs. Tamba asks.

"They are doing quite well. They will be here for the wedding, of course. Naturally they miss their mother but they are now also in love with their new mother-to-be."

Jamina keeps a straight face but shakes her legs, embarrassed.

"Your sister and brother will be here, too, I gather. At the time of your mother's funeral, only my husband came, so I don't even know what they look like. But then, even Jamina does not know them. So we will have a lot of catching up to do."

"Yes, indeed. As for Elizabeth, after you meet you will think you've known her for a long time. Peter is more reserved. But he is also very friendly and easygoing. I gather your son in the US is coming as well?"

"Yes, thank God. We have not seen him for five years now. He keeps promising to come and then something happens and he must postpone. But he says that will not happen this time. He says he is anxious to meet this man that Jamina finally thinks is good enough for her to marry."

They finish eating and move to the family room to relax. Mrs. Tamba turns to John suddenly and says, "Oh, John, I'm sorry; I forgot to tell you that my husband sends his congratulations to you on your new assignment. I also neglected to extend my congratulations. We are really happy for you and expect that you will do a great job."

"Thanks, Mrs. Tamba. I expect the job to be challenging, especially since I am going to push for greater transparency."

"Well, good for you. My husband thinks that if things continue the way they are going, you will be one of the leading candidates to succeed your father. Will you like that?"

"You know, Mrs. Tamba, if the majority of my party wants me as their candidate for the presidency, I will not say no. But really, I have not thought of myself as one of the candidates that the power brokers in the party will nominate for the post."

"Don't underestimate yourself, John. Anyway, the next few years will be interesting for you."

"That's an understatement, Mrs. Tamba."

"If you decide to go for the big job when the time comes, my nephew, Mahdu, will be one of your supporters. He has told my husband that he and a few others in the cabinet and in the party at large are already planning on bringing the subject up with you. But don't tell Mahdu that I told you this. I was not supposed to know."

"Of course, Mrs. Tamba, you have not told me anything."

"How is your father doing?"

"He seems happy, now that the elections are over. But he was disappointed that he did not reach the 60 percent mark. That was his target. He understands that the people want to see better performance during this term."

"I guess he can now work on leaving a favorable legacy. It must be so hard to run this country."

"Yes, but if you seek power then you must find a way to overcome the difficulties."

"I suppose you are right, John. My husband has the same attitude. He keeps saying to fellow chiefs, when they complain about the difficulty of the job, that if the job is too hard for anyone, he should abdicate his chieftaincy and go back to being an ordinary citizen."

After relaxing a little longer with the ladies, John takes his leave. A few minutes after his departure, Mrs. Tamba asks Jamina, "Does Rabena Karam still work as the confidential secretary for John's father?"

"Yes. In fact, you will see her on Saturday. She will be here with Vivienne. I asked her to join us, because she has been saying she wants very much to meet you."

"Your father knows her ex-husband, although they have not been in touch for some time now. The man, a brilliant lawyer, has been out of circulation. I gather he became an alcoholic. But they say he seems to be trying to get back on his feet. Remember, I told you that the word went around that Rabena and the president were having an affair?"

"Yes."

"Did John hear that rumor?"

"Yes, he did. He told me about it. He said he and his brother and sister believe their father, who denies that anything of the sort has ever happened between him and Rabena. Also, they say if there was truth in it, their mother would have stopped it."

"It's not so easy to find out when your husband is doing such a thing with someone working that closely with him."

"I'm sure. But I believe John's father, too. The man is too conservative. Anyway, John says that he does not really mind if the two of them get together. All he wants is for a reasonable time to elapse between such a time and his mother's death."

After a brief pause, Jamina says, "Incidentally, I found out from Rabena that she and a few friends are launching a new organization called NARROW, which stands for Nigasilian Association for the Rights and Respect of Women. And you know what their motto is? *Eliminate the Gender Gap*. She will probably talk about it on Saturday. If she does not, I shall bring it up and ask her to tell you more about it. She is trying to recruit Vivienne. She basically has me in already as an active participant. She said that she and her friends were inspired by what John was doing in mobilizing the youth."

"Yes, of course."

"So, I told John about NARROW. And then I said to him, 'You are going around talking about misery here and misery there; isn't the gender gap also a miserable situation?' You know John can be funny. He looked at me and said, 'You see, that shows I'm only a man.'"

"So, what did you say?"

"Oh, I said to him, 'No, that's only part of it. You grew up in a house where your sister was given equal access to education. She is now a full-blown professional, earning a good chunk of money. She has never been subject to wife abuse or rape.' Then he said, 'Yes, that's true, but I also observe what's going on with women in this country.' Anyway, forget about John. For me, personally, my own view is that we should focus on equal education and pay and employment opportunities. Then a lot of other gender biases will slowly disappear."

"In other words, you would not want to continue with NARROW if it were to fight against polygamy and clitoridectomy, for example."

In some parts of Nigasilia, clitoridectomy is the custom. Increasingly, even in those parts of the country, many are opposed to it, for reasons including health concerns. But the authorities have not been willing to address the issue at a national level, despite pressures from activists both inside and outside the country.

As for polygamy, in Nigasilia, Muslim men are allowed to marry up to four women, while most of the tribes allow their men to marry, within native law, as many wives as they want and can afford. The only other constraint is the willingness of the women to participate in a polygamous marriage. Increasingly, many of the women do not accept being part of polygamous relationships.

Jamina responds assertively to her mother's remarks. "Exactly. But I would worry about wife abuse and rape."

"Sure. Education does not seem to help in those areas, unless we mean special cultural education."

"Unfortunately, that's the truth. And the cultural education should focus mainly on the men. The women would just need to be taught that they do not need to stay in an abusive marriage, especially when they can support themselves."

On Saturday, Jamina has arranged for Rabena and Vivienne to spend the afternoon at her house. After their late lunch, they might go for a walk on the beach. Mrs. Tamba leaves tomorrow for Wombono.

When Vivienne walks in, Mrs. Tamba says, "Vivienne, are you pregnant? Otherwise, marriage seems to be treating you very well."

"So Jamina did not tell you? Yes, Mamma, I am pregnant, since February."

"Congratulations! So what does your husband want? It's usually the men who seem to care."

"Actually, Santie does not care either, since it is the first one."

They hear Rabena and Jamina goes to the door. Soon she brings Rabena inside and introduces her. "Mamma, this is Rabena."

"I'm very pleased to meet you, Mrs. Tamba. I guess you have come to see if Jamina is surviving. It's a lot of hassle for her, I'm sure."

"Yes, but I find that she and John seem to have everything in order. I also came down just to bond with her a little. Even though we talk on the phone all the time, I miss her."

"So, I guess that you are looking forward to grandchildren."

"Yes, thank you. I have always thought Jamina deserves her own children."

"I'm sure she will make a good mother."

"Jamina tells me you have a daughter in college in America. I hope she is doing well."

"Yes, she is. And she calls regularly because she and I were always so close."

"What is she studying?"

"She wants to go into either dentistry or biochemistry; she is not sure yet which one she will end up choosing. For her undergraduate degree she is majoring in chemistry. She had to do some catching up when she went. But she is all right now. That is one good thing about the US; they have summer school. So if you are serious, even if you start a little behind, you have the opportunity to catch up."

"That's good."

Rabena turns to Vivienne. "Vivienne, how is Santie doing? So you decided to desert him for the girls today?"

"He deserts me for the boys all the time. I don't know what those men talk about in their gatherings. They probably end up drinking too much anyway."

"You are not the only one who wonders about that. But they run the world, or so they think. Maybe they discuss matters of great importance to the human race." They all enjoy the cynicism with a big laugh. And then Vivienne brings them back down to earth.

"And probably girls, too."

"Of course, but do you care?"

Mrs. Tamba interjects. "When my husband worked for the government, he would socialize with the boys a lot. I came to the conclusion that it was important that one does that to get on in the community and even at work. Now, of course, he no longer engages in that kind of socializing."

"Vivienne," Rabena says, "my husband socialized quite a bit with his colleagues. He also is a Freemason. But he worked very hard. In fact, I honestly think that the pressure of his work drove him to excessive drinking. It was sad to be there and feel helpless to do anything about it."

Vivienne observes the look on Rabena's face and moves on. "Mrs. Tamba, do you think that Jamina could become a chief someday?"

"Yes, of course, if she is interested."

"Right now," Jamina says, "all I am interested in is completing a master's degree in botany and continuing with my teaching. Chieftaincy is not on my radar."

Mrs. Tamba asks, "Rabena, tell me about this women's organization that you are launching."

Jamina butts in. "Ladies, let's go eat. Rabena can continue at the table."

They settle down to a sumptuous lunch of roasted peppered chicken, shrimp in a traditional Nigasilian sauce, fried plantains, sweet potatoes, and mixed vegetables. Rabena picks up where she left off.

"Yes, Mrs. Tamba, we have established a working group to draft the constitution and proceed with registration and mobilization. The group includes Dr. Janice Kotombo as chairperson, the lawyer Alimatu Tana as general secretary, Betty Mongo as treasurer, Jamina as deputy chairperson, and me as organizing secretary. There are ten of us in all in the steering committee. We want to launch NARROW on August 3. By then we should have finished the draft constitution and registered it. So far, some thirty other women have signed up as ready to join from day one. We want to get at least one hundred to start. When we launch it, we plan to invite John to be the keynote speaker."

Jamina's mother asks, "What will be your main focus?"

"Equal education, jobs, and employment opportunities; equality in property distribution; and better enforcement of laws on the books relating to spousal abuse and rape."

"So you are not going to address polygamy and clitoridectomy."

"When we debated them in the steering committee, we came to the conclusion that education will lead to the disappearance of those two practices over time. We see it already happening, especially in the case of polygamy. Most of the well-educated women marry according to Western law, and not one of them is in a polygamous marriage, even where the husband is free to marry under native law."

Mrs. Tamba says, smiling, "So the men have only the alternative of girlfriends."

None of the younger women say anything in response.

After a moment, Rabena asks, "Jamina, are you and John going to leave for your honeymoon immediately after the wedding?"

"Actually, we are not sure that we need to go anywhere for our honeymoon. We have two houses here. Also, we want John's boys to spend a good part of the summer here. But if we do go, we will spend the time mainly in the Washington, DC, area and in New York."

"So how many weeks will you be gone, if you do go?" Vivienne asks.

"About three weeks."

"Wow, Mrs. Tamba, then you could be a grandma sooner than you think."

Jamina laughs. "I thought you were going to ask if that was not a long time for John to leave his post. We don't need to go to America to make a baby. Just look at you."

The women finish their meal and decide to take a walk on the beach.

Mrs. Tamba is worried the walk may be exhausting for Vivienne, but she assures everyone that it's all right.

When they begin their stroll, Mrs. Tamba says to Rabena, "This NARROW could be very good in helping the government keep its commitment to the education of the girl-child. My only concern is that until we get free education, the majority of parents in this country will still have problems sending their children to school. They will still be left with having to make that difficult choice of which child to send. It is this choice that typically forces parents to select their boys over the girls. Those parents that can easily afford to send all their children to school don't discriminate between boys and girls. As you know, most of our people think that women can find men to take care of them but that it is against tradition to have a man depend on a woman. NARROW may find itself having to fight for free primary and secondary education as part of its agenda."

"Mrs. Tamba, you have a good point. We ourselves believe that the cost of sending children to school is the root cause of discrimination against girls. Maybe we shall make the fight for free primary and secondary education part of our agenda. Jamina, what do you think?"

"I agree. Otherwise, among the poor, the scales will remain tilted against the girls."

Rabena turns to Vivienne. "I assume that you will join our movement, too?"

"In spirit, of course, the answer is yes. In practice, I have to think about it. There is just so much happening around me these days. But I really will try."

"Well, take your time. We will not pressure you. Jamina will keep you informed, I'm sure."

As the women watch the fishermen bring their nets in, Mrs. Tamba turns to Jamina. "Jamina, John was talking about promoting summer camps in Nigasilia. But he never thought about beach volleyball and surfing. We could easily train people to win Olympic medals in beach volleyball. You know, your father first discovered it watching the Olympic games on tape at the American embassy in Lamongwe. He then drew my attention to it. I had a long discussion with him about how much of a sport it really is. Anyway, if it is a sport, we can certainly do it, too."

"Oh, Mamma, we have a lot of potential that we are not exploiting in this country. John says whenever he brings such subjects up, people say we don't have the money."

"Isn't that true?"

"John does not think so. He thinks that it's all about discipline, being more efficient in our use of resources, and deciding our priorities."

"He may be right."

Vivienne puts in a word. "We have so many people who are adept at swimming and canoeing. All we need is organization and coaching and we can have people ready to compete at the Olympic level."

"I agree," Jamina says. "But, again, our politicians say we have no money."

Mrs. Tamba, a little excited, says, "In that case, maybe we need a nongovernmental association to take the leadership."

"So I see we need another movement here," Jamina jokes. "We should ask John to start organizing a voluntary sports association to address such issues."

"Jamina, why not?" Mrs. Tamba asks. "Talk to your man about it."

"I'm afraid he might get serious and start another project."

"You have a point," says Mrs. Tamba.

A few days following the meeting with John, STRONG presented to the leaders of civil society organizations the final draft of the manifesto to be distributed by the Unified Civil Society Movement (UCSM) of Nigasilia. There was intense debate on the content and the political action called for in the manifesto. There was unanimous agreement on the socio-economic variables to be monitored, on the annual meetings to assess the progress made by the government, and on the issuing of a press release on the UCSM's assessment.

There was deep division over the need for, or the nature of, any unified political action. The majority of the participants preferred to leave such action to individual members of civil society or, at a minimum, to individual civil society organizations. Some felt that the kind of political action called for in the manifesto was too radical. Others felt that political action for a whole unified civil society could not be based on such a single issue. But most felt that such action on this single issue would divide the movement. Political party loyalties, for example, can be strong.

It is now Monday of the last week of May and the STRONG leaders would like the manifesto to be issued in the first week of June. Once more they look to Minister John Bijunga for help. They ask for a meeting in his office and he obliges them.

John immediately appreciates the arguments against trying to insist on a unified political action. The civil society organizations in Nigasilia are not financially strong and are divided. Yet they all agree on the socio-economic variables. That in itself is a major achievement, which should not be allowed to go to waste. They will struggle in the future over the decision on whether the progress made in socio-economic development in any year is satisfactory or unsatisfactory. There is no reason to bring in the additional problem of having to take unified decisive political action against the political party in power.

"Ladies and gentlemen, you have done well. You have come a long way in trying to put in place a system that will enable Nigasilians to assess how well their government is improving the lives of ordinary Nigasilians. You will face many issues as you try to implement the program you have designed. No doubt there will be borderline cases when you will have differences of opinion as to whether the overall performance of the government should be rated satisfactory or unsatisfactory. You may be wise, in fact, to sometimes simply use the rating of 'not satisfactory.'"

John pauses and looks at his guests, who conjure up the image in his mind of participants in a small post-graduate seminar.

"So my first suggestion is that you include that as a possible rating: 'not satisfactory.' A different issue is that it will be a major annual challenge for you to come up with precise quantitative measures for the ranges of performance that you will regard as satisfactory, not satisfactory, or unsatisfactory for each of the nine variables and for the overall performance. I will be available to you for consultation on that exercise as well. I would suggest that you select some committee to be in charge of that exercise."

John pauses, in case the young people want to ask questions. But they all look relaxed, with a couple of them nodding approvingly. So, he figures they are in tune with him and happy.

"So that was the second suggestion I wanted to make. I have also listened to the arguments for and against unified political action. I would err on the side of promoting unity and consensus. So, my third suggestion to you now, is that you forget about unified political action. Leave that to individuals and to individual civil society organizations to decide for themselves."

The STRONG representatives look at each other and signal by nodding their heads or raising their thumbs that they are willing to accept all three suggestions. They thank the minister and leave to finalize the manifesto. It will be issued as the joint product of the Unified Civil Society Movement, UCSM, and signed by the chairperson of each organization. There will be an introduction stating that though the manifesto is the brainchild of STRONG, it has been developed with the full participation of the other signatory organizations.

As the young people leave his office, John slumps into his chair and talks to himself in his usual way. "Praise the Lord. I think these guys have got it right. If the people build pressure on the government to improve socio-economic performance, we will certainly see progress."

John recalls the discussion he had with his father when Tubo Bangar was going to London to plead for aid money. "But I still have to deal with aid dependency. I think I am in that battle alone, at least for a while. I have to build the case to convince my cabinet colleagues to reduce aid dependency. Our message to the aid donors should be simple: 'Go sell the food somewhere else and give us the money to build dams, storage facilities, and feeder roads for our agriculture, and drastically cut down on foreign consultants as components of aid packages.' Yes, let them give us the money to train our people, including sending them to study abroad if necessary. And when we give scholarships to Nigasilians to get serious training abroad, they have to come home and work for at least four years. If they do not come, they have to repay the scholarship or we will revoke their passports. If any one of them gets a scholarship, from or via the government, he or she must either give us our money back immediately, with interest, or fulfill the work obligation. We will give them freedom to select where they work. But it must be here in Nigasilia, for government or business—no NGO or international organization or foreign embassy."

John gets up from his chair and resumes his soliloquy. "As for this customary land tenure system, my number one ally will be Dumomo Frah. Maybe I should encourage him to take the leadership. But deep down I know the chiefs are not going to give up the power the colonial masters handed them. I guess change will have to come in the old-fashioned way, via a land reform revolution. But that may not come before a hundred years from now. In the meanwhile, yes, there will be changes somewhere else in this cursed system. But why should I hang around and suffer the agony of watching it all happen at a snail's pace?"

He scratches his head as if he is mad with his dilemma. Then he feels he must calm down.

"Okay, for my dad's sake . . . but only during his reign."

On Monday, June 3, John arranges an early meeting with his father.

"Dad, I would like cabinet discussion on certain proposals that I have. They are topics that you and I have been discussing for the last year or so, with the possible exception of one. I can prepare a cabinet paper covering all four. Maybe we won't be able to fit the discussion into one meeting, but we can have a special cabinet meeting over a couple of days to cover them all."

"So, what is suddenly so urgent, John, if you and I have been discussing these subjects during all these months."

"Dad, I can't function here unless we make some definitive decisions and take action."

"So what are these decisions and actions, John?"

"Like forming a national council on socio-economic governance and giving it more than an advisory role. Like insisting on proper cost-benefit analysis in our decision making over budget allocations, recognizing STRONG and giving it a substantive role in governance, and reorganizing the Anti-Corruption Commission and getting it to focus on prevention and addressing corruption in the whole society—government, civil society, and business."

"John, we don't need a cabinet meeting on the cost-benefit analysis issue. You have a lot of leverage in that area. Write a paper on that issue indicating how the departments should structure their requests for funds, so that you can compare the benefits and costs to the economy across items of expenditure within and across departments. On that basis your department will make the budgetary allocations. Once the detailed draft budget is out we can all then have a discussion that is focused and concrete, looking at the actual numbers in front of us. What you are really trying to do is make the whole process transparent, logical, and operational within a coherent framework. And with that, I agree with you."

"Yes, you are right, Dad. My fear is that people will not want to cooperate to give us all the relevant information or to answer any follow-up questions that we have."

"Well, I was not quite finished. Once you draft a paper on the procedures, you will send it to every cabinet minister and, of course, to the VP and me as well. Then we will all give comments, and you can revise the paper. Once the paper is written, we will put it all in the form of an order from me. We will need a cabinet meeting only if there are serious objections to your ideas; for example, on how you want people to structure the initial requests. But I would be surprised if their comments and your revision will not handle everything without the need for an elaborate cabinet discussion. Like every year when we put the numbers together, we will have a lot of discussion. The difference now is that you might end up helping by making the allocation criteria more transparent."

"Okay, so you want me to confine the cabinet paper to the other three topics."

"Yes. But there should be only a few pages devoted to each topic. I don't think you need more than two to three single-spaced pages of explanations on each one. All you are trying to do is state why you want what you want. Don't try to answer any potential objections. When they are brought up, then you can respond."

"Okay, Dad, you have been of great help."

"So when would you be able to get your paper circulated?"

"This week."

"Then let's discuss them next Friday, the fourteenth," the president says as he thumbs through his calendar.

After a brief pause, the president looks at his son with a very serious look over his face.

"Now, I have also been thinking, John. In five years I leave office. What are your long-term plans?"

"What do you mean?"

"Would you want to continue in politics here, or would you rather do something else?"

"Probably something else."

"Why?"

"Because I won't be able to stand the likely leader of our party."

"Then you can form your own party or compete for leadership within our party."

"A third party has no chance, and I have no chance within our own party. The reasons are the same. Those who go into politics in this country do not do so in order to move the country forward fast, and those who would be attracted to my party would be no different."

"So, your problem is with our pace of change."

"Ultimately, yes. We don't know how to prevent people from going into politics primarily for the power, position, and perquisites. Even worse than that, I believe that the people who are single-minded in the pursuit of power, position, and perquisites dominate our politics. The system is incapable of preventing politicians from being corrupt. And we don't know how to create and implement a system where we achieve objectivity, hard work, and discipline in government management. Our system is nothing but a grand patrimonial system. Yes, there are honest and straightforward people in our government. But they do not run the show. Once our party members see that I will insist on certain rules, processes, and procedures, they will not give me the leadership position. For exactly the same reason, the politicians who know how to succeed in our system will not join me in any third party initiative."

"And you are not willing to compromise?"

"What do you mean?"

"I mean govern like me. Not to insist on getting everything at once but making sure that you are making progress in the right direction."

"Yes, Dad, I am not willing to compromise in that way."

"Unfortunately, if you try to shove certain things down the throats of people, they will say okay and then sabotage your plans when they get to the implementation."

"In other words, they will not swallow the medicine, and they will spit it out when you give them your back?"

"Yes, John, they will spit it out."

"I am fully aware of that."

The president seems baffled as to what to say. So John breaks the silence.

"When I told you some minutes ago that I would rather do something else five years from now, that's only half the answer. The other half is that I will do the something else somewhere else, not in Nigasilia."

"Why, John, why?"

"Because I do not want to be like a doctor watching a patient die from refusing the medicine. I am not masochistic enough to relish such an experience."

The president, with a serious expression, says, "I understand, John. I understand."

The Unified Civil Society Movement manifesto is sent to John on the same afternoon, June 3. The members of STRONG inform him that it will be sent to at least the five leading newspapers for immediate publication. Then the youth will try to publish the manifesto as a small booklet, neatly designed, to sell to the general public.

Titled "Holding Government Accountable for the Socio-Economic Welfare of Citizens," the core of the manifesto reads as follows:

We, the members of the undersigned Unified Civil Society Movement (UCSM) of Nigasilia, are committed to ensuring good governance by all sitting governments of Nigasilia. In that light, we intend to hold all governments accountable for the standard of living of all Nigasilians. We shall conduct an annual assessment of the government in power using the following nine indicators for Nigasilia and the Nigasilian population, using data validated by credible sources, including the United Nations Development Programme, the World Bank, the International Monetary Fund, and the International Labor Organization:

* Infant mortality
* Death from childbirth per thousand
* Life expectancy of the average Nigasilian
* Literacy rate of Nigasilians above the age of fifteen
* Average years of schooling of Nigasilians above the age of twenty-one
* Proportion of Nigasilia's population with access to safe drinking water
* Electricity production per capita in Nigasilia
* Proportion of population with access to electricity
* Real income per capita

We call on all civil society organizations in Nigasilia to unite behind the above set of indicators to judge government performance. We demand that the government annually publish data on the above socio-economic variables, as validated by one or more of the above-mentioned international organizations.

The unified civil society movement will meet each year and vote on whether it considers the progress made by the government during the past year in each of these above-mentioned areas satisfactory, not satisfactory, or unsatisfactory. The movement will hold a news conference at the end of the annual session and issue a press release as well.

If progress is judged unsatisfactory over a four-year period of the same government party, then the movement will declare the overall performance of said party in improving the socio-economic lives of Nigasilians as poor, and urge all Nigasilians to take that into account as they vote in the next election.

John drops by to visit with Jamina in the evening. He tells her about his discussion with his father.

"So, at least he is happy you plan to be around until his term ends?"

"Yes, he is happy."

"Well, are you?"

"I'm not sure."

"So, what is really bothering you now?"

"Well, I do not honestly believe that I will succeed here, and I find that too painful to admit."

"You are minister of finance and economic development. Tell me why you will not succeed."

"Because a military commander cannot win a war all by himself. He needs good and committed generals, lieutenants, and ordinary soldiers."

"So?"

"Okay, look. I'm going to be pushing these people so that we increase investment and the efficiency of investment, raise the quality of education and training of people, and better manage our natural resources. My ministry will work with the other ministries in designing the policies. But when it comes to implementation, my colleagues and I will not be there to monitor the implementing ministries. They can be incompetent, corrupt, and do different things from what we agreed. And they could cover it all up. There are great limits to what I can do when it comes to implementation."

"So, this is it. You do not trust the implementing ministries."

"I do not trust the culture and discipline in those ministries."

"Have you discussed this with your dad?"

"Not forthrightly as I should, but I have broached the subject."

"What is preventing you from being clearer?"

John grits his teeth. "I thought he would understand my meaning."

Chapter 14

June, the big month, is here. The whole of Nigasilia is looking forward to the wedding of Jamina Tamba, daughter of Chief Jawana Tamba, to John Bijunga, son of President Samuel Bijunga.

John's sons, Donald and William, are the first to arrive in the first full week of June, straight out of boarding school.

"You must be hungry now," John says upon their arrival. "Dinner will be ready soon. I asked Ms. Tamba to join us. Is that all right with you?"

"Yes, Daddy," they reply in unison.

"So what do we call her when you are married?" Donald asks.

"You can call her Mom, Mommy, or Mommy Jamina, whatever you prefer."

William looks at Donald as if to say, 'You decide.'

"I like Mommy Jamina," Donald responds. "But sometimes when we think that is too long we will call her Mommy."

Jamina soon arrives and the boys rush to her and embrace her warmly. Jamina returns the favor with three kisses each.

Donald asks, "So, Mommy Jamina, what will you call yourself when you get married?"

Jamina looks surprised and raises her eyebrows at John. John does not know whether she is shocked at the question or at being addressed by Donald as Mommy Jamina.

John answers for her. "She will still be Jamina Tamba, so she will be Ms. Tamba. That's what I prefer her to be."

Now Jamina is surprised because she had never thought about what she would call herself after getting married. But she likes the idea of maintaining her name. She does not think of it as having anything to do with women's liberation. She is well-known in Nigasilia for her work in the Conservation Society and she is the daughter of a well-renowned chief. Of course, she can call herself Tamba-Bijunga. Actually, she loves that. But she is afraid it may be too much for some people.

After a silence that seems like an eternity, she says, "Yes, that is right. I shall take whatever name your daddy suggests."

"Good," Donald replies, "we like that. That is what many women in America are doing now."

Jamina is dumbfounded. "Oh, I see. Well, we women in Nigasilia cannot allow ourselves to lag behind the women in America, right, boys?"

"Right."

They settle down to dinner. It is rice cooked in a special Nigasilian style. Gravy of onions, peppers, tomato, tomato paste and spices is prepared in peanut oil to which white rice is added with sufficient water to cook it. Then as the red rice simmers, a smattering of the sauce from the stew with which the rice will be eaten is added, which further enhances the flavor of the rice. Nigasilians call it Jollof rice. The stew with which the rice will be eaten usually contains chicken, beef, and pig's feet.

William takes one bite and says, "This is one meal I miss at school. I enjoy Jollof rice. I think we eat too much potato at school. I think we should eat more rice and pasta. They asked us for comments on our meals and I said that on my form."

Donald adds, "I just mentioned the rice. They will not know how to prepare Jollof rice. But I am surprised they don't serve something like plantains."

"Plantains are not so well-known among the majority of Americans," John says. "But I think they should give you a fair share of rice and pasta. I'm sure the other boys will complain the same way as you have done. The school will adapt. After all, it is not a great change of direction that they are being asked to make."

Jamina has been smiling throughout the boys' complaints. "Well, I hope the school reacts to your comments. If they want any help, I can prepare some recipes for them as far as sauces are concerned, to accompany white rice. Jollof rice will be too difficult for them. Anyway, you will have a lot of rice while you are here. I hope you boys are ready, like last summer, for a lot of activities. Your dad has a lot planned for you, apart from all the fuss surrounding the wedding."

"We will start slowly, though," John promises. "Your granddaddy, as usual, is anxious to see you. So tomorrow evening, the three of us will go visit him. Then, on Sunday afternoon, the four of us will head for one of your favorite beaches. Remember that during the next two weeks a lot of family will be dragging you around. Aunt Lizzie and Uncle Peter will want to have some time with both of you. Of course, you will get to meet Mommy Jamina's parents, Chief Tamba and Mrs. Fatima Tamba. During the last week in June and the whole of July, the four of us can be together as much as we want. We may decide to go to the US sometime in August for a short holiday, but we may instead simply stay here. At least we will all four spend the whole of your summer together."

Elizabeth and Peter arrive later that week with their spouses. They will be staying at the president's house for the three weeks they have come to visit. When the group arrives at Jamina's on Saturday, the usual introductions take place, followed by chitchat about the visitors' trips, jet lag, and Elizabeth's children, who have been left behind to participate in various summer activities. Only Peter and Kiraney have brought their twelve-month-old baby girl. John's siblings and their spouses comment that Jamina has a very beautiful house. At the end of the tour, Elizabeth remarks, "Jamina, you have very good taste. You have decorated this house so elegantly. I can now understand why John says that he prefers to come and live in this house. There is more room than in that government house and you will begin to have children soon."

"Yes," Jamina says, "I want to have them as soon as possible."

"That is never a bad idea. How many children do you want?"

"Oh, I think two would be enough. I told John that I would then have four."

Everyone laughs. A servant takes the orders for drinks and Jamina invites everyone to sit and relax.

Kiraney asks, "Jamina, you have a brother who lives in America, right? Is he coming for the wedding?"

"Oh, yes, he won't miss it for anything. He comes on Monday. He is very anxious to meet John. He tells me that he has been hearing nothing but good things, and not only from me, either."

Soon they all head for the table to have a dinner of sweet potato leaves cooked in palm oil with smoked fish and a smattering of beef. The meal is served with Australian Shiraz, a wine that goes very well with that dish, beer and mineral water. Then they have fruit for dessert. Mundu Sasay, Elizabeth's husband, asks, "Jamina how is your work with the Conservation Society?"

"It is going well and is very interesting indeed. Among other things, I help to make sure that we Nigasilians keep things under our control without fighting with experts from abroad. Because, you know, we receive a lot of foreign assistance, and these Western experts usually think they have all the answers. This annoys some of our university lecturers and professors."

"Yes, I understand. But do you have to travel around the country a lot?"

"I do, especially during school holidays. But I find that my work is making my students more interested in biology than they would otherwise be. I bring lots of samples and pictures for them. Some of them understand the ecology of this country better than many of the university students. And now with videos, we come up with films that would make even folks from the National Geographic Society jealous. The girls are also developing an interest in our natural environment, which I certainly lacked in my youth. I am beginning to interest the teachers in other secondary schools, especially, by sharing the videos that we make."

"So I guess you will become challenged in your time management when you start raising kids."

"You are right. But this is Nigasilia. If I am stressed, I will simply telephone my mother and she will leave the chief and come down immediately."

"Yes, as far as that is concerned, you are quite right."

"John also tells me that you and Rabena are active in the initial stages of this organization you call NARROW," Peter interjects. "What's that all about?"

"It is simply about eliminating gender gap, especially in education, pay, and employment. We will push for free primary and secondary education so that the poor people in this country will not have to be faced with the choice of which child to educate beyond a certain low level. I think that is a very important thing, because the parents typically discriminate in favor of the boys, hoping that the girls will find a man to take care of them."

Kiraney asks, "What about expulsion for pregnancy? Isn't that a form of discrimination?"

"Yes," Jamina responds. "There is a two-track policy that is beginning to attract supporters. For schools that are coeducational, if the boy responsible for the pregnancy is in the same school, some principals have announced that when the girl is being kicked out, the boy will be kicked out as well. Then, for all schools, there is increasingly a policy of allowing the girls to have their babies and then return to school, if they want to."

"I think that's more equitable," Kiraney says. "Of course, the girls still get stuck with caring for the babies, because the boys invariably are hopeless and their parents are not typically kind to the girls, either."

"Yes. And you know, Kiraney, we still do not have sex education in the schools."

"Jamina," Mundu Sasay asks, "I have not checked the latest statistics on the subject, but is the incidence of HIV and AIDS a serious problem here right now?"

"The answer is no and yes, Mundu. It is no in the sense that the incidence is, on face value, very low right now. It is yes in the sense that it is growing, and some people are even afraid that the full extent may not be known. But most doctors feel that the incidence is still very low. We are taking the ABC model—Abstain, Be Faithful, and Use Condoms—very seriously. We are getting lots of foreign assistance in that area as well."

"Yes" Mundu adds, "there are many governments, aid agencies, and NGOs around the world willing to give money for work on all aspects of prevention. The saying 'Prevention is better than cure' cannot be truer."

Jamina asks, "John, did they remember to ask about coffee or tea?"

"Yes, but we did not give a clear answer. I think everyone wants coffee."

As Jamina leaves for the kitchen, Elizabeth turns to John. "My dear brother, that is a fantastic girl you found."

Jamehun arrives exactly one week after John's boys. John drops by in the evening of the following day to meet the brother of his fiancée, but he leaves the boys at home. They will meet their uncle-to-be another day. It was Jamina's suggestion. She thought that it would be better, so as not to restrict the conversation among the adults.

As they sip their before-dinner drinks, John says to Jamehun, "I hear your girlfriend is a registered nurse and works at the university hospital. That must be very interesting."

"Yes, it is. But it is also demanding work. Part of the problem is the shortage of nurses, which seems to be a worldwide phenomenon. Then, with malpractice suits so prevalent in the US, everyone needs to be very careful."

"You know, although these malpractice suits may have gone overboard in the US, sometimes I think we need something along those lines in this country. The father of a friend of mine, for instance, was admitted to one of our better hospitals. The nurses were so inattentive to his calls that he had to reach for his bedpan himself to urinate. You know, that man fell from his bed, hit his head, and lost his speech. It was downhill for him until he died some months later. In such a situation someone should suffer financially for their gross negligence. Here, for such things, whether they happen within the public or the private facilities, the doctors, nurses, and the hospitals go scot-free. If you ask the ordinary people in this country what we should do, they will simply say, 'Oh, leave them to God, they will get their punishment from the Almighty.' Well, I like the US style."

"Indeed," Jamehun comments, "that's why the doctors and the hospitals are all laboring under huge insurance bills."

"We don't even have the insurance programs for that sort of thing here," John notes. "This place is really backward, you know. Of course, to be fair, if people start suing for malpractice here, the insurance companies will begin to write policies, because the doctors, I'm sure, will begin to run for such cover. But then again, I'm sure we will also discover that our legal system is totally underdeveloped in that area, almost completely bereft of appropriate laws to address the issues. We have a long way to go in this country. Everywhere I turn I see backwardness and archaism."

"Jamina has told me that about you. But she says that you are determined to help mitigate the backwardness."

At the table, John continues questioning Jamehun. "So how old is your daughter now?"

"She is just five."

"That's a big girl. Soon she will be in first grade."

"Yes. It's also time to have another."

"Then why don't you?"

"My girlfriend says that will come after we marry."

"And when will that be?"

"In a few months, we hope. It will be a quiet one."

"What's your girlfriend's name?"

"Angela. You know, I have wanted to marry her all these years, but she said she wanted to be sure."

"But you have been living together and have a child. What did she want to be sure of?"

"That's what I asked her. But I got no reply. She is the sweetest thing. So, when she said she wanted to be sure I had to allow her."

"I guess you had no other choice."

Jamehun then asks, "When you first came home, you did not want to be a minister, just a technical expert trying to improve economic policies in general. Now, you are minister of finance and economic development. What made you change your mind?"

"I came to believe that my dad was serious about improving governance but did not have enough support within the cabinet. Second, I came to see how he was seizing every opportunity he had to push up people that were committed to his cause, and to push out people who were corrupt or simply inept. He trusts me and my judgment. Third, he volunteered, without my prompting, to bring my old department within the new ministry. You see, I think they have not been serious about doing solid economic analysis. Now I can do that."

John pauses for a sip. Jamehun can see he is not yet finished.

"Fourth, my dad convinced me that I can influence things more by being in this ministry than where I was before. No other minister can ignore me now. It is not merely because I hold the purse strings, because the president can order me to give another minister the money he or she wants. It is because now I can push for revenue and expenditure rules, procedures, and standards to which everyone must conform. And then, once we agree, even the president will be embarrassed to order me to violate the agreed framework. In brief, I can further my goal of making good economic policy making the normal order around here, rather than the exception, which it has always been."

John surprises Jamina. He is being very positive about his situation. She turns and smiles at him.

"That's great," Jamehun says. "But you know that you will have your detractors, and they will try to fight you."

"Yes, I am preparing myself for the fight. To tell you the truth, I have been wondering if that process will change me and if I will become more like a wild animal with a mentality of trying to get them before they get me. I hope not. Your sister will alert me, I'm sure."

"A lot of people do believe that it is possible to be a tough leader without being inhumane."

"Well, that's what I'm hoping."

"You'll make it. Like you said, Jamina will be watching you. I hear also that our cousin, Mahdu, is in your group. Well, he will also help you stay tough and humane at the same time."

"Thanks, Jamehun. Thank you very much. Anyway, we will get many opportunities to talk some more while you are here. My boys are anxious to meet their uncle-to-be. They say if you are half as nice as your sister, their Mommy Jamina, then that would be enough for them."

☓

On Friday, June 14, the cabinet meets to discuss John's paper, which his father had asked him, a few days ago, to circulate to all the ministers. All twenty-six cabinet ministers are present, plus the president and the vice president. No deputy minister has been invited to this meeting. John's cabinet paper had been circulated for comments, and John received feedback from fifteen of the twenty-six. John will be asked to open the discussion on each subject, responding to the comments received.

Once John thought through his proposals in drafting his paper, he decided to drop the request for a national council on socio-economic governance. Instead, in the spirit of some compromise with his father, he suggested that the government publish, every year, data on socio-economic variables including those suggested by the Unified Civil Society Movement. He also suggested that the government meets every year with UCSM to discuss the performance related to the socio-economic variables.

"I want to thank you all for your comments. I understand the unease that most of you feel with elevating STRONG or the UCSM by official recognition. I also agree that when it comes to validation, if the international organizations are slow in validating the figures, we should simply rely on data verified by Statistics Nigasilia, which after all is a department under the Ministry of Finance and Development. But I do not agree that publishing the indices would be enough. We need to give the populace the satisfaction of knowing that our publishing of the data is not merely an academic exercise and that the data mean something for our policy formulation and implementation. Therefore, I would like to suggest that at a minimum we agree to hold an annual conference on national socio-economic governance in which we discuss the published indices, among other subjects. I also wish to suggest that the Ministry of Finance and Development, working in close consultation with other ministries, be placed in charge of the list of indices to be published, and also of organizing the annual conference."

The president looks around. No one seems eager to comment. So the president says, "Okay, we all agree. John, you can go ahead and start organizing those events."

They turn to the Anti-Corruption Commission issue and John again must react to comments of his cabinet colleagues.

"Most of you who comment do not seem to be happy that I want to have the Anti-Corruption Commission stop prosecuting corrupt individuals and focus almost exclusively on procedures, rules, and organization to control corruption in the whole society, including civil society and business. Basically, you agree that the prevention focus should be strengthened. But you want the commission to focus mainly on government and to continue its prosecution activities. I am willing to concede that maybe we should leave the prevention work outside government to others, such as our regulatory agencies, the membership of civil societies, and the shareholders of the businesses. But I am not convinced about the prosecution work of the commission. So far, all the information I have on so many countries in the continent is that these commissions have become an instrument to go after opponents of the sitting government, including those in the ruling party who have fallen out of favor for reasons unrelated to their corrupt behavior."

Claudia Sandeh, the minister of labor and social security, responds. "John, as I commented to you in my memo, you do make a strong case for strengthening the rules and organization for prevention. But we do need to have a way of prosecuting offenders, and right now we have no alternative but to use the commission. As a compromise, we should add something, in the bylaws perhaps, that states that the commission should take care to ensure that the cases chosen for investigation of actual corruption, and the decision of who to prosecute, are not motivated by politics or any form of bias."

The president looks around to see if there are any other comments. "John, do you have any response?"

"Let's work with the general sense of the meeting. I buy Claudia's points. At worst, once we put the suggestions into effect we shall be able to observe what happens in practice."

The following day, Saturday, the president calls John to drop by the house for a quick lunch. "So, how do you think things went yesterday?"

"All right, I must say. I'm still worried, though, that I will find it difficult to monitor implementation. Daddy, this is where you will have to come in. You should find a way for people to report to you on a constant basis on the implementation, and you should develop a validation system to check on the accuracy of their reports."

"Do you think the annual conference on socio-economic governance will help?"

"Yes, Dad, it will. I plan on inviting civil society organizations, business leaders, and academics to participate, in a way that will bring out clearly the successes and failures of our implementation."

"We might also learn something from those conferences that will improve our policy design, don't you think?"

"Yes, of course."

"So, what else?"

"Well, I have given up on the land tenure system. I will let it evolve until it explodes when the common people see the inequities in the system as it operates in practice."

"I knew that's where you were going to end up. It is a difficult issue. The chiefs do not want any change. Challenging them is a big burden for any political leader to take on right now."

"Yes, I know. Again, we have to wait for pressure from below. But when that comes, the system will have to deal with mass revolt, not some movement directed by the educated youth and civil society organizations."

"Well, I will let future presidents worry about that."

"Or we can get rid of the chieftaincy institution."

"I won't even entertain a debate on that subject."

"I know, Dad."

On his way home John drops by to see Jamina. The boys had spent time with Jamina and then with Vivienne during the day. When John arrives, Jamina says, "So the meeting went well, yesterday? I did not hear from you."

"Oh, sorry, I was exhausted."

"I guessed as much."

"My colleagues were very polite. I already expected that from the written comments they sent me. And I am proud that I was willing to compromise as well."

"So, you see, you can work with them."

"Yes, I can, up to a point. My overall attitude has still not changed."

"And it won't, John, I know."

"So how did the boys do today?"

Jamina had taken the boys to visit Vivienne at work, since the Customs Department is open on Saturdays as well. Vivienne took them around to see the customs offices, without disturbing any activity, and then took them to see ships docking at the port.

"Great. Vivienne actually arranged for them to go see the officers' quarters on a big cargo boat."

"That's interesting. I have been on cruise ships a couple of times, once with Cecilia before the kids and once with the kids as well. But I was never privileged to go to the officers' quarters."

John then asks Jamina, "So what do you think now about going on a honeymoon?"

"Sounds all right if you can spare the time. Where have you decided you want to go?"

"My suggestion would be London, Washington, New York, and Boston, in that order. We can take the kids to New Hampshire and then fly back via Boston."

"What dates were you thinking of?"

"Leave, say, middle of August and arrive here again no later than the end of the first week in September. I have an approximate itinerary written down. I shall let you handle the details, if you approve."

"Well, my dear," Jamina says, looking a bit flustered, "right now I am thinking only about the wedding. I shall get to this honeymoon thing after that."

"That's all right, dear; that's all right."

David and Frances arrive on June 17. Two nights after they arrive, Jamina invites them, through John, to her house. Apart from John, Jamehun is also at the dinner. David, of course, met Jamina when he was in Nigasilia to cover the elections. He introduces her to his wife.

"Jamina, I am delighted to meet you," Frances says. "David has said nothing but glorious things about you."

"Frances, it is my great pleasure to meet you. I have also been hearing great things about you from John. Let me introduce my brother, Jamehun, to both of you. He resides in North Carolina. He is a computer scientist."

"Pleased to meet you," both Frances and David reply, as they shake Jamehun's hand. David adds, "No doubt you also are here for the wedding."

"Yes, but I will spend six weeks here, since I have not been home for five years. My mother, especially, has been complaining."

David asks, "Are you married yet?"

"No, I was waiting for my big sister," Jamehun replies with a chuckle.

"Sure," Jamina jokes. "The good news is that he is actually thinking of getting married very soon."

Jamina invites everyone to sit and then turns to Frances. "I gather that this is your first trip to Africa. Nigasilia is very pretty but I am sure that there are other African countries that would probably leave you with a better first impression of Africa."

"Why do you say that?"

"Many African countries hide their poverty better than we do. For instance, they keep their capital city cleaner and better supplied with electricity."

"That's an interesting point. Sometimes people do gain an impression of a country by what they see of the capital. In the US, though, Washington, DC, is a beautiful city but most people coming from abroad are more interested in New York, San Francisco, Hollywood, Beverly Hills, or Los Angeles. I guess that is the advantage of a big country like the US. Not everything of interest to tourists happens to be located in the capital city. But you do have cases like the UK and France, among big countries, which are exceptions. When people go to the UK, they are interested mainly in London."

David adds, "I think being a federal country is also part of the difference. The capital of Switzerland, which is a small country, for instance, is not the main attraction among cities in that country. Zurich, Geneva, and Lucerne are greater attractions than Berne."

"Anyway, Frances," Jamina interjects, "John tells me that after you see all the scenery of Lamongwe and its environs, you and David will explore some of nature's gifts outside of Lamongwe. John has organized some bookings and arranged for people to help you."

"Well, Jamina, I gather you were of great help, too. John says that you are very active in the Conservation Society here and know the geographical terrain much better than he does."

"That's true," Jamina says, smiling, "but I am helping him to catch up. His one disadvantage is that he is not a biologist. But then, he sees the economic aspects and educates me on those."

The servant takes their drink orders. Frances starts the conversation again. "Jamina, David was right. You have a very beautiful house. What are you going to do with it when you get married?"

John answers for her. "She has invited me to stay here and I have accepted with pleasure. I will give up my government house. This house is very big. I was surprised that a woman who wanted to be a nun built such a humongous house."

Jamina cannot let that go unanswered. "Well, Frances, thank you for the compliment. Actually, John knows the answer to his puzzle, because I gave him the answer before. When I got the money from my grandfather, I built this house as an investment. I was going to build a smaller house as residence for myself. Then I found out the problems that landlords were having with tenants and how badly some of the rented houses were being treated. So I decided to keep the money for my small house in a money market account in England and to postpone the decision. I have simply not got around to the final decision. This has been aggravated by the fact that I have come to enjoy all the space here. John made a good point to me though. He said that since I am not living abroad, if I rented my house to some foreign embassy or NGO, things should work out all right. I will be here to monitor the situation and many such tenants tend to leave every two or three years. Anyway, I will now have a reason to just stay in the house, right, John?"

"You are right, dear."

The food is ready and Jamina invites everyone to the table. Soon after the first dish is served, Frances says, "John, what do you miss most since you came back?"

"The opera, the symphony, the theater, bookstores, and museums—especially art museums—constant electricity supply, good roads . . ."

"Is that all?" Everyone laughs.

"No," Jamina adds, "he forgot to add a real post office."

"Ugh, yes, that takes the cake. We have no real post office system in this place. You can see, Frances, that I did not name anything that is nature's gift. We have plenty of that here."

"But, John," Jamehun says, "we can bring those things that you miss here, too."

"Yes, but they require cooperation and much more order than we have here."

"And money, too," Jamehun says with a tinge of protest in his voice.

"Yes, money is important. But it is not money that is keeping all those things out. It is the lack of cooperation and organization by the human beings of Nigasilia."

"What about taste, John?" Jamehun asks.

"Taste may be slightly important. But I doubt that it is very important. Take the case of opera. I am not asking them to produce *Aida* or *The Marriage of Figaro*, although I would not mind it. My basic point is that we have the potential to have our own opera or theater on our own subjects and using our own artistic cultural attributes. We just have not got around to it yet and I am still waiting to hear a justified excuse for our failure."

"Then, John, what do you enjoy most about being home?"

"Without a doubt, Frances, it is the opportunity to help in the economic development of the country of my birth. The good fortune of having my father as the president has made it possible for me to contribute. That, I believe, is the main factor behind my potential to reap some real satisfaction from working here."

"You say potential; does that mean that you are yet to realize the benefit?"

Jamina looks at John and smiles. Frances, of course, has heard from David some of John's frustrations.

"Frances, I was just being honest. It is not so easy to convince people here to move fast in making changes. Right now, I seem to want to move faster in economic management and governance reforms than everyone else I meet. And *that* I honestly find frustrating."

David turns to Jamehun. "You have not been home for many years now. Do you notice changes? Do some stand out?"

"Oh, yes. I think urbanization is increasing. Lamongwe is far more crowded than when I was here five years ago. Lamongwe is also much dirtier than when I was last here. Maybe the two are related, but I suspect that sanitation services have deteriorated. I'm glad that those who have been here all this time feel the same way. Another thing I notice is the flood of used clothing. I am surprised that there are still many tailors around, although I suspect the number is not increasing with the increase of population."

"Well, my brother," John remarks, "we are a used goods depot and it's going to get worse before it gets better. Used vehicles, used computers, used machines, just name it. Obviously, as you say, used clothing hits you immediately. But used vehicles will get your attention, too. We have too many breakdowns, and junked vehicles are abandoned on the sides of many narrow streets, aggravating traffic jams."

After a pause, John asks, "But Jamehun, isn't the number of electricity shortages worse now than when you were here five years ago?"

"Yes, you are right, John. In fact, it is the most disgusting. I watch how much Jamina spends on fuel for the generator. It is incredible, really. Your government has to work on that."

"Yes, we are trying. But I doubt that things will improve significantly within the next couple of years."

Jamina changes the subject. "Frances and David, John said you sent your two boys to camp. Soccer camp, I believe?"

David responds, "Yes, it was their choice. They love soccer."

"I understand that soccer is catching on in the US, although John tells me that it will never be really big there. Why is that?"

"It is a question that many people have asked but no one has come up with an answer. My view is that it has something to do with the American temperament. But I cannot place my finger on what it is about our nature that makes us go for baseball, American football, basketball, and hockey, but not soccer."

Jamina says, "John wants to start summer camps here, too, American style. He wants something for his two boys to do during the long summer months. He thinks the idea will catch on in Nigasilia. He plans to extend it to other sports as well."

"What do you think, Jamina?"

"I think John has something there. There's no reason we can't have successful summer camps here."

As they leave with John, Frances says, "Well, Jamina and Jamehun, thanks for a great evening. Jamina, I wish you luck over the next few days. We will see you two at the wedding."

Two nights before the wedding day, the president hosts a dinner for the nine members of the two families. As Jamina and John arrive with the other three members of the Tamba family, the president first shakes the hands of both the chief and his wife and then hugs Jamina. To Jamehun, he says, "You must be the one from America, Jamina's brother. I'm pleased to meet you. What is your name again?"

"Jamehun, Mr. President. It's my privilege to meet you, sir."

"Well, welcome to all of you. Chief, I assume that your beautiful and efficient daughter is taking good care of you."

"Yes, Mr. President, she is doing an excellent job."

"Now, you have not met my other two children. This is Elizabeth, who lives in England, and this is Peter, the youngest of the three, who lives in Canada." Elizabeth and Peter shake hands with Chief Tamba, Mrs. Tamba, and Jamehun, and then the two siblings introduce their spouses.

The president invites everyone to sit and gives the nod to the servant standing nearby waiting to serve drinks. With so many new acquaintances, the party spends a lot of time asking each other about their respective families, work, and day-to-day lives. Soon it is time to go to the table.

After everyone is comfortably seated, the president begins the talking. "Chief, as I told you before, I am very pleased that you and I will become family. You have a wonderful daughter. She is a real role model. And to top things, she has been a real asset to me in helping to make sure John stays around here to support me in my work."

"Well, Mr. President, let us say that you and I are both lucky. For a long time we wondered whether Jamina would find a man that she wanted to marry. Fatima and I had started to blame ourselves for raising her in such a manner that no man would meet her standards of uprightness. Brilliance and good looks are easier to meet. But uprightness—to find one young man among Nigasilians with an adequate amount to satisfy Jamina—I, for one, was not optimistic."

"Chief, thank you," John says.

The chief continues. "And John, your willingness to stay is going to matter a lot to this country. Look at the way you are inspiring so many of the young people. I think that's good. We hope that you can motivate other Nigasilian professionals in the diaspora to come home and help."

The president says, "Chief, let's ask our diasporan children here what it would take for them to come home and help."

Elizabeth takes the floor. "Dad, Chief Tamba, as you might imagine, this is not a novel question. It is a question being asked and answered every day in the diasporan communities of African countries all over the world. I suspect that, by now, we know the answer. I'm not talking about those who are running from conflicts and persecution, but normal people like us around this table. I would say it is income, facilities, and standards. Income is obvious. We go abroad because we can earn higher incomes to meet expenses for educating our children, better lifestyles for ourselves, and savings for retirement. Mundu, here, is a doctor. The professional satisfaction of having up-to-date medical facilities is enormous for him. He feels far more fulfilled as a doctor. The same goes for an engineer like Peter, the computer scientist like Jamehun, the financial analyst like Kiraney, and the architect like me.

"The other side of the facilities calculation has to do with facilities in our everyday lives, whether we are talking about facilities to repair our cars, shops for ordinary consumer goods, or, as John would say, bookstores and post offices. When it comes to standards, I think that demand tends to kick in after we have been abroad for some time. Then we begin to fuss about workmanship, cleanliness, efficiency, timeliness, all that kind of stuff. John sent me a copy of his commencement speech. I saw a bit of that sort of complaint in there as well."

Jamehun decides to jump in. "Elizabeth, you summarize correctly what keeps us out. I suspect that many Nigasilians would still return home, even with the attractions of income, facilities, and standards abroad, if there were signs of even a modicum of progress in this country. Many Nigasilians would prefer to be home—perhaps even the majority of them—if there were serious signs of real progress in our development."

Kiraney agrees. "I think you have a point, Jamehun. This, in a sense, is what African diasporans mean when they talk about wanting to see significant progress. They want their country to cross some threshold, because they want decent income and reasonable facilities and standards. But here's another issue, Mr. President and Chief Tamba, which diasporans debate all the time. In fact, it is a dilemma for them. If such a high fraction of the leading professionals of these countries go and live abroad, how will these countries make enough progress to cross that threshold to trigger a net inflow back?"

The president nods. "I guess you are asking if we are in a vicious circle."

"Yes, Mr. President. Are we?"

"Well, look, there is no alternative but for the ones who stay here to work very hard and turn things around to get the ball rolling. Then we can begin to attract the diasporans back, first in small numbers. As we make more progress, we shall begin to get larger numbers flowing back. Many, like John here, who have thought about that question, say that we should begin with those who are fifty and above and have worked abroad for some fifteen to twenty years and with no more school fees to pay. That means we must seriously improve our medical facilities, because those older people will be especially concerned about that."

Mrs. Tamba looks at Mundu and asks, "What's your specialty?"

"I am a cardiologist."

"I'm sure if you came home you would have almost the whole field to yourself."

Peter butts in. "That means he would probably have no facilities to work with."

"It's not that bad, Peter," the president replies. "It's not satisfactory by any standard but there is something with which he can work."

John joins the discussion. "I notice that no one has talked about that big group of diasporans, the unskilled. The welcome mat is not exactly spread out for them in the advanced countries and they lack jobs at home that pay them living wages. They are not worried about facilities and standards. For them it is income, income, income. We, as Africans, should be ashamed that we have a whole group of people who risk their lives to go find work abroad because we can't provide work for them here. So what do we do for those? They are not the ones I want to see leading social movements here."

The president is eager to reply. "John, we are not forgetting the un-educated youth. We know that they need education and skills training as well as job opportunities. That's why we want the skilled diasporans to come home and help. Even foreign investors will be impressed by all those skilled diasporans around to man the factories and the workshops and service centers."

John presses the president. "So there you have it. We have a vicious circle. How do we begin to create a virtuous circle to solve the problem?"

Peter cannot resist teasing his brother. "But John, I thought that was why you decided to come home and help—to help solve that problem."

"Yes, but I need support. And I am not getting enough of it."

There is silence and John senses the reason. "Well, our dear dad and a few others excluded, of course." Then, after a deep breath, he continues. "So, I intend to ask a lot of people a lot of questions and to motivate them to come up with the answers themselves. That way, I will kill two birds with one stone. I shall deflect criticism that I think I have all the answers, and I shall get them to feel a sense of ownership of the solutions."

Most of those present do not understand what John is trying to say. But the chief understands and is in agreement. "That is exactly the approach I take with my people."

"Chief, is the celebration in Wombono going to be big?" Elizabeth asks, in a tone that makes clear that she wants to talk about something else. "I heard the one for the engagement was very big. The way John described it made me feel sorry I was not there."

"Yes, the engagement celebration was big. But Jamina says we should not have another big celebration. She says that, after all, most people feel the two got married that day."

"Well, I hope you will have some local dance groups and musicians perform for us. I really miss such cultural events here."

"Yes," the chief interjects, "your brother has told me. Maybe you should become a promoter of such things in London. What's the word I am looking for again?"

"Impresario?"

"Yes, that's exactly the word, Elizabeth, thanks."

"It's a good thought," Elizabeth agrees, "but I doubt I will have the time to do a good job of it. For one thing I will need to have things around here organized as well. Maybe I should discuss it with you, Jamina. Oh, but you have your Conservation Society and now you are also getting involved in this new women's group. So, Jamina, I guess that rules you out, too."

"Not necessarily. But you are right, perhaps. When I add my teaching job, I will then have no time left for John." Everyone laughs. "Still, the idea is a good one and I shall make sure that you and I discuss it further."

"Elizabeth, you see, this is how ideas develop," the chief says. "I'm sure there are people both here and abroad who will be willing to join in any initiative you two can come up with."

"You are right, Chief."

The president is interested in this particular subject.

"You know, along these lines, I have been floating the idea among members of my cabinet that we should look into formal and informal ways to spur cooperation among our diasporans and locals in many business areas. That will not be anything new. I see it happening in more and more African countries. Here, at this table, for example, we have an architect, an engineer, and a computer scientist; there are all kinds of possible business partnerships that we can think of in those three areas that would involve people living here in Nigasilia working with Nigasilians abroad. I'm almost sure the banks will be willing to lend to such enterprises. John was even telling me that such partnerships in certain areas can connect with global networks—what they call value chain relationships, whatever that means. I realize that credit will not be easy because interest rates are so high here, but I am sure that there are ways around that problem, including banks abroad helping with the financing. I have also asked my legal people to look at our laws on limited liability partnerships and other relevant legal issues to see how we can improve the enabling environment."

"Mr. President," Kiraney comments, "I think one of the biggest problems in the past with such relationships is that the diasporans complain that the local partners are often just out to steal from them. You know, to cheat them."

"We have to find a way to make that less of a problem. Maybe I should organize a national debate, beginning with a conference, on the issue of promoting business cooperation and partnerships among diasporan and local Nigasilians. Building trust and reducing corruption could then be among the issues addressed."

"Mr. President, that sounds like a great idea. What happens is that we have these ambassadors calling meetings of diasporans and pleading for them to invest in Nigasilia. But when some diasporans raise the issue of theft and corruption, among other things, the ambassadors typically give short shrift to the questions. So, diasporans have reached the conclusion that many of the ambassadors have a history of corruption. To tell you the truth, Mr. President, if I may make one suggestion to you, as I sit here, it will be that you vet thoroughly the ambassadors that you send to the advanced countries."

"Thank you, Kiraney. In fact, your brother-in-law, who will be one of the organizers of the conference, tells me the same thing. Unfortunately, we do need concrete evidence of corruption, not simply anecdotes, before we take action against our public officials. One of the things I have asked your brother-in-law to do in the coming year, in cooperation with the attorney general and the Anti-Corruption Commission, is to vet, again, the ambassadors we have in these high-profile countries, precisely to look at this issue of their possible history of corruption. We have been hearing things about a couple of them. But I am not going to mention any names until I have stronger evidence."

It is June 22, 2002. The big day has arrived. It seems like yesterday when John decided to come home and help. John had made the decision in June 2000 when he came home for his mother's funeral. But he actually came on February 1, 2001, which was not a very long time ago. Still, that leap of faith placed John on the trail that led to the wonderful union that is about to be solidified and transformed into a blissful covenant today. Mahdu Kontana feels particularly elated, because it was he who introduced the two and he was convinced from the start that they were two souls meant for each other. He is sorry that it was the death of John's wife that has made such a union possible. But he is sure that the spirit of Cecilia will be with them on this day and throughout their marriage.

As for the Bijunga gang, before they leave for church, they all gather for prayers. They want to have a moment of silence, just among themselves, and together, in memory of Mrs. Bijunga. Tears flow from their eyes in that brief moment. Then the president breaks the silence. "My dear Matinbi, wherever you are, I know you are looking down on John today. You would have been proud of the choice he has made. I know that your spirit will be with them today and throughout their marriage."

The motorcade soon departs from the president's residence to the Roman Catholic Cathedral of Lamongwe.

At Jamina's house there is also a quiet moment before the four Tambas leave for the wedding. They gather in the living room. Mrs. Tamba serves Jamina a tot of cold water for good luck. "Jamina, never forget who you are and where you came from. God will help take care of you. Do your best to make the marriage work. But remember, when you need support, we will be there. I give you all the blessing I can bestow as a mother. Now let's go get God's blessing of the marriage."

And off to church goes the bridal party motorcade. When the bridal party arrives, there are throngs of people waiting. When Jamina steps out of the vehicle, elegant in her white bridal dress and pearl necklace and earrings, there are cheers and cries. "This," they chatter, "is a state wedding indeed." Some speculate about where the dress and pearls came from, and how much they cost. Well, Elizabeth brought the dress, as a separate piece of cargo, from the UK, and it cost a lot of money, which the Tambas duly paid for. The pearls are gifts from her grandmother, which Jamina has been storing secretly.

By the time Jamina stands imposingly at the entrance, ready to begin the procession, the church is already packed. Unfortunately, only those with invitations are allowed to enter the church. The guests include, apart from family members, cabinet members and their spouses, several ambassadors, including those from the US and the UK and a number of African countries, representatives of the UNDP and the European Commission, several teachers from Jamina's school, and close friends of the couple. The weather has cooperated. It is sunny and the humidity is not too high. There is hardly a cloud. A light wind enhances the pleasantness of the atmosphere. The air is clean.

John and Jamina were determined to have their wedding start on time. And that they are able to do. At the exact hour of 2:00 p.m. local time, Jamina starts her march down the aisle, side by side with her papa. The chief is wearing a white gown and white cloth cap and is holding his chieftaincy staff. John and Jamina have opted for processional music that is familiar, even if too popular for John's taste. John would have loved to have had a string quartet play the second movement from Haydn Opus 76 no. 3 ("The Emperor Quartet") while Jamina is entering. But there is no string quartet in Nigasilia to play that kind of music. So, as processional music, they have decided to stick with the "Bridal March" from *Lohengrin* by Wagner. For the recessional music, they stay with the familiar "Wedding March" from Mendelssohn's *A Midsummer Night's Dream*.

Jamina and John discussed carefully their choice of readings from passages of the Bible, guided by recommendations of their tutoring priest. For the Old Testament reading, they have selected Song of Solomon 2:10–13. For the epistle, they decided on Philippians 4:4-9. This choice took them the longest to settle. They realized that a favorite of Nigasilian Christians is 1 Corinthians Chapter 13. Many Nigasilian Christians can probably recite all thirteen verses from memory. Jamina loves it, too, but came to realize that John did not really want it, because he hears it at so many weddings. In considering alternative selections, John was uncomfortable with readings that tell wives to submit to their husbands. "It is all right to tell the wives to submit to the Lord," John joked with Jamina, "but I am not lord of anything." As for the Gospel, that was easy for them. They both love the Beatitudes, and thus the choice of Matthew 5:1–10 was straightforward.

As the service progresses, John is very impressed at how seriously the choir has taken the whole affair. Here they are, singing from one of Mozart's masses. They will also have an anthem. From the Mozart

Mass they sing the Kyrie, Sanctus, and Agnus Dei and they do so in Latin. John is flabbergasted. "Pleni sunt coeli et terra glòria tua" is so much more uplifting than hearing the mundane "Heaven and earth are full of your glory."

The bishop of the cathedral decides to give the address, and discusses marriage from the perspective of a contract under law, a union under God, the apogee of a love relationship, and a crucial element for the survival and stability of the community and its values. He says, to the congregation and to the bride and bridegroom, that when you marry in a church, you capture all of these elements in one fell swoop. To the newlyweds he stresses that the covenant or legal contract aspect of the wedding is all well and good. "That is a kind of protection of our rights as individual human beings. But we as Christians hold the belief that a wedding should be sealed with God's blessing. We also stress that His love is a crucial lubricant sustaining the relationship. Moreover, we underscore that cooperation and trust must exist as major enabling elements."

The bishop urges them to take prayer seriously. And he expresses his wish that the marriage be blessed with as many children as the two wish for themselves. To the members of the congregation, the bishop says, "While it is true that you are here to participate in the celebration of the wedding, you are here also as witnesses, witnesses in the eyes of the law and in the sight of God. Moreover, you are here as testimony of your commitment to support a successful marriage."

The reception is held at a newly built grand hall near Lumpimo Beach. It is operated by one of the hotels situated nearby. John and Jamina have decided that they will not keep their guests waiting for a long time before they make their appearance at the hall. In fact, they will have pictures taken quite close to the hall. It is a pretty area and they will not have to struggle for backgrounds they fancy, including the scenery of the beach on one side, and the hills hovering beautifully on the other. Guests will be served drinks and hors d'oeuvres as they enter the hall. Then they will be handed their table numbers. The couple has asked the disc jockey to play the music at a very low volume to give the people the opportunity to have civilized conversations.

By the time Jamina and John reach the hall, everyone is seated and enjoying hors d'oeuvres. There is plenty of everything to eat and drink. Jamina and John enter, everyone rises, and they march down the aisle to the high table, with the accompaniment of soft music. The chairman of the ceremony is Stephen Mongo. He makes a few opening remarks, and then invites the bishop to say a short prayer. When the bishop takes the microphone, he asks everyone to stand and observe a moment of silence for Mrs. Bijunga, late wife of the president, and for Cecilia, late wife of John. After the bishop prays, the master of ceremony advises everyone that meals will now be served, and the waiters proceed to the task. At the end of the main dish, the chairman invites the couple to come forward for the cutting of the cake. There is a wide selection of desserts. Once the cutting of cake is done, the guests are asked to proceed to serving tables, located at four corners of the hall, and help themselves. Coffee and tea will be served by the waiters as the guests return to their tables.

It is soon time for the toasts. There are four in the program—to the bride and groom, the parents of the bride, the parents of the groom, and the guests. For the toast to the bride and groom, Mahdu Kontana has the honor. "Ladies and gentlemen, nothing delights me more than to have the honor to propose the toast to these two beautiful people—beautiful in looks, mind, and spirit. John first laid eyes on Jamina in my office. They chatted for only a few minutes and John was convinced he wanted to know this lady some more. I organized the first date and we all three ate lunch together. The rest, as they say, is history. I tell you, from the beginning I knew that John was the man my cousin was waiting for. They are meant for each other. Jamina, of course, I have known all her life. I don't know of a more upright and decent lady. So, without much ado, let us all rise and drink to the health of these two great people and wish them nothing but success in their married life."

First Jamina and then John get up and thank Mahdu for his kind words and for the role he played in getting the two of them together. They also thank their parents and siblings.

As for Jamina, she says with that calm, lovely, confident tone of hers, "Mahdu, thank you for being not only a great cousin but also a true friend. And thank you, most of all, for being right about John. He has turned out to be, indeed, the man for whom I was waiting." She thanks her parents for her upbringing, not only for her schooling, but also for infusing her with the right values. "You left me with a determination to help people and to contribute substantially to the development and well-being of women and girls, of my community, and of Nigasilia. Above all, you have guided me by your great example as parents. I hope that I shall be able to do the same for my children." Then she turns to her brother, and with a big smile says, "As for you, Jamehun, thank you for being a truly gracious and loving brother."

John, among other remarks, says, "Mahdu, I won't disappoint you." He thanks his parents for their love, attention, and patience. "There is no doubt that my parents deserve most of the credit for any success that I have achieved and will achieve in life. They instilled in me certain values that continue to guide me. As for my siblings, well, they know I love them, and I can always count on them for emotional support."

The toast to the bride's parents is given by Chief Modibum, one of the chiefs who had been involved in the dispute that Chief Tamba had mediated. He tells the guests that he has known Mrs. Tamba since she married Chief Tamba and knew Chief Tamba even before then. "It is no surprise," he continues, "that these two people have produced a woman in the person of Jamina, a brilliant young woman of style, elegance, and tremendous discipline and commitment to nationally and socially important causes. It is the patience, discipline, and exemplary behavior of her parents that have gone a long way toward making Jamina such a role model for our women. It therefore gives me great pleasure to propose the toast to these two wonderful parents of Jamina Tamba. Please rise and drink to their health."

Jamina's father, in response, thanks Chief Modibum for his kind words; Mahdu Kontana, his nephew, for his great judgment and foresight in seeing that Jamina and John are well suited for each other; and to the guests for coming out to support them in their joyful moment. Then he turns to John. "John, we have not known you for very long but our interaction with you has brought us nothing but pleasure. We are as optimistic as we can possibly be that the relationship with Jamina that you have formalized here today will be a happy and fruitful one. We welcome you into our family. We have no doubt that our daughter will be a good wife to you and you a good husband to her. I wish you both all the best."

The vice president, Kamake Tigie, gives the toast to the parents of the bridegroom. He was the president's choice. "Ladies and gentlemen, this is a great honor for me, giving this toast. The late Mrs. Bijunga was a true leader. She was not only a brilliant scholar, but she took seriously that she should unite people in pursuit of higher goals; in her case, for the improvement of the socio-cultural environment in this country. I see those same leadership qualities in John. I know, therefore, that Mrs. Bijunga's influence on John has been deep and long-lasting. As for John's father, well, you all know him. He is an unquestionably great leader. He not only believes in uniting us in pursuit of higher goals for our society, but he is a man of integrity and decency. Again, I see those same qualities in John. Now we all know how he got them. So, I invite all to rise and drink to the health of our dear President Bijunga and his family."

The president in his response thanks the vice president for his compliments and kind words, and joins Chief Tamba in thanking Minister Mahdu Kontana for his role in bringing John and Jamina together as well as the guests for their support. He continues, turning to Jamina, "You know, by now, how much I admire you. You are very welcome into our family. I have no doubt that you and John will have a very successful marriage and that John will treat you with the great respect and dignity that you deserve. I wish the two of you the best of times ahead."

The toast to the guests is the honor of Jamina's brother to give. He thanks the guests for their presence and their support, reminding them that without their attendance, the celebrations would not be as complete or as gratifying as they will be today. He says he hopes they will all enjoy themselves and that this event will be etched in all of their memories for the rest of their lives. He thanks them for the pile of presents stacked in the small room reserved for the gifts. He says he can visualize Jamina and John over the next few weeks having much pleasure unwrapping them. He asks the members and close relatives of the Bijunga and Tamba families to rise and drink to the health of these "resplendently attired and extremely generous guests."

Vivienne responds to the toast. She says that most of them who know the couple well have been waiting with enormous anticipation for this great day. There is no doubt in their minds that these two wonderful people deserve each other. Hence, the guests are extremely happy that they have all been invited and are able to come and join in the celebrations. They are sure that today will be a day they all will remember for the rest of their lives. She ends her speech with further words of gratitude as well as best wishes. "I would like to thank Jamehun for his kind words of appreciation and praise for the guests and to wish John and Jamina a very happy and fruitful married life."

The MC announces that the floor will now be open for dancing. The first pair on the floor will be the newlyweds. They will be joined on cue by the rest of the wedding party, and then by close relatives. Finally, everyone will be invited to join. The MC informs the guests that there is still plenty to drink. Snacks will be served a little later.

The party continues until John and Jamina decide that it is time to go home. Members of the wedding party, as well as the Bijunga and Tamba family members, have been invited to Jamina's house before they all depart for their separate homes. Vehicles hired by Jamina and John will be available to take home those of the wedding party who need rides. Even the president comes to Jamina's house. When everyone arrives, John announces that the two of them intend to spend tonight and the whole of next week at his house. Then they will make their move to this house, which will become their permanent residence.

By his announcement, John calls to mind the last formal stage of a normal Nigasilian wedding—the husband takes the bride from her house to his. Mrs. Tamba quickly seizes the opportunity. "John, you have to take your bride home now. Jamina, your husband is ready." And all jump to their feet and shout "Hurrah!"

And so ends what has been a glorious day in the lives of John and Jamina. As they drive to John's house, with great expectations, they pray that it is also the first day of what will become a marvelous future for the two of them together. Yes, there is much uncertainty surrounding John's decision to stay in Nigasilia, the governance work to which he has committed himself, the future of the leadership of the party, and his relationship with his boys. But they stop thinking about the future the moment they open the door of John's house. They immediately send Donald and William to bed.

As they undress that night and look into each other's eyes, words cannot characterize adequately the exhilaration that runs through their bodies. For John and Jamina, this is no time to contemplate the future.

The parents of the couple have had a lovely day as well. For President John Bijunga, in particular, this is a truly blessed day. Even up to a few weeks ago, there was a question in his mind as to whether John would not prefer to return to America and his ivory tower. The president wished to have his son around, but he also wanted John to appreciate the constraints the president faces and to be patient. The president has lost sleep wondering how he could get his son to understand that there was no point running back to America, but rather for him to appreciate that he was an essential element in a rainbow of forces that could succeed in improving governance in Nigasilia. The president knows that he owes a great debt to John's friends in the cabinet, to Jamina, to the youth of STRONG, and to many in the Chamber of Commerce for helping John see that he could make a difference by staying home. The president can only hope that indeed his analysis is correct. Deep down, he is confident that he is right. He saw it in John today, his demeanor, that, yes, he is going to be around for some time. For how long, no one can be sure. But he is not going back to America very soon. Of that, the president is certain.